# For Better or Hearse

# AVA HUNTER

*For Better or Hearse*
Copyright © 2024 Ava Hunter

All rights reserved. No part of this publication may be reproduced, distributed or transmitted in any form by any means, or stored in a database or retrieval system, without the prior written permission of the author.

*For Better or Hearse* is a work of fiction. Characters, names, places, angst and incidents are a work of the author's imagination and are fictitious. Any resemblance to real life events or persons, living or dead, is entirely coincidental and not intended by the author.

ISBN: 979-8-9897906-2-3

Cover Design: Leni Kauffman
Editing: VB Edits
Formatting: Champagne Book Design

# Also by Ava Hunter

*Babymoon or Bust*
*For Better or Hearse*

### Nashville Star Series
*Sing You Home*
*Find You Again*
*Love You Always*
*Need You Now*
*Bring You Back*
*With You Forever*

### Runaway Ranch Series
*Tame the Heart*
*Rope the Moon*
*Burn the Wild*

# Playlist

Shadowboxer | Fiona Apple
Parting Gift | Fiona Apple
Knee Deep | Zac Brown Band
What He Didn't Do | Carly Pearce
I Got You | The White Buffalo
Left Alone | Fiona Apple
Vampire | Olivia Rodrigo
Daredevil | Fiona Apple
I Bet You Think About Me | Taylor Swift
Girl with One Eye | Florence + The Machine
Please Pardon Yourself | The Avett Brothers
What Am I Gonna Do | Chris Stapleton
Scared to Start | Michael Marcagi
Delicate | Taylor Swift
Cry Baby | Janis Joplin

# Dedication

*For the weirdos. The left out. The lone wolves. Those who found themselves in the darkness and the doubt and bloomed. You're perfectly dreadful.*

*For my cousin. For always matching my freak.*

Psst.
The next page contains trigger warnings.
Please skip if you wish to avoid spoilerish content.

## A Note from Ava:

Dear Reader,

Please know that while most of this book is fun and bright, the characters also deal with themes of loss, grief, mortality and love. A supporting character suffers from cancer. There are discussions of death and infidelity.

If you're sensitive to subjects such as these, please use this warning to make an informed decision about whether to proceed with the story.

As always, take care of yourself. Your mental health matters.

With big love and all good wishes,
Ava

# I.

## DOOM

# Chapter One

Ash Keller's job is to ruin things.
Most especially this wedding.
Most especially Nathaniel Rhodes Whitford.

In her hands, Ash carries a file. *The* file. A document she uses to vet those she's hired to break up. As a professional wedding objector, she requires proof. Concrete evidence, like the Roswell incident or the JFK assassination. Otherwise, she won't touch the job with a ten-foot pole. Sure, she ruins lives, but she ruins lives with purpose.

As Ash steps up to the door of the church, she groans. Why does it have to be a church? A prim and proper two-hour Catholic affair is most definitely not up her alley. Why couldn't he get married on top of a mountain or at least a place where she could parachute in? Each time she sets foot on sacred ground, she feels like she'll spontaneously combust.

Inhaling a hard breath, she grips the handle. The door opens with a tired sigh. A crescendo of music echoes down the long corridor. She settles her stomach. Steels her spine.

And walks.

Or rather, stomps.

Clad in fishnets, she storms down the aisle. Her lovingly worn combat boots squeak loudly on the marble floor, echoing through the archaic space, as she storms for the altar. The aglets of her eternally untied laces snap and bounce. Her red lipstick is bright and as blaring as the music coming from the organ. The heart in her chest beats hard and fast. So hard and fast, in fact, that the guests can surely see it through the bodice of her dress.

Of course she dressed up. It's a wedding. Although not for very much longer.

Halfway down the aisle, she hears it. The priest is at the "If anyone wants to oppose..." part of the vows.

It's so very seventeenth century of him.

"Wait!" she shouts, lifting an arm like she's volunteering as tribute. A thrill unfurls inside her. She's timed it perfectly.

*I object.* The two most powerful words in the English language.

Because the person voicing them wields power. Vengeance. Not participating. It pisses everyone off.

As she nears the altar, confused murmurs erupt around her. Guests twist in the pews to glimpse her better. Groomsmen—LA's top five blandest white guys—in dark jackets turn her way. Women in long beaded gowns sneer. The dresses and suits they're wearing probably cost more than her monthly rent.

The long walk down the aisle feels like she's walking the plank. Her great, furious boot stomps aren't helping her either.

Through it all, Ash faces front and center. Zeroed in on the bride. By now, she's a pro at this. Avoid eye contact with the family. Keep emotions out of it. Get in. Object. Get out.

Or run like hell. Depending.

She knows what she's walking into. She's been well debriefed by her client.

The Whitfords. A prominent wealthy LA family. Their accolades and accomplishments make her itch. Doctors. Owners of fancy businesses and expensive cars and straight Trident white teeth. They're into snobby hobbies like skiing and golfing. No doubt they run a 5k on Thanksgiving and each of their children has a trust fund. It's only a matter of time before one of them gets fingered for a white-collar crime.

Gripping the folder tight, Ash slows her stampede.

She surveys the bride. Camellia Barrister. So clean-girl aesthetic. Impossibly beautiful in a fresh and effortless way, unattainable to mere mortals. In addition to her placid expression, she wears a stunning mermaid tail organza with a sweetheart neckline that amplifies her busty cleavage. The diamond tiara nestled in her slicked-back bun reminds them all that she is and always will be a princess.

The groom, dressed impeccably in Ralph Lauren, angles in and murmurs to his bride. Then Nathaniel Whitford fixes his piercing gaze on Ash, one stern eyebrow raised. "Who the hell are you?" His voice is clipped, machine-gun style. The irritated intensity of his expression sends a burning sensation through her ever-tightening chest. It feels like he's judging her, untied laces and all.

Her heart stutters to a stop along with her feet.

Why can't he be ugly? Like Harlequin baby ugly?

He's like Harlequin romance. GQ brooder with a jawline that could slice through glass. Golden-bronze skin. Wheat-colored hair like a swirl of butterscotch ice-cream. The cavalier no-big-deal flip in the front. An obscenely, unfairly tall asshole. One of *LA Times'* most promising doctors of the year.

And a cheater.

"Hello?" Nathaniel's no longer looking at her. Instead, he scans the crowd. "Can we get security here?"

"Seriously?" she hisses, shooting him a glare. "Security? What is this, the CIA?"

"At my wedding," he replies, chin lifted and eyes hard, "yes."

Ash hops to the side, moving closer to Camellia. "I'm here to show you something, Ms. Barrister."

She opens the folder and holds it up, making sure Nathaniel can't see its contents. Ash hands over the folder, even as Nathaniel's glare burns a hole in her face. By the time this is over, she'll look like one of those Victorian women who burned to death in flammable dresses.

Heat blooms in Camellia's cheeks as she scans the incriminating photo, but she keeps her expression neutral. A minimalist tactic of the rich and famous, Ash supposes.

"Oh, come on," Nathaniel snaps, a vein in his forehead pulsing. "This is ridiculous."

Camellia looks at Ash, her brown eyes burning with relief.

Ash closes the folder and pulls it tightly against her chest.

"Nathaniel," Camellia says in a silvery tone, tipping back. Away from her groom. "We should...talk."

"Right." His voice is strained. His ice-blue eyes darken. "Talk."

That's when his broad shoulders and golden head swivel Ash's way. As he studies her, something greasy and wormy turns over in Ash's stomach. The bite of pain on his face has her taking a step back.

Fuck. She wasn't expecting that.

Suddenly, she begins to sweat.

From the shadows, a man in a suit emerges, earpiece in place and attention set on her.

*Shit.*

Ash turns. Every person in attendance is whispering now, hands to their mouths in quiet, delighted shock. There's the flash of a photo. Camellia tugs on Nathaniel's hand, urging him to a back room. An older man with a shock of white hair has rocketed up, phone to his ear. If his furious, blustering expression is anything to go by, it's time for Ash to move her boots. There are nearly five hundred people here. She scans the first five pews, the immediate family there, then, almost desperately, shifts her focus to the exit.

And then she fucking runs.

Door. Exit. Now.

Before the entire Whitford family riots.

The slaps of her boots and laces echo down the aisle, metronome along with her heartbeat.

When the massive wood door slams shut behind her, she slumps back against it. Ash sucks in great gulping breaths. The air tastes like smog, the May sunlight so bright she can barely see. She is glad for the distraction, even as she tries to convince herself that what she's just done is not the lowest level of low. The Whitfords will thank her for it later. They will. Thank her for all the hymns, blessings, verse readings and divorces she saved them from.

The thought hums in Ash's ears, fizzles out before she can believe it.

Fuck. What's wrong with her?

Most times, guilt is not a factor. Today is an anomaly.

It's the church. The eyes of God. Making her quake. Objecting to weddings in backyards, beaches, bars is so much easier. Here, where her soul is up for judgment, even if she doesn't believe in the big guy up in the sky? It makes her insides twist and her airway tighten.

*You're messy, Ash.*

Sweaty and hounded, she squeezes her eyes shut. Her blood is on fire. Fumbling around in her purse, she grabs a granola bar. Crushes it in her fist.

*It's just a job.*

It's what she wishes someone would have done for her. She's saving them. She'll never let another person go through it. That almost-walk.

With Jakob, she learned the rules of love.

She learned that less of herself was more.

She learned on a moonless night who else was sleeping in her bed.

Hot guilt pumps through her, so loud she can hear it in her ears.

"Fuck." Ash doubles over, gasping at the gray sidewalk cracks of LA. "Fuck."

Later that night, flopped in bed after devouring a carton of chicken lo mein and wrapped in a soft southwestern-pattern cardigan, she picks up her phone to respond to a text from her cousin.

**Tessie: Well? How'd it go? Did you burn up upon entry?**

She feels like she did.

With a sigh, Ash rereads the message, then tosses her phone on the nightstand beside her gory true crime novel.

Suddenly, she isn't so eager to reply to Tessie. Today was nothing to laugh or brag about. Not like the time she interrupted a serial-cheater's wedding. The job where the drunk uncle in the back of the pew shot up, threw the keys to his Thunderbird into the aisle and screamed *Take the money and run, son!* thereby cementing her all-around good faith in her career choice.

It's haunted her all night.

The sight of Nathaniel Whitford's face as she bolted for the door of the church.

It wasn't what she expected at all. Not from a man who'd been brazenly caught on camera in a strip club. It was the complete opposite of guilt.

It was pain.

Staring at the ceiling, Ash chews her lip, her nervous tic. A hot shower feels necessary. Along with a Brillo pad to scrub the slime from her skin. Today, she was a bad person. And not just in the oops-I-fucked-up-and-accidentally-dropped-a-baby kind of way. Bad in the I'm-taking-a-magnifying-glass-to-a-jar-full-of-bugs-and-I-fucking-love-it kind of way.

Is she really helping?

Or is she the girl who breaks hearts to make her own feel better?

Who knows? Right now, Ash doesn't feel anything.

Least of all good.

# II.

# GLOOM

# Chapter Two

*Three Years Later*

Hollywood Forever is hopping. Tourists stroll the lush grounds. The scent of honeysuckle floats in the light breeze. Sparkling June sunlight ripples across the Garden of Legends Lake. Ash wishes for clouds. She's burning alive in her boots.

Still, she smiles and waves goodbye to her tour. The last of the day. As she walks toward her favorite bench, she inhales. LA. It's where she comes from. Deep in her blood, endless sunshine and summers and smog. Hook it to her veins.

Nearby, a couple snaps a photo of the grave of Johnny Ramone. She could fill a library with her love for Los Angeles, and particularly the cemeteries.

Not only is Hollywood Forever Cemetery the resting place for many of the biggest stars of Hollywood's golden age, but it's Ash's favorite place for peace and quiet. For many, a walk among the dead is macabre, but to her, it's peaceful.

Wiping sweat from her brow, she stops over a grave, her black combat boots dusty from her trek outside. She looks down at her new acquaintance. Jayne Mansfield.

Celebrities at their most human. She could take a lesson.

At the ping of her phone, Ash retrieves it from her pocket and smiles.

**Tessie: Poop disaster averted. Call incoming.**

As promised, the FaceTime call comes through. Like clockwork. Ash never misses a call with her cousin. No matter how many blowouts or babies or deaths. No matter the daily drudge.

It's their commitment to each other. Ash would never survive this life without Tessie.

She's the most important thing in her universe.

Tessie, sparkling-eyed and fresh-faced and definitely not sweating, blinks at her from the screen.

"Lay it on me, preggo," Ash says.

"What about…" Tessie makes jazz hands. "Tallulah?"

Ash makes a face. "Absolutely not." After her mother saddled her with the absolute worst name in the world, Ash refuses to let Tessie do the same to her child.

Tessie sighs and waves a hand around her belly. "It's the hormones. I swear I like the strangest things these days. Ask me about my obsession with bee pollen."

Tessie's two-year-old son, Wilder, toddles in the background. "Aunt Bash, Aunt Bash, Aunt Bash," he chants, making Ash sound like a destructive video game villain.

She leans into the screen, wishing she could reach in, grab her cousin and squeeze. "How is my favorite tiny human?"

Tessie laughs. "Which one?" she asks, palming her belly. "Bear or…"

"The barely formed." Ash pokes a finger at the screen. At Tessie's round belly.

"She is currently the size of a banana and subjecting my bladder to a myriad of spectacular sucker punches."

Ash tosses her head back and hoots. "Solomon's mountain man sperm really claiming that uterus."

At a large kitchen table covered in design boards and Pantone chips, Tessie grips her belly and lowers herself into a chair. Even five-months pregnant, she's the epitome of Vogue perfection. Glossy blond hair, bright brown eyes, tan skin with a sprinkling of freckles over the bridge of her nose.

Ash is her opposite: dark, moody and pale as hell.

As kids, their mothers called them white swan and black swan cousins.

Not only because of their looks.

Late, Ash.

Early, Tessie.

Chaos and confusion, Ash.

Calm and order, Tessie.

They could have taken lessons from each other; instead, they egged each other on in all the best ways.

"I miss you," Tessie says, her brown eyes suddenly full of a soft sadness.

Ash's heart expands at the words.

Since the moment her cousin and best friend moved to Alaska two years ago, their distance has been a gaping wound in her soul. Despite what feels like an entire continent between them, the lock and key of their friendship has stayed strong. They still have their rhythm. It's just shaken up and stirred thanks to babies and miles and that thing called life.

Though Ash is always homesick for her cousin, Tessie is where she's supposed to be. Alaska. Getting railed daily by her bearded mountain man.

"I miss you too." Ash takes a seat on her favorite bench. Beneath her feet, the grave of Fay Wray. "God, what I wouldn't do to teleport you a hug right now."

"Well?" Tessie's eyes, now brimming with doubt, flicker to the phone. "Are you packed?"

Ash raises a hand. "Hold, please."

Overhearing a tourist searching for the grave of Judy Garland, Ash points her in the right direction. Saturday afternoon, and the cemetery is packed with tourists studying maps in the bright sunlight and the sweltering heat.

"Do you think I'm packed?" Ash says, coming back to the conversation. "Or do you think my suitcase is lying in the bottom of my closet, filled with vintage copies of Nancy Drew and dried-up sea monkeys?"

Tessie squeals in protest. "I absolutely can*not* with you right now."

Ash, knowing last-minute packing goes against every bone in Tessie's perfectionist body, smothers a smile.

"How can you not be packed?" Her cousin huffs. "You leave tomorrow."

"I am a one-woman show. You know that. And I have more important things to worry about."

"Like Augustus."

Her heart squeezes. "Like Augustus."

Her newest client, Augustus Fox, is a wealthy hotel magnate. He's flying her and his family to Hawaii for one last family vacation. It's the oddest job she's ever had.

And Ash is the odd-job queen.

She tried. Tried hard to do the thing known as the American dream and make something of herself.

After high school, she enrolled at USC, where she did poorly. Couldn't sit. Mind too wild. She dropped out. Meanwhile, Tessie excelled, working her ass off in school while waitressing to pay for it and eventually flourishing in her interior design career.

Ash spent most of her twenties playing Russian roulette with entry-level positions, taking the first humdrum desk job she could find, one after another. She burned through seven in her first year. And she hated them all. With the burning passion of a thousand fiery suns. The butt-in-a-chair-and-work mentality. Corporate ass-kissing. The part of life where a person is required to get a paycheck in order to live.

It was too rote. Too boring.

She longed to do something unhinged and beautiful.

Eventually, that need led her to death.

The first death that hit hard wasn't personal. It was Princess Diana. Her mother and aunt cried. Big tears that rivaled the tears they'd shed when they watched *Steel Magnolias*. It confused young Ash. It fascinated her. She was glued to the TV. The funeral. That envelope sitting atop the casket. *What was in it? What did it say? Would Diana ever really know?* She asked Tessie what she thought happened to people when they died. Her cousin responded with a shrug and an *I don't know*.

Ash didn't know either. So she went to the library. She read book after book. Had all kinds of questions. *Where do we go? Does the big man in the sky greet people with cocktails and high fives? Or is it an endless black nothing?*

And then, when she and Tessie were seventeen, death hit closer to home. Her Aunt Sophie, Tessie's mother, passed.

Core memory there, that feeling of her stomach sinking. That knowledge that nothing in the world she knew would ever be right again. The sight of Tessie collapsing to her knees in the hallway of the hospital and sobbing with her entire soul, *I don't know how to do this*, and even though her words scared her so fucking badly, set a fire loose in her chest, Ash took her in her arms and swept her off to all-night movie marathon.

Her mom was sad. Her best friend was sad. She was too, but all Ash wanted to do was heal them. Help. Only, she didn't know how.

Over the years, Ash honed her craft. Her job search skills. Off-jobs, this time. Dog walker. Art model. Say what you want about LA, but she has had one fantastic job after another. After discovering she had a talent for crying on cue, she started her own business. She became a professional funeral mourner. Then, after her botched relationship with Jakob, she expanded into professional wedding objector.

A profession she abandoned three years ago.

Nathaniel Whitford and his dagger-eyed glare haunt her nightmares. The pain on his face. What she did. Everything about it was icky. *She* was icky.

She didn't like herself in that period of her life. Jakob's betrayal launched her into her villain origin story. It changed the trajectory of her life and influenced the decisions she made. Objecting to weddings, hurting people even if they deserved it, were very bad decisions. She fumbled. Eventually, she worked to course correct.

The change began soon after the Nathaniel Whitford almost-wedding. While she was attending a funeral, working as a professional mourner, she met a woman who was a death doula. They had coffee after, and the prospect pulled her in. It felt like a *hell yes*. Every aspect of it—the freedom of care she could offer, the lack of strong regulations that came with working in an office, the fact that death is the most natural part of life, yet somehow generates so much fear.

Two weeks later, Ash enrolled in a death midwife certification and earned the first degree she's ever had.

After two years, she can confidently say that her death doula gig is no longer an odd job. It's her passion. A calling she's honored to have found.

New leaf.

Helping, not hurting.

"Remind me again," Tessie says, bringing her back to the conversation. "You're gone for how many days?"

"Fourteen-ish." Ash squints, working to recall the itinerary she's barely scrolled through. Go-with-the-flow is more her speed. "We fly out tomorrow morning at nine and land in Honolulu."

"God. I wish I could come and rot on a beach with you."

"I wish you could too," Ash says, then groans. "Why couldn't I get a client who likes snow in the Alps?" She thrives among new people. She just doesn't thrive in subtropical climates.

Tessie snorts. "You hate snow too."

"True. But I could be sitting in a lodge with blankets and fuzzy hats and spiked hot chocolate."

"Adorable fuzzy hats," Tessie adds wistfully. Then she shoots a narrowed gaze at Ash. "Think of it as payback for ditching me on my babymoon."

Ash rolls her eyes. "I will never hear the end of it, will I? Even if you are carrying the second of Solomon's brawny heathen spawn."

A low rumble of a growl. "I heard that."

Solomon comes into view, leaning in from one side, his burly flannel-clad shoulder blocking Tessie's face.

The way Solomon sets a plate of food in front of his wife, then sweeps a kiss over her lips, makes Ash's cheeks warm. Her cousin looks for all the world like a lovesick teenager. It's impressive. Clearly, Solomon Wilder has mellowed Tessie out with that extra-large dick of his.

"God, I'm such a whore for your love story," Ash muses.

Tessie laughs. Ash smiles.

Love.

It's all she ever wanted for her cousin.

Herself? She'll steer clear, thank you very much.

Solomon sweeps a lock of hair behind Tessie's ear, and that's when she catches a glimpse of the dark circles under her cousin's eyes.

Ash frowns, and a niggle of worry worms its way through her. "Are you sure you're sleeping enough?" she asks, suddenly hating the distance between them. "What's wrong?"

Scowling, Tessie presses palms to her stomach. "You're as bad as Solomon."

"She's fine," Solomon says, giving Ash a look of mutually assured overprotection.

Memories of that time, Tessie near death, always leave her feeling panicky and breathless and anxious. The closest to a breakdown she's ever come. Her own death doesn't scare her. But her cousin? The one person she needs in this life, the only person who's ever understood her, who never questions her weird, who loves her fiercely even when she doesn't love herself? Her close call almost ended Ash.

Nothing will ever happen to Tessie again. Not on her or Solomon's watch.

Tessie smiles after her mountain man, then turns her attention back to Ash. "Are you okay?" Her voice gets hushed. Her brown eyes burn with worry. "Going to Hawaii?"

Ash's stomach plummets, then snaps back into place. Hawaii is one of many bad callbacks to her relationship with Jakob. Do not pass go. Do not flash back. Do not let your reptilian brain run down that track.

She swallows hard.

"I'll be fine," she says. "Of course, I hate that we're over the ocean. Have you seen my algorithm?"

"You almost went to Mexico," Tessie points out.

"Mexico was different. And that was for you."

"You're there for your client, but *you* try to have fun too. Don't reserve your amazing good moods exclusively for me. Don't forget sugar. Find a graveyard. Oh! Better, a haunted lighthouse. And call me every day so I know you haven't fallen into a volcano."

Ash smiles at Tessie's frazzled mom energy.

"Go on a date while you're there. Have fun with a hot surf instructor."

"I don't have time for dates."

Tessie wiggles her brows. "Just the dead?"

Ash looks down at the grave beneath her boots. "Something like that."

# Chapter Three

SUITCASE WHEELS SCREECH ACROSS TILE FLOOR. Overhead, fluorescent terminal lights hum. The heavy carry-on and roller bag weigh Ash down like anchors.

All the sunscreen and floppy hats in the world have been successfully packed. Because Ash doesn't tan like Tessie. She fucking crisps.

Up ahead, Augustus breezes through the Honolulu airport. In his patterned cardigan, slim-fit trousers and loafers, he looks like a member from the Rat Pack. The gold band he still wears for his late wife, Rosalea, glimmers on his ring finger. He keeps a tight hold on his carry-on with his age-spotted hand. He wouldn't let her carry it. No matter how many times she asked. He might appear fragile, but the man's strong like bull.

"Coming, Ash?" He glances over his shoulder at her with a chuckle. His determined yet casual stride says *I am a man with money and damn good taste*.

"Coming." She tugs at her roller bag and then promptly stumbles over her boots.

*Damn Tessie*. She never should have let her cousin talk her into that second bag. But if she's into blaming things, she also never should have had that second tequila on the plane.

She shakes her head, trying to catch her breath, then hustles up to Augustus, who's clearing the space ahead of her like he's Usain Bolt.

This is Exhibit A of her theory of why the man will truly never die. Even with a slow-growing form of brain cancer, he is a nonstop force of nature. Overseeing his boutique chain of hotels. Poker games at the legion every Sunday. He never stops.

Augustus Fox. A man larger than life. Rich. Decisive. No bullshit. He's also the kindest and most interesting man she's ever met. The stories he tells her about Hollywood and Vegas in the '70s are like catnip. She's 90 percent positive he muled for the mob. He claims to be in possession of a money clip that once belonged to mafia don Carlo Giacomo. She 98 percent believes him.

Six months into their relationship, Augustus is a part of her daily routine. They met at a funeral of an old-school Hollywood actress he swears he almost married. Ash was working part time as a mourner, and after she flung herself on the grave and was dusting off her shoes, Augustus said, "I like your style."

Then he hired her, and that was that.

Now, on his good days, she plays chess with him in his posh Beverly Hills bungalow. She accompanies him to chemo on his bad. In a matter of weeks, he became family. This wise old man who makes tea for her, calls her dear, and has the most magnificent wine collection she's ever seen.

Officially, Ash is his death doula. Though she likes to think of herself as a personal death bouncer. Regardless of where her clients are in the process, they don't have to do the game of death alone. She's there. To help plan, to advocate, to spend the last moments with those who have no one. Whatever they need. Hand massages, spiritual readings, traveling halfway around the world on a tropical vacation. It's what she does.

Sure, it's an unorthodox arrangement, but it is also an honor.

It doesn't hurt that being Augustus's death doula comes with a lifesaving amount of money. Literally. With the cost of insulin supplies astronomically high, she needs to bank every penny she can.

"Okay," she huffs, bringing a hand to her chest. Her heart has never known this much exercise. "Debrief."

Augustus barely turns, his lips pulling into a smile. "Debrief? We prepped on the plane."

"Then a refresh," she croaks. Her mouth is dry and sweet. She wishes she could stop at a bathroom to clean herself up. She doesn't trust her fuzzy tequila-riddled memory. On the plane, Augustus gave her the lowdown on each family member who'd be joining the vacation. *To be prepared.* That warning had been ominous, to say the least.

His nod is brisk. "My daughter."

"Claire. Also called Claire Bear. You love her, but you'd love her more if she hadn't settled for, and I quote, that 'deadbeat, dead-eyed sorry excuse for a husband.'"

"Impressive. And accurate. My son-in-law." Augustus's voice hardens. "Don."

"Don," she repeats. The name drips from her lips like poison. "Part Frankenstein, part day trader, all asshole. We couldn't take the private jet because he called dibs first. And as you repeated numerous times on the plane, you will not save him from a shark attack, and I am banned from doing so as well, which is exactly my type of petty."

Augustus's bark of laughter echoes through the terminal. "Would you believe it was the tequila talking?"

Ash swats at him lightly. "Augustus, I think you're a lying liar."

As is her habit, she palms the bag slung around her waist. Checks to make sure she has her insulin pens. One long acting and one short acting. Another set tossed in just in case she gets stranded on a desert island.

"Tate," she says.

"Youngest grandson. Goes by the unfortunate nickname Tater Tot. He's using his inheritance as a podcast startup."

In unison, she and Augustus groan.

"Horny," Augustus continues. "Every time he crosses a state line, he sees it as an objective to get laid."

A stranger rams into Ash's shoulder, pulling a curse from her. She spins around to glare at the offender. Walking backward, she says, "How do you know all this? Somehow, I doubt it's in the family manual."

His blue eyes sparkle with a glint of mischief. "I have little birdies."

Ash laughs. Of course he does.

The annoying chime of her phone blares from her purse. A warning from her continuous glucose monitor, or CGM, that her blood sugar is either high or low.

"Sugar, my dear?"

"Nope." She swirls a finger. "Not yet. Keep trucking."

They continue their trek through the terminal. Ash resumes her debrief.

"Delaney. Baby of the family. Only granddaughter. Actress of slasher films. If she offers to give me a tarot reading, I am to politely decline." Ash rattles off the details, ingrained in memory, for this two-week vacation.

With a nod, Augustus puts a gentle hand on her elbow and stops her, pulling her into a nook near a water fountain. "Listen, Ash. I love my family. But they are like sharks. When one of them takes a bite out of you, the rest of them can smell it."

Ash fights the swell of anxiety rising inside her. What is she walking into? God, what if they're the Firefly family?

She shakes off the thought. It's only two weeks. And it's for Augustus. She can survive almost anything.

"I will be on guard," she says. "But I will also be on my bullshit."

Augustus cackles. "That's why I like you, Ash. You sting."

"Oh good," she huffs, fighting with the strap of her carry-on. "I love being likened to a swarm of wasps."

The older man's expression drops into melancholy. He steps closer and grips her shoulder with a firm hand. "This is my last chance, Ash. To make sure they're okay." His voice softens. "Because how can I leave this earthly plane without doing everything I can to protect them?"

The words are said with such a sad caress of longing that it makes her heart ache.

She sees this a lot. The end-of-life wrap-up. It's human nature.

Fix regrets. Mend bridges. Get things in order so that the dying feel some semblance of control, no matter how small.

Which is where Hawaii comes in.

For once, Augustus has nothing on his calendar—no medical tests, procedures or treatments—and he scheduled the trip to fit between his six-week chemo appointments.

Augustus, a developer of boutique hotels studded across the West Coast, has arranged for his family, as well as Ash, to visit each of the resorts he's built in Hawaii. One last vacation before he gets too sick to enjoy it. And she's to act as a kind of mediator between him and his estranged family.

Augustus arches his craggy brows and sighs. "We're loud, Ash. Loud in love, loud in anger. For the last few years, it's been decibel levels. And not in the good way." He looks at her, pleading. "I need to see us all together. One last time."

A wave of softness hits her in the gut, but she refuses to get emotional. At least until the end. She takes her vibes from her clients. If they want her to rail and sob and curse the world, she will. If they need her to be a hard-ass, to be unaffected and stoic, she can do that too.

It's why she's good at this.

Only with Augustus, she's not ready.

Augustus isn't either.

She squeezes his hand. "You will. We're going to see your hotels, have a fucking party and wrangle your family."

His lips part. The mournful look gone. "I couldn't have said it better myself, my dear."

They begin to move again. Up ahead, the baggage claim beckons. A voice over the loudspeaker reminds travelers that suitcases and strangers don't mix.

"Oh, and I forgot to tell you," Augustus booms. "My oldest grandson will be joining us. It was touch and go for a while there, but he was finally able to get time off work."

"The more the merrier," Ash adds. As he should. What kind of monster can't take work off for his grandfather's last trip?

"Don't tell anyone." Augustus's voice is jovial. "But he's my favorite. Even if he is a doctor who works too much."

"Favorite. Doctor. Noted." She nods. Logs the info away in case she needs an adversary. Or a tourniquet.

Ash trips over her suitcase, the laces of her untied boots tangling in the wheels. She swears as the overpacked bag on her shoulder jerks her into a 360-degree spin. "What did you say his name was again?"

"I didn't," Augustus says, keeping his focus fixed on where they're headed. "Nathaniel."

Her whole body freezes. Ice courses through her veins. She tries not to choke on her own tongue. "Nathaniel. That's, uh, short for Jonathan, right?"

Augustus doesn't reply. He's already shoving through the sliding doors that lead to the baggage claim area. "He's here," he exclaims with a kind of giddy little kid excitement.

Ahead of her, Augustus is pulled into a hug by a very tall, very broad, beige-ish figure.

She tilts her head up.

And up.

*Holy shit. Holy fucking shit.*

Ash stops. As does her heart.

*This cannot be fucking happening.*

The man letting Augustus loose from a hug is none other than Nathaniel Rhodes Whitford.

His eyes land on her, and he freezes too. The moment is like that terrifying jump cut at the end of a horror movie.

As Nathaniel takes her in, shock creases his expression. And then it slowly morphs into a more suitable look. A scowl full of loathing and disgust.

"You've got to be fucking kidding me," he says.

In response, Ash's entire body locks.

His eyes of pale-blue ice skim over her body. And not in a sexy way. In a how-you'd-look-at-someone-if-you-were-plotting-out-their-murder type of way.

"You're the driver, right?" Ash asks, even though she knows he's not the driver. Unless Augustus is very into giving out free hugs to just about anyone.

"The grandson," Nathaniel bites out, his jaw as rigid as his posture.

Ash stiffens as if her body's filling with cement.

That voice. Stern. Curt. It's haunted her memory. Sure, he said less than five words to her that day, but those words were sandblasted into her brain.

Ash takes him in, her gaze shrewd. Unfortunately, the man matches the memory. As unfairly good-looking as she remembers. Obscenely tall. Muscular and broad-shouldered. Thick, wheat-colored hair that would make any normal woman want to rake her claws through it. Expensive chinos. The white linen shirt shoved up to his elbows exposes tan, corded forearms, an expensive dive watch. She could huff the Ivy League stench wafting off him. Which is unfortunate, because it's obvious his face card is never declining.

Augustus looks from her to Nathaniel. "This is Ash."

She stiffens, bracing for the blow. For Nathaniel to reveal to Augustus that she's a home-wrecker. A terrible person.

Instead, all he says is "Ash? Just Ash?" He looks down at her with an expression of distaste. His upper lip curls. "Like soot from a chimney?"

Ash bristles but quickly shakes it off. She won't give him the satisfaction of letting on that she's uncomfortable. "The best kind."

His brow lifts. "And you're a…"

"A death doula. Your grandfather's."

Nathaniel surveys Augustus, doubt etched all over his grim face. Then he turns back to her. Amused now. "So, essentially, you're unemployed."

Asshole. Of course employment would be the first topic on his mind. This man has probably never missed a day of work in his life.

Fine, then. She can give as good as she gets. Ash shoots back, "I wasn't aware Hawaii had a welcome committee that insults its tourists."

She squares her shoulders and turns to Augustus. But Nathaniel beats her to it. He takes his grandfather's bag. Tries to pluck hers off her back like the caveman he is.

"I got it." She locks her arms and pulls the bag tighter, but the sight of his long fingers and tan, well-veined hands is enough to knock her off-kilter.

She turns her head with a cringe. Please, god. Delete image.

"Grandpops," Nathaniel says, his voice affectionate but still rough, "I think you could do better."

Ash rolls her eyes. *Grandpops.* Of course he'd have an adorable nickname for Augustus.

Nathaniel heads for the exit, Augustus at his side, and she follows. She doesn't attempt to keep up with them. The more distance kept between them, the better. Disgust emanates off Nathaniel in waves. He's gritting his teeth so hard she's afraid he'll need reconstructive surgery.

Holy fuck. She's always believed in kismet, but this? Flying halfway around the world only to discover that Augustus's favorite grandson is Nathaniel Whitford is truly the coup de grâce. It's the worst karmic retribution she's gotten in her thirty-three years of existence.

There's no talking, no expression on Nathaniel's face as he leads them to the car. Only a hand on his tie, tugging it loose like it's constricting him.

He's a robot. A scowling, stomping lithopedion.

They pass through the sliding doors. All at once, they're outside. Ash hisses at the sticky air and brilliant sunshine. Her all-black attire is instantly clammy and uncomfortable.

"Interesting," comes a grim voice. Nathaniel's sharp gaze skims from her boots to her sheer long-sleeved lace bodysuit. "I should have known you were catlike in all of your reflexes."

Ash bares her teeth. "Cats are one of the top apex predators of this world." She jerks her bag back when he reaches for it again. "Show a little respect."

His brow furrows. "Are you always so full of fun facts?"

"I am a walking encyclopedia."

She scrutinizes the car. A big, black luxury SUV. Outside the passenger-side door, a driver waits, and relief fills her. She wants this conversation over with. More importantly, she wants air-conditioning. She's sweating bullets. The heat's sweltering. So different from LA. It's like she got dropped into the middle of a sauna. Everything on her body is a puddle.

"How nice of you." She gestures at the driver. "Making the world feel your wealth."

"It's a rental," he grits out.

Ash yanks on the handle of the car door and throws him a withering glare over her shoulder.

Nathaniel pauses at the passenger side. "You know," he says, squinting at her in disapproval, "not dressing like a plague doctor would help with all the sweating."

Ash snorts. "At least I'm not dressed like *American Psycho* in paradise."

There's no comeback. Just a shutdown. Nathaniel flexes a fist, looking like he's charging up his violence using photosynthesis.

Maybe she went too far.

Maybe.

Either way, she chases away that flare of guilt. He's a cheater. He doesn't deserve sympathy. Or niceness. Not from her.

Releasing an impatient breath, Ash crawls into the back seat. It's dark and cool. She wants to burrow into the leather like a field mouse who loves a good sand dune. In her bag, her phone pings.

On the other side of the tinted window, Nathaniel helps his

grandfather into the car, gripping Augustus's hand with a tenderness that makes Ash's throat pinch.

When the bags are loaded, Nathaniel takes a seat in the middle row and leans forward to give the driver directions.

The car begins to move as Augustus settles in the third row beside her.

Her phone's obnoxious CGM alarm chimes yet another warning. This time she listens and pulls it out to check the reading. Her blood sugar is seventy-three and dropping. Tequila and an airport trek have done a number on her.

"You know," Augustus begins, angling closer and momentarily distracting her. "If there was one thing I liked about you when we first met, it was the way you lunged for the altar."

Her jaw drops, along with her stomach.

"Holy shit, you knew," she hisses. Her eyes snap to Nathaniel, who sits stiffly in front of them.

"I knew *of* you."

"Augustus, you cannot fucking be telling me that I am stuck on vacation with your grandson whose wedding I pretty much atom-bombed."

"The more the merrier. Isn't that what you said?" Augustus grins like the Cheshire cat.

She elbows him. "You're lucky you're dying."

In the seat in front of them, Nathaniel makes a kind of choking noise.

Augustus merely shrugs. "I can't say I agree with what you did, but I'm sure you have your reasons. Camellia was never up to snuff, in my opinion."

She covers her face and sinks deeper into the seat, her chest constricting. "Oh Jesus, Augustus."

"I can hear you, Grandpops," Nathaniel says. He crosses his arms, but he doesn't turn around.

Hit with a tidal wave of panic, Ash tilts closer to Augustus.

"I have to meet your entire family. *Tonight*. At dinner. And they all know what I did."

"I'll be there." He pats her knee. "You'll be fine."

*Fine.* Right. That's what serial killers say to their victims before they drive them down an old winding road to meet a garden shed full of meat hooks.

Her CGM alarm chimes again, but the reminder isn't needed. Her body is already screaming at her. The fire of her blood. The sweat on her brow. Shit. She drops her phone back into her bag and digs through it for a granola bar. Once she's got one in hand, she tears off the corner and takes a huge bite.

Nathaniel loops his arm over his seat and peers over his shoulder. "Like I said, it's a rental. If you're going to eat in the car, can you please try not to fuck up the upholstery with your crumbs?"

"Apologies for the inconvenience of being a type-one diabetic," Ash says calmly but sharply. "I can drop dead if you prefer."

Her response is met with nothing but silence from Nathaniel. Good.

Ash collapses against the leather seat and turns her face to the window. The granola bar sits heavy in her stomach. The jagged cliffs and emerald-green foliage of Honolulu flash by. But she can't appreciate its beauty, much less concentrate on it. Not with her blood sugar in the shitter and a disaster of a dinner looming on the horizon.

From the corner of her eye, she catches Nathaniel needling his brow like an icepick has just made its mark.

And it has.

She's the icepick.

## Chapter Four

NATHANIEL CAN SPOT DISASTERS FROM A MILE AWAY. A damaged wellhead soon to leak oil. A patient saying *I don't feel well* moments before they collapse. And this, this vacation, will be a disaster.

He should have known. When it comes to his family, nothing is ever easy.

Less than a day ago, he decided to take leave from his post as a remote-site doctor on an oil rig and join this so-called family vacation. Typically, he uses the four weeks off to travel the world. Surfing in Australia. Scuba diving in Belize. Family time isn't his strong suit. Not with the Whitfords. Close confines with his prick father, his mother—who has looked like she's on the verge of a nervous breakdown for years—his horny little brother and his attention-starved little sister? Just the thought is enough to make him itch.

And yet he came. He rallied.

For his grandfather.

A decision he already regrets. This whole situation is absurd.

This girl. Ash. What was his grandfather thinking, inviting her? She wreaked havoc on his world. Wrecked his fucking wedding. Sent his life into a spiral for a good year. He doesn't know a damn thing about Ash whatever-the-hell-her-last-name is, but now that she's inserted herself into his grandfather's life, he plans to make it his mission to figure out what the hell she wants.

Either that or drop her on a desert island and leave her to the birds.

To her credit, she's already a pain in his ass. It takes a lot to snap that thread of patience. Full moons and emergency room patients have nothing on this girl.

An hour in the car together, and his nerves are fried. The crunchy wrinkle of the granola bar. The tap-tap-tapping on her cell phone with those long black nails. Her ability to joke warmly with Augustus while simultaneously ignoring Nathaniel.

It pisses him off.

But now that he's here, he can't leave. All he can do is wait it out.

"We're all checked in," Nathaniel tells his grandfather as the driver pulls up to the curb of the hotel. "Delaney can't get off set until Tuesday, so she'll be here then."

With a chuckle, Augustus pushes out of the back seat. "Delaney will be Delaney."

Nathaniel climbs out quickly and grips his grandfather's hand. His stomach pulls tight as the older man shuffles forward, gait unsteady. This isn't the outcome he wanted. When Augustus was first diagnosed with cancer, Nathaniel flew to LA every weekend he could. Threw himself into finding him the best doctor, experimental treatments. He hoped for a miracle, because he's not ready for his grandfather to go.

"Fuck, fuck, fuck."

Nathaniel cranes his neck and homes in on Ash, who's muttering *fuck* like it's the lord's prayer. As she leans forward to scoot out of the back seat, crumbs scatter from her lap. Still cursing, she flails, trying to capture the granola bar wrapper that's being manhandled in the breeze. Her wild mass of black hair swirls like a cloud of doom. She looks up, catching him watching her, then scowls. Scowls some more.

"Shit." She waves a hand in the air. The move causes her to drop her purse on the curb, where its contents scatter. Phone. Packets of lavender tea. A baggie of little peanut butter Ritz crackers. A pair of 3D glasses. "Go in. I'll catch up."

He sighs. She's a fucking mess.

On their way inside the open-air lobby of the Rosalea Montage resort, Nathaniel takes in the familiar sight. He's been to nearly all his grandfather's hotels. As a child, he, along with the rest of his family, stayed for weeks during the summers. All Fox Hotels have the same immaculate vibes, décor, hospitality. The Rosalea Montage resort, perched at the edge of a seaside cliff, is no different. Decorated in colors of muted turquoise and cream, the fifteen-acre beachfront property screams luxury and elegance. Attracts a pampered and peaceful clientele from all over the world.

Beside Nathaniel, his grandfather stands taller than he has in a long time, his expression proud.

"Just like you remember?" he asks, a smile tugging at his mouth as he hands his grandfather his key card.

Augustus chuckles. "I remember you right there. You ate too much shave ice and puked in that planter."

A warm fondness blooms in Nathaniel's chest. "It wasn't my finest moment."

Augustus gives him a wry side-eye. "You sure you don't want it?" he asks good-naturedly.

Nathaniel slings an arm around his shoulder. "Not at all, Grandpops."

Unlike Nathaniel's father, Augustus leaves it at that. No pushing for corporate takeover.

Nathaniel is content on the ocean.

Away from his family. Keeping a free life. He'll never trap himself again.

For a second, he loses himself in the tranquility of his grandfather's hotel. The crash of the ocean outside. The warm sun casting shadows through the eaves.

And then he hears it.

The sound of great, gigantic boot stomps.

Instantly, the peace of the hotel is shattered. The concierge frowns. The people in line at the check-in rubberneck their way.

Nathaniel bristles, instantly annoyed. Christ, that noise. No matter how many times he's tried to acid wash his brain, he can't get the sound of Ash storming through the church like some vengeful wraith out of his head.

Scowling, he turns. Across the glossy marble tile, her boot laces dance and dart.

"Fuck," he mutters.

She's oblivious. And she looks ridiculous. Like some gothic black cat of a girl. Oversized combat boots. Short black skirt, long-sleeved black bodysuit. Despite the absurd outfit, he can't help tracing over the specks of color on her pale frame. Colorful tattoos cover her thighs. Flowers of all varieties. Higher up, a pop of a neon pink bra strap accentuates her fair skin. The kohl cat eye slashed atop her lids gives her a feral look. All that, combined with her violently blood-red lips and her doomsday cloud of jet-black hair, makes her look like she's a dark harbinger of doom.

Again, what kind of name is Ash?

Her boot stomps silence as she stops beside Augustus, and the open space goes deafeningly quiet. Briefly, her gaze flicks to Nathaniel. A look equal parts intrigued and disinterested. Her big gray-green eyes and those long black lashes cause his stomach to flip. A sensation he could do the fuck without.

"Boots are untied, Bigfoot," he barks in a hard tone.

The arch of her brow is cool. "Maybe you'll get lucky and I'll break my neck."

He runs a hand down the front of his shirt. "Your commitment to your early death is impressive."

"I am nothing if not an agent of chaos." Done with him, Ash scans the lobby. "This is real, Augustus. Impeccable. Like chef's kiss."

Nathaniel rolls his eyes but holds his tongue. By the way his grandfather lights up, he's clearly delighted by Ash's compliment.

As Augustus goes on about his hotel's amenities, the three of them make their way to the elevators that lead up to the tower suite. His grandfather's reserved a block of rooms on the seventeenth floor. They all share a balcony that Augustus likely hopes will maximize family togetherness. Apparently, running into a family member unplanned and unannounced is what the man is aiming for.

All the doors to the rooms are closed. So much for the welcome wagon. Tate's probably sleeping off a hangover, but Nathaniel doesn't share that fun fact with his grandfather.

"Ash and I will stay here," Augustus says, swiping the key card against the sensor.

He swings the door open, and they step into a generous two-bedroom suite. The living room is outfitted with woven throw pillows and a teakwood coffee table. In the corner of the room, across from the fully stocked minibar, rests a ukulele. Across the walls, framed vintage postcard prints of Hawaii. The luggage has already been delivered. The curtains have been opened to expose the balcony and highlight the spectacular views of Diamond Head.

Ash strolls into the room, brows lifted. "Holy shit," she breathes. "Fuck yes, Augustus." She pumps a fist, revealing a little white disc-shaped sensor on the back of her arm. "Slaying it again."

"Take the bedroom with the best view, Ash," Augustus calls in a jovial tone. "I've been here many times, my dear."

Without argument, and with a great grunt, she heaves her suitcase onto the bed of the room she's chosen. The minute she pops the latch, the luggage explodes. The bed is instantly peppered with big, dumb floppy hats and bottles of sunscreen. Itty bitty bikinis. Lacy underwear. Suddenly, Nathaniel is picturing her doing backstrokes in the resort pool. His gaze dips. Freezes on a toned thigh streaked with brilliant color and violence. A heart and a knife blooming in a bed of flowers.

Nope. This is not okay. Absolutely the fuck not.

Smearing a hand down his face, he clears his throat and moves to the center of the living room. Away from Ash. He needs a topic of conversation other than this strange woman's underwear. "How are you feeling?" he asks his grandfather.

Augustus tsks, brows raised. "No cancer talk."

Nathaniel releases an impatient breath. "Grandpops—"

"You want to talk about it, we'll talk. Over much whiskey. But I'd like to have fun on this vacation, and I expect that you'd prefer that too."

It's the way of his grandfather. Demands. Well-meaning demands, but demands, nonetheless.

He shoves his hands into his pockets. "Are you sure about this?"

Augustus leans, wearing a conspiratorial smirk. "Sure about what?"

His gaze flicks to Ash. Out on the balcony, leaning so far over the railing as she surveys the path down to the ground, he can't be sure she doesn't have some sort of death wish. The impractical urge to go to her, to move her away, runs through him like electricity.

"Are you sure about *her*?" He can't keep the bite out of his voice.

"I like Ash and all her fucks," Augustus says with an adoring chuckle. "She tells it like it is. She's macabre. She's quirky. She's—"

"Feral," he finishes.

Augustus tuts. "She's exactly what this family needs."

Annoyance ripples through him. He doesn't like it. This girl is a relentless force of chaos. Everything that can get under his skin and threaten his planned and orderly world. Worse, his grandfather is clearly enamored with her.

Augustus presses his lips together and glances at Ash for a moment. "She was in the wrong, doing what she did in the way that she did it, but tell me she was *wrong*, and I'll send her home."

It's that *wrong* in his grandfather's pointed tone that holds all the truths Nathaniel's never admitted aloud.

A muscle flares in his jaw. He won't. Can't say it.

When Camellia called off the wedding, it wasn't relief that hit him. It was a sensation more like being put out of his misery.

Still, that stubborn streak of anger runs through him. Anger at Ash. It's not so much that she broke up the wedding. It's that she had the fucking gall to do so. That in the eyes of Camellia and her family, he's been branded something he's not. That he still doesn't fucking know who hired Ash to cause the chaos she did.

Augustus goes on, his expression earnest. "I know you have your reservations, but I want Ash here. Her presence fills me with a great deal of warmth."

Fuck. Begrudging his grandfather this is something he'd never do. Not when he's been looking forward to this vacation. Not when he clearly enjoys the girl.

And yet…

He can't stop from voicing his concern. "Grandpops, what if she's some sort of con artist?"

A husky voice pipes up, making his stomach lurch. "Con artist?"

Ash and her cloud of hair slink around the corner. Her stare is stony as she takes a step forward.

"I may be a lot of things. Ill-reputed. Disheveled. A Scorpio. But I'm no con artist." For a split second, she looks genuinely hurt.

Nathaniel wonders if it's all an act. "That's up for debate," he argues.

His grandfather narrows his eyes on him, then turns his attention to Ash, his mind clearly spinning. Of course it is. This is the man who bought Delaney a pony on her tenth birthday, all because their father forbade pets. It's in his blood to meddle.

Brows cinched, Augustus squeezes Ash's arm, then Nathaniel's. "Get along or don't. Either way, we're meeting for dinner at seven. I've booked a table at the restaurant." He hobbles toward the bedroom, grumbling as he does so. "And now, if you'll excuse me, I'm going to pop out for a minute."

With an affectionate smile, Ash watches as Augustus departs. "That man's red flag is if he says he's going to 'pop out for a minute,' it means he's going to take a nap."

Nathaniel bristles. It irritates him that she knows his grandfather so well.

Ash turns to Nathaniel. She looks him up and down. Scrunches her face up in a way that could be misconstrued as adorable. "Let me guess. You unpack your suitcase the second you get home from vacation."

"And you're an off-putting person who likes the sight of murder."

She crosses her arms, lets out a purr of agreement. "Guess there's only one way to find out."

"I'm impressed," he says. "You went from weddings to hearses. Times must be tough."

She colors. "It wasn't my finest moment, okay?" She chews her lip, then shakes her head like she's already regretting her decision to speak to him. "Listen, Nate—"

"Nathaniel."

"Fine. *Nathaniel.*" Even the way she draws out his name, in husky, honeyed, ice-cold syllables, grates on him. "I understand why you're pissed at me, but do you think we can maybe co-exist? If not peacefully, at least not maliciously? For Augustus?"

"Of course," he grits out, annoyance simmering in his veins. "I won't even know you're here."

A relieved sigh pops out of her mouth. "Good."

Nathaniel asks, "What did you say your last name was again?"

"I didn't. Keller." She digs her fingers into her biceps. "Why? Planning to do some reconnaissance?"

"I might." He adjusts his rolled shirtsleeves. "Wouldn't want you to screw my grandfather over."

Gaze narrowed, she steps close to him. So close her breasts sweep against his chest. Hurt flashes in her green-gray eyes, her voice as cold as an icy wind. "I would never do that."

"I'll be on you," he warns. He takes a step back. The burning touch of her lingers. "The entire trip."

She cocks a brow. "Like a barnacle."

"See you at dinner, Bigfoot," he says dryly. Before he goes, he takes a second to revel in the brief flash of panic that crosses her face. God knows he could spar for hours with her, but she's not worth it.

At least he finds a modicum of comfort in the knowledge that she has to meet his family. He can't wait to see the shitshow that is tonight.

For the next two weeks, he plans to do to Ash what she's done to him.

Make her life a living hell.

## Chapter Five

THE DEVIL WORKS HARD, BUT NATHANIEL WHITFORD works harder.

The man's ready to kill her. Either it's a throttling with his massive, well-veined hands or a shot-put direct into the ocean from their shared balcony. He could do it. The muscles he's hoarding—unfairly toned biceps and ridiculously rippling pectorals—are evident even in the stern button-up he's wearing.

And what did he call her? *Bigfoot.*

Scoffing, Ash tosses her dresses into a drawer without bothering to hang them up. Everything's wrinkled anyway.

Clearly, petty nicknames are the best he can do.

Not that she blames him for his anger. Her actions back then were abhorrent. But he did a shitty thing. He should be pissed at himself, not at her.

Her mind leaps to the photos her client gave her. Nathaniel at a strip club, positioned far too familiarly with a girl who resembled a Bratz doll. Big eyes, bigger lips.

An icky, strange feeling suddenly settles in her belly like a lead ball. She's on vacation with strangers. Worse, those strangers are the *Whitfords*. Dull, straitlaced millionaires who get what they want with a snap of their spoiled fingers. Her only ally is Augustus.

Puffing her hair out of her face in frustration, she eyes the fluffy white bed. A nap. A nap would be good for regeneration. But if she sleeps, she and Augustus will miss dinner. And she won't give Nathaniel Whitford the satisfaction of thinking he's scared her away.

With that vengeful thought, she rallies. After a scalding hot shower, Ash checks her blood sugar and towel dries her hair. She's midway through her lip liner when her phone buzzes.

*Tessie.*

"Help," Ash says into the device. "What do you wear to a dinner party where you need to be cool, calm and collected, but you're also dining with the family of the man whose wedding you crashed?"

"A paper bag." Tessie already knows the story, thanks to Ash's frantic text during the car ride to the resort.

Ash snorts as Tessie stifles her own laughter. "Get serious. I'm having an existential crisis in paradise."

"I am serious." Tessie adjusts Bear in her arms. He's climbing over her like she's a carousel ride.

"Fuck." Ash paces her bedroom, already sweating again from nerves. "They're going to take one look at me and tar and feather me in the square. And why wouldn't they?" she mutters. "They're rich and I'm just a rag. They have perfect 401(k)s and make meaningful charitable contributions, but only for the tax write-off. And they do the turkey trot on Thanksgiving. I will bet you a thousand bucks."

Tessie laughs, her dark eyes dancing. "Done."

"Don't get me started on Nathaniel. He's this ugly, sour, morose doctor with a chip on his shoulder."

Tessie arches a brow. "Ugly?"

With a flap of a hand, Ash averts her eyes. She regrets saying anything. "He's one of the worst single, tall assholes I've ever met."

"Of course he's unbearable. You ruined his wedding." Tessie's lips tilt in a frown. "Have you considered apologizing?"

"Never," Ash hisses. "You're as bad as Mom."

Her cousin lets out a thoughtful hum. "Aunt Bev knows the truth."

Ash rolls her eyes, even though Tessie is right. The ever-present voice of reason, her mom, always ensures solid advice. Especially after Tessie's mother died. She has always been there for Ash. To reassure her that her odd jobs and pastimes are valid, that she isn't one career away from being on Feet Finder.

"Now," Tessie orders with a giddy determination, "show me your clothes. I will style you from afar, and you will appreciate it."

"Ruthlessly use me," Ash crows as she sets her phone aside.

Once her hands are free, she lays out her dresses. Stares at the dark jewel colors that suddenly make her feel like a monster who's swallowed the sun.

Phone in hand once more, Ash pans the collection. "Well?"

"The dark green slinkshow of a sundress." Tessie peeks over Bear's shoulder. "Add a gold necklace and hoops. Flip-flops."

Ash wrinkles her nose and fights a shudder. "I don't have flip-flops."

"Wise decision," Solomon says, popping in to steal Bear away from Tessie. "Your chances of being hunted by a seagull are low, but never zero."

"See?" Ash says, lifting her chin. "Bearded baby daddy speaks the truth."

Tessie sighs, and when Solomon dips close and kisses her brow, she smiles.

Ash flips her phone's camera so the dresses are on screen again. "Which green? Emerald?"

"Evergreen."

Leave it to her cousin to get picky with her Pantones.

Tessie nods her approval. "It's giving big main character energy."

Ash scowls. "I don't want to be a main character. I want to be that statue in the corner of the room that sometimes gets mistaken for a ghost and scares the shit out of people."

When Ash is sure Solomon's out of eyesight, she strips. Then she slides the slinky green dress, snakelike, onto her curves. Once it's in place, she holds the phone up and takes in her reflection in the mirror. With her wild hair and red partially painted lips, she looks…

Messy. The thought hurts.

"Ash?"

She doesn't reply. She can't. Not with the way she itches in her skin. That age-old feeling of not belonging. Even the suite is too fancy for her. Polished and pretty and light, when all she has is dark edges.

Fuck. She hates this feeling.

"You look beautiful, but you also look like you're going to puke," Tessie says gently.

Ash swallows, stares at her reflection. She doesn't think she could get any paler. "I feel like I'm going to puke."

"Okay, okay. Sit down. Water," Tessie cries. Ever since she became a mother, she's been obsessive about hydration.

Screw the water. Ash's anxiety is bouncing all over the place. She collapses on the edge of the bed and sucks in one shallow breath after another.

Somewhere in the suite, the creak of a door. Augustus is awake and on the move.

"I'm fine, I'm fine, I'm fine," she tells Tessie, desperate to erase the look of doubt on her cousin's face. "If loving Jakob taught me anything, it's that I will be *fine* no matter the situation." She flaps her arms, airing out her armpits. "See? I'm not even sweating. I'm going to have a mai tai and hang with some vengeful strangers who hate my guts, and at the end of the trip, we'll all be best fucking friends."

"Ash—"

"*Tessie*. It's going to be *fine*. It's an adventure. Paradise. It's not trauma; it's spicy sadness."

Tessie needles her brow. "Only dogs can hear you right now."

A knock at the door startles her. "Ash, my dear?"

"Go." Tessie blows a kiss at the screen. "And remember: observe, do not absorb."

"Right," Ash mutters. "Observe."

After she hangs up, she goes to the mirror and finishes her

lipstick. Bright, matte lips of red. Ash narrows her expertly lined cat eyes at her reflection. She looks menacing and unaffected and unloved. Like a vampire from the Middle Ages.

Good.

If there's one thing her ex taught her, it's that love is a kind of death. Ash wants none of it. The happily-ever-after belief system perpetuated in fairy tales is a farce. Because eventually it all ends.

She glares at her reflection.

All she and Nathaniel have to do is avoid each other. It's that easy. It's not like they'll be paired in water aerobics or shipwrecked together.

She chews at her lower lip as her stomach flips.

"You are not a mess," she tells herself. "You are very much all the fuck put together."

***

"We are fused," Ash tells Augustus. She keeps her arm linked through his and holds tight. "Do not let go of me."

A gruff chuckle. "Don't choke, Keller."

An inhale. A steeling of her spine. *She can do this. She can.* She may get knocked down, but she's like one of those creepy clown punching bags—she pops right back up.

The Whitfords sit at a round table on the oceanfront terrace. Right in time for sunset. The sky is stained lavender and pink. Palm trees sway in the breeze. The air is clammy and warm. The crash of the waves creates a chaotic symphony amid the silence.

It should be a view to *ooh* and *aah* over. Instead, every person at the table is on their phone. No one's paying attention. Or talking.

Except for Nathaniel.

He's lounging in his chair, looking like he's been personally styled by Hades himself.

His head snaps up, his lip curling at the sight of her. He scans her face, then his eyes dip to her breasts.

She flushes. Damn Tessie for this dress.

"You're late," he announces, those pale-blue ice shards piercing straight through Ash.

His annoyance has her bristling. Has her flashing back to those tiny, petty insecurities.

Messy and late and flaky. Everything Jakob said she was.

Never sticks to one thing, never stays in one place.

Once again, truly fuck that man.

"Dad." The word is barely more than a whisper. A woman who looks like she's the epitome of green smoothies and Pilates stands from her chair and wraps Augustus in a hug.

Ash hangs back, keeping a respectful distance. When he pulls away, Augustus beckons her forward to make introductions.

"Ash, this is my daughter, Claire."

Claire is dressed in a long ivory pleated skirt and a silk tank top. Her platinum hair is twisted into a chignon.

Pushing down her nerves, Ash smiles. "Hi, Claire." She sticks a hand out. Steadies it. "Mrs. Whitford," she amends.

Claire's palm is soft and warm in her own. "Ash." Claire's confused gaze bounces between Ash and Augustus. "And she's your—"

"Death doula," Ash says, intercepting the topic before it grows two heads. It never gets old. Especially in LA. Everyone assumes she's Augustus's much younger gold-digging lover. "I am, as they say, a way to bridge the gap between life and death for your father."

Silence. For entirely too long.

"Christ, Augustus," comes a resigned sigh from the table. Don, who looks like a reincarnated 1920s oil tycoon in Nike shorts and a tech fleece jacket, finally looks up from his phone. "Morbid, don't you think?"

A guy in his twenties sporting a modest buzz cut and a bowling shirt—Tater, she supposes—snickers. "Man, that's creepy."

Nathaniel gives the man who must be his brother a scathing look. Probably for acting like Don's parrot.

"Morbid, maybe, but necessary." Augustus shuffles toward

the table, mirth in his eyes. "I told you over the phone that I had hired someone to help navigate the end-of-life process. That's why Ash is here."

"It's your dime," Don says to the older man, giving Ash a look like she's an unemployed freeloader.

Claire squints at her, her blue eyes cool. "You look…familiar."

Her throat instantly goes tight. Nerves spark under her skin.

"That's because she is." A hard voice speaks up then.

Ash cringes at the conversation hijack. *Shit.*

Nathaniel leans forward in his chair. His long form a panther ready to strike. Vengeful eyes, eyes that Ivan the Terrible would be envious of, stare her down. "She's the one who interrupted my wedding."

As soon as he says it, she wants to saw her own head off with piano wire.

More silence.

"Oh, holy shit." Tater covers his face with his hands and cackles. "This is fucking going in the podcast."

Sure, she didn't expect a red-carpet rollout, but being gaped at like she's the reincarnation of Rasputin is a bit much.

Nathaniel wears an amused smirk, clearly pleased with himself.

Claire lets out a sharp breath. "How could you?"

Ash isn't sure if it's directed at her or Augustus.

Regardless, her stomach falls. Sweat mists her skin.

Don's face is twisted in disgust. He scans Ash, his lip curled. "You've lost the plot, Augustus."

Augustus dips his chin and grips the back of a chair with white knuckles. "I won't stand for you giving Ash hell all night," he says, his voice laced with stubbornness. "The past is the past, and she is here as my guest. We all deserve a fresh start."

From the look of revulsion on Claire's face, Ash is about as fresh as a two-day-old diaper.

Eyeing Ash, Augustus pulls out a chair and nods, motioning for her to sit. Unfortunately, the spot he's chosen is next to Nathaniel.

Wordlessly, she obeys the man.

As Claire and Augustus argue using fake polite voices over whether she deserves to be here, Ash grips the table tight and holds on for dear life, even as her heart takes off at a gallop. Breathing through the panic, she tries to conjure the conversation she had with Tessie before she came to face the firing squad.

*Observe, do not absorb.*

Beside her, Nathaniel is rigid. His posture makes it obvious he'd rather be anywhere than here.

That makes two of them.

She feels like a snack stuck in a vending machine with no hope of rescue. Unloved. Uneaten.

"You're still sweating."

The smug voice has her slowly turning her head.

Nathaniel angles in. Only a few inches separate them. The geometry of his face is insane. Stern brows. Chiseled cheekbones. Her sense of self-preservation is nonexistent when he's well within punching distance. As well as smelling. It's unfortunate, because his unholy scent is too damn fantastic for words. Like sun and sea with a hint of pine.

"No thanks to you."

She's boiling. And Nathaniel sits there like a smug blue-eyed bastard with his sharp, square jaw and perfectly mussed hair, while she feels like a drowned river rat paddling in a sewer for dear life.

"I hope you're happy with yourself," she grits out. "Your entire family hates me now."

"They would have hated you anyway."

She doesn't know whether the statement makes her feel better or worse.

He shrugs. "I think I deserve some form of payback. Even if the punishment doesn't fit the crime."

Ash grips her butter knife. "And what would?"

A wicked smile curls his lips. His voice is rough, murderous. "I can think of a few things."

As waiters swoop in to set bottles of fancy water and expensive wine at the table, Ash drops the knife and picks up the heavy menu. Her arms strain to hold it upright.

"Shield?" he observes.

She eyes his excessively smug face over the entrée page. "Battering ram."

Nathaniel takes a long drink of his beer, one brow cocked. "Is that a threat?"

Ash opens her mouth. Before she can snap back, her attention's diverted by Don.

"Just tell me one thing, Augustus," he's saying, "is she in the will?"

"Whoa." Ash sets down her menu with a thump. "Just so everyone knows, I do not need to be in a will. Anybody's will."

Augustus, seated between Claire and Ash, frowns. "If Ash is in the will, that is for me to know."

Don grumbles. Tater cocks his head and inspects her.

Ash stares back, unmoved.

"She looks like a Manson girl," he says suspiciously.

Ash perks up. Holy shit, if this dinner conversation takes a turn for Charlie Manson, she will not be upset about it.

Claire drains her wineglass. "Manson girls are not polite conversation, Tater."

Nathaniel sighs and slumps in his seat.

Augustus lifts a hand. His soft voice is laced with vulnerability. "This is not to be a sad trip; you understand me? It's a celebration of life, but *before* I die. A farewell party, if you will. I want to be around to enjoy it. I want us to spend time together."

Ash takes in the faces around the table, expecting nods of agreement, maybe tears. There's only awkward tension, averted eyes.

"Hikes. Tours. You can't do much of that, Dad," Claire says

softly, tapping a manicured nail against her wineglass. The crystal sings out.

"Maybe not," Augustus agrees with a lift of his chin. "But I'll be there. Something I haven't done well in the past."

"It's never too late," Ash says, sitting straighter, "to start over."

For a second, Nathaniel's attention lands on her. His sharp jaw tightens a fraction.

Tate leans back in his chair, scratching his belly. In his belligerently bright shirt, he looks like he does the weather in Belize. "As long as it's only two weeks. I got shit to do back in the States."

Nathaniel needles his brow. "Jesus Christ. We are in the States, Tate."

Ash narrows her eyes at Tate, tempted to scream at him. At all of them. Shock them out of their snooty, self-absorbed ways. This isn't just some free vacation. This could be their last chance. This is a gift. To spend time with Augustus. Sure, he could have many long years left with treatment, but nothing is ever guaranteed.

She wills her nerves to steady, then palms Augustus's shoulder. "Are you okay?"

The older man straightens the buttons on his dress shirt. "It's fine, my dear."

"What?" she blurts. "No. It's not fine." She twists in her chair, scanning the table.

She can't take the look on Augustus's face. Crestfallen. Dejected. This is why she's here, right? To intercept? To mediate. Her purpose here is to make Augustus happy. Fuck everyone else.

"Look," she says, and all eyes land on her. "I realize you all want to tear into me like a pack of hyenas, and we'll be stuck together long enough for you to do that. But Augustus planned this trip for *you*. You can schedule an appointment to yell at me in private, but for now, for these next two weeks, do you think I can just get a universal mulligan and we can all have some fucking fun?"

Claire squeaks.

"She's right."

The deep voice sends a shiver up her spine. Stunned, Ash slowly turns to look at the source of backup.

Nathaniel arches a brow at his grandfather, silently conveying a message Ash can't decode, while ignoring Ash like a tall, dutiful asshole. "We're here, Grandpops," he says stoically. "And this trip is all yours."

Grudging murmurs of agreement come from the remaining Whitfords.

Eyes alight, Augustus drums the table, looking peppier than he did seconds earlier. "I appreciate that, my boy."

*Favorite grandson.*

Ash can't help but study Nathaniel's tall, lean frame as the metal chair he's lounging in practically groans under the weight of his muscles.

*Cheater.*

A vision of Nathaniel cozying up to the Bratz doll renews her anger, and she wills her eyeballs to disconnect from their optic nerves.

A waitress approaches with their appetizers. Oh, thank god. Food.

Mini crab cakes and potato chips with crème fraîche and caviar.

*Fuck. This dinner from hell is never ending.*

She looks up from her plate. "How many, uh, courses are there again?"

"Five." Nathaniel's lips curl up at the corner. "So get comfortable, Bigfoot."

Ash narrows her eyes, holding his stare. "I will."

"Good."

"Good."

The sun has set. In the distance, the spark of lightning. Instead of conversation, the only sound is the clanking of utensils as they eat their tiny appetizers. The Whitfords' uncomfortable stances make them look like they haven't eaten dinner together in years.

As if, in this family, conversation is reserved only for discussions about politics or professions. Not like a meal at her house. Loud and laughing. Ash and her mom and Tessie DJing their favorite songs while her father goes on and on about his train collection.

Ash sighs. She can't take another minute of Claire clutching her pearls and giving her the evil eye.

If no one else is willing to start a conversation, then she will.

Lips twitching, she side-eyes Nathaniel, ready to harass this rude, unfeeling robot. "How's life in the ER, Doctor Whitford?" she croons.

His eyes slice to her before his head does. "I don't work in the ER anymore." His words are choppy, like he's grating up glass. But he doesn't volunteer further information.

That's new news. Last she heard from her client and the papers in Los Angeles, he was an ER doctor set to take over his father's successful plastic surgery practice.

"So what do you do?"

Don sets his utensils down with a clatter. "Yes, Nate. That's what I'd like to know."

Nathaniel takes a bite of his crab cake and chews slowly before replying. "I work on an oil rig. The *Sophia Marie*. You know that, Dad."

"Tell your father about the new position," Claire urges with a small smile.

"Yes," Ash says, at the same time Nathaniel says, "No."

Interesting.

A muscle flexes in Nathaniel's jaw. His eyes, lit by the glow of the tiki torch, flash. "Not tonight, Mom. It's not a sure thing, anyway."

Ash props an elbow on the table and her chin in her palm. "I'd love to hear about your life at sea. Are you, like, a pirate doctor, Nathaniel?" She arches a mocking brow. One she hopes makes him see red. "Are you skilled at treating scurvy?"

The glare he gives her is a snake ready to strike.

Don blusters a laugh, his chest puffing out. Then he stares Nathaniel down like they're two lions in the jungle. "Because that's far more useful than taking over the family business, I suppose."

Fuck.

Shamefaced, Ash ducks her head and focuses on her plate. In her attempts to gently annoy Nathaniel, she inadvertently made friends with a far worse devil. The only time Don's looked up from his phone or his meal to make conversation has been to rag on his son.

As drinks are refilled, appetizer plates are exchanged for fancy cheese and fine china in the promise of the main course to come.

While Don waxes on about the new plastic surgery practice he's opening in Malibu, Ash's phone beeps.

She checks her blood sugar. Sighs. Traveling always throws her schedule and her body out of whack.

As a type-one diabetic, controlling her blood sugar is a bitch. It's not black or white. There's no rule book. It's not eat-one-Oreo-and-your-low-blood-sugar-will-go-up-twenty-points. It's all trial and error. What worked yesterday may not work today. Exercise, stress, hormones, even her time of the month, all play a role in that funky dance of the ups and downs of blood sugar.

She opens her purse and groans when she realizes it's empty. In transferring her belongings to the tiny baby purse Tessie forced her to pack, she's forgotten her granola bars. Normally, she'd wait for dinner, but since it doesn't seem to be happening in the next century, she needs sugar. Her go-to to raise it quickly is juice, although any sort of sweet will do.

She looks around for a waiter, then scowls. Nathaniel's bogarting one like the man is his own personal assistant.

Don drums his fingers on the table. "I still think you should get off the rig, Nate, and take over the Malibu practice."

Nathaniel turns from the server, his voice low. "That's not what I want, Dad."

Augustus sets down his wineglass. "Let the boy live, Don."

Ash watches Augustus, notes the fatigue in his eyes. The hand to his temple. He's getting one of his migraines. The conversation is wearing *her* out; it must be a struggle for Augustus.

A harrumph from Don. "Easy for you to say. You're not the one who has to watch him throw away his life."

Beside her, Nathaniel laughs tightly. "Because you're an expert on what a good life looks like."

"I know what success looks like." Don jabs at the air with his fork. "And let me tell you, Nate, it's not you."

A muscle jumps in Nathaniel's jaw. His lips are flat, pressed together, white. He looks to the left, contemplates the ocean.

Regret curdles Ash's stomach. She feels as if she's set off a bomb that's been long dormant. The Whitford family dynamics are more like family dynamite.

Her phone's CGM alarm chimes again.

The sound of a chair scooting back has her looking up.

"Oh, don't go." Claire's standing, holding on to Nathaniel's arm with an intensity that makes Ash think she hasn't seen her son in a while.

"We'll catch up," Nathaniel says in a strained voice. "We have two weeks." With that, he kisses his mother. Then he crosses the terrace and disappears into the restaurant.

Moments later, the entrées appear. A glass of orange juice is dropped in front of her.

"I didn't order this," she tells the waiter.

"For you," he says, nodding across the terrace. "From that man who just left."

Sighing, Ash slumps in her seat and grudgingly picks up the glass of juice Nathaniel ordered. "Fuck."

## Chapter Six

A BURNING OIL RIG WOULD BE BETTER THAN THIS. Nathaniel's trapped on a barstool next to his idiot little brother while Tate drones on about his plans for his podcast's launch.

"It's a startup right now," he chatters as Nathaniel stares into his whiskey. "But we're working on the funds to get it off the ground."

*Working on the funds* means Tate is planning to ask their father for money from his inheritance.

"Do you think Dad will say yes?"

*Absolutely. Then he'll use it against you your entire life.*

Nathaniel keeps that thought to himself, instead nodding as he reaches for his drink. The resort bar is packed, thanks to the unending amount of rain coming down outside.

As it always does, talk of his father has Nathaniel bristling. Maybe that makes him an asshole. Or maybe it means he's long since given up on making the man proud.

His father's soulless Beverly Hills plastic surgery practice is not the legacy he wants. Vapid women clamoring for nose jobs and butt lifts. Even if the plan—his entire life—was to take over the family practice. He took a job in the ER, allowing him to put his father off for years, but after the breakup with Camellia, he finally said fuck it.

He resigned his position at the prestigious hospital, gave up his loft and Mercedes, and went to live as a doctor on a floating oil rig off the coast of California.

He has Ash to blame for all of it.

She fucked up his life when she came storming into that church.

Only he's not sure *fucked up* is the right term. Admitting that grates at him. Has for the last three years.

A flash of black catches his eye. Ash. She's standing in the corner, perched at the window like a disheveled vagabond. She stares out into the pouring rain, arms wrapped tight around her slender, bare shoulders.

A grin tips the edges of his lips. He was right. She is a cat.

"What do you think of the Manson girl?" Tater asks.

He swirls the whiskey in his glass. "I think she probably lives in a spider web or something."

His brother chuckles. "She's tight, though. You gotta admit that."

Nathaniel pauses mid-sip, a prickle of irritation running the length of his spine. "What exactly is *tight* about her?"

Wicked gleam in his eyes, Tate snaps open his mouth.

"You know what?" Nathaniel says, lifting a hand to cut his brother off. "I don't need to know."

He already does.

She's a demon. The prettiest demon he's ever seen.

He's not proud to admit that her body in that slinky dress briefly short-circuited his brain tonight. How could it not? He'd have to be a corpse to remain unaffected.

Tate grins at him. "She looks like she bites."

Christ.

Nathaniel drags a hand down his face. One day, his horny little brother won't piss him off. His stupid hobbies and grating commentary about the female species won't irritate him. And on that day, he'll be free.

At least dinner was entertaining. For that, he'll give Ash credit. She sucked it up and took his family's shit. She gave back as good as she got it. Defended his grandfather. But that doesn't mean he's taking his eyes off her. He doesn't trust her for a second.

"You think Grandpops has lost it?"

"Grandpops is doing what he thinks is best." Nathaniel rubs his jaw. "And unfortunately, he thinks hiring an emotional support"—he zeroes in on Ash again—"*creature* is the way to go."

Tate gives an easy shrug, like he hasn't yet caught on that their grandfather is not long for this world. Reality doesn't get through the cracks of Tate's existence. Not until it's too late.

Feeling eyes on him, Nathaniel glances at the demon woman again. Locks gazes with her.

Before he can warn her away with a glare, Tate lifts a hand to his mouth. "Ash," he bellows. "Over here."

Brow arched, she considers them. Her expression wars between interest and *ugh*. Then, slowly, with a wary look, she prowls their way.

"Gentlemen." She sets her ridiculously tiny sequined clutch on the bar top and slips onto the stool beside Nathaniel. The way she shifts to adjust her dress causes the slit to fall open, exposing more tattoos, a flash of the curve of her ass.

*Good Christ*, he doesn't need this right now.

"Bar has a dress code," Nathaniel says, rerouting his attention to the bartender. "Doesn't include drowned rat."

She side-eyes him. In his periphery, her expression looks like one of amusement, or maybe irritation. He can't tell.

"I was on the beach," she says, wringing out her hair on the bar top. Small puddles form. "I tried to run but got caught in the downpour. Doubled back."

His eyes drift to her boots. They're covered in sand. Does she own a pair of flip-flops?

Her husky voice floats on the air around him. "I would recommend living a little. Have you tried it? You would love it."

Huffing, she moves to grab a stack of napkins just out of reach. She stretches out on her barstool. Wiggles her fingers. Flattens those red lips and looks at Nathaniel.

"A little help here?"

"Maybe I like watching you struggle."

Her eyes glow, more green than gray in this moment. "You would. A true sadist."

With a grunt and a wrenching stretch, she snags a stack of napkins and blots her pale face. The way water runs off her skin in rivulets tugs at his stomach. He grips the bar top with white knuckles, tamping down on the reaction. Her lipstick sticks.

*What would it take to get it to come off?* With a slight shake of his head, he banishes the thought.

When she's dry and the napkins are drenched, she sighs. "You're not going to make this easy on me, are you?"

"No," he says. "I'm not."

With a slight, devious smile, Ash says, "Sounds like you have too much time on your hands."

Nathaniel bristles. Wills his muscles to unclench. He's stuck on an oil rig for weeks at a time. He can suck it up and stick it out with this girl who aggravates his senses. Mostly the murderous side.

Her face does this pretty, pinched scrutinizing glare that makes him feel like he's burning up on the surface of the sun.

The bartender sets a martini in front of her.

Tate leans past Nathaniel, says, "Bottoms up."

Tate's three objectives in life are to get people laid, get people drunk, and get people on his podcast.

"Thank you." The honest smile Ash flashes in response makes Nathaniel's stomach flip in an extremely fucked-up way.

"Funny, I didn't get a thank-you," Nathaniel says coolly. "For earlier."

"I didn't want your juice," she shoots back.

"Well, you needed it."

"Congrats on your show of chivalry. You ticked off one box." She sips her martini, then studies both men. "While we're here, Augustus wants me to ask each of you to write down your favorite memory of you and your grandfather together. I'm helping write his memoirs."

Tate gapes at her, jaw slack. "Man, that's crunchy as fuck."

Nathaniel sets his drink down. Hard.

It's too close. Too in his face. He's accepted that his grandfather won't be around forever, but this girl is like an omen. A chaotic, disheveled presence he doesn't want to stomach, let alone include.

Nathaniel rolls his neck out. Irritation creeps over him. "Kind of personal, if you ask me."

"He's dictating. I just type. I'll compile all the stories in a book for anyone who wants it." Ash throws him a wicked smile. "And don't worry, Nathaniel, your little third-grade poker party secret is safe with me."

"Christ."

Tate snickers.

Ash continues with a shrug. "He wants to fix it, control it, because that's—"

"Augustus," Nathaniel says.

"Wow, finishing each other's sentences." Tate guffaws, drums on the bar top. "That's a match made in—"

"Hell," Nathaniel snarls.

Ignoring him, Ash cocks her head. Purses her lips. Examines Tate. "You're the one with a podcast about…potatoes?"

Nathaniel grinds a fist against his forehead. "Please don't ask him about it."

"That's right. Tater Talks."

Her eyes widen. "Wow. Really cashing in on this lifelong nickname, aren't you?" She dips her chin. "I respect that." Then, leaning into Nathaniel, she lowers her voice. "Do you think your grandfather really knew Carlo Giacomo?"

He's already shaking his head. "No idea."

Bored, likely because he's no longer the subject of the conversation, Tate stands and stretches. "Gonna head out. Can't take much more of this doom and gloom talk." He claps Nathaniel's shoulder. "Think I'll rustle up some fun. You comin'?"

Nathaniel shakes his head. Fun to his brother is a podcast, a vintage porn mag and a bag of beef jerky. "Funned out for the day."

"Yeah, yeah." Tate slugs down the remains of his drink. "If I can bail tomorrow, you best believe I'm on it." He turns his focus to Ash. "What about you? You want to come?"

Nathaniel stiffens.

As if she's considering it, Ash runs her finger around the rim of her glass. Then she says, "Think I'll stay and harass your brother for a while."

"Cool."

"Oh, and Tate—" Ash slips off the stool and steps into Tate's space. Gripping the collar of his bowling shirt, she yanks him down to eye level. Her pretty face threatening, her teeth bared, she says, "If you go this entire vacation without having a true one-on-one with your grandfather, I'll come to your podcast and beat the fucking shit out of you with your microphone."

With that, she lets him loose.

"Fuck," Tate breathes in what Nathaniel swears is amazement. Then he turns on his heel and beelines for the exit.

Ash hops onto her stool again. Slides her martini closer. "We need a task force that stops white men from starting podcasts for no reason."

He chuckles. Barely.

They sip their drinks. Outside, the rain comes down in droves, the tin roof a lively melody of percussion.

"I'm sorry."

Surprised, he blinks, unsure he's heard her correctly. "For what?"

She wrinkles her nose. "For inadvertently taking Lucifer's side tonight." Her soft eyes sweep over his face, drop to his lips. "Your father."

She splays her hand on the bar top. Long fingers. Long black nails. What would those nails feel like scraping down his back?

Fuck.

It takes all the willpower he has to fight the heat creeping through him and force his mind back to the conversation. "My father's a world-class asshole, but I'm used to it by now."

"We all have to excel at something." Ash props an elbow on the bar and evaluates him. "As much as I loved listening to the sound of your family silently sawing through their meat, is it always like this?"

"What? A complete disaster? Pretty much," Nathaniel admits, frowning at his drink. "I don't want my grandfather to be disappointed. If this doesn't turn into what he wants."

There's no way his family will recognize this for what it is. One long goodbye. One last chance to bond.

"What do you mean?" Ash asks.

"We don't relax," he warns. "We don't lounge. Every hour of every day is scheduled, planned. Because we are nothing if we don't strive for excellence."

Ash's eyes flash, but her lip curls up like she's amused. "No sightseeing? No poolside lounging? No gluttonous buffets?"

"Only vigorous activities that detract from building a bond or actually having conversation." In his family, vacation is a duty to get through.

She chews her lip, considering. "On a scale of one to my-soundtrack-is-the-*Rocky*-theme-song, what are your holidays like?"

"Turkey trot," he says grimly. "On Thanksgiving and Christmas."

"I fucking knew it," she whispers. She looks panicked and defeated, and even though it should make him smile, it doesn't.

A few silent minutes pass, and finally, curiosity gets the best of him. "A death doula. What exactly does that entail? Communing with the dead?"

He's asking not because he's curious about this weird, feral girl, but because of his grandfather. It's his duty as the oldest grandchild to do his due diligence. At least that's what he tells himself.

Ash tucks a hunk of black hair behind her ear. "I am but a mere carrier in your grandfather's astral plane of life."

He rolls his eyes. "English."

"Fine. I'm his death bouncer, so don't fuck with him." She inclines her head, eyes swimming with challenge. "I don't do medical stuff. I'm there for him. If your grandfather wants to discuss his childhood or just tell fart jokes for an hour, I'll be there. I'll listen." She brushes a puddle of water off the bar. "It's another way to navigate grief."

He regards her for a long moment. "And what makes you the expert in grief?"

"Everyone's an expert in grief." The gray flecks in her green eyes catch the soft overhead lighting. "We just don't know it until it fucking hits us." Ash plucks the olive out of her glass, pops it into her mouth. "You're a doctor," she says, chewing. "You try to stop death."

Nathaniel has to tear his eyes away from those blood-red lips. "Postpone it."

"I love Augustus," she says, her voice thick. "Your grandfather's a firecracker. He's stubborn and strong, and I think he'll be around for a long time."

It takes effort to swallow past the rock in his throat. "What I don't get is how one goes from love to death."

She averts her eyes. Says nothing. Though a flush creeps up her chest and neck.

He swigs the last of his scotch, twists into her. Ready to get one thing out of the way first. Maybe it's the alcohol talking. Maybe it's because the question has bothered him for the last three years. Either way, he can't stop himself from asking.

"Who hired you?"

Her kohl-lined eyes widen, and her breath catches. "Excuse me?"

Fuck. She's even prettier when she's stunned. If he had to guess, she doesn't give her emotions away easily.

"Who hired you to break up my wedding?"

Those full red lips part. "I don't give away my sources."

He snorts. "Who are you, Lois Lane?"

"It's called client confidentiality. A concept you should understand." Her sharp tone wards off further questioning.

But it doesn't stop him from persisting. "That's cute. Pretending you give a damn about someone else's feelings."

Her cheeks flush. But Ash recovers quickly, turning to meet his accusing gaze. "I'm not the one who cheated on my fiancée."

He clenches his jaw. Derision and anger pinprick his skin. "Right. Because you automatically assume you know everything about me based on a bullshit rumor."

"It wasn't a rumor; it was true."

"Was it?"

He holds eye contact. Looking away from her feels like a dare.

When she says nothing, he laughs bitterly. "You like this too much." He lifts his drink to his lips, only then realizing it's empty. "Breaking hearts. Hurting people."

Ash pales. "I made it better." Her voice is small, distant. Like she's trying to convince herself. "People should know before—"

She cuts off abruptly, bites her lip.

"Before what?" he demands.

After the briefest hesitation, she licks her lips, says, "Before they get hurt."

Silence.

Ash rises from her stool. Smooths her damp dress. "Anyway," she says softly. Almost sad. "I don't do that anymore."

Arms crossed, he nods at the windows. "Rain's stopped."

He's riled her on purpose, told her what he thinks of her, made it clear he wants her to go. But now that she's watching him with that hard stare of hers, he's more uncomfortable than he anticipated.

Dropping her gaze, Ash curls her hands around her arms like she's protecting herself.

Her expression—fragile, sad—causes a strange herky-jerky kick to his heart.

Then, without another word, she turns and goes.

Nathaniel eyes the trail of sand she leaves in her wake, winces at the hard clop of her boots.

Why, suddenly, is he not so sure he's glad he chased her off?

## Chapter Seven

THE NEXT MORNING, THE WHITFORDS PLUS ASH make the short trip to Makalapua Palms.

What used to be the headquarters of the Fox Hotel Group is now an authentic working coconut farm nestled in the verdant green hills of Hawaii. Augustus insisted a visit here was the way to kick off their vacation.

For twenty minutes, the older man leads the pack, detailing exactly where on the property his company used to sit. They stroll through the lush farm and past the quaint shack where coconuts and snacks are sold while Ash holds up the photos she pulled together before they left the resort, comparing the black-and-white snaps to the current scenery.

"Back in the seventies, when we opened our very first resort in Maui, this is where our office was located. Of course, now the head office is in Los Angeles, but this is where Fox Hotels began."

Augustus spreads his arms out as if he can scoop up the land and hug it. Pride shines in his eyes. Ash smiles, but when she notices the fond way Nathaniel watches his grandfather, her mood quickly sours.

Ugh. Having the same emotions as Nathaniel Whitford is nauseating.

"So what happens to the company?" Tater lowers his phone and tugs an earbud out. "Who gets it when you kick it?"

"Tater," Claire hisses, clutching her designer bag to her chest.

Nathaniel glares. He looks like he wants to bowl his little brother's head under a bridge.

Augustus chuckles. Death doesn't faze the man, nor do rude

questions. "Not to worry. I have made the necessary arrangements for the takeover of my empire."

Nathaniel laughs, and Ash jumps at the sound. "So humble, Grandpops."

Augustus's eyes dance with mischief. "I've been told it's my second-best trait."

Ash regards Claire. "Don't you want it?" A brave question, considering the woman can't stand her, but the curious blurt of her mouth knows no bounds.

Before Claire can respond, Don's blustery guffaw cuts in. "Not my wife. She knows more about her afternoon iced coffee than running a business."

Ash narrows her gaze. She's never wished for telekinetic powers more than she has since she met him. Fire. Just his face. All fire.

Augustus nudges her shoulder. "What do you think, my dear?"

"I think…" Ash says, looping her arm through Augustus's, "it's a pretty fantastic legacy."

He smiles, his blue eyes crystalline in the sun. "Thank you, Ash. I think so myself."

The crow of a rooster and the scent of plumeria flowers fill the air.

Augustus checks the time on his Breitling. Turns to his family. "We have a few hours until our scuba session. Why don't we explore the farm? I've arranged for lunch and a coconut carving."

A bored sigh from Don. He puts a hand on his round stomach. "Crafts, Augustus?"

"I happen to love arts and crafts," Ash lies to spite the man.

Ghost tours, graveyards, give it to her. Hikes and water activities with the Whitfords? Hard pass. But she's here for Augustus. No complaints.

Amid the thrum of low murmurs, the group splits off. Tater

takes a phone call while Don does a virtual interview about how dimpleplasty is the hottest trend in Hollywood.

Ash meanders, examining the trees, studying the coconuts. The sky spills out golden light. Hawaii's beauty stuns. She drinks in the fresh air. It's not downtown LA. No drunk children. No naked men covered in feces.

Cute, happy, quaint Hawaii. Nice. Safe.

Hot.

Really hot.

"Fuck," she grumbles, wiping her damp brow.

It's an overcast, balmy day, and yet she's sweating. Her feet, in her boots, burn.

"—a shame you're on this trip by yourself, Nathaniel." From the grove of trees, Claire's voice floats.

Ash freezes. Her heart thumps against her sternum.

"Mom, where am I supposed to meet someone?" Nathaniel. Exasperated.

"You met Camellia in France."

"I met Camellia because of Dad."

"Yes, but it'll happen again."

"Who says I want it to happen again?" he says, tone dark.

Ash cranes to catch a glimpse of him through the trees. Shoulders tight, he paces.

Claire's voice oozes disappointment. "That's not true."

A long sigh. "I'm just trying to get through this trip, figure out this job situation."

"Are you sure it's what you want?"

"I don't know, Mom." From his pocket, the buzz of a phone. "I have to take this." Palm fronds crunch. He's on the move.

Fuck.

Ash turns, scrambling over her boots to break into a run. The last thing she wants to do is get caught eavesdropping.

It's not until she breaks through the grove of palm trees that she releases the breath she's been holding. The dark tone in

Nathaniel's words weighs heavy on her. The fickle beast of guilt whispers in her ear.

*You did that. You.*

She shuts her eyes, absorbs the pain.

Then she slogs her way up to the small shack. Outside the building, an employee has set out coconuts, wooden bowls and various tools that look like instruments of death.

She looks over one shoulder, then the other. The rest of the Whitfords are hovering by the SUV, on their phones, like one second of enjoyment will rot their robot-like shells. Hell, she is here in paradise, on Augustus's dime. She's not missing a minute.

She sits at a picnic table, relishing the shade thanks to the frond-covered eave above.

An employee approaches with a tray of coconut water and coconut meat. With a thanks, Ash asks about the coconut craft. The young woman gives her instructions on how to harvest her own coconut meat. Points at a machete.

"Really?" Ash asks, a zap of delight sparking through her.

"Really, ma'am." The employee brings her hand down in a sharp, swift cutting motion. "You hack it."

Ash lifts a brow. "Impressive."

When the employee disappears into the shack, Ash reaches for the handle of the machete.

"Might need a waiver," a low voice says, the sound sending a shiver up her spine.

Ash cuts him a glare. Ignores her body's traitorous response. "I am very experienced in the art of cleaving."

Nathaniel strides up to her, one big hand clenched around his phone. He's dressed like a sexy grandpa from the '60s. That swirl of wheat-gold hair. The trousers. The tight black T-shirt that screams *I am riddled with abs and biceps!*

Her blood churns. In rage. In indignation. In attraction. *What?*

No.

Never.

Her heart stops as he brings his long, tan fingers closer. Carefully, he plucks at her hair and comes away with a piece of palm. She flushes.

He eyes it, then lets it flutter to the dirt between them. "And clearly the art of eavesdropping as well."

*Smug bastard.*

"How was your call from Lucifer?" Ash croons. "Did you receive instructions on how to proceed with the devastation of humanity?"

Ash looks up from the coconut, noting the ever-so-slight curl of Nathaniel's lips.

"Sorry to say, devastation is imminent."

Ash hums, ignores him.

"Late night, Bigfoot?" he asks, brow cocked. "You look tired."

Ash eyes him warily. She's certain he's 11 percent human and 89 percent homicidal robot.

"I slept like a baby." A lie. After their heated conversation in the bar, she slept like shit. She dreamed up no less than fifty scenarios where she is wrong and he is right.

What if he *is* right?

What if she hurt him for no reason at all?

Ash stands from the table. Moves into prime coconut position. Rests her knee on the bench, her thigh tattoo shifting with the movement. Her frayed cut-offs—tossed over a one-piece bathing suit—expose more of her ass than she'd like in this awkward position, but it's for the good of the coconut.

Glancing over her shoulder, she finds that Nathaniel's also thinking about her ass. If the way he's ogling it is any indication. She smirks. He's not the only one who can catch a person in the act of self-destruction.

"That's a very shameless stare, Doctor Whitford."

Instantly, his eyes snap to her face. His Adam's apple bobs.

"Don't flatter yourself," he says, the hunger in his expression morphing to discomfort, then disdain.

Ash evaluates him from behind her dark sunglasses. She'd need a chisel and a hammer to get him to smile.

The wind kicks up. Drags with it a familiar, lovely scent.

"Mmm." Ash smiles. Breathes deep. "It smells like the Amalfi coast. Lemon. Cedar."

Nathaniel blinks. His jaw slackens.

Hit with her own bout of annoyance, she crosses her arms. "You think you're the only one who travels? So small-minded of you."

The edges of his lips twitch. Barely.

Thanks to her mom's job as a flight attendant, Ash is well versed in the art of traveling. She and Tessie both have seen the world. One of her favorite trips was to the Madonna Inn on her sixteenth birthday. They wore vintage dresses and ordered a bottle of champagne even though they were underage.

"First time in Hawaii?" Nathaniel asks.

"Hawaii's one of the few places I haven't been." Her heart gives a twinge, but she wills it to flutter away. Then she rests her palm on the coconut in front of her.

Nathaniel mimics, palming his own coconut.

She has to fight to keep her breath from catching. Christ. His hand is the size of her face.

Lucky patients.

"That looks wrong." Brow furrowed, Nathaniel gestures to the row of knives and chisels beside the coconut. The machete's blade gleams in the sunlight.

Ash snorts. "Okay, I didn't realize I was speaking with the CEO of coconuts."

"We should get someone." He cranes his neck, searching for an employee. "I can't believe they just left you alone with an arsenal of weapons," he mutters.

"Don't be silly." Ash's pulse quickens in excitement as she

grips the sticky handle of the machete. "This seems completely safe."

Beside her, Nathaniel watches her carefully, his face a mask of grim disapproval.

"Don't you want a Hawaiian coconut fresh from the farm?" she asks with a wicked smile.

A curt nod at the shack. "Go buy one."

Ash squares her shoulders, affects a scathing tone. "That would be the Whitford solution, wouldn't it? Buy something. Have someone fix it. Hop on your private jet and purchase a small island."

Nathaniel's response is an eye roll and nothing else.

"I, for one, take coconut carving very seriously." Ash lifts and lowers her arm, gauging the heft of the weapon. "Did you know you have a better chance of being killed by a falling coconut than by a shark?"

"Great." Nathaniel rakes a hand through his hair. "Another fun, macabre fact."

Ash brings the machete up over her head, focus lasered in on the furry fruit on the table. "Damn right."

Her arms are still lifted high, ready to slice straight through, when Nathaniel nudges a finger against her coconut.

Horror swamps her as it slowly rolls off the table and splats on the ground.

"Oops."

He's smiling.

"Fuck," she swears at the ruins of her coconut. All its decadent, snowy white meat exploded on the ground.

She yanks off her sunglasses and whips her head to him. "Wonderful. Genuinely the exact behavior modeled by toddlers. Lack of impulse control. Tantrums."

"Looks like you got your work cut out for you, Bigfoot," he observes, stepping away.

"You Tall Asshole," she seethes. She cannot stand this man. He needs to remain at least ten feet from her at all times.

She jabs a nail at the mess on the ground. "Clean that up."

Nathaniel chuckles. "Make me."

She glowers at him. "Make you what? An early grave? Gladly."

With a smirk that pushes her right over the edge, he glances over a shoulder, says nothing.

On vengeful instinct, she palms Nathaniel's coconut and hefts it. As she's considering the best way to hurl it at the back of his head, a soft voice says, "Ash?"

She freezes.

Shit.

Claire blinks at her. She's caught Ash in the act of second-degree homicide on her first-born son.

"Hi, Claire." She lowers her hand. The coconut drops and does a slow wobble around on the table.

The older woman studies her, blue eyes icy.

Ash shifts, uncomfortable. Forces a smile. "I know you think it's weird, what I'm doing for your father, but if you ever want to talk—"

"I will never talk to you about a thing."

Heat springs to her face. The words find their target across every part of her body. Heart, chest, stomach. All suffering the effect of the verbal sucker punch.

"You may be here for my father," Claire says, tilting her chin with a regal air, blond hair perfectly in place despite the thick tropical air. "But I'd like you to stay away from my son. You've done enough damage."

Ash swallows. Her heart pangs. She feels like a piece of shit. "I know."

Claire turns and walks off.

She sighs up at the bright blue sky. Fucking great.

No one wants her here except Augustus. Loneliness settles

like a lead weight in her stomach. In her legs. Sure, his family is exhausting and pretentious, but she'll gladly suffer through it for him. Not only is it her job, but she loves Augustus.

She can do this.

She takes a long, long breath, imagining Tessie's voice in her ear. *Observe. Do not absorb.*

But that's exactly what she's doing. Absorbing every barb, every glare from Nathaniel Whitford and his big, dumb, handsome, stupid face.

There's no way this trip could get any worse.

## Chapter Eight

"This is incredibly, most definitely, worse."

The sound of Ash's smoky voice sets Nathaniel on edge.

Together, the two of them stare up at the chalkboard sign on the beach that proclaims: Get Fishy With It Snorkel.

The name is ridiculous.

He crosses his arms. Lifts a brow at the woman beside him. "What's wrong? Can't swim?"

The second he asks it, he internally groans. Why is it he can't go more than thirty minutes without getting drawn into a conversation with her? He's curious about her, even if he doesn't want to be.

She's mean and chaotic and an infinite pain in his ass.

"Oh, I can swim." She pulls her phone out of her woven beach bag. "I just prefer to bob on the water with a beer as opposed to sleeping with the fishes."

"Swimming."

She cocks a brow. "That's what you think."

An instructor steps up, dropping mesh bags full of snorkel gear on the sand. On his other side, his mother and Tate. Both look more interested in the buckets of chum than the snorkel instructions. His father went back to the hotel, while Augustus rests in a chair on the beach. Through the entire lecture, Ash taps on her phone.

When they're finished, he tilts closer to her. "Did you get all that?"

The slice of her eyebrow arch could cut. "Ugh, deciding to talk to you was the mistake of my life."

With that, Ash stalks away from him. Cold shoulder at the ready.

A muscle jerks in Nathaniel's jaw. She doesn't want to talk to him. Fine. It's not his fault she's chaos waiting to happen.

Yes, he'd protected her fingers when she was wielding that machete. The possibility of her hacking her fucking arm off had his heart gearing up for a widowmaker. But that doesn't mean he likes Ash Keller. He just prefers this vacation to have as little drama as possible.

Ahead, she slips her shorts off. The move has his body locking up. He can't help it. His attention is set on her tattooed thighs. Fuck. The one-piece black swimsuit she wears should be modest and boring. Instead, it clings to her lush curves, her soft breasts. Turns him into a teenager all over again.

And he's not the only asshole watching her. Every single man on the beach—except for Augustus—stares.

Brazen fucks.

Shaking his head, he looks away, toward the water. He could use an ice-cold dousing right now.

Curses drift on the breeze.

Nathaniel focuses on Ash again.

Irritation, amusement prickle him as he watches her upturn the bag of gear. She's like a cat, slowly nudging an object to see what it's all about. Flippers, goggles, life jackets. Gingerly, she picks up a life jacket. Anchors it around her waist.

He sighs, needles his brow. It's upside down.

She'll never survive the day.

"Let me," he says, crossing the sand toward her.

Ash regards him, eyes swimming with suspicion, holding the life jacket to her chest. "Why? So you can sabotage me and I'll plunge to a watery grave?"

"If I wanted to kill you, that's not the way I'd do it."

Her sharp brow arches. "I'm intrigued."

"I'm certified." He takes the jacket from her, pissed that she doesn't trust him. Pissed that she'd blindly launch into an activity without thinking it through. It's insanely irresponsible. The ocean's dangerous. Just like those damn boots she wears. Death traps. "On the rig, you have to be certified in scuba."

"Ah, an expert in everything. Why am I not surprised?"

He closes his eyes briefly, exasperated. "Three in the morning, out on the rig, someone gets hurt, has a heart attack, falls in, I have to go in after them. It's a basic requirement of the job."

When her only response is a quiet scrutinizing look, he slips the life jacket over her slender shoulders. "If you were listening, you'd know it's a buddy system."

Sharpening the knife of her voice, she says, "I'm not your partner." She stands on tiptoes, craning to see behind him, bringing her breasts a hairsbreadth from his chest. "What about Tater?"

He bristles, irritation pricking at the back of his neck. "Tate will get two feet down before he panics and flails." He tightens her life vest. Extra-tight.

Ash, to his satisfaction, gasps a pained breath.

"Might even take you with him. So either you buddy up with me, or you go sit your ass on the beach. Those are the rules."

Ash glowers at him in utter disdain. "I'd rather have bamboo sticks shoved under my fingernails than spend this vacation with you." Her husky voice gives his dick a little nudge of encouragement.

He drops his hands, ignoring the electricity that sparks when his fingertips skim against her soft skin. "That makes two of us."

Scowling at him full blaze, she turns on her heel in the sand and stomps toward the water.

He grinds his jaw as he goes to follow. Immediately, his mouth goes dry. Deepest fantasies unlocked. Still, he keeps breathing. Walking. It's all he can do.

Two thin stripes run up the backs of her calves all the way to the tops of her thighs. Like the seams on pinup stockings topped with little bows.

Nathaniel scrubs a hand through his hair. Christ. She

just walks around with those out for anyone to see? It's getting ridiculous.

It's the sexiest goddamn thing he's ever seen.

It's also the moment he knows he's fucked.

A violent ringing sounds out across the beach.

Wide-eyed, Ash turns and races back toward him. She crouches over her towel, pulls her phone from her bag, silences it. "Shit." Attention fixed on her phone, she waves a dismissive hand at him. "Go find another buddy. I'm out."

"Everything okay?"

Why does he even care? Doctor instinct. That has to be it. That and nothing else.

Her smile is brittle, forced. "My blood's just…fucked up."

He scans her pale face. "Your blood sugar's high."

"Yeah. Just when I think I've got the hang of this thing…" With a groan, she plops onto the towel. Waves again. "Go. I'm a big girl. I'll be okay."

The desire to stay with her hits him like a hammer, but he says nothing. Only moves on toward the beach. He and Ash Keller don't mix.

Still.

He can't help but glance over his shoulder at Ash. Catches her as she gives herself an injection in the thigh, right in the middle of a beautiful blooming iris.

## Chapter Nine

It's in the wild blue moonlight of the witching hour that Ash's thoughts take over. When her anxious brain catches up to her mouth. When she wakes in bed and panics about-slash-ponders life and death and everything in between. That article she read five years ago about the swarm of murder hornets. And where exactly is her birth certificate? Has Jakob stepped on a rusty nail and gotten lockjaw yet? She replays the conversation she had with her mom before she left for Hawaii. When she suggested that maybe Ash should get a job with health insurance benefits so she doesn't go broke before she's fifty. How existing in LA while existing with diabetes is like playing Russian roulette with her money. Rent or insulin? Her parents would never say it, of course, but they worry. They care. She knows that, even though she's thirty-three years old, her mother still logs on to her CGM app to check the spiking trajectory of her blood sugar.

Maybe her life isn't as together as she tells herself it is. Maybe it never will be.

Ash shoves the thought from her mind. She has this. Her life gripped with both fisted hands. Even if 75 percent of her brain space is taken up by what-ifs, grudges and so many ways to die before a person's time.

Ash stares at the ceiling, her mind whirling. Inhales. Exhales.

Everything's okay. Tessie is fine and she is fine and Augustus is fine. They will all live long and beautiful lives.

She pushed Tessie. Pushed her right into the arms of her flannel-clad mountain man. She helps her clients, but she doesn't know how to help herself.

Sometimes it's as if she's still that little twelve-year-old. Newly diagnosed and unsure about everything. Especially herself. She's an acquired taste, like fernet or oysters. Never fits in. Too weird. She was never all the fishes in the sea. She was the junky thing found in the bottom of a drawer. And that was *before* her diagnosis. After? Friends didn't get it. They dropped off, quit calling. Either thought she was weird or got weird about it themselves. Ash learned then that when things got hard, people who love her will let go. So it's better if she does it first.

She believed that for a long time. And then she met Jakob.

Ash met Jakob, a financial controller at a credit union, at a brewery during horror movie trivia night. On paper, they shouldn't have worked, but they quickly discovered that they liked the same crappy music, shared a hatred of crowds and had insane chemical bliss. He was like cling-film against her skin; she couldn't pry him off. Eventually, they moved in together. Got engaged. Ash never thought she'd be planning a wedding, but she was. And she did.

Except she never truly saw Jakob.

What he didn't do.

What he did do.

He always made her feel like that lonely kid left at the lunch table.

Jakob. Even his name means supplanter and deserter. And he lived up to the moniker. He replaced Ash. With a different woman. A better woman.

Even now, years later, the memory lingers. Stings.

Coming home to find him with another woman. The "fucking hell, Ash," he bleated in surprise. Like it was her fault she walked in on them. The sight of the woman's bare ass as she ran from the room. The smell of her honeysuckle perfume.

That night, she got drunk and lit her wedding dress on fire in her bathtub.

She gave back the ring. Tessie helped her move out and wore a *boys suck* manicure for six months.

She thought she'd be okay. She had survived worse. It was only when Ash found out Jakob had taken the girl on their honeymoon that it was like her world blew up.

After that, she could have starred in a new season of *Snapped* all on her own. She quit her job, got a new tattoo and blew through her savings to travel the world. Before then, she was certain she wasn't the kind of woman who'd let a man and a bad breakup make her go AWOL for six months. She was wrong.

Every emotion—betrayal, rage, grief—she went through it at warp fucking speed.

It wasn't fair. Cheaters like Jakob get to survive. Love again. Fuck another person over again. While their victims have to wear the battle scars. Even all these years later, Ash has guilt that *she* did something wrong. That she's a fool because she didn't see it. That she wasn't *enough*.

In the end, it all comes back to that, doesn't it? That she was too much, too messy.

If not for Tessie, who pulled her back from the pit of a black hole, those thoughts would still eat her alive.

*He made you disappear,* her cousin said. *Come back to us.*

So she did.

Tessie and Ash's mother were relieved. Only now, in hindsight, can she recognize all the times they tentatively broached the subject that Jakob might not be as fucking fabulous as Ash thought. But she never heard them. That's love.

Obsessive, disgusting denial.

Only her father lived in ignorant man-bliss. *He was good to you. He made you laugh, Ash,* her father would say, turning a page in his paper, while her mother shot daggers at him from the kitchen. Later, she would pull Ash aside to say, *We love him, but your father is an obtuse buffoon.*

"He laughed at me," she told her dad later. "Not with me."

And she was right.

Jakob didn't get her. They were a match made in paisley shirt and plaid pants. Absolutely awful. But the worst part was that Ash let him change her. Let him make her feel bad about herself. Let him shame her for the things she wanted.

Slowly, she got her life back together. She focused on jobs she loved. Not what Jakob thought she should do. The wedding objecting, Nathaniel, were casualties of her relationship. Once her vengeful plot twist was satiated, she found her calling as a death doula.

It's been a long road.

Finally, she's set her focus on what matters. Her family. Her dreams. Her freedom. She refuses to give her heart to a man ever again. To be anything but herself for anyone else.

Falling in love did nothing but make her look fucking stupid.

Ever since Jakob, her heart has been wrapped in thorns. Stopping it from blooming. Though she wouldn't get rid of them if she could. She likes those thorns. They cut. They protect.

She doesn't love Jakob anymore. She's haunted by him. Because isn't that what past relationships are? Ghost after ghost after ghost? And what do ghosts do? They haunt. They linger. They freak the fuck out of people when they least expect it.

Once, when Ash was on a New Orleans ghost tour, she was sure she'd seen a ghost. It crossed the room and held for a heartbeat. That glimpse of possibility, and then it was gone. After, she was left wondering if she was crazy for seeing it. If she imagined it.

That's what love is.

An apparition.

It exists, until it doesn't.

From the next room over, Augustus snores.

Does Nathaniel snore too? If so, is it as room-shaking as his grandfather's? Is his preferred method of murder throttling or suffocation by pillow?

Ash sighs. She's wide awake. The whirring of her brain won't be silenced. It's on a tilt-a-whirl ride to anxiety land, and she's the lone passenger.

Restless, she rises. Checks her phone. Finds a late-night text from Tessie that asks: *Lavalier?*

*That's a necklace, preggo*, she replies. *Not a name.*

Ash checks her blood sugar and then tiptoes out of her room. Quietly, she slides open the door to the shared balcony. Steps out barefoot into the gaping dark, leaving her darker thoughts behind.

In front of her, the white sand beach is just visible. The salty ocean breeze and tropical flowers are fragrant in the balmy night air. The moon shines with bright uncertainty, illuminating the jagged peaks of Diamond Head.

It's so unlike LA. No street noise. No sirens. No arguments over parking spots. Except for the crash of waves on the beach, there's silence.

Ash peers over the balcony at the beach below.

"I wouldn't do that if I were you. For reasons I don't understand, my grandfather seems to like you."

At the grating voice, she tips her head back, groaning. She can't escape him.

In the dim light, she squints. Finds Nathaniel. He sits in a deck chair, clad in gray sweatpants and a black T-shirt.

"Lurking in the dark?" Why is she not surprised he blends in so perfectly with the shadows?

"It took you long enough," he says dryly, rising, "to realize you weren't alone out here."

She arches a brow. "Planning your attack?"

He laughs, a husky, calm sound. "Not yet."

"We're on the same sleeping schedule." She bats her eyes at him. "This could get messy."

He grunts unhappily.

Angling forward, she rests her forearms on the railing. "You know, I was just lying in bed thinking about how you owe me a coconut."

"Saved your fingers from a massacre. You can thank me later for that."

She snorts. His doctor's ego knows no bounds.

"That's Diamond Head crater," he offers, appearing at her side.

She stiffens as he grasps the railing and looks out into the dark. She looks straight ahead, telling herself not to think about how their elbows are touching, how she can feel the scorching heat from his tall asshole of a body. "We're hiking it tomorrow."

"Wonderful. More exercise." Ash's gaze abandons Nathaniel and finds the moonlit beach. "Did you know Hawaii's a hotspot for suicide tourism?"

He turns, mouth agape, and blinks at her.

"It's the charm about Hawaii." Her smile is feline. "Every place has a dark side."

Pinching the bridge of his nose like he's pained, Nathaniel sighs. "How did you get so weird?"

She laughs, unoffended. "My mom's a flight attendant. My father's an accountant. Instead of forcing me to play sports, they let me be me, and now I'm this person who has no talent or ambition. All I do is float through life like an unsatisfied wraith."

"That's not how I pegged you."

"Oh? Do tell. I'm afraid I won't be able to live my life until Nathaniel Whitford tells me what he thinks of me."

Nathaniel lets out a soft laugh. "I'm still forming a consensus."

Without looking over, Ash says, "While you do that, there's this lighthouse in Kauai. It's supposed to be haunted by ancient spirits."

"Haunted lighthouse, noted."

Finally, she glances over at him. Takes in his strong jaw, those stern brows. "I went to the Paris catacombs when I was fifteen. Changed my life."

His eyes snag on hers, his mouth curving into something like a grin. "I can see how those skulls would have an impact."

"When I was ten, I was so unhinged about Jack the Ripper and Lizzie Borden that my mom had to go to a parent-teacher conference about it."

His jaw tightens with tension, and he shifts, straightening up. "I don't think my father's ever been to a parent-teacher conference."

"What about your mom?" Ash asks, tilting her head. "She seems like she misses you."

His face closes up like he's sorry he's overshared. "Work keeps me away from civilization," he says, his voice low, gravelly.

"Does it get lonely? Being out on the high seas?"

He looks out at Diamond Head. In the blue moonlight, the angles of his face are almost exaggerated. The sharp jawline. Lush full lips. The crooked bridge of his nose.

Lust rushes through her. Flips her stomach over in a wild sort of hunger.

Shit. She looks away.

When he speaks, the words are lighter than she anticipated. "Nothing a pirate can't handle."

Ash bites her lip. Searches for a fitting response. Miraculously, they've been having a civil conversation for at least four minutes. A world record.

Before she can say anything, Nathaniel's striding toward his balcony door.

"Make sure you don't freeze to death," he warns. With a hand on the doorknob, he gives her a once-over.

Ash smirks. "You wish."

A quiet snort. He steps into his room and disappears.

Left alone in the balmy night air, Ash wraps her arms around herself, willing that funny feeling in her stomach to dissipate.

But even long after she's gone back to bed, it lingers.

## Chapter Ten

Nathaniel follows several paces behind Ash as they file out to the van before dawn. At his grandfather's insistence, they're headed to watch the sun rise over Diamond Head.

"Shit," Ash swears, as her pack tilts.

Nathaniel sticks a hand out, catching a bottle of sunscreen in midair. She tucks a lock of hair behind her ear and murmurs a soft word of thanks.

Leaning in, Nathaniel spies glucose gels, sunscreen, and bottled water. At least she came prepared. Except for her attire. This morning, she's clad in an oversized hoodie and tight tan shorts. The laces of her boots are untied, click-clacking on the stairs as she boards the van.

Tater takes the long back seat, sprawling out to listen to his podcasts. His mother and father sit separately. Nathaniel and Ash are crammed into one bench while his grandfather sits in front of them.

Leading the pack as always.

"Here we are," Augustus says, handing out pamphlets.

He's bright-eyed this morning, while Nathaniel slept like shit. Apparently, Ash did too. Late last night, she was on the phone, then again early this morning. The walls are fucking paper-thin, and she's as loud as a car engine. Their run-in on the balcony flashes across his mind like a subliminal message—part confusion, part annoyance. He hates that he's intrigued by her. Hates that he wants to know more.

Eyes on the pamphlet, his mother says, "I hear the views of Waikiki and the ocean are beautiful during the sunrise."

Augustus chuckles fondly. "Up early to get the wiggles out. Remember we'd always say that, Claire?"

"Is this a good idea, Dad?" his mother asks, brow furrowed as she closes the brightly colored paper. "The hike sounds really taxing. Are you sure you can do it?"

"He can do it," Ash adds, flipping through her own pamphlet. "Exercise is good for him."

His father's lip curls. "Are you a doctor, Ash?"

Ash shifts in her seat. Her pretty face tightens. "No, but I've been to several of Augustus's appointments."

"She's right," Nathaniel cuts in, giving his father a glare. Although he's not sure why he's playing defense. Not for this girl. Maybe because he's seen the way his father treats the help, and the way the man pokes at Ash pisses him off.

Augustus squares his shoulders. "Until I start falling over, I'm on this earth to move around."

With a noncommittal hum, his mother turns her face to the window, like she's trying not to process the knowledge. If there's one thing the Whitford family excels at, it's denial. If they don't acknowledge it, it never happened. After his failed wedding, it took his mother a year to ask about what really happened with Camellia.

"How long is this hike, Augustus?" Sighing, Don checks his Rolex. "I have a consult at one."

Nathaniel rolls his eyes. "Dad. I think you can make time."

"You're bringing down the vibe, Don," Ash adds, her face full of mischief. "If you took the time to read the pamphlet, you'd know the hike lasts between thirty minutes and an hour."

Nathaniel bites back a laugh.

That rebellious say-anything streak of Ash's sends a pulse traveling through his dick.

Fuck. What the hell's wrong with him?

Don appraises him, his derisive gaze on his face, before moving to Ash and then back to his phone.

Ash leans in. "Is he silently carving up my face in his head?"

Nathaniel nods. "Without a doubt."

"How big do you think he'd make my breasts?"

He swallows, his mouth suddenly dry. "I'd prefer to leave your breasts out of this."

She smirks.

Head lowered, he can't help but take in the hem of Ash's short shorts. Her pale thigh covered with bright, blooming tattoos. What would it feel like to trace the petals of a rose up her thigh to her—

Fuck.

Self-loathing fills him.

Her pretty face. Her high cheekbones, the slash of red lipstick, her wild mane of hair, those sharp nails. Every little thing about her screams untouchable. Mean. Feral.

He's too close to her. She smells like grapefruit and spice. Nutmeg. He should stop huffing her scent, but he can't. It's all so strange. She's not even his type.

The van ride goes on. Tirelessly. Uncomfortably.

"So, Ash…"

His mother picks at her nail. Searching for a topic to break the silence. Nathaniel knows the feeling. It's been so long since he's been with his family, he doesn't know how to act. Maybe he is a robot. The thought of Ash being right irritates him even more.

"How long have you been doing"—his mother waves a hand helplessly—"this?"

"I got my certification two years ago at the Sacred Crossings Institute in Los Angeles." Her words are bright, proud.

His father examines Ash over his phone. "Isn't that like some touchy-feely school?" The look of disdain he gives her is one normally reserved for his own family.

Her smile slips. She looks to the ground, her eyes suddenly glassy. "Something like that."

Her feelings are hurt.

Fuck his father.

A swell of protectiveness rises up in him. The urge to defend her takes over before he can stop it. "It's a good school," he says. "I've read about it in the journal."

He didn't. He knows nothing about the school. What he does know is that he'd do anything to get rid of that sad look in her eyes.

Don grunts.

Ash remains silent, shoulders tense, her face now turned to the window.

Her defeat bothers him. More than he'd like to admit.

Beside him, Ash, voice low and husky, says, "I appreciate the lie." Her eyes are still on the passing scenery.

Nathaniel swallows hard. He wants to tell her he's sorry. Sorry that his father's an asshole and that being combative, competitive, is the fucked-up way his family bonds. But he keeps his mouth shut.

As the drive continues, Tate bitches and moans. If Delaney doesn't have to be here, then why does he? Like he's a five-year-old all over again instead of a twenty-six-year-old with a pornstache.

His mother sits, unmoving, with those same glassy, bored eyes from his childhood.

Christ. His family is so fucked up.

They just can't pull it all the fuck together for his grandfather, can they?

Finally, thankfully, the van pulls into the parking lot.

Without missing a beat, Ash whistles, long, loud and sharp.

The van goes silent.

She pops out of her seat. Surveys the group with a feline-like smile. "You all ready to fucking roll?"

At the word *fuck*, his mother makes a tiny squeak of protest in the back of her throat.

Nathaniel laughs, his earlier annoyance at the ridiculousness of his family chased away.

Ash's gray-green eyes meet his.

His chest tightens. All because of her.

After disembarking the van at Diamond Head, Nathaniel zips his pack. Ready to go, he scans the parking lot. Early morning, the lot's crowded with tourists and guides. The breeze is warm, and birds chatter overhead.

Ash fumbles with her own pack. The wind whips her dark hair, like a feral mane swirling around the crown of her head. With a growl, she settles her backpack on her feet like she's a penguin ready to nest and arranges her things.

"Hey," Tate says to Ash, holding out his black North Face pack. "Same pack." He holds out a fist to bump.

She obliges. "Twinsies," she says with a grin.

Nathaniel rolls his eyes.

And then she slips her hoodie off.

Instantly, his brain scrambles.

She's in a tiny crop top. That combined with the Lara Croft–type shorts and the colorful tattoos snaking her thighs, does something warm and unwelcome to his stomach.

After cramming her hoodie into her pack, she stands tall, dips her head back, and stares up into the sun. "Great," she mutters, shielding her eyes. "No shade."

Nathaniel smirks. "Good thing you brought your big, dumb floppy hat."

She scowls. "Good thing I did." With exaggeration and gusto, she plops the straw hat on her head.

Frowning, Nathaniel assesses her attire. The shoes are a complete walking hazard, her hair defies the laws of physics, and the floppy hat obscures her vision. Great. It makes him itch. Makes him want to get down on his knees and tie those fucking laces. And maybe get a closer look at those tattoos.

"Watch your boots," he growls. "I have enough to worry about with my grandfather."

Ash plucks her pack from the ground and shrugs into the

straps. The look she gives him is pure venom—eyes narrowed to slits, nostrils flaring. She checks her blood sugar, swiping her phone against her sensor. It makes a ping, and she takes in the reading.

"You have sugar?" Christ. Why is his tone suddenly soft? Why does he feel the need to check on her? "I don't want to get to the top and have to carry you down."

After what he swears is a low growl, she pulls herself up straighter. "I am perfectly capable of surviving on my own, fuck you very much."

With that, the hike begins. It's an out and back trail, so they keep to the right of the crater as they ascend up the winding paved road.

Don looks at Tate, his expression full of challenge. "Bet you I beat your best time up there."

Tate hoots and mimes the Running Man. "You're on."

Nathaniel holds back an eye roll as his brother and father peel away from the group.

"So much for family togetherness," Ash mutters beside him.

"Tell me if you get tired, Dad," Claire says.

"Should we tell a story?" Augustus suggests. "While we hike?"

Ash bobs her chin. "If you have the lung capacity for it, absolutely."

"Why Hawaii for your hotels, Grandpops?" Nathaniel asks. He's heard bits and pieces, but never the entire story.

Augustus's eyes twinkle. "You, Nathaniel, ask the good questions."

"It's because of Mom."

Nathaniel's eyes slide to his mother.

"That's right, Claire. Your mother and I spent our honeymoon here."

At Ash's sharp intake of breath, Nathaniel glances over. She dips her chin, then turns away, her focus suddenly fixed on the far side of the crater.

Augustus continues, nostalgia staining his voice. "We loved it here, so when we saw a listing in the local paper, we decided to check it out on a whim. When I saw the land, I knew I wanted it to be home base for my hotels. To bring out that sense of peace, of paradise for our guests. But…after Rosalea died, I moved the company to LA. I couldn't bear to come back." He inhales a hard breath. "But now…it's time. Some of the happiest moments of my life took place here, and I'd like to share them with you."

Despite her smile, his mother's hesitation is palpable. She'd never admit it, but Augustus has never been the father she needed. He missed birthdays and he hired nannies to cart her around. Nathaniel's own father missed more birthdays than he can count. He's experienced that stinging, lonely feeling that settles in a person's gut and refuses to leave.

Maybe she should open up to Augustus. Maybe that's what his grandfather wants, what this trip is for.

"Is it true Carlo Giacomo was an investor on the down-low?" Ash asks. She's once again affected her go-to expression, a look of fearless cool. "That he had a key that opened any suite when he needed it?"

Augustus's sharp laugh echoes around them. "That, my dear, is a story for another day."

"I don't know why you keep humoring them," Claire says with a smile.

The group stops at the base of a set of stairs.

"Oh god." Ash stares at the steps, her shoulders slumped.

According to his pamphlet, there are seventy-five.

He peers at her. "What's wrong, Bigfoot? You look scared."

She turns in his direction. Arches a brow. "Scared of a mountain? Please. I used to practice math with my dad."

"You two go on," Augustus orders. He looks from Ash to Nathaniel and back, like they're in cahoots. "Claire and I will meet you at the top."

"Are you sure?" Ash says as they're hit with a gust of wind. She frantically grabs the brim of her hat to keep it from being sacrificed to the volcano. "I can stay."

"No. You two have fun."

Ash frowns, probably doubtful of the promise of fun, but they continue on.

Another brisk breeze flows past, bringing with it scents of plumeria and salty sea air. Nathaniel inhales, his muscles burning, relishing the exercise.

Beside him, Ash huffs. "Why do people over six feet always walk so fucking fast? Do you have something to prove?"

"Only that I'm the master of the universe."

She snorts.

His lips twitch at the extra-long strides she takes to keep up with him.

"Did anyone ever tell you that you hike like an injured animal?" Nathaniel asks, nodding at her unlaced boots.

"Oh fuck off," Ash says, but her laugh is husky. "I didn't realize everything would be a contest. Well, I have news for you. I'm the least competitive person you'll ever meet. Especially when it comes to a hike."

He arches a brow, deciding to stop battling his curiosity. "How so?"

"If I don't care about it, I don't care. If there's nothing in it for me, forget it. Now a hike with a bar at the end of it? Sign me the hell up. A beautiful waterfall that may or may not be haunted by the spirits of vengeful lovers? Sure." She breathes a laugh. "A hike where you find a dead body at the end of it…mwah." She kisses the tips of her fingers. "It's like spaghetti in Italy."

"Nature," he grunts, "is what gets me moving."

"Great. You love nature. Congrats." Ash puffs a lock of hair out of her eyes. "I swear to god," she grumbles, "of all the lies Augustus has ever told, *this hike is easy* is the boldest."

Nathaniel hides a smirk. She's breathing so hard she can barely get the words out.

At a pit stop, Ash bends at the waist, palms on her bare thighs. Her hat falls into the dust. "Oh for fuck's sake." With a growl, she snags it from the ground and smashes it into her pack. "I thought I was entering my big hat era, but I was wrong."

Nathaniel waits for her to catch her breath before proceeding. Even he can admit, the climb is not for the faint of heart. The terrain is made even more treacherous by the two-way traffic. Selfie sticks, joggers and slow walkers clog the narrow path.

Ash straightens up, only to be knocked off the pathway by an errant jogger. Over the top of her head, Nathaniel shoots daggers at him with his eyes. Fucking asshole. Thinks he owns the goddamn road.

Without thinking, he puts a hand on her hip, moving her out of the way of traffic.

"You ready?" he asks, watching her with a careful eye. "Or do you need an escort to the bottom?" The last thing he needs is for her to keel over.

"Ready."

They begin again, side by side once more.

"Okay," Ash says when they're halfway up the summit. "Since Augustus isn't here, you have to entertain me."

Entertain her? Sure, he'll bite. "What'd you have in mind?"

"*Truth/lie*. Augustus and I play it all the time."

He blinks. "You do?"

"We do."

"Fine."

Her face brightens. "Okay. Truth or lie. Would you rather fight one hundred chickens or a bear?"

The question's so out of left field that he bursts out laughing.

Ash blinks at the sound, seemingly stunned for a moment, and then smiles. Her red lips curl, catlike, at the corners.

"Isn't this really Would You Rather?" he asks.

"Listen. It's whatever I want it to be. It was invented in a closet on a very drunk Friday night. The rules are lawless. Can turn on a dime." She throws him a half smile that makes his throat tighten. "Well?"

"A bear." Nathaniel trades places, moving Ash onto the inside of the path. If one more person knocks into her, he's going to lose it. "It's one target."

"What ambition." She struts forward, keeping pace with him. "Your turn."

He stares at her for a long minute. The bright sunlight brings out the shimmery blue undertones of her black hair. "Your real name."

He swears at himself the second the question's out of his mouth. Why does he even care? Why is he so curious about this girl? And why does he keep clocking her bare shoulders and the sunburn that's barely begun?

The glare she gives him could scorch the sun.

"You don't expect me to believe it's just Ash. Plain old Ash."

The tips of her ears turn pink.

Nathaniel grins at her uncomfortable expression. So, he is right.

That plump, lower lip juts out. Defiant. Stubborn. "What's wrong with plain old Ash?"

"There's nothing plain about you."

"Careful." The sly arch of her eyebrow. Her curious attention sweeps over him, her green-gray gaze glittering in the sun. Like fog after a summer rain. "It almost sounds like you're admitting I'm *interesting*."

A shrug, even as he internally berates himself for his comment. "You call it interesting. I call it predictable."

She swirls a finger. "How so?" The smoky purr of her voice has his cock flexing.

"If I had to guess, I'd say your favorite color is black and your favorite holiday is Halloween."

"You forgot something."

"What's that?"

"I drink the blood of little children by candlelight."

He chuckles, enjoying himself. And that's when he remembers he's fraternizing with the enemy. The woman who destroyed his life. The thought shoves his mind, his emotions, back three years.

"Another question then." He grinds his teeth, soaking in the echo of that pain. "Who paid you? To interrupt my wedding."

Her body locks up. She stops, and the humor in her expression vanishes. "We're still on that?"

The way her eyes shutter has anger simmering in him. She's already remembering what she thinks she knows about him.

Ash studies him intently. "You have psychopath eyes, you know."

He lets out a sound of frustration. "Probably because I want to murder you."

She watches him, lip caught between her teeth. The strap of her tank top has slipped down. Instead of making her look reckless or messy, she looks vulnerable and soft. It pisses him off.

"C'mon, let's go," he barks. He's done with this game.

---

Another fifty-four steps, silence, and two tunnels later, they make it to the top of the Diamond Head Observation Station. A clear day, the view stretches on forever. Beneath them, the Honolulu sea front. Navy-blue waves lap at the shore. Nothing but sun, sky and surf.

"The lighthouse," Ash breathes, sounding awed, as she draws up beside him. She points at the base of Diamond Head, where a white lighthouse stands. "There it is."

"What do you like about lighthouses?"

Fuck his life. The questions keep coming.

"They're mysterious." Her cheeks are red. The wind whips her hair, and she fights to control it. "Imagine saying you live in a lighthouse. Life goals unlocked."

Nathaniel angles his head. Says nothing.

Ash lifts her phone, side-eyes him. "No pictures?"

He crosses his arms. "No."

"Wow." She purses her lips. "You can even suck the joy out of a photo. Fascinating."

With that, she snaps her photo and walks off.

Rolling out his shoulders to release the Ash-induced irritation built up there, Nathaniel shucks his pack. He stretches and drinks from a bottle of water. Checks his phone. There's a text from his mother that says she and his grandfather called it quits at the second set of stairs.

Pack secured once more, Nathaniel studies the map as he elbows his way through the photo-snapping crowd. In his periphery, Ash is holding her phone up to the sky like she's trying to signal the aliens to take her back to her home planet.

The game was clever and chaotic; he'll give her that. But it unraveled before it even got started. His fault. He brought up the wedding, instantly fueling the animosity between them. Maybe it's not Ash he's pissed at. Maybe it's himself. Because it still bothers him. Not because he still loves Camellia, but because he has an innate need for closure.

And he refuses to let his grandfather's pain-in-the-ass death doula get under his skin. Thirteen more days, and he's free of her.

Ash paces the chaotic space, phone to her ear. When someone knocks into her a second time, spinning her around like a top, Nathaniel stifles a growl and trudges her way.

Unbelievable. Can she be any more oblivious?

"What are you doing?" he asks tightly.

"Trying to get service." She props one of her boots on the edge of a rock. "I have a standing appointment. If we're late, we text."

He bristles. Heat floods him. Excellent. She has a boyfriend. Not like it matters. The guy, whoever it is, has his hands full.

Still, his idiot mouth opens, and he asks, "With who?"

An honest kind of happy crosses her face. Her smile wide and full.

Startled, Nathaniel falls silent, and the burn in his throat intensifies. It's like the parting of a curtain. A special glimpse into Ash Keller.

"The one," she says.

His gaze jerks to her. "The one?"

"The *one*." Her face brightens, and she holds a hand up, palm out, to the sky. "It's like your soul sister. The crème to your coffee. The Nancy to your Sid. That one person who'd bury a body for you or take a bullet." Her voice is earnest as she asks, "Don't you have that person?"

Nathaniel has never known a person like that, let alone *had* one. Not his brother, sure as hell not his father. Even his so-called best friends from college were little more than acquaintances. Even his relationship with Camellia was mechanical. Nothing says *our love is for show* better than a paid article bragging about their engagement in the *LA Times*.

Ash's husky voice breaks through his thoughts. "Sometimes I think it's all you need in the world. If you have that one right person in your life, you can survive anything."

Curious now, Nathaniel keeps at it. "What have you survived?"

She looks at him, sharp. "What makes you think I have?"

Then she's turning. Pulling herself up on a rock, using a tree branch as both leverage and balance.

"Anyway, Tessie is my cousin. Love of my life. Apple of my eye. Currently pregnant and incubating an absolutely feral fetus. And if I do not reply ASAP to this name suggestion, her baby will be called Leviathan and I will forever have this on my conscience."

"Is that who you were talking to last night?"

She freezes. "You heard me?"

Of course he heard her. She's the loudest living thing on the entire planet. Her jovial and smoky laughter. Soft muttered swears. Whispers with his grandfather. Every word from her mouth, regardless of its volume, annoys him.

"Walls are thin." He presses on. "And you're extremely loud."

A smile blooms across her red mouth. She laughs, the boisterous sound filling the air like fireworks. "I am truly an elephant at heart."

It totally fucking works.

He smiles.

He can't fucking believe it. Christ. What is it about her? Her weird. Her quirk. Her brazenness to just *be*. Her *IDGAF* attitude and ballsy demeanor antagonize and intrigue him all at the same time.

She's a fucking Rubik's Cube. No, strike that. She's more of the puzzle box from *Hellraiser*.

He spears a hand through his hair, watching as her laces tangle. "I wouldn't do that."

"Do what? Harness the power of the satellites for service?" She stretches higher. Scoots farther back on the rock.

In a flash of foresight, Nathaniel sees it coming. Too close to the edge. Her boots have no traction. The rock's slick as hell with morning dew.

Crossing his arms, Nathaniel inhales sharply to push the emotion, the worry, aside. And yet he drifts closer to her. A strange tug in his stomach. Ridiculous. She's ridiculous and reckless, and how his grandfather puts up with her is beyond him.

"Ash. Get the fuck down." His tone is sharp, efficient. The kind he once used on the battlefield of his emergency department.

The bite in his voice has her eyes widening.

Then she sticks her tongue out at him and hops off the rock. "Killjoy." She's still too close to the edge, but she's on the ground again, at least.

*Thank fuck.*

She takes a step toward him, but as she does, a tourist wielding a rogue selfie stick knocks into her. Knocks her off balance.

Knocks her to the edge of the cliff.

The heel of her boot slips on loose gravel. She gasps and grabs at the air.

And then she screams.

## Chapter Eleven

Nathaniel yanks Ash into his chest before she can tumble down the sheer face of the cliff.

"Jesus Christ, Ash." His rough voice grates against her cheek. "You almost died to send a goddamn text."

"Tessie," she croaks. Her voice is faint amid the dizzying rush in her head.

His tennis shoes crunch on the gravel as he moves away from the ledge. Nathaniel's racing heart pumps hard against hers. A perfect sync. A rhythm she wants to pretend is so not happening.

How he did it, she'll never know. It took seconds, not minutes, to clear the space between them. He snatched her up before she could go over the side of the cliff. She squeezes her eyes shut and presses her face into his neck.

She wants to cry. Instead, she's distracted when she gets the most amazing whiff of Nathaniel's natural scent. Internally, Ash is a 360-degree eye roll. Of course the man doesn't wear cologne. He naturally smells like the sea and sun. Of fucking course.

She whimpers. Her brain forever chemically altered with one hit of him.

"You're okay." He squeezes her tighter. "You're okay. I've got you."

Eyes watering, she nods, nods, nods.

It's so goddamn embarrassing, clinging to him like a deranged koala, but she can't help herself. Nathaniel's solid, tall form is like an anchor. A reassurance that she didn't just literally drop dead.

"Am I alive?" she gasps.

"No, you're in heaven, and even the angels don't want you."

That pulls a laugh from her. "But what if?" she whispers.

His body rumbles with a brusque chuckle. And then he's sliding her down his warm frame until her boots touch steady ground. When he sets her gently on her feet, she looks over her shoulder at the drop. "Holy shit, I don't—"

A broad palm cups her face. Moves Ash's gaze, up, up, up.

Vaguely, she's aware of people staring. Hushed murmurs of concern. There's a whole world around them, and all she can see is him. All she can feel is him. The way his big thumb skims her chin, how his long fingers tangle in her snarled hair.

"Ash?" Nathaniel's ice-blue eyes shoot to hers, full of concern. Not the annoyance from earlier today. "You okay?"

His response causes her stomach to tighten. She clamps down on her emotions. Fights to control her breath. The last person she wants help from is him.

"I'm fine."

His soft expression sharpens. "You're an idiot." The words are harsh, but she doesn't miss the tremor in his voice.

"Your bedside manner is impeccable." With a huff, she shoves a hunk of hair out of her face. "I bet your patients beg for a timely death."

With a dubious grunt and a tense jaw, he inspects her. He's back to annoyed. Doctor Robot. That's him. And that's why he's doing this. Checking her over like she's a glass-jarred specimen.

"Holy shit, that was next-level death defying."

Both Nathaniel and Ash bristle. Slowly, they turn their heads.

The offender wielding the selfie stick is back, Hawaiian shirt and all. "I got it all on video," he says, lifting the stick in victory. As if that was his sole mission. To push Ash off a cliff for the sheer sake of views.

Almost killed by a rogue TikToker. She'll never live it down.

Ash flinches as the selfie stick whizzes past her ear.

"Get that fucking thing out of her face, asshole," Nathaniel snarls, shoving the stick and the man backward.

Eyes wide, Ash bites her lip. Not Nathaniel literally confirming he can fight.

"I just want her name for the video—"

"Take your fucking stick and keep moving unless you want it up your ass," Nathaniel snaps, stepping in front of her to block her from view.

"Fuck you, dude." With that, the guy storms off.

Ash looks up at him, brow cocked. "Impressive. Violence before lunch."

He blows out a hard breath. "Fucking people." Placing a hand on her elbow, he steers her toward a less populated area. "Let's get the hell out of here."

His stern, bossy tone steamrolls her stomach.

She nods, straightening up, convincing herself to rally. And then a weight's lifted from her, literally. Nathaniel slips her pack down her arms and hooks it around his broad shoulder.

"You don't need to be any more off balance." With those words, he drops to his knees. Lifts his eyes. "And you don't need to break your neck either."

Feeling almost lightheaded, she stares down at him. "Nathaniel, you don't—"

"You almost fell down a fucking cliff," he grits out, "because of your goddamn boots."

Before she can argue with him, he wraps his warm, broad palm around her right ankle and sets her boot on his thigh.

Ash stiffens at the feel of his hands on her.

Head bowed, face furrowed in concentration, he ties her laces. His long fingers dexterously loop the bows. He tightens them extra-tight, as if he's angry. To steady herself, she places a hand on his shoulder. In the morning sunlight, the honey-wheat hue of his hair, the flex of his jaw, do something ominous to her heartbeat.

Because, holy shit, is this the hottest thing a man has ever done for her? On his knees tying her shoes? Yeah, right. Ash shakes herself out of her moony daze. He's treating her as if she's a toddler. He's behaving exactly as a doctor should. This does not mean he cares. Because a man like Nathaniel Whitford doesn't care about anyone but himself.

She's pulled from her ridiculous thoughts when Nathaniel lifts his head. She watches as his gaze roams over her tattoos. Stiffens when his thumb strokes across her calf in a sweet, calming motion. He shouldn't be touching her there. And she should absolutely not be enjoying it.

He looks up at her, his eyes lasered firmly on her face. The air changes between them. Electrified. Intense.

Ash sucks in a breath, wanting to push him away, wanting to push herself into him all at once. "I think you throttled the laces enough," she says quietly.

With visible effort, he removes his hands from her and dusts dirt from his pant leg. Then he rises to stand tall over her. "There," he says. His biceps ripple. He's so close she can feel the heat radiating between them. "If you fall now, it's not on my conscience."

"That's presuming you have one."

Fuck. It's the wrong thing to say.

Nathaniel's face wipes clean of its softness, hardening into an emotion she can't place. Seething anger maybe. Irritation.

Distressingly, it upsets her that she's upset him.

Despite her dislike of moody billionaire doctors, she opens her mouth, determined to take it back, but she's too late.

Nathaniel lets out a humorless laugh. "Here." He shoves a solid object into her hands.

She looks down. Blinks. It's her phone. Her throat goes tight. He even managed to save that.

"Your one and only will be glad to know you only barely survived."

Then he turns abruptly, and his tall, broad-shouldered form disappears down the stairs. His pace is brisk and brutal. One Ash has no hope of keeping up with.

She gnaws at her lower lip. Looks down at the phone clenched in her hand. At Tessie's text that says *Mabel?* and exhales. Glances over her shoulder at the boulder, the warm sear of Nathaniel's touch echoing across her skin.

In the moment she slipped, it's like a life she didn't know she wanted flashed before her eyes.

---

The first thing Ash does when she gets back to the hotel is head to the pool. The trip down Diamond Head was much faster than going up. The van ride back to the hotel was full of awkward silence. Augustus pressing her and Nathaniel for photos of the view, a summary of their experience. All Ash could do was show him the lone photo she took. Nathaniel ignored her the entire way back.

Opposite seats. Cold shoulders.

Perfect.

She needs that.

A return to her senses.

Not the strange, swoony feeling in her stomach.

Ash rolls her neck out and claims a lounge chair. If there's one thing a near-death experience calls for, it's time poolside.

The Whitfords broke to do their own thing the second they got back to the resort. It's only day two of vacation, and already, they're foaming at the mouth to get away from one another.

After placing an order with the server—a very, very large piña colada, stat—Ash gives herself a quick shot of insulin to combat the upcoming sugar rush. Then she reclines on a lounge chair and takes in the scene.

This is better. How vacation should be. Sitting in the sun and judging people. A little boy with violent red hair runs back and forth across the pool deck, banging a plastic shovel against a sandcastle bucket. Seagulls claim leftover sandwiches. Hikes that nearly kill her and rude doctors who want to do the same should be forbidden.

Distressingly, before everything—including her—went south,

today was fun. Sure, it was death defying and involved more exercise than she would have liked, but she enjoyed herself.

The thought disgusts her.

She let her guard down. She laughed. She told Nathaniel about Tessie and the truth/lie game. They bonded. No. She wouldn't consider it bonding exactly. More like hate-enjoying each other's company.

She reminds herself of who he is. He's a man like Jakob. A cheat. A liar. A person who hurts others because all he cares about is himself.

She is here for Augustus. For a job. She cannot create more messes in her life. Casual, clean chaos is all she will allow herself.

The heat of the sun coasts over her. Even with the umbrella providing a modest amount of shade, small torches have implanted themselves beneath the skin of her shoulders. Sunscreen failed her. Ash flicks a look at her boots. They're kicked up on the lounge, mocking her for being an idiot without sandals.

*Untie them. It's easy. Just untie them and let your feet breathe.*

And yet...

Nathaniel tied them. It feels like undoing something that's only just begun.

Which means absolutely nothing.

Nothing except—

Movement in front of Ash startles her, and she nearly drops her piña colada.

"Shit," she swears, sinking lower onto the lounge chair.

Speak of the devil.

Nathaniel strolls to the poolside deck. His board shorts sit low on his hips. His teeth white and gleaming as he grabs a towel from the bin.

Eyes closed, she groans. She can't escape him.

When she opens them again, he's diving into the pool. He swims its length and then emerges in a perfect Bo Derek *10* run, minus the problematic braids.

Strangely entranced by the rivulets of water streaming down his body, Ash sips her piña colada. Allows herself a moment to shamelessly ogle.

Ugh.

Too perfect. Too infuriating. Too tall. If this were the Dark Ages, he'd be the healthiest specimen of man. Tone and tanned and muscled. Broody and most definitely ready for the Crusades. If only she could send him into battle, never to return.

"Christ," Ash mutters as Nathaniel towel dries his abs in what feels like slow-motion. God, is this a scene from a *Baywatch* movie?

Her stomach flips, and she growls a reminder to herself to cool it.

She'll literally rip her eyes out of her face if she doesn't stop checking out Nathaniel Whitford.

Is this how it will be at all the resorts? Stalked by his absolutely flawless body?

"Disease," she mutters. "I have a highly contagious disease. It's the only valid option."

This morning, he was like a German shepherd, shifting into protective mode. Tossing the TikToker aside like he was a pesky gnat. Something tells her if he had taken a swing at the guy, he'd likely be sleeping for a year.

Ash shifts uncomfortably, resisting the urge to take a dip into the shallow end of the pool. She shouldn't have liked that macho display of dicks out. And yet…her stomach feels gooey and warm every time she replays it.

Fuck. Why are all her emotions jumbled?

The memory of Nathaniel sprinting the distance and pulling her into his arms is seared onto her brainstem.

He wasn't worried about her. Was he?

To distract herself, Ash pulls out a magazine from her beach bag. She flips through the spreads, but she can't help but peek at Nathaniel over the edge of the pages. His effortless glide through the water. Sunkissed forearms. Those sexy veins running from his biceps down to his hands.

He's soaking wet, but so is she.

*Focus, Ash.*

Resisting the urge to fan herself with the magazine, she reroutes her attention to a twenty-page spread about cryptids.

Miraculously, she loses herself in the article. She's been successfully reading for ten minutes when the lounger beside her squeaks. "Catching up on *Cryptozoology Weekly*?"

"Monthly, actually," Ash deadpans. "Only so much can happen in thirty days."

Nathaniel takes it from her, holds it at arm's length like it bites. He cocks a brow, squints dubiously at the centerfold.

"Which one's your favorite?"

Delighted by the question, even though Nathaniel looks like he regrets it, Ash lifts her sunglasses. "Bigfoot. He is truly the OG of the cryptid world. Hairy. Smells. Has a whole forest to himself. And yours?"

When he opens his mouth only to look baffled, she laughs.

"Nathaniel," she says, "you disappoint me. How do we hope to ever have cryptid discourse if you can't name a single one by heart?"

He rolls his eyes but says nothing. Just leans back against his lounger.

Ash slurps extra loud on her straw in the hopes of driving him away.

The only thing she gets is an unfairly handsome brow furrow.

With a withering sigh, she tosses the magazine on the seat near her feet. So much for peace and quiet. "Why are you here, Nathaniel? Can't you just let me lounge poolside in peace? Don't you have family to annoy?"

He takes in her boots, then surveys her face.

He points at the beach. "Tate's up there right now." In the bright blue sky above, a parasailer flails. "My mother's at a massage, and my father's probably virtually carving up the face of a pre-teen girl."

Ash lowers her sunglasses, squints at the sky. "Over under odds Tate gets attacked by a seagull?"

Nathaniel's lips flatten into an almost smile. "Twenty-to-one." Then, in a disappointing move of modesty, he pulls a shirt from his gym bag and shrugs it on.

Ash sits up on her elbows. His shirt's plastered to his damp skin. All those toned muscles beg to be free. "Why would you wear clothes? You work so hard to earn validation from the female species."

Shaking his head, he sets his beer on the table. "I think the female species will survive."

"You're too handsome." She appraises him. "Maybe you need a scar."

He raises an eyebrow. "What'd you have in mind?"

She can't help the wicked grin that crosses her face. But it's wiped away when her lounger is rocked. Ash snaps her head to the left.

The redheaded little boy smirks at her and slams his shovel against the metal frame of her chair.

Ash flinches at the sound. Then growls at him.

With a squeal, he takes off.

"Weird-ass little kid," Nathaniel mutters.

"He's like Chucky roaming the grounds, minus a murder weapon."

The boy runs over to a woman in big Jackie Kennedy sunglasses. But those aren't what snag Ash's attention. It's her sandals. Strappy, jelly-like flip-flops covered in spikes. They're right up Ash's alley.

Nathaniel nods at the sandals. "You like those?"

*Love them.*

She shrugs. "They're fine." She will never admit her feet are small forest fires in her boots. Nathaniel needs no more fuel to add to his ammunition.

He laughs. Something soft, quiet falls between them.

Ash inhales. Fights the sudden tightness in her lungs. She has to do it. Be bigger. It's the only human thing to do. Because, like him or not, he did save her life.

"Thank you," she says softly.

His response is a confused frown.

"For earlier," she clarifies. "For not letting me fall to my untimely death."

"You're a pain in my ass," he replies. "But even I wouldn't shove you off a cliff."

Ash arches a brow. "That statement does leave room for you to hire someone with all your billions."

A chuckle rolls off his lips. "Despite what you think, I'm not that entitled."

Her phone chimes.

Forcing her attention from his unfairly gorgeous face, she leans over to the small table and silences the warning from her blood sugar monitor.

Nathaniel's eyes sweep over her, linger on her sensor. Attached to the back of her arm like a Frankenstein bolt. A long time ago, she'd be self-conscious. Now? Her diabetes is not *the* thing. It's just *her* thing. A part of her that's overall cooperative, even if, at times, it's a pain in her ass. She deals. She survives. She conquers. Sugar is not death. Everything in moderation.

"How do you like that compared to the finger prick?" Nathaniel asks, brows high.

Her heart briefly stutters at the question. "It lets me feel like I have a life."

He nods like he understands. "When were you diagnosed?" Before she can answer, he holds up a hand. "Don't feel like you have to answer. I'm a doctor. I'm naturally—"

"Nosy," she finishes.

Expression soft, he says, "I was going to say curious."

"I don't mind."

Nathaniel butting in, being interested, is more than she ever got from Jakob.

"I don't need the gory details, Ash," Jakob said when she tried to explain it to him once.

She shifts on the lounger. Well aware of the meager inches separating their bodies. "I was twelve. Height of middle school, so you know, the timing was"—she smacks her fingers with gusto—"chef's kiss."

Nathaniel's presence, his intense gaze on her, doesn't slow her down. No. Surprisingly, it makes her want to talk to him.

"I didn't know what was happening. For a few months, I felt off. Thirstier than normal. Tired. I passed out in school. I was in a coma for a week, if you can believe that. I almost died. Clearly, I didn't. But it did get me out of gym class for a month. Bright side, right?"

Gently, Nathaniel says, "Jesus."

The memory comes to her with ease. She's thought about it every day since she was diagnosed. Tessie, shaking her, screaming *Ashabelle!* like the sound of her full stupid-ass name would be enough to snap her out of the coma. And maybe it did, because it's the only thing she remembers about that awful time in her life.

Her heart pounds as she goes on. "It took a bit to understand what I was dealing with. I hated it, hated myself. At the time, it was like a scarlet letter embedded on my forehead. Everyone knew. It's all they wanted to talk about. All they worried about." She traces a finger over the rose on her thigh and takes a deep breath. "It really fucking sucked. Everyone acting like I had glass bones and paper skin. They thought if I touched a piece of sugar, I'd drop dead. Or they excluded me from birthday parties because suddenly, I was no longer normal."

Nathaniel's frown deepens, his shoulders sinking. "They did that?"

"Oh yeah. Kids are mean." She smiles. "But then my parents put me in a camp when I was thirteen, and it was like a bong hit for every one of my senses. Every camper, every counselor there had it. I wasn't alone. It was normalized—as much as you can normalize diabetes."

A strange softness washes over his handsome features, his usually icy blue irises warming.

Ash drops her stare, takes a sip of her slowly melting piña colada. "It's cheesy, but now it's just me. Diabetes doesn't control me. There is nothing I can't do. I've lived an awesome fucking life so far. I can still eat chocolate, have a beer, travel the world, and almost fall off the sides of volcanoes."

Nathaniel chuckles. Then scrubs a hand across his jaw, contemplative. "And all of this plays into your morbid obsession with death?" Not an ounce of judgment in his tone. Just stark curiosity.

Ash sobers. Squints at him. "It's not an obsession. Technically, it's probably existential OCD, but what's so wrong with caring about death anyway? Babies, marriages, first homes. Those are big life events. Death is too. Everyone deserves their last wishes."

He assesses her quietly for a moment and then says, "That's an interesting take on it."

She bites her lip as a prickly defensiveness that always hit when she was with Jakob crashes over her. "There's nothing wrong with that."

He pins his gaze to hers. Frowns.

Her stomach blooms with heat at the intensity of his eye contact.

With a sigh, he says, "I didn't say you were wrong."

Inhaling deep, Ash calms her tongue and her defenses. It's a strange sensation. A man listening. Looking at her in a way that makes her think she could tell him anything and he'd accept it.

Maybe Nathaniel Whitford's one positive attribute in life is that he pays attention.

He tilts his head. "Where's your big, dumb floppy hat?"

She snorts. "Trash. Why?"

"You're getting burned."

"Despite what you may believe, I have lubed up many a time."

At her answer, Nathaniel clears his throat, and she smirks at his obvious discomfort.

Ash lowers her head, inspects the pinkening tinge beginning to bloom on one arm. "My skin is repellant, I swear. The sun hates it."

"That's because the sun down here is a menace."

"I could say the same thing about you."

Brows raised, he flattens his mouth and gives her a look. "It's because of all the sand. It reflects the sun." He dips his chin. "Turn around. You missed your shoulders." When she hesitates, Nathaniel's mouth quirks to the side. "Melanoma is a real risk."

"My god, you have such a boring doctor brain." Breath held, Ash moves onto the edge of his lounge, giving him her back.

With a chiding sigh, he grabs the bottle of sunscreen. Into his hand goes a large dollop, like a stigmata in paradise.

One big, warm palm lands on her back. Ash tenses. Hisses a breath at the contact. "Should you be doing this?" she goads. "Touching me?"

"Ah," he says, tone dry, "I forgot the part where you spontaneously combust at human contact."

"You never know," she murmurs. Then, horrified to feel her lips parting in something like a smile, she flattens them.

Almost delicately, his hands skim up the backs of her arms to her shoulders. Jesus. The grip in his hands. Long fingers, broad palms.

He begins to rub.

Oh. *Oh.*

The sun, the rum heat her face. There's a lovely little pulse down below she hasn't felt in such a long time.

Nathaniel flexes his hand, moving his fingers just so to tuck an errant lock of hair behind her ear. Warmth coils and curls. She glances over her shoulder at him.

"Careful," she warns breathlessly. "You get to my throat, you give it a quick throttle, and it could all be over."

It's all her brain can do. Tease. To chase away their strange yet welcome closeness. Her defenses are down, and she can't even help it.

"Don't tempt me," he says, sounding strained.

Ash leans into the slow rhythm of his touch. Leans back. Closes her eyes, soaks in the feeling of being braced by his large palm.

Nathaniel makes a noise deep in his throat as his thumbs smooth up, tracing the arc of her shoulder. It's a delicious sensation. The gentle search of his hands, tracing over her bare skin, inking pulse points. Breaking boundaries.

She wants more. Wants it harder. Him against her. Like paperweights.

"Ash," he says, voice catching, fingertips on the curve of her throat.

"What?" she whispers. A lick of heat curls up her spine, and she shivers. "What is—"

"Nathaniel!"

The sharp bleat of his name sends her heart jumping and breaks the spell between them.

Nathaniel jerks back from her, his hands slipping over her shoulders, his touch disappearing. She twists, taking in the sight of him. He looks like a man come out of a trance. Face flushed, hair damp, rumpled and caught off guard.

He scans the pool, then goes stiff.

Ash follows his line of sight.

Realization hits her with sinking-gut shock.

Slowly, she looks back at Nathaniel, who's gaping as well.

Standing on the poolside deck, nearly naked in a long shimmery cover-up, with vibrant pink hair, is the Bratz doll. And she's headed straight for Nathaniel.

## Chapter Twelve

"You're here," Nathaniel says, meeting Delaney in the middle of the sun deck.

"Oh my God, it's so freaking good to see you," Delaney squeals, throwing herself into his arms to squeeze the life out of him.

He holds her at arm's length to evaluate her better. "I thought you couldn't get away until Tuesday."

"Don't tell Mom, but..." Delaney's lips split into a grin. "I stole half the props on set and got fired."

He massages his brow. "Christ, DeeDee."

"Don't worry. My publicist is on it," she says. "They have to bring me back. I get shanked in prison in episode seven." She wiggles her brows. "And then disemboweled."

Nathaniel shakes his head. His little sister—younger by ten years—snagged a role as an inmate in a limited run series on HBO. While working as an intern on a set, she happily sat through a production of the producer's daughter's kindergarten play, and in the end, she got the part.

She's truly the personality hire of the office and the Whitford family.

Aside from his grandfather, DeeDee's the one family member he can tolerate. Even if she does arrive half-naked to every family event and can't keep her hands off the valets.

Delaney scans the pool. Puffs out her chest. "Do you think people recognize me?"

"If you wanted to be undercover, I'd rethink the hair," Nathaniel replies drolly. With her short pink guillotine haircut and sparkly rainbow cover-up, astronauts in space couldn't miss her.

"Never. The hair is my calling card." She regards him, curious. "So, how's it going, big brother?"

"It's...going," Nathaniel replies.

Her gaze drops to his sunscreen-covered hands. "Looks messy."

His mind spins with thoughts of Ash and what he was in the middle of. Rubbing in that goddamn sunscreen to the point of distraction.

Using the towel Delaney has slung over her shoulder, he wipes off the remaining sunscreen. Guilt twists in his gut. As if he's been caught in the act. But the act of what? Helping a woman who's so clueless she can't even take care of herself? Never mind how fucking good she felt beneath his hands. Smooth and warm and soft.

"Ooh, is that her?"

Nathaniel snaps out of his reverie.

In his periphery, across the pool deck, there's a flash of yellow. Ash. She's gathering her things, smashing the magazine and towel into the beach bag like she's planning to melt into the shadows before anyone can see.

"That's her," he says dryly.

It's a given that Delaney got the scoop about Ash from his mother or Tate. News in their family travels fast and usually incorrectly.

Delaney, hand shielding her eyes, surveys her. "She looks like she could cut you."

"She *would* cut me."

"Hey!" Delaney waves that same hand. "Over here."

Fuck.

Nathaniel freezes.

Ash freezes.

She turns in slow-motion, her posture rigid. Then, with narrowed eyes, she heads toward them.

The world goes quiet for half a second.

Staring is wrong, but it's all Nathaniel can do. Those high cheekbones, that sun-yellow bikini, her long bare legs covered in tattoos. The bounce of her creamy white breasts as she sashays his way. She's like an eclipse. Dark and light. Terrifying and fascinating. A once-in-a-lifetime event to remember before it's gone.

And suddenly he's surprised to find that yellow is his favorite fucking color.

"Slinking away?" he asks.

She settles beside him, wrapping her arms around her middle. "Slithering."

Nathaniel frowns. Her voice is tight, her lips pressed in a flat line, eyes straight ahead. He can't deny that it bothers him. The sudden cold shoulder. The refusal to meet his gaze.

He nods. "This is my sister, Delaney. Delaney, this is Ash."

"Hi," Delaney chirps, stretching out her hand. "Call me DeeDee if you're nasty."

"This is your *sister*?" Ash takes a wobbly step back, pushing her sunglasses on top of her head. She sounds horrified and uncertain, as if the words don't compute.

Nathaniel clears his throat lightly. "One and only."

Wide-eyed and suddenly paler, Ash finally takes Delaney's hand and shakes it. "Hi," she says in that low, smoky voice of hers. "Nice to meet you."

Delaney stares at Ash. She's practically bouncing on her toes, like she's ready to erupt. "I swore I wouldn't. But I am."

"Am what?" Nathaniel asks.

Delaney traces Ash's form. "Vibing with her."

Nathaniel groans. The last thing he needs is for the two of them to bond. Between Ash and his sister, he has enough problems.

Delaney tilts her head. "You're a Scorpio, right?"

Wordlessly, Ash nods.

"You like tarot?"

Ash opens her mouth. Before she can answer, Nathaniel snaps the air, intercepting his sister before she can start.

"Let's. Not."

With an elbow to his ribs, Delaney pouts. "You suck the fun out of everything. You're boring."

"That's what I told him." Ash smiles, but it's wan, tired.

Delaney giggles, pleased to have someone on her side. "I know, right? One time in Chile, all I wanted to do was…"

As Delaney prattles on about all the ways Nathaniel has been the most boring brother in the history of the world, he catches a glimpse of a streak of sunscreen on Ash's shoulder. He reaches out to rub it in, but catches himself at the last minute.

Ash half turns toward him. Her smile is brittle, panicked. "I—I have to go."

Nathaniel scrutinizes her. "Is everything okay?"

Her pale cheeks burn red, and for once, she doesn't have a cryptic comeback. Towel clutched to her chest, she takes a step backward. "I—I should check on Augustus."

His stomach tightens in a knot. Concerned, Nathaniel moves to follow. "Ash—"

She turns away from him, and then she's racing toward the door that leads into the hotel and away from whatever spooked her.

---

After a shower, Nathaniel meets his family for dinner in the lobby. His father's hired a driver to take them to a Michelin-star restaurant on an adjoining beach.

Hands in his pockets, Nathaniel paces the marble floor while his father describes in detail the call he took today. He does his best to look bored, but he can't help looking up and over every time the elevator chimes.

He's waiting for it. The sight of the stomping black cloud of Ash on the arm of his grandfather.

When the elevator doors open for the fifth time, there's only Augustus.

"Where's Ash?" he barks, unable to help himself. Unable to shake that prickle of annoyance. Of want.

"Too much sun," Augustus says with a cheery grin. "She's taking it easy in the room." Eyes twinkling, he turns to Delaney. "Hi there, sweetheart."

"Grandpops," Delaney squeals, throwing herself into Augustus's arms.

Dinner's unbearable. His father picks apart the last few episodes of Delaney's show while Delaney agrees with every single fucking offensive word. Why wouldn't she? For the first time in God knows how long, she actually has thirteen minutes of her father's attention. Nathaniel carries the conversation, volleys the dialogue between his mother and grandfather, as futile as it is.

Augustus keeps trying to mend fences. No one seems to want to reciprocate. Nathaniel's not sure what to do. Except wish Ash were here. She'd have a solution. Make jokes, lighten the mood, at least piss off his father.

It's only been two days, and already, she's the sole person ensuring no one bolts for saner pastures.

He's certainly not leaving, but that doesn't mean he isn't counting down the days until the vacation is over and he can get away from his family. This isn't a feasible or workable emotion. This is about survival. Even med school wasn't this hard.

An email pops onto the upper left corner of his phone screen. He checks it with bated breath. But it's not the email he's been waiting for.

It's why he's applying to the North Sea, right? To get away?

Halfway through coffee and dessert, his mind has strayed to Ash again. To their conversation at the pool. To the people who made her feel like an outcast. What he'd give to throttle them. Fuck those people. Anyone who can use someone's health condition as a reason to exclude them. It's fucking cruel.

He admires her for going through all that so young. Despite

the slight cynical edge to her voice, so much of her holds resilience. Bravery.

The image of her wary—and then stunned—expression at the pool keeps playing across his mind like a GIF.

His stomach fills with annoyance. Worry. Did she at least get dinner? Christ. He doesn't like anything about this. His Ash-centric brain doesn't like the thought of her not eating. Doesn't like the way she all but ran away from him today. It doesn't sit right.

As soon as they finish dinner and get back to the resort, Nathaniel heads to his room. His first stop is the balcony, where he hopes to find Ash. And do what? Talk? Trade banter that stings and then some? It's either talk to her or give in to Tate and listen to his podcast.

But the balcony is dark and empty. The curtains to her room are drawn. He lifts a hand, hovering, wanting to knock, but thinks better of it.

So he sits. Thumbs through his phone to check his email for word about his job application. But he finds he couldn't care less.

For once, the North Sea isn't on is mind. Neither is figuring out an early exit from this trip. Instead, he's consumed with thoughts revolving around a different subject entirely. One that doesn't make him want to run away.

It's Ash. The macabre girl with the blood-red smirk.

After an hour on the balcony, he stands to go. The moment he's on his feet, the light in her room turns on. He waits, heart pounding, listening to the crash of waves, hoping for a glimpse of her scowling face, and then the light flicks off.

## Chapter Thirteen

I T'S HER. THE BLUE-HAIRED, SEQUINED STRIPPER FROM the photo her client gave her.

The photo Ash took as absolute proof. Proof that allowed her to object to the wedding.

Only it wasn't an affair.

The woman was Nathaniel's sister.

His fucking *sister*.

The look on Nathaniel's face that day—that confused, hurt expression that's haunted her nightmares for the last three years—floats through her mind once again, and her guilty heart shrivels up and drops into her stomach.

"Fuck," Ash whispers to her pale reflection in the mirror. "Fuck, fuck, fuck."

---

She's watching the patio light flick on and off like some sort of drug dealer signal when Tessie calls. Flopping onto the bed, Ash slides her finger over the screen of her phone and lets out a heaving sigh as a hello.

Skipping dinner seemed like the best option. She couldn't face Nathaniel without a game plan, without dissecting her emotions, her fuck-up. And she needs her cousin to talk her through it.

"Well?" Tessie says, sounding harried. "Let it rip." All that's visible are her nostrils. The camera jostles like a found footage film and then steadies.

Ash squints. "Are you in the bathtub?"

"I'm in my overwhelmed mommy era," Tessie hisses. Fully

clothed, she pulls the shower curtain around her. "I have to hide every chance I get."

After explaining what happened at the pool, Ash says, "Nothing, and I mean nothing, will ever top the shock of this reveal. The audible gasp that came out of my mouth when I saw her..." A shudder racks her at the memory.

Tessie studies her, head tilted and dark eyes thoughtful. "So you're saying you feel bad?"

"Of course I feel bad." Ash chews her lip. "I ruined people, Tessie. I actively worked to dissolve a union with malicious intent."

"You're not a serial killer, Ash."

"It feels like it."

"You were hurt. After Jakob."

The hardness in Tessie's voice brings back flashes of the moment she physically tackled her cousin on the front lawn of her parents' house to keep her from rushing to Jakob's apartment with her power saw. "We've all been where you've been," Tessie continues. "Where we want to fuck up the person who hurt us. And sometimes, when we can't, we take it out on everyone else."

"I was in the wrong, though. All this time, I thought he was a devil, a cheater, but—"

"But he's tolerable."

Ash scoffs. "Hell no. He's literally the worst person I've ever met. But he is taller than me. So there's that."

"Not a cheater. And he's tall? And he saved you in a rockslide? I don't know, Ash." Tessie's brown eyes sparkle. "Sounds like Nathaniel Whitford might not be the worst."

"I don't like this. This opposite thing we're doing. I'm the one who gives advice, and you're the one who complains."

Tessie laughs. "Tough. I'm your vacation fairy godmother living vicariously through you." With a grunt, she reclines in the tub. Rubs her belly. "Take a photo of him for me. I want to see what he looks like."

Ash stifles a laugh. "Hard pass."

Tessie pouts. "Please, I'm bored, and Solomon has no plan to leave my side for the next four months."

"You love it," Ash hisses.

"I heard that."

There's a growl in the background. Then the shower curtain is torn open. A grinning Solomon stands tall behind Tessie. Peggy Sue sharks along the side of the tub. Bear screeches and hurdles over the edge. Tessie squeals and bobbles the phone as she hugs him to her with her free arm.

"So what do I do?" Ash shouts, knowing she has about five seconds before it's chaos.

"Apologize," Tessie orders as she's rocked by her son and her image goes blurry. "It's the oldest trick in the book. And guess what? It works!" Tessie and Solomon erupt in wild giggles before the screen goes black.

Ugh, they're too cute for words. Heart sinking, Ash tosses her phone onto the nightstand. She hates everything about this day.

Once again, the light to the patio flickers on. Then the silhouette of Nathaniel's tall frame passes by her room. He's waiting. Most likely to murder her. And she wouldn't blame him. That fifty-foot drop to the beach sounds pretty good right now.

The light flicks off.

Her blood churns faster in her veins as her thoughts spin out.

The photo she saw was a setup.

Her client lied to her.

It means what she did was very, very wrong.

It means she can't lump him in with Jakob anymore.

It means Nathaniel Whitford is not the worst.

She is.

---

"Please don't take my horsey," Ash says, sitting cross-legged on her lounge chair. "I like it."

As they sit in companionable silence, Augustus examines the chessboard on the small table between them. Then her horse is knocked over.

"Apologies in advance."

Two more moves, and Augustus has checkmate.

Ash throws her hands to the sky. "You're a cruel and cunning man, Augustus." Trying to beat him is a futile objective. As pointless as arguing with a toddler or trying to wear socks with sandals.

They're spending their last few hours in Honolulu at Waikiki beach.

Obviously, she's avoiding Nathaniel. Not an easy feat, since they're both stuck on this two-week trip. Dodging him is awkward and uncomfortable and makes her feel like she's in hiding.

She's not angry at him anymore. She's angry at herself. For being wrong. For being played. For being an asshole and hurting him.

Ash quirks a brow as Augustus resets the board. "Are you sure you didn't hire me just to kick my ass in chess?"

"My dear," he says with a smile, "I hired you because you kick *my* ass."

"I will never understand this game." Ash squints in disapproval at the brown and white checkered board.

The sun spreads golden across the sand. A server delivers lunch. Fries and club sandwiches and palomas. Before they can dig in, a frisbee nearly sideswipes their drinks.

The little redheaded Chucky boy from the pool appears.

Ash shoots the kid a glare, tosses the frisbee back in his direction, then forces her attention back to her companion. "How do you feel?" She reclines on the lounge, and Augustus does the same. Her eyes dip to the beach, to Nathaniel, golden and muscled, catching a wave out at sea.

Goddamn that body.

She clears her throat. Regroups. "Do you feel like you're getting quality family time?" If not, she needs to know whose ass to kick.

He sets his hands on his thighs. "I didn't expect to. This trip is more about watching them. Taking things in. Making plans." His bushy brows lift. "Claire and I—our relationship has not always been the best. After Rosalea died, I tended to pull away."

"Do you think it's fair..." Ash begins, hesitant. She and Augustus are close. She is giving him a commitment to the end of his life, but she can't be sure she's not crossing a line. "To put it all on your dead wife as a reason for your behavior?"

"You know, Ash..." Augustus strokes his chin. "I don't." He inhales, determination sparking in his eyes. "I want them all to have the time of their lives. Money is no object."

She stops him with a firm hand to his arm. "Maybe that's the problem. You're focusing on money, not your family. Don't be like that old white man from *Jurassic Park*, Augustus."

He nods. "Denial."

"Bingo."

"I was absent. I was unavailable." He scans the beach, finds his daughter. "I don't think she's ever forgiven me."

"Maybe Claire needs to hear you admit that."

He lets out a tired sigh. "Maybe she does."

After passing Augustus his lunch, Ash snags a fry. Pops it into her mouth. Muses as she chews. "I think...if you honor some of your dreams, try to fix some of your mistakes before it's too late, it'll put you and your family in a better place."

"I missed my daughter's birthdays growing up. Every one. I don't think I've been there for a single one since she was two."

It's clear in the tone of his voice. How something so small still stings so very much.

"She must have been upset."

"She was."

Ash perks up, ideas churning in her head. "What if...on the

last night of the trip, you had a birthday party for her? Not just a birthday party, but the birthday party of all birthdays. It's like an apology, but with cake."

Augustus's pale-blue eyes spark with excitement. He hoots a laugh. "You know, my dear, I think that's your best idea yet."

"So you plan it, and if you need it, I'll help."

He arches a brow. "That's not in your job description."

She scoffs. "It's not, but I'll still help. I am a master at all the random things. Not to mention, I love a good party."

"It's a beautiful idea, Ash."

"What else?" she asks as she covertly takes a second to inject herself with insulin. "We're writing your memoirs." It's what the two of them have been doing on their brief rests in the hotel room. "We're in your resorts. What else do you want?"

"I want my family to be prepared."

A rock lodges itself in Ash's throat. The thought of Augustus dying is a punch to the solar plexus. He hired her early in the process, so she's here for the long run. Still, some part of her hopes. Hopes that with the chemo, there will be a miracle.

"I want my oldest grandson, who gets a month off at a time, to come home. I want him to stop running halfway across the world to escape the past."

Ash smothers a smile. "You're meddling, Augustus."

A harrumph. "I'm an old man. I deserve to meddle." He sighs and adjusts his hat.

Ash frowns up at the umbrella. The sun's beginning to edge out the shade it provides. "He's in LA." She dusts sandwich crumbs from her fingertips. "That's hardly halfway across the country."

"Soon, he'll be far away from us all," Augustus says, lowering his head. "He applied for a position on a North Sea oil rig."

Ash swallows hard. Her thoughts, her eyes, drift to Nathaniel. Strange emotions slice through her chest. Emotions like concern and worry and panic.

It sounds dangerous, but he's a doctor. He'd take care of

himself, right? Put others first, that's their creed. It makes sense that Nathaniel Whitford would risk sinking to the bottom of the ocean for a career change. He's an idiot.

"Maybe those are his dreams," Ash muses, tearing her focus away from Nathaniel.

"Perhaps." Augustus offers her a small smile. "What about you? What are your dreams?"

Ash blinks. "This isn't about me."

"Yes, but I want to know about you," he says, laying a hand on her wrist.

Silence ripples as Ash considers it. Why the hell not? She needs a voice of reason. Why not Augustus?

"I did a bad thing," Ash admits. She peers toward the lip of the beach. Nathaniel rising out of the ocean like a great scowling Poseidon, biceps tight as he carries his surfboard to land. "To your grandson."

Augustus follows her line of sight. "Maybe. Maybe not. Either way, maybe he needs to hear you say that." His tone is mild, but there's a fair hint of scolding in it. Or maybe it's smugness.

Ash scoffs, narrows her eyes. "Using my words against me is unfair." Then she sighs.

"I thought the wrong thing. I did the wrong thing. I fucked up."

"Like I tell my operations team, my managers, my marketers, when the so-called shit hits the fan," Augustus says, his tone calm with reflection, "I don't care about your mistake. I don't care about what went wrong. All I care about is that you fix it."

Ash's eyes land on the beach again. *Fix it.*

There has to be a way.

---

Ash trudges down the beach, sand in her boots. Research. Due diligence. It's what she should have done three fucking years ago.

Delaney's on the beach, snapping selfies in poses that look more like scenes from a torture museum.

"DeeDee, hi," Ash says as she approaches. Before she can work up the nerve to say more, her shin is violently smacked.

"Fuck," she mutters as a frisbee falls to the sand in front of her. The sharp sting of plastic burns.

Eyes narrowed, she scoops it up and flings it back in the direction of Chucky. Hopeful of a direct hit to the face. Little menace.

Delaney snaps a bubble. In her visor, dark glasses and floral beach cover-up, she looks like a sexified version of a poker player. "Oh goody, you are nasty." She contorts her arm. Another selfie snap. Then a fast scroll through her phone. "Ugh, my IMDb page is so lackluster."

Ash sits on the edge of Delaney's beach towel. Scoops up sand in her hand and lets it fall. "So, uh, I hear you're an actress."

Delaney's face lights up.

"And, uh, I was wondering." Ash screws her face up, pretending to think hard. "I thought I saw a movie with you where you had blue hair and this, like, sequined bikini…"

Delaney perks up. "Oh yeah. That was *Neon View*. I was a stripper called Belle Beaver who was fighting for custody of her kids." Forgetting about selfies, she tosses her phone onto the towel. Sits beside Ash. "I also had a torrid affair with the director, but don't tell anyone."

Ash can't help but smile, despite her internal turmoil. She's beginning to understand Delaney. The woman is a master at dramatic words, exaggeration, and affairs.

"Can I show you something?" Ash asks, holding up her phone. "But it's like the CIA. You can't ask questions, or I kill you."

Delaney breaks out in a wicked smile. "I'll bite."

On her phone, Ash scrolls back to her downloaded images. Pulls up the photo she used to bring Nathaniel Whitford down.

Drawing back, Delaney wrinkles her nose. "*Ew*. This photo."

True to her word, DeeDee doesn't ask where she got it. She's more concerned with—

"Why does it look like I'm grinding my brother's crotch?"

Ash laughs. "I had similar thoughts."

Delaney taps the screen. "I remember this day. This was on set. We filmed at Go Go Girls."

She knows the place. Ash drives by the legendary LA strip club at least once a month on her way to the cemetery.

Delaney frowns, her brows bunched. "Nathaniel was in town. He had just gotten leave from the rig." A happy smile tugs at her lips. "He always tries to see me when he can. He brought me lunch from Tender Greens."

Ash's stomach sinks farther. Fucking fantastic. Every single tidbit of information she's receiving about how great Nathaniel Whitford is ups the guilt factor. Already, she's annoyed.

Delaney makes a face. "God, this photo is *yikes*." She and Ash both squint, tilt their heads. A misplaced angle that looks so much like a lap dance. A stolen kiss. "Those booths are like trying to cram into a sardine can."

"Fuck," Ash bemoans. She collapses beside Delaney. Guilt's a hurricane-level spiral. "I fucked up his wedding."

Still looking at Ash's phone, Delaney moans even more pitifully. "I fucked the director, and he never cast me again." She tilts her head. Brightens. "I still have those shoes, though."

They share a laugh.

Nathaniel passes by in her periphery. She avoids eye contact, refuses to let her head swivel in the direction of his chiseled body. To let him see the guilt in her eyes. The utter fuck-up that she is.

*Messy*. She's always been messy.

Slowly, Ash studies Delaney, looks at her phone. "How come you don't hate me like everyone else?"

DeeDee drops her voice. Leans in to stage-whisper. "You have good vibes." Her blue eyes narrow. "The person who took this didn't."

Clandestine conversations beneath palm trees. It's what Ash is good at.

Phone to her ear, she waits. It rings and rings, and then the call goes to voicemail.

"Hi," she says, the single word shaky. Her heart thunders in her chest. "It's Ash Keller. I'm sure you remember me. I mean, how could you not, seeing as how I saved your life and all." Fuck. When she's anxious, she rambles. Calming herself, she inhales a breath. "I need to ask you something. Call me back." She pulls the device away and taps End.

"Truth/lie," a deep voice says in her ear. "You can't stand it when people pay with exact change."

"Jesus!" Jumping, she turns and scowls.

Nathaniel, golden and bronzed from the sun, stands not two feet away, one eyebrow cocked.

"You'd think being so very tall and assholeish, you'd lurch rather than quietly sneak up on your victims." Ash tosses her hair. "And truth. You got me. I mean, the time it takes to count it all out? Sadistic."

He smirks.

She glowers. Hating herself. Hating how her sneaky eyes run over Nathaniel. The expensive diving watch on his wrist, the wet suit half pulled down that long frame of his. The wheat-colored hair darkened by the water. So what if she could lap water out of the grooves of his abs? Eyes above his neck, please.

In return, Nathaniel's heated gaze dips to her two-piece, bringing a scorching heat with it, before moving to her face.

So they're attracted to each other. Big deal.

"You missed dinner last night." His voice is thin, flat.

She tilts her chin. "I wasn't aware that I had to spend every waking second with the Whitford clan."

"My grandfather's paying you. It's the least you could do. Spend time with…with everyone. Make an effort."

She rolls her eyes. "Is that on your family crest? 'Make an effort'? It's so extortionist of you."

Before he can reply, she turns and trudges across the sand. She needs air. An escape from her guilt. From Nathaniel Whitford.

Naturally, the man follows. Even at a slow lope, he keeps pace with her. "How does all that sand feel in those boots?" She can hear the laughter in his voice.

To spite him, she continues struggling across the beach, huffing in her big black boots. "Phenomenal."

Only she doesn't get far.

A groove in the sand causes her ankle to roll.

Nathaniel's quick, grabbing her by her elbow. "You know," he says, steadying her. "The smart thing to do would be to leave the boots off."

She scoffs. "They are my power suit."

At the sound of a shriek, they both turn. The little redheaded kid from the hotel is barreling toward them at breakneck speed.

This time Ash is ready for it. She snatches the frisbee in midair.

The little boy stops in front of her, grunting and making grabby hands for his weapon of mass destruction.

"Kid. I'm gonna be real. I am at my fucking limit." Ash squats down. Bares her teeth. "You hit me again with this frisbee, and I will personally eject you from this world, understand me?" With that, she flings the frisbee into the sea.

The little boy blinks at her, then turns, screeching to run toward the ocean.

"What if he can't swim?" Amusement tinges Nathaniel's voice.

"He'll learn. Or not." Tucking a lock of black hair behind her ear, she looks up. "Now tell me a truth." She gives him a once-over. Her lips curl, feline. "Where do your balls go when you're in a scuba suit?"

Nathaniel chokes, then laughs. "Jesus, Ash."

"Ash, huh?" She props her hands on her hips. "Whatever happened to Bigfoot?"

"You'll always be Bigfoot to me," he says.

Ash finds herself smiling. Finds herself heating in places that haven't been lit in a very long time.

She doesn't have to hate him anymore. What a disappointment.

Even more disappointing? The realization that she's attracted to him. The sheer sight of his handsome face has her mind, has her heart, drifting.

She can smell the sea on his skin. See the glimmer of sunlight reflected in his blue eyes. That sharp jaw is dusted with an inappropriate amount of scruff, like he hasn't bothered to shave since he got here.

She lets out a trembling breath. Purging lust. Guilt.

"Listen, Nathaniel—"

She opens her mouth to apologize, to confess, but it's all swept away when she notices Nathaniel's attention is focused elsewhere.

It's set on something across the sand, away from her. Lasered on the spike-sandal-wearing woman from the pool yesterday. Blond. Tan. Mother to Chucky.

An all too familiar pang hits her heart. It makes sense. That's the type of girl Nathaniel needs to be on vacation with. Pearls. Perfection. Mess free.

Because he is a perfect specimen of a man, while Ash is a weird globule to be stepped in on the sidewalk.

"No ring. Go talk to her," Ash goads.

He lets out a dry laugh. Looks her way. "And become stepfather to Chucky? No thanks."

Ash gives a cavalier shrug, ignoring the fire that burns in the pit of her stomach. "She looks like your type."

Nathaniel's face holds only a strange reflectiveness. His eyes are locked on her face. "I wouldn't be so sure about that."

She blinks up at him, the thorns around her heart briefly vanishing at his words.

"C'mon." He watches their van pull into its designated pickup spot. A lopsided smile tugs at his lips. "You don't want to miss the bus, Bigfoot."

And then he's gone, headed toward the showers, leaving Ash with a soft smile on her face and an uneven beat in her heart.

## Chapter Fourteen

His room's quiet. Too quiet.

He and his family checked into their hotel on the Big Island earlier this afternoon. Royal Grace Resort is one of his grandfather's triumphs. Floral, lush, and jewel toned. Tropical chic meets modern city.

After a day at the beach and then a winery tour, they're all ready to call it an early night.

At ten o'clock, Nathaniel's out on his balcony. Like the last hotel, he's got a spectacular view of the ocean. Salty sea air. Above, the stars sparkle extra-bright against the inky sky. A lush tree canopy frames the sky. A slice of a silver moon. Despite the million-dollar view, annoyance beats through him. He doesn't share this balcony with Ash and his grandfather. They're on the floor below him.

It shouldn't matter.

But he's used to her sounds. Soft muttered curses. Banging. Talking to herself.

It's sociopathic of him to be so attuned to her. But she's a body on this trip. And an interesting one at that. Making that little kid cry today...

Nathaniel chuckles and stares into the dark.

*She looks like your type.*

Why the hell did he reply the way he did? The idea that Ash thinks he only wants blondes in high heels annoys him. That couldn't be further from the truth.

In fact, he can't help but be drawn to Ash.

She's excessively goofy and earnest and maybe a little off-putting with her positive attitude and mean sense of humor.

She's a mix tape blasted to the max, and even then, he wants to crank the dial until it snaps.

The woman is entirely too beautiful. The husky sound of her voice. Those blood-red lips. Her feral black hair. That impossible-to-ignore yellow bikini that breaks every synapse in his brain.

He's hated her since the moment she objected to his wedding. Now, she's the only one he wants to talk to on this trip.

He's teetering on the verge of an emotion, a discovery, he can't describe. It's dangerous. Not to mention confusing as fuck.

After Camellia, Nathaniel doesn't do confusing. As an emergency physician, he was an expert in triage. Only he was constantly triaging and re-triaging their relationship. What he *thought* it was is not what it was. There were times that he felt like he was a window dressing. Along for a ride. Camellia's ride. He won't be miserable like his parents. He can't make that mistake again.

A frantic, hammering knock—*rap, rap, rap*—jerks Nathaniel out of his feverish state.

"Nathaniel? Are you in there?"

*Ash.*

Flames rising in his chest, he crosses the room in less than a second. He lunges for the knob. Throws open the door.

Ash stands on the threshold, hugging herself. In the bright light of the hallway, her eyes are a kind of earthen moss. She's in a robe that's too big for her. Tied carelessly around the waist, one shoulder slipping low. Long bare legs. Her hair a wild, careless tangle.

"Nathaniel," she gasps, her voice low, gravelly.

"What's wrong?" he says, alarmed.

"It's Augustus. He has a fever."

Cold sears his stomach.

"I think he's sick. I didn't have your number. I didn't know what to do, so I—"

His hands land on her shoulders, cutting off her wild ramble. "Slow down."

She sucks in a breath. "Can you—can you get your fancy doctor bag and come help?"

The corner of Nathaniel's lips tug. "You assume I have one?"

She props her hands on her hips and stares at him. Waits.

"Fine," he grumps, crossing the room to pull out the small satchel he brings with him in case of emergencies.

She brightens, a smile of vindication on her face. "I fucking knew it."

"Pain in my ass," he snaps, before softening his voice for her. "Come on, let's go."

Ash gives him a grateful look. Together, they head for the elevator. He tries not to notice, tries not to feel the absolute lock of his body as her small hand slips around his as they rush down the hall.

---

"Well?" Ash makes a sound of distress when Nathaniel exits Augustus's room. She sits on the living room couch, hands tucked between her knees. "Is he okay? Is it the cancer?"

"Not cancer," he says. He sets his bag on the bar. "My grandpops has all the classic symptoms of sunstroke."

"Sunstroke?" A relieved breath puffs out of her. "Oh, thank god." Then her face clouds. "This is my fault. I should have made sure he was—"

"It's not your fault." He doesn't want her to blame herself. "My grandfather's stubborn, and he's also a grown-up. The sun down here gets most people."

She studies him, her eyes swimming with worry, her full bottom lip pulled between her teeth.

"You did the right thing," he says, wanting that worried look off her face. "Coming to get me. He'll be okay. A lot of water, air-conditioning and rest."

"Good," she says, voice trembling. "Because it'll only take me five to seven business days to recover."

She looks toward the open balcony door where a warm breeze blows, but not before he sees a sheen in her eyes. Fuck.

*Go. Walk out the door.*

He doesn't. The expression on her pretty face, so forlorn and lost, keeps him here. His legs won't physically move. He doesn't want her to be upset or sad. And he sure as hell doesn't know what that says about him.

He eyes the bar. "Drink?"

"Running straight to whiskey as your main life hack?" Her eyes sparkle, clearer now. "Yes, please. I approve."

He pours two fingers of amber liquid into a glass. Then another. Curling his hands around them both, he crosses the room. Once he's lowered himself down beside her, he hands her one.

"Thank you," she says, accepting it. She studies Augustus's closed bedroom door. Lets out a long rush of breath. "I'm not ready. I'm really not ready for this."

Surprise has his eyebrows lifting. "Isn't this your job?" There's no malice in it. Only a question. Curiosity.

"Yes." Ash frowns, brows pinched. "But with everyone else, it was quick. Only weeks. But with your grandfather..." She trails off, a small smile tugging at the edges of her lips. Earnest. Honest. There's no con in her smile. She deeply cares for his grandfather. The thought sears something deep inside him.

"I'm going to stay," he says.

That's all it takes for her tense expression to change to relief.

"To monitor him," he elaborates. "If that's okay with you."

She nods. "I would really appreciate it." With that, she takes a long gulp of her whiskey and shivers. "Tastes like fire."

He lifts the glass to his lips. "Feels like it too."

They sit side by side, their hips, outer thighs touching.

"So." Ash's attention is heavy on him. "This rig of yours. Is it dangerous?"

"It can be."

She tilts her chin. "I read about what you do for work."

He lets out a small chuckle. "Stalking me? Fits the pattern."

"It's dangerous."

"I like danger. It's—"

She gasps. A mischievous smile curls her lips. "It's your middle name, isn't it?"

He rolls his eyes. "You looked it up?" Funny, how his heart beats double-time at the thought.

"I did. I now know more about water circulation and storm tides than I ever needed to." Her eyes meet his. She arches a dark brow. "I read up on Byford Dolphin."

A laugh escapes him. "Jesus. You picked the worst of the worst."

"What can I say? I like my morbid facts." Ash sips what's left of her whiskey. Tilts her head, causing her long black hair to curl around her shoulders. "What's it like?"

"Most times, it's boring. We play cards. Bullshit. Do standard check-ups. But then there's work. I thrive on the chaos when it happens."

Ash asks him, her voice quiet, "Have you ever saved anyone out there?"

"Yeah." His lungs squeeze tight, making it hard to breathe. "I have." He should stop talking. But she's looking at him in a way that he likes. In the eye. With interest. It's a trance she puts him in. Her closeness, her warmth. He's not sure how she does it.

He scans her curious expression for a heartbeat, then takes a deep breath and continues. "One time, a crane fell, triggering an explosion on the rig. We were in a rescue craft picking up survivors that had managed to swim out. We did what we could. We triaged there since we couldn't set up on the helideck." He swallows. The memory a haunted whisper in his ear. "But we got too close to the debris. The propeller got caught, and our boat was engulfed. It threw our crew and the survivors into the water. We were picked up from sea an hour later. Two of my crew died."

Beside him, Ash has gone still. Her face pale. "That sounds horrifying, Nathaniel."

He leans back against the couch. "It can be. But I like the chaos of it. The long hours. The distraction. The schedule." He rubs his jaw. "Four weeks on. Four weeks off. After Hawaii, I'm going to Peru to hike the Inca Trail."

Ash cradles her whiskey glass in her palm. "Augustus says you're running away."

He fixes her with a look. "Is that what you did all day? Discuss me?"

A pink flush creeps into her cheeks. "Among other things." She tilts her dark head at Augustus's door. "Your grandfather wants you to be happy."

"I will be. One day." He gives a quick laugh. "But I know he'd like to see it now."

Ash doesn't respond right away. Eventually, though, she clears her throat. "So listen. Can I tell you a truth?"

"Truth away."

"I think you're unhappy because of me. Because of what I did to you." She looks down at her lap, her hair falling like a curtain, obscuring her face. A weary growl pops out of her mouth. "It wasn't nice. And it wasn't right."

Nathaniel's heart suspends itself in his chest. Thumps hard against his ribs.

Looking up, she studies him from beneath her long dark lashes. "I thought I was doing the right thing. Saving marriages before they got wrecked. But only if they needed it. And I thought yours did." Ash balls a fist. Bulldozes ahead. "I believed the wrong thing about you, Nathaniel."

He glances at her. "This almost sounds like an apology."

"It is. I fucked up. I made you pay for—" She catches herself, stops. A sadness, an emptiness, reveals itself in her eyes, an expression he hasn't seen before.

A hot poker jabs him in the jugular. "For what?"

"Nothing." A sharp inhale. "I'm sorry. I am truly sorry for what I did to you."

Nathaniel stares at her like he's never seen her before.

The words land between them like a shock. Tentative. A peace offering.

Eventually, he organizes his thoughts. Finds his voice. "Thanks," he says quietly, turning the whiskey glass around in his hand. "I didn't expect that tonight." But damn if her apology doesn't mean everything.

"I never should have been doing it anyway," Ash admits on a sigh.

"Why were you?"

Her mouth twists to the side. Sharp and savage. "Let's just say young, dumb love."

His jaw clenches. "Tell me. How'd you come to that conclusion? That you were wrong?"

At first, it looks like she'll evade his question. Then she shakes her head. Says, "Before you say anything stern and scolding, I swear I never took on a job without evidence. Proof. I didn't just break up couples willy-nilly." Chewing her bottom lip, she searches his face, mossy irises misty. "There was a photo of you with another woman. It looked bad. But yesterday, when we were at the pool..." She inhales a breath, then bursts out, "It was Delaney in that photo. She was on the set of her movie. Blue hair. Strip club."

A murky memory surfaces, of Delaney hopping over him to sit beside him in the booth right before hoovering the salad he had brought her for lunch. It makes sense. It also explains why Ash reacted the way she did at the pool.

"I didn't know it was your sister," Ash insists. "I thought it was some...some trollop. My whole criteria got thrown off. My radar." Her brow furrows. "I'm usually really good with things like that."

Warmth spreads in his chest. It's stupid, but he's relieved. That she knows the truth. And why? Why does Ash Keller's opinion of him matter? He'll forget all about her after this vacation.

"Will you tell me?" he asks. "Who hired you to object?"

She drops her gaze, taps her whiskey glass with those long black nails. "I can't. I'm sorry. Client confidentiality."

He sits with that. Understands. Despite the thread of disappointment that weaves through him.

Smearing a hand through his hair, he leans back against the couch. Ash does the same.

The truth about Camellia is like a lock box. Only he holds the key. Moments like the one at their rehearsal dinner when he held his breath as Camellia downed a shot of tequila when no one was looking and said, "Let's get this over with."

Everyone thought Ash ruined his life. Including him. But she didn't.

*He* ruined his life.

Agreeing to take over his father's practice when it was the last thing he wanted to do.

Putting that ring on Camellia's finger.

It was all him. And he's been so angry for so long. Blaming it on Ash. But deep down, it wasn't her he was angry at.

The thought has him looking up at the woman in question. Their eyes meet, a quiet sort of calm there.

"You did me a favor," he says.

Ash's sharp intake of breath is audible.

"With Camellia. But I'll never admit that again." He clears his throat. "Does that ease your conscience?"

"Somewhat." She spears him with a grateful look. A timid smile. "If it makes you feel any better…I stopped after that."

"Gee, thanks," he says dryly.

"Again," she says. "I'm sorry."

He sets his glass down. Folds his arms across his chest. "You should go to bed."

She's apologized enough. No more.

"No way. If you're in it, I'm in it." She gives him a half smile, her eyes dark and sleepy.

With a sigh, she curls up on the couch, her body, still swaddled in the robe, brushing against his thigh.

His blood heating, Nathaniel surveys her lean frame. Unlike his body. Rigid, stiff, robotic.

The last thing he needs to do is touch her. It's bad enough he's attracted to her. The bulge in his fucking pants mocks him.

Talk about something else. Anything else.

Attention drawn to her boots, sitting in the corner of the room, sand caked on the soles, he says, "Boots won't last."

"Ugh, you're so right." Her low, husky laugh ripples over his body. "I have to empty a pile of sand from them every time I take them off. I could fill an hourglass."

His gaze darts to her mouth, curved and feline. He forces the hard knot down his throat. "My number," he says abruptly. "You should have it. Just in case."

"Mmm," she hums, handing over her phone. Nathaniel plugs in the numbers, giving himself the name *Tall Asshole*.

When he gives it back, Ash laughs. "What does this mean?" she teases. "We hate each other significantly less now? Only 97 percent of the time?"

Nathaniel rolls his eyes. "Ninety-five," he replies. "My grandfather likes you. And you're good for him. I think there's a chance we can get through this trip without tossing each other into a volcano."

"What if I want to be tossed into a volcano?" she replies, without missing a beat.

He fights the smile tugging at his lips. "That can be arranged."

"Ten more days," Ash murmurs, stretching out on the sofa. She rests her head on the armrest.

Vaguely, ridiculously, Nathaniel wishes it was his shoulder.

"Not friends, not enemies," she says. "Frenemies. A good old-fashioned truce."

"A truce," he agrees, scanning the room for a blanket to cover her with. He finds one draped on a chair across the room, but he doesn't want to move. Can't move. Isn't willing to disrupt this tentative peace between them. Their bodies bridged. Connected. Ash's feet tucked under his legs. Her knees against his thighs. Her tired eyes fluttering shut even as she fights to stay awake.

*Ten more days.*

He can do ten more days.

What a fucking awful liar he is.

## Chapter Fifteen

Bright sunlight. Dry mouth. Whiskey headache. Ash wakes curled up on the couch in a fetal position and covered in a soft blanket. She blinks away the veil of sleep and pushes up on her elbow. Swiping her phone from the armrest, she checks her blood sugar.

She listens. It's quiet. The only noise the crash of the ocean through the balcony door.

Her eyes fall closed at the memory of last night. Nathaniel's large frame beside her smelling of sunlight and sea. In charge and calm. She appreciated him last night. More than he knows.

And then she scowls.

The interaction shouldn't be lingering in her mind. It's silly. Stupid.

Never mind that she apologized, that he came through when she needed him.

Frenemies. That's it. That's what they are.

That's when her bleary gaze lands on a shoebox on top of the coffee table. She sits up and slides it toward herself. On top of it, a piece of hotel stationary pad with the words *Hope you can still stomp in these, Bigfoot.*

She opens the box, pushes aside the tissue paper and gasps. Then laughs.

Inside, she finds a pair of black spiked, studded sandals. Violent and vixenish—just the type she would wear if she liked sandals.

They're too expensive. Fancy hotel boutique wrapping from Rosalea Resort. Which means he must have bought them before they left.

Her face heats.

She should return them, should march back up to his room and say *no, thank you,* because Nathaniel Whitford and nice things do not go together.

She swallows hard. Forces back all emotion. It'd be stupid to return the shoes. She needs them. They're her style, and surprisingly, her size.

She slips them on. Holds her breath.

The sandals scare her and thrill her all at once.

Because she can't think of a time when Jakob was this thoughtful. When he went out of his way to give her something she needed, even when her attitude was the worst. The thought makes her itch, has her biting down hard on her lip.

She doesn't know what to make of the gesture. Doesn't know what to make of her heartbeat.

Not only did Nathaniel take care of Augustus last night, but he bought her shoes. Fucking spiky shitkickers that put a little flutter into her heart. They're stylish…and yet…they're perfectly her.

A door cracks. Augustus, dressed for the day, steps across the threshold of his room. He stops when he sees her, crosses his arms.

"New shoes?" He's smiling.

Ash shoves a hand through her wild cloud of hair and groans. "Don't say it."

Augustus cackles, his eyes twinkling conspiratorially. "Another day."

Ash inhales. "Another day."

---

After a chartered ride, they spend the morning hiking Bird Park Trail. Nathaniel leads the pack, walking ahead with Augustus, keeping his distance. It's just as well. It's best if she avoids the man's nearness and smug glances and salty sea scent. She will hang at the back of the family like the weird little barnacle she is.

After the hike, they head to Hapuna Beach. At a reserved spot, they find lounge chairs, shaded picnic tables and box lunches waiting. The half-mile stretch of white sand is crowded with people. A tiki hut sells shave ice, spam sandwiches and cold drinks.

The Whitford family drifts. Claire to shop, Don back to the hotel to work, Delaney and Tate on their phones.

Ash groans. It's like herding cats. But Augustus wears a content expression as he takes a seat in a lounge chair to work on his memoirs.

Ash helps get him comfortable. Water. Pens at the ready. A big fucking umbrella.

Maybe this is what he wants. To watch. To enjoy. To just be. Sometimes clients prefer that. But it makes Ash ache. If only the Whitfords knew how lucky they were. If only Augustus's family would behave like *family* during this one last trip.

Augustus holds his notepad out and away from him, wearing a thoughtful frown.

"How are you feeling?" Ash asks.

"You know already." He squints at his handwriting.

Ash hovers near him, heart throbbing, biting her lower lip. His doctor mentioned his vision and his focus could change because of his cancer.

She reaches for the pen. "Do you want me to—"

"No," Augustus says. "I may be slow, but steady wins the race." His tone is light but resigned.

Ash chews her lip.

Augustus tips his head back and tuts. "Go on." He lifts a hand to shoo her away. "Go be Ash."

She has to physically make herself move to leave. She can't fix everything. No matter how much she wants to.

At the picnic table, Ash sets her beach bag down. She's just taken a seat when a shrill beeping pierces the air. With a whip-quick hand, she silences her CGM alarm. Damn the downward spiral of her blood sugar. She digs around in the melty cooler, searching for a Coke. Then stops herself when movement near the shave ice stand catches her attention. If she needs sugar, she's going to sugar this right.

In line, Ash waits, thankful she's already lathered on the sunscreen. She shivers as the breeze kicks up. Surveys the ocean. Water's one sport she enjoys. Lounging on beaches in California with Tessie. Paddleboarding or surfing, it's all a source of calm, of home, for her. She'll have a shave ice and let her blood sugar come up to normal, then go for a swim.

"Tell me a truth, Ash," a velvety voice says in her ear.

She smiles, then remembers who it is, and lets it morph into a groan. "Your murder. On the beach with a harpoon."

Nathaniel laughs. A bright sound that has her heart pumping double-time. Sharp and electrifying. His laugh makes her want to drink it down.

Mouth curving upward, he leans in. "Your favorite flavor. Something disgusting, I'm sure."

She bats him away and rolls her shoulders back. "No doubt yours is bitter and paranoid." A shrug. "Guess we'll never know, because you dislike anything fun or delicious."

Shamelessly, her traitorous eyes flick to him. Nathaniel unbuttoning and rolling the cuffs of his linen shirt is the near equivalent of a *Baywatch* beach run. In the sunlight, his hair is a dark caramel. The scruff on his jawline competes with his full lower lip for sexiest feature of the year.

"Didn't hear you stomping back there, Bigfoot." His smile is smug, blue eyes triumphant.

"Sandals are adequate, even if they were too expensive." She stares into the sun, sacrificing her retinas so she doesn't have to make eye contact with Nathaniel. She'll never let on how much she loves them. How they're so perfectly her. How her feet have been cool and comfortable all day.

"Since you seem hellbent on killing yourself, I thought I'd upgrade your footwear." He looks down at her feet. "They suit you."

"I'll still never stop wearing the boots."

Nathaniel grins tightly. His arms cross to fold around his biceps. "I'd expect nothing less. Stubbornness."

Ash yawns, cups her mouth, feigning boredom. Cranes forward to see what's holding up the line. "To what do I owe this displeasure?"

"Hiding out from my siblings." With a long-suffering sigh, he shakes his head. "Delaney wants to read lines. Tate's after me about listening to his podcast."

Ash peers over her shoulder, takes in Delaney and Tater, who are sitting at the picnic table scrolling through their phones.

"Listen, I detest a himbo podcast bro as much as anyone, but maybe it'd be good to give Tater the benefit of a doubt. Maybe he just wants you to listen to him." She shrugs. "Sometimes when people are annoying as fuck, it's because they want attention. Maybe he just wants you to like him. People will do all kinds of things to be liked."

Nathaniel goes completely still. If it's possible, those broad shoulders get even broader. He glances back at his brother, brow furrowed thoughtfully.

"They're younger, right?"

Nathaniel's laugh is humorless. "Yeah. By ten years."

She can picture it. The Whitfords at the family dinner table. Nathaniel home from college, stern, broody, focused. Delaney, whimsical and sweet. Tate, stupid yet endearing. Young kids vying for Nathaniel's attention. Nathaniel so focused on getting the fuck out, he doesn't see.

She's probably overstepping. But it's always been in her to fix. Fix her blood sugar. Fix her heart after Jakob. Fix Tessie after her mother's death. She can fix this too. Sure, she might find herself at the bottom of the ocean after this conversation, but she'll take that chance.

She turns to him. "You're running. You don't give yourself to people. It's understandable. Your father's a nightmare, and the jury's still out on your mom. But maybe your siblings..." She should stop talking, stop rambling, but after last night, it's like she has a window into the hard shell that is Nathaniel Whitford. It fascinates her. "Maybe they deserve you. Maybe they want to know you. Or, if you want to get away from your family so badly, maybe you should cut this vacation short and go on your hike."

With a hard swallow, he blows out a breath. "You talk a lot."

The line inches forward. Barely.

"Your grandfather," she begins. "Do you think he's having fun?"

He crosses his arms, lets out a tired sigh. Her gaze lingers on the bulge of his biceps. "I think he wants *us* to have fun."

"Maybe we should run interference and force everyone to spend time with him." Ash clears her throat. "In the name of the truce."

"The truce." Those two words are staccato, brusque. Like he's already regretting their agreement. But stern tone or not, his gaze meanders over Ash.

Once again, the alarm on her phone screeches. Ash scrambles to silence it, then surreptitiously checks her blood.

"Fuck." Her blood sugar's now sixty-five.

Nathaniel suddenly sobers. His hawklike gaze has caught her reading.

Then a broad palm cups the small of her back. "C'mon," he barks, gently ushering her forward. His expression has turned intent, his moves sharp and quick.

Horrified, mortified, she says, "I can get a Coke, it's really not—"

He's moving again. Leaving her there. Cutting everyone ahead of them. Ash covers her face. In low tones, he speaks to the person at the head of the line, who nods, assesses Ash.

Nathaniel turns over his shoulder, searching for her. He waves her up.

"I'm sorry, I'm sorry," Ash says as she passes the people. "He's a nepo baby. No one ever said no to him when he was a child."

When she reaches him, Nathaniel lifts a brow. "What flavor?"

"Oh, uh, root beer."

A strange expression crosses his face. Shock, surprise, maybe. Then he turns back to the server and places the order.

"Here." He hands the server a wad of cash and takes the shave ice. "For hers and everyone we skipped."

Ash looks at him from beneath lowered lashes. The gesture has her heart pumping in a slow, grateful cadence.

Nathaniel moves close to her. Once again, his broad palm has attached itself to the small of her back. The warmth of it has butterflies swarming in her stomach. Ash wonders what that big, tan hand would feel like drifting over her bare skin.

Oh god. What's wrong with her? She's lust addled. Lightheaded. And not because her blood sugar is low.

"Thank you," he says to several people as they pass down the line. "We appreciate it."

"We?" Ash snorts. "There is no we."

"Eat," he orders as they approach a picnic table. Square jaw locked tight, he hands her the shave ice. "Now."

Sitting, Ash does as she's told. The shave ice is cold and icy and sweet-bitter and probably exactly what Nathaniel Whitford's heart tastes like. Delicious.

From his seat across from her, the man himself watches, wearing an intent expression.

Ash eyes him warily, waiting for more. For a scolding lecture about the perils of low blood sugar. It's been the bane of her existence for so long. For so long, she's been treated as if she's fragile or weak because of her diabetes. When it gets low, people always assume she's irresponsible. The reality? Controlling it is one of the hardest things she's ever had to do.

It's the kind of thing a person can't understand unless they've been there, and Ash wouldn't wish it for anyone else.

"You're here to help my grandfather," Nathaniel says in a low voice. His pale-blue eyes, warmed by the sun, stay fixed on her face. "But that doesn't mean you can't take care of yourself."

For a second, she can't speak. His words have carved her to pieces.

It should be triggering, even the smallest worry over her diabetes. It isn't. Not with him. Nathaniel's offering to help and doing it in the most alpha not-at-all-attractive-way he knows how. Taking charge. Being calm.

"Okay," she says quietly. "I will."

"Good."

It's a fleeting second. The space warming between them.

Ash's bench is rudely rocked as Tater, baseball cap twisted to the side, drops beside her. "Really going hard on that sugar, dawg."

"She has low blood sugar," Nathaniel snaps. With well-practiced big-brother ease, he turns a death glare on Tate. "You don't need a dissertation on how it works."

"It's okay." She's always happy to talk about being a type-one diabetic. "It's not a death sentence," she tells Tater. "We can have sugar. Like everything, it's in moderation."

Tate blinks slowly, nods. "Cool, cool."

Nathaniel's blazing gaze skims her face. The look twists her insides into heart-shaped bruises. He rests his hand on the tabletop. Those long, strong, tan fingers inches from hers. His palm is big as hell. A tap on her ass would probably sound like a microwave being slammed shut.

Fuck. Stop.

Why is she thinking about Nathaniel's hand and her ass in the same brain sentence?

Ash licks faster, but the move only creates an image in her mind of her tongue scraping down the side of Nathaniel's well-scruffed face.

Holy shit. She needs an exorcism. Clearly, she is diabolically horny.

"Ash?"

She swallows, pulled out of her trance by Nathaniel's rough voice. "What?"

He tilts his head to the side, eyes dim with concern. "Better?"

She inhales. "Yes." Her blood feels less on fire.

The bench is rocked again. This time Delaney plops herself down beside Nathaniel. She takes in Ash, the shave ice, sniffs the air, then smirks. "You got his favorite."

Ash blinks. "What?"

"Root beer. It's Nathaniel's favorite flavor of anything."

Surprised and horrified, Ash swivels her head to Nathaniel. He's frozen, jaw tight.

Her mouth tugs into a half smirk. "Looks like we're twinsies."

One large hand smears down his face. "Please don't say that," he mumbles.

She holds the shave ice out in offering. "Lick?"

He groans. "Especially that." He blows out a breath and pushes a hand through his hair. "Fuck," he says, looking frazzled. Then he abruptly stands and walks off.

Delaney evaluates Ash with shrewd eyes. "You annoy him."

Ash laughs. "That's what I like to hear."

"He talks to you, at least." Delaney props her chin in her palm. Picks at the box lunch. A wilted ham sandwich and a bag of chips. "More than us."

Ash smirks. "It's not really talking as much as arguing into oblivion."

A bark of a laugh escapes Tater. "He can't wait to get the hell off this island."

"Can you blame him?" Delaney looks wistful. "Remember when Dad used to allow us to express our personalities?"

Tater guffaws. "Definitely in the embryo stage, dawg."

Ash splits a look between the siblings. It feels like she's at the children's table at Thanksgiving. Which, in truth, is the best place to be. It always has the hottest gossip. Not to mention, less drama and fewer political conversations.

"Ugh," Delaney groans. She throws a dramatic hand to her face. "And now I have one brother with a podcast and another who's determined to kill himself in the North Sea." She swivels her head to Ash. "How gross is that?"

Ash laughs, though her heart pounds in her ears and fingertips at the memory of her conversation with Nathaniel last night. "It's just the ocean."

Delaney's eyes are wide. "No, it's not just the ocean." She reaches for her phone. Pulls up a TikTok video. "They say it's the most treacherous sea in the world. Look at this vortex."

On screen, the sea's in an angry mood. A ship battles against devastating waves until it's eventually engulfed completely. It capsizes and then slowly sinks beneath the waves.

Tate gapes. "Damn, dude."

Ash opens her mouth, but nothing comes out. Worry weighs down her bones, her breath.

She shouldn't care. But she does. It's dangerous, and he's an idiot.

She scans the beach, finds Nathaniel in the crowd of people. God, he's obnoxious. He drives her crazy.

Delaney shudders. "You couldn't pay me enough money." She exits TikTok. Stands and says to Ash, "Swim?"

## Chapter Sixteen

NATHANIEL COMES BACK TO THE PICNIC TABLE JUST as Delaney and Ash head for the beach.

With an aggrieved sigh and a wary look at Ash, he sits. She's at the shore, wearing cut-off shorts and that yellow bikini. Her long black hair hangs, disheveled, down to her waist.

When he's around her, his headspace is frazzled. His breathing uneven. He hasn't been on his game the last four days. He needs orderly. He needs planned. Ash Keller is none of those things.

She's beautiful. So beautiful that she scalds his blood. But even better, she's a morbid beauty with a smart mouth. It turns him on. He loathes himself.

Beside him, Tater bangs a fist on the picnic table, making Nathaniel scowl. "You're not pitching it without me, dawg. I put the podcast together. I need to be there."

Nathaniel side-eyes his brother, the phone pressed tight against his ear. It's rare for him and his siblings to make conversation. Family is dutiful, not familiar, as his father often reminds him. Delaney's daddy issues, Tate's insecurity, all stem from their father's country club rules for raising a family.

"Damn it." Tate stabs his phone screen, tapping End, and runs a hand through his light-blond hair. With a disgruntled expression on his face, he bites into a crusty ham sandwich. Crumbs scatter across his Jimmy Buffett muscle tank.

Ash's words weave their way through his head. *Maybe he just wants you to listen. Maybe he just wants you to like him. People will do all kinds of things to be liked.*

He gets it. It's easy to understand when he thinks of all those nights, when he was a kid, that he waited up for his father. Nights when his father said *five more minutes,* but five more minutes turned to ten, and ten eventually turned into too many years too late.

Christ. He's taking advice from a girl who's chaotic neutral at best?

And yet.

"So, uh." Nathaniel shifts, scratches at his neck. "What's this podcast about?"

Tater's head jerks back so fast Nathaniel can't be sure he doesn't have whiplash.

Jesus Christ.

The surprised look on his brother's face sends a wave of shame through him. Fuck, Nathaniel is a piece of shit.

"So, uh, we plan to touch on a different topic every season. But the first is all about potatoes."

Nathaniel nods. It seems like the right thing to do. "Potatoes, huh?"

Tate's scowl deepens. "We have a meeting set up with a producer. But now RJ wants to move it to tomorrow. Little weasel's trying to hog all the glory, when I'm the one who came up with the idea."

Nathaniel sucks in a hard breath, barely reining in his impatience.

"You think you can shut up about the podcast for the next week and try to enjoy the trip for Grandpops?"

Tater's glower quickly morphs into a smirk. "What do I get out of it?"

A black eye. A black eye is what the kid's going to get out of it.

"He has cancer," Nathaniel snaps. "Make him fucking happy for once in your life. Christ."

"Damn, dude," Tater says, wounded.

They stare at each other, both frowning.

Breathing hard, Nathaniel massages the bridge of his nose. "You hang out with Grandpops; I'll listen to your podcast."

Tate's eyes go wide. "Really, man?"

Nathaniel was serious when he and Ash called a truce. He wants to make this vacation great for his grandfather. He won't fail him. "Really."

"All five episodes?"

Christ. The slow death he's dying inside. Still, Nathaniel hides his flinch. "All five episodes." He jabs a finger at Tate. "No phone at dinner or any time Grandpops is around. And you fucking make conversation with him and mean it."

His brother holds up his hands in an "easy there" gesture.

"Seriously, Tate."

"Dawg, fuck, yes." Tate shoves the rest of the ham sandwich into his mouth and chews. "You got a deal."

With a grin, Tater picks up his phone and types out a text message.

As if Nathaniel's inquired, he says, "I've been trying to wrangle this girl for a while now, and she's at a party out in NoHo."

"Wrangle. What is she, a cow?"

"The way I see it, it's the perfect way to weed out a woman. Interested. Not interested."

"What do you mean?" Nathaniel hates himself for asking, but dammit if he isn't curious.

His brother leans in, grinning. His eyes glitter like he holds all the secrets of the universe. "My theory is, when women get drunk, they want their man. If you're not getting a text or call when she's drunk, you're not the one she wants."

Maybe Tate has a point. Maybe he's an idiot.

Tate scans the beach. "What about Ash?"

Nathaniel gives him a dry look. Tamps down the lightning strike that courses through him at her name. "What about her?"

Now they're both surveying the beach.

Silence falls.

Ash is kicking off her shorts, leaving her in nothing but that painted-on bikini. At the sight of her perky ass, Nathaniel is hit with a strange, primal urge. To make his way over to her and give her a playful slap on one tight cheek.

What does she taste like? In the morning and at night. And what would those pouty red lips feel like against his? Despite his better judgment, he can't help but imagine running his hand over all that smooth creamy flesh and kissing his way down her thighs. Does she steal the sheets, or does she share? She seems like the type to take a long nap after a day on the beach, not because she's lazy, but because she's like a cat and prefers to bask in the sun, and goddamn if he'll interrupt her.

"You think she's looking to…you know?"

Nathaniel snaps himself out of his ridiculous thoughts. "What?" he asks through gritted teeth.

Tate gives him a knowing grin. "You think she'd be interested?"

No. She wouldn't be.

But nonetheless, a pang of irritation rises at the thought of Tate taking Ash out.

Nathaniel scowls at him. "In you?"

"Sorry, dawg. Read the room wrong." Tater lifts his hands, giving him a conciliatory look. "You get first dibs."

Nathaniel opens his mouth to tell him he doesn't want first dibs. He isn't interested in Ash.

Only, nothing comes out.

Until last night, he wasn't sure about her.

Now? His self-control is deteriorating at a rapid pace.

Nathaniel feels dumber for having listened to Tate's entire spiel on women and the ways of the world, but it's the least he can do for his grandfather. And Ash.

*Ash.*

Fuck. Why is he even thinking about her right now?

He empties his head of her and looks toward the ocean. On the water, a sailboat slices with swift delicacy. The sky is bright and blue. A group of surfers carry their boards up to the rocks.

"You want to kayak?" he asks Tate, in desperate need of a distraction. "We could take Grandpops out."

Tate shrugs. "Sure, man. Whatever." His little brother is like a Labrador retriever. Eager to please. Always has been.

For the next two hours, the brothers, along with Augustus, tour the cove. No phones, minimal conversation. But within minutes of being on the water, Nathaniel's mind clears. The beach has always been his source of calm. In LA, he has easy access. Living on the water on the rig is another world entirely. On the *Sophia Marie*, he has to be level-headed and prepared at all times. Aware of what he can and can't control. The sea. The weather. But he can stop blood. Restart a heart. Stay away from his family. Ash. The predictability of life gives him focus. An escape.

Back on shore, they get Augustus into his lounge chair, then make sure he's covered by an umbrella and has water.

Once his grandfather is settled, Nathaniel straightens up. Ridiculously, his first thought is to scan the beach for Ash. He's looking for that Pavlovian flash of yellow when the blast of a whistle cuts through the noise on the beach.

The sharp alarm, the urgency, kicks his adrenaline into overdrive. The masses are on their feet. Many are wading out of the ocean. Now choppy and wild, waves crash onto shore. Ominous clouds are rolling in quickly. A man in flamingo swim trunks helps a pregnant woman to shore.

Nathaniel stops a lifeguard who's hurrying by, scanning the water. "What's going on?"

"Riptide rolled in," the man says, lifting his whistle once more to his mouth. "We have to get everyone out of the water."

Augustus is suddenly beside him, his face etched with concern. He grips Nathaniel's shoulder. "Where's Delaney? Ash?"

*Ash.*

Swallowing the burn in his throat, the panic, he scans the beach. Where is she? Even wading in knee-deep water can be a death sentence with a riptide.

Frantically searching the shore, he sees her sandals.

Alarm speeds through Nathaniel's senses. Those overpriced spikes of doom sit on the sand just waiting for someone to step on. Without Ash.

The blood drains from his face.

"Stay here," he tells his grandfather. Then he's running, racing down to shore. Elbowing his way through the rushing crowd, his heartbeat jackhammers in his ears. He plows into a person scurrying past. Without bothering to apologize, he moves the woman roughly aside.

Where is she?

Helplessness twists at his gut. Frantically, Nathaniel whips his head left and right. Trying to pick out a teeny, tiny yellow bikini has never been more frustrating.

And then his heart stops. Sound ceases to exist.

Christ. What if she's in the ocean? Of course she's in the ocean. Because it's Ash. Carefree and careless. And always primed to give him a heart attack.

He vaults over a towel, a beach bag. Finally, he finds himself at the edge of the shore. He's hurling himself forward, ready to go in, when a hand wraps around his bicep and he's yanked to a stop.

"Are you an idiot? What are you doing?"

Chest heaving, he whips around. Every muscle in his body is strung tight.

Ash is there, wide-eyed, staring up at him. Water sluices down her frame, her long black hair hanging over one shoulder. Tamed for once.

"I couldn't find you," he rasps.

The instinct she triggers in him is primal. He reaches out, slides his arms around her slender waist to pull her to him. The moment she's in his arms, his tension ebbs.

His heart pounds, on fire, as he takes her in. Soft, dewy skin. A hint of a sunburn on the tops of her shoulders. Her pretty face a mix of amusement and confusion.

"Are you okay?" Fuck. Somehow his hand has attached itself to her cheek. Cupping it like it'll help him feel better. "You're not hurt?"

The look she gives him is incredulous. A rosy flush spreads across her cheeks. Her eyes darken, long lashes fluttering. "I was in the bathroom, you Tall Asshole." Despite her words, her tone is soft.

She's still in his arms. He pulls her closer. Reassurance she's okay. Reassurance he didn't know he needed.

The exhale he lets out shakes them both. "Thank—"

Nathaniel's words are cut off as he's shoved roughly back and away from Ash.

"Thanks a lot, Lancelot. I could have been dying, and you just bulldozed me out of the way." Delaney's eyes flash fire, her hands propped dramatically on her hips. "You don't even think to look for your little sister when there's practically a tsunami on the beach? What were you doing?"

His mouth works. No words come out. That calm, decisive cool he's perfected in the ER is gone. He's too muddled to respond, a volatile, overreacting mess.

Ash smothers a smile and wiggles her fingers. Slipping her feet into her sandals, she takes one more careful glance over her shoulder at him. Then she runs up the beach to Augustus's outstretched arms.

As the sound of the ocean crashing against the beach rushes back to his ears, bone-deep awareness hits him like a brick.

Ash.

She's the first one he looked for.

# Chapter Seventeen

**IT'S STUPID NOT TO USE YOUR NUMBER NOW.**

Ash tries not to smile at the text from the *Tall Asshole*. Instead, she focuses on the chessboard in front of her. She and Augustus have been engaged in an unending battle for a little over an hour. She makes her move—defending the d5 pawn with another pawn—and then discreetly taps out a quick reply.

**Who is this? Satan?**

**Funny.**

When Augustus peers her way, his brow lifted in curiosity, she waves her phone. "Your grandson."

"Ah." He goes back to studying the board.

Ash smirks at the bubbles appearing, disappearing, then—

**Can you meet for a drink on the beach?**

Ash bites her lip and stares at the text. It's probably a bad idea. After the way Nathaniel reacted to her on the beach today, her thoughts have been mushy oatmeal. Why did it turn her on? The emotion on his face—she misread it, right? She had to have. Today, on the beach, there was a tremor in his voice meant for her.

Augustus chuckles, pulling her back to the moment.

Shit. She looks at the board, sticks a hand out, takes in her impending doom. "Don't—"

"Checkmate."

Ash puffs a lock of hair out of her face. Scowls. "Damn it."

"There. Now you have to go," Augustus instructs.

After waving off her efforts to help, he pushes to standing and hobbles slightly before righting himself. Ash watches him closely.

Today was a long day for him. Without a doubt, he'll be moving slowly tomorrow.

He chuckles all the way to his room. "Enjoy, my dear."

The bedroom door shuts with a soft click.

Ash rereads the text. A drink? Why? To engage in a battle of wills? Or to continue their tentative truce?

Either way, she can't let him win, nor can she be the one to break their temporary peace.

She absolutely has to go.

In her room, Ash rifles through her suitcase. She can't go to one of Augustus's fancy hotel bars in sweats and mismatched socks.

As she searches, she can't help but think about Nathaniel's heated eyes on her earlier today. Tracing her breasts, the shape of her thighs, her hips. And then—awareness. Worry. The way his big hand palmed her cheek and stayed there.

She wants to see that look on his face again.

Soft. Suddenly, she wants to be soft.

She slips on a semi-sheer black tank bodysuit with a low neckline that reveals an adequate amount of cleavage. Then she adds a leopard print sarong with a sky-high slit that exposes her tattooed thighs. Her hair's wild from the salt and sea, so she leaves it be. All she needs now is a slick of mascara, a flick of a cat eye, and dark cherry gloss.

When she's finished, she assesses her reflection. Too much? Not enough? She'll let Nathaniel judge.

Her brain is muddy. Confused. Why is she even doing this? Playing this game? Regardless, it's the only game she wants to play. The way his eyes grazed over her. Witnessing it. Teasing emotion out of a seemingly emotionless Nathaniel Whitford.

Rile, react, repeat.

She likes it too much to stop.

Ash shakes her head, clearing it, and checks her blood sugar. Then she slips into her sandals and heads out.

She walks the few minutes to the bar on the beach. A swanky

tiki-haven with a righteous view of the Pacific crashing on the cliffs. Sunburned tourists take up most of the chairs, but there's one vacant. One meant for her. Right beside Nathaniel.

Seated at the bar, studying his phone with laser-like interest, Nathaniel looks handsome and confident. Dressed down in linen pants and a white button-up. Cuffs shoved up to his elbows. The high arches of his cheekbones are so unfair she wants to puke.

Watching from the shadows, Ash smothers a smile. He picks up his phone. Puts it back down. Drums a little beat on the bar, then does it all over.

Nathaniel Whitford antsy. Never thought she'd see the day.

There's a pulse between her legs as she slides onto the barstool. His masculine scent surrounds her instantly. Salt. Sea. Sun.

"Margarita? Cheeseburger?" At the sound of her voice, he straightens. Turns. She leans in conspiratorially, gesturing at his order. "Could you be any more cliché?"

His eyes snap to her face. That strong muscle in his jaw pulses. He sets his phone down before she can see what he's looking at. "Keep laughing, and I won't share my fries."

It's impossible not to notice the way his gaze dips, lingers on her colorful thigh, the gentle slope of her breasts, her lips.

"Fry hoarding is a victimless crime," she drawls as she snags one. She pops it into her mouth.

He zeroes in on her lips as she chews, a half-smile turning up the corner of his mouth, then lifts his hand to signal the bartender. "What can I get you?"

"Tequila. In a fancy as fuck glass."

"You heard her," he tells the bartender. "Tequila in a fancy as fuck glass."

Ash laughs aloud, and in response, Nathaniel's smile grows wider.

"Is it weird?" she asks. "That your grandfather owns these hotels? Like do you have to fight the billionaire urge to scream your wealth and privilege at the sky?"

He makes a noise that could pass for a chuckle. "You have an obsession with billionaires."

"Maybe I do." She arches a brow. "Or maybe it's just you I'm obsessed with."

He cocks his head, squints, and her heart stutters.

Feeling like she's said too much, gotten too close, Ash breaks eye contact. "Augustus's hotels are all so beautiful." She exhales as she scans the bar. The darkness of the ocean and the sky blur as one. "It truly is paradise."

"That was his goal," Nathaniel murmurs. "Make every hotel feel like it's your home." He nudges the tequila the bartender set on the bar top closer to Ash. Golden liquid in a champagne flute. "Wait until you see the hotel in Maui. That's one for the books."

Maui. It's like a brief blip in the center of her brain. That whisper of *Jakob*. And then it's gone.

Ash sips her tequila. A shot of fire to her belly. "You ever think about taking it over? His hotel business?"

"No. I prefer putting people back together over picking out carpet samples." He takes a drink of his beer. "I talked to my brother today," he says simply.

She looks him over, surprised at his uncharacteristic openness.

"I told him I'd listen to his idiotic podcast if he shut up and hung out with our grandfather."

She hums. "I think…that's a very selfless act."

"I'll take what I can get." The words are clipped, gruff.

Fuck. They're having an actual conversation. Sitting without sniping. Their easy closeness sends a ripple of fear down her spine, has her shifting uncomfortably in her seat. Nathaniel has the ability to draw her secrets or worries out of her with an ease she's never experienced. It's like breathing. Natural.

Ash takes a long sip of her tequila. "Tell me a truth." She tilts her head. "Do you still think I'm a con-artist ghoul?"

"No. Not anymore." There's a ragged edge to his voice.

Ash flushes at the sound. It's the tequila. Has to be. The heat of it spreads through her like a sun, warming her insides, her heart.

"My turn." Nathaniel twists on his stool to look at her. "What are you afraid of?"

She ponders it. Takes another sip. "I'm afraid of nachos."

He barks a laugh, looks surprised at the sound, schools his expression.

She continues. "They're pointy and comprised of an amalgamation of sauces and shapes and textures that can't be discerned."

Nathaniel stares at her. Blinks.

She draws back, narrowing her eyes. "What?" she asks. "You're looking at me like I'm—"

"The most fascinating person I know?"

It catches her off guard. Jettisons her defenses. Steals her breath. When was the last time she heard something so beautiful? Has she ever? "Really?"

"Really."

She places her chin in her palm. Considers him. "I make sense to you now?"

"Yeah." He dips his chin. "You do."

Her eyes shut. When she opens them seconds later, the smile's still on her face.

"That makes you happy," Nathaniel says, continuing to stare at her. "Why?"

Why? Because she's always been too much to so many people. Or not enough.

She's horrified when tears spring to her eyes.

Quickly, blinking fast, she looks away. Oh god. Oh fucking shit. She's never affected like this. It must be the tequila. This is why Tessie always warns her away from the stuff. One sip, and she loses her marbles.

"Ash?" Nathaniel's tone is inquisitive, etched with concern.

Two late-night stragglers stroll in, the movement and noise

garnering their attention. A man wearing a frilly white shirt and a bandanna, and a woman with biceps bigger than bowling balls.

"Looks like the party has found us," she murmurs, relieved at the interruption.

"That's how Paul Walker died," the man says. "The government took control of his car and killed him."

"Joel, you're embarrassing me," the woman huffs. "No more conspiracy theories."

The man, Joel, scoffs. "Oh, twenty years of marriage, and you suddenly think you're too good for me?"

"Holy shit," Ash gasp-whispers. She grabs Nathaniel's bicep. "Are we witnessing a marriage mid-breakup?"

"What are we working with here?" Nathaniel angles closer, voice laced with humor. He grins, causing the corners of his eyes to crinkle.

Ash dips her head. Wills the image to be deleted from her mind. Hotness overload. "We got a guy who looks like a pirate and a woman who looks like she could take him down with her bare hands."

Ash sinks lower. Squints at the couple.

"Oh, she will," she predicts. "End of the night, he's going into the Pacific. And she will claim that insurance money and run off to Bora Bora."

The man, trying to spin the annoyed woman around on the not-a-dance-floor, backs into Ash's chair, rocking her forward.

She steadies her tequila.

Amused, she turns to Nathaniel. "Do you ever think about how drunk people lack the core strength to sit on barstools?"

"You want to take a walk?" Nathaniel asks, putting a hand on the back of her chair. Annoyance furrows his brow. He glares at the blundering man as if he has a personal vendetta. "On the beach?"

At her nod of assent, he helps her off the stool. One palm pressed gently against her shoulder, he guides her out of the bar.

Seconds later, they're on the white sand. Balmy air and the scent of plumeria surround them.

"Wow," Ash breathes, lifting her champagne glass in a toast. She drags her attention from Nathaniel and takes in the ocean. "Drinks on the literal water. Hard to beat."

He appraises her. "Tell me."

"Tell you what?"

"How you would beat this."

Her heart stumbles a little at his deep tone. She really should have left the tequila at the bar. "That sounds like a challenge."

"Maybe it is."

She thinks on it. A little shock of glee fills her. "I don't think you can. Tequila. The stars. The dark. The Very Tall Asshole next to me. They're all bad ideas."

"You," he says, the single word making her breath hitch. In the moonlight, the angles of his face look like they've been chiseled from stone. He's so good-looking, it's debilitating.

"I'm a bad idea?"

He takes a long sip of his beer, drags a hand through his hair. "You aggravate me." His gaze drops to her lips.

Her heart takes off, hammering at a furious pace.

Flirting. They're flirting with something. Most likely disaster. Either way, Ash should go. Take her tequila and run.

Instead, she lets out a breath. "Is that good or bad?"

"Good." His voice thickens. He moves in closer. "I think."

The ocean crashes against the shore. A breeze kicks up, ruffling her hair, obscuring her vision.

Nathaniel reaches out. One big hand caresses her cheek, sweeps her hair behind her shoulder, taming it. Instead of pulling away, he inches closer. Long fingers hold her jaw. Eyes turning heavy-lidded.

Ash waits, hesitant, anticipatory. Her body sizzles.

It's the throttling he's been waiting for.

Her lips part. All the air escapes her lungs. She tips her head back, eyes him. "Nathaniel. If you're going to ki—"

His mouth lands on hers. Every one of her protests smothered. There isn't an ounce of hesitancy in his kiss. It's only warm and hungry and addictive. He grips the edge of her sarong with his free hand, using it as leverage to pull her closer.

Her champagne flute thuds to the sand.

She has better things to do with her hands.

She clings to those broad shoulders. Arches into his touch, deepening the kiss. Offering more of herself as Nathaniel unleashes a deep, tortured sound from the back of his throat. It's hot as hell, sending shivers through Ash. He feels *so* good.

Too good.

Next thing she knows, he parts the slit of her sarong, his hand roaming. A big palm squeezes her thigh. This time it's her turn to make some sort of wicked, desperate sound. Because his lips taste like lime. His sea-salt scent makes her head spin.

"Kill," she gasps into his mouth when she pulls back. "Not kiss. I was going to say kill."

"Not yet," he rasps against her lips. "I'm not done with you."

Ash laughs darkly. And then Nathaniel's mouth is back on hers.

She opens her eyes while she's kissing him. Her heart pounds. God, he's so fucking beautiful. He looks so hungry. And she's feeding him. The thought causes her to whimper.

She closes her eyes, digs her nails in and intensifies the kiss. Might as well. She's had just the right amount of tequila.

He growls in response. Slides a hand up to cup the curve of her throat. Sweeps his thumb over the back of her neck. Slow and teasing. "God's sake, Ash," he groans, but his tone isn't exasperated. He sounds…turned on. Ravenous.

Heart rate spiking, she clutches the thin fabric of his shirt. Yet instead of shoving him into the ocean the way she's imagined, she glues him to her. She feels delicate against this ridiculously massive body of his.

"Ugh," she mumbles, even as she holds him close. "We can't do this."

"Why not?"

"Because we hate each other."

"Liar," he murmurs, smug. With his thumbs, he grazes her collarbone—a primal motion that curls her toes. His jawline is dangerous, and so is his kiss. So sweet. If she lets him get too close, there's no telling what she'll let him do to her.

Heated gaze raking over her face, he pulls back a fraction. "It's a lie."

She blinks at him. Unsteady and confused and overheated. Doesn't he hate her? Doesn't he still hold a grudge?

As if in answer, his mouth lands on hers again.

Ash stiffens. Expecting apocalypse, the entire collapse of society the minute his arms lock around her waist.

But there's only bliss.

Sweet, beautiful bliss.

A little murmur of joy pops off her lips. Wordlessly, she nods. Gives in.

Kissing. They're only kissing.

A good idea. She hasn't had a blistering make-out session since…well, since she hooked up with her roommate at that German hostel.

Wait. No.

A bad idea.

What is she doing?

She's kissing Augustus's grandson. Making a mess of things like she always does.

Whatever exists between them, this isn't what she meant when she suggested a truce.

Abort mission. Abort kiss. Abort everything about tonight.

"Nathaniel," she murmurs.

As she tries to pull away, he tugs her back into his arms. He's hot, hard. The length of him presses against her like a brand. Only, instead of lunging for his lips for the third time like a feral kiss-starved hell beast, she stops him with a hand to his shoulder.

"No." Her lips pulse from his kisses. "It's the truth. We hate each other."

They assess each other, both breathing hard now.

Nathaniel bites his swollen lip. Reaches out to run a hand down her shoulder. "I don't hate you."

The hangdog look on his face will haunt her for the rest of her life. At this rate, she'll never get him out of her horny nightmares.

Torn, Ash tucks a lock of hair behind her ear.

Sure, they could continue this enemies-with-benefits thing for the rest of the trip. A distraction—or better, a reward for suffering through their time with the Whitford family—but then what? It ends. That's where it goes. Nowhere.

Easy enough, right?

Except she doesn't deserve Nathaniel. Not even a quick, casual hookup. Not when she did what she did to him. Guilt burrows a hole inside her. Devours her like flesh-eating bacteria. She hurt him and she could hurt him again. She can't do that to him.

And she can't make any more mess of her life than she already has.

Besides, she and Nathaniel, they don't compute.

He is Vlad the Impaler, and she's Elizabeth Bathory. They do not exist in the same century.

Hands on her shoulders, Nathaniel steps into her. Frowns more deeply. "Tell me why."

"Because of Augustus."

Every ounce of emotion drops off his face. Like a whiteboard being erased. "Right," he says, suddenly rigid. His hands fall away from her body. The loss of him stings.

Shaking her head, she twists away from him. The burn in her heart intensifies. "I mean your grandfather is paying me to be here.

I shouldn't fraternize with…" Heat fills her face, that pulsing spot between her legs, but she forces herself to look at him. "I'm here for Augustus. No one else."

A muscle in his jaw snaps tight. He runs a hand over his mouth, stifling a groan.

She bites her lip. Glances down. "I apologize for your raging boner."

He exhales, chuckles. "You have no idea."

Ash backs away. "I—I should go."

"Yeah." The heat in his eyes is still there. It scares her.

He doesn't try to fight her on it. It's relief. It's disappointment. It's both.

Nathaniel gives her a head start. Then she's walking, stumbling, running across the sand like she's trying to leave Past-Ash behind. A mistake. She's made a very bad mistake. And she doesn't know if that mistake is the kiss or the not-continuing of the kiss.

All he is is a heart interruption. Ash thumps her chest. Time to get back to her regularly scheduled beat.

Even if a little voice in her head tells her that it's impossible.

# Chapter Eighteen

If only he still wanted to push Ash into a volcano.

Or a crevasse. Or a crack.

It would be so much easier.

Time of day. It's what he's not getting from her right now. It's only been twelve hours since the kiss, and during every activity they've participated in, Ash has treated him like a pariah.

Skipping breakfast, sitting at the far back of the van. Even now, on the quarter-mile hike to the waterfall, she lags behind, walking with Augustus. She's like a ping-pong ball bouncing farther and farther away from him the closer he gets.

Amazingly, befuddlingly, she's gone from the woman he wanted to scrape from his memory to the woman he can't stop thinking about.

Her distance puts him on edge.

It's unfair how much he misses her presence. He didn't realize how bored he'd be on this trip without her.

And after last night, he's had a deeper glimpse—a literal taste—of Ash Keller, and he likes it.

Too much.

The trail to the waterfall is steep and rocky but not nearly as treacherous as Oahu. His brother and sister bicker in low tones behind him, trying to hike while searching for cell service.

He glances over his shoulder.

Augustus and Ash follow the pack. She's in her boots. Untied, of course. The strap of her yellow bikini pokes out of her tank top. Shimmering sunlight catches the tattoos on her legs, flashes of color in the dense, balmy jungle. Even from a distance, the splash and crash of the waterfall can be heard somewhere up ahead.

Jesus. That bikini, that thigh tattoo haunt him. In the best possible way.

"I don't like that girl," his mother says, marching beside him.

Nathaniel's gut pulls tight. "She's here," he says with a shrug. "She's doing more than most of us for Grandpops."

"I just…" His mother regards him, eyes sad. She places a hand on his forearm. "After what she did to you."

Of course his mother wouldn't see how bad he and Camellia were for each other. Not after being married to his father and putting up with his bullshit for so long. Even now, his father's not here. His mother would never say she's upset with his father for bailing for the third time on this trip, but Nathaniel sees it in her eyes, her posture.

Behind them, there's a bright burst of laughter from Ash. The husky sound of her voice sends a jolt of electricity to his cock.

Christ. Suddenly, he's hit with a desperate need for her to look at him. For her to pay him any attention at all.

Truth is, it's getting harder to pretend that he has it out for Ash Keller.

Unable to stand it any longer, Nathaniel falls behind his mother to join Ash and Augustus.

"I hear you're in need of some better company," he says, linking arms with his grandfather.

Augustus chuckles.

Ash rolls her eyes. "Your grandson is truly a terror," she snipes, holding on tight to Augustus's other arm.

Nathaniel arches a brow. "Says the girl who scares little children."

Briefly, her gaze flicks to his.

There it is. That glimmer of a smile. Or annoyance. Either way, he'll take it.

"I was just telling Ash," Augustus says, "all about that money clip I got from Carlo."

Nathaniel chuckles. His grandfather is notorious for his tall tales. "You expect me to believe that? All these years, and I've never once seen it around your house."

"Ah, but it's a legend."

Ash shakes her head. "I feel like I'm getting hazed by this family."

He skims his eyes over her, noting the Band-Aid over her sensor. His stomach pulls tight. "What happened to your sensor?"

Ash tsks. "So nosy." Then she says to him, "The water always makes it come loose. But I patched it with my very best MacGyver skills."

Nathaniel considers it. "We could fix that." His mind's already on it. Pathetic.

Ash looks curiously at Nathaniel over the top of Augustus's head. Instead of the tense awkwardness he's braced himself for, an intimacy hangs in the space between them. Calm. Warm. Tentative. Like Ash's body last night. That slow curl into him, hands on his shoulders, that red mouth landing on his lips like a bomb.

He doesn't know what it means. All he knows is he has to talk to her.

Alone.

When the trail ends and they funnel out onto the beach, Ash gasps. Stretched out in front of them is a massive rock wall where a large waterfall crashes into the swimming hole below. Farther back, calm, crystal-clear turquoise waters lead into numerous lagoons and shallow enclaves. A line of large rocks borders the shore edge. The beach is sparsely populated, an "intimate gem," their guide claims.

"Now this," Augustus says, "is what it's all about."

Claire, her face soft, wraps an arm around his shoulders. "Oh, Dad."

The group spreads out. Doing that awkward family thing that looks like togetherness while they actually ignore each other until it's over.

Book in his hands, Augustus sits on a boulder in the sun. Tate sits beside him, grudgingly laying his phone down.

When Nathaniel glances over, he catches Ash's eye. She gives him a slight smile. God help him. The warmth that pours through him is shameful.

"Tarot?" Delaney singsongs, bouncing beside Ash and waving her deck.

"No," Nathaniel and his mother say in unison.

"What's so bad about Delaney's tarot?" Ash asks him.

"We've all avoided it since the time she pulled the death card for Don, and two days later, he had to close his Costa Mesa practice."

Claire shakes her head. "It was very ill-advised."

"The universe did 90 percent of the work," Delaney argues.

Ash laughs.

With a shake of his head, Nathaniel tugs his shirt off and tosses it onto his pack. As he strides by Ash, he says, "You going to swim or crisp in the sun?"

She scoffs. The flash of mischief in her eyes makes his dick twitch. "Again with the competition. If you're so worried, I'll show you up, just say it."

He leans in. Notes the shiver that goes through her. "Had to find some way to get you speaking to me again, Bigfoot."

Lips curving in a smile, she lifts a creamy white shoulder. "Hasn't been that long."

Twelve hours and two minutes. That's what he wants to say, but he doesn't.

Jesus.

When did it get like this?

She's driving him wild, and she's completely oblivious. Or maybe she isn't. Maybe she just loves torturing him.

Speaking of torture...

Ash strips out of her tank top, shimmies out of her shorts, in one quick motion. And there it is. Her yellow bikini shines bright. The beacon of his ever-constant erection.

"Fuck," he mutters. Heart pounding, he tears his gaze away

from her perfect breasts. Only it doesn't get far. It gets caught on her perky ass as she struts away from him. Slender curves and creamy white flesh.

He stares, entranced.

Ash hops on a rock that juts over a lagoon. Eyes closed, she kicks out a leg like she's testing the temperature of the sunlight.

His breathing grows shallow. She's so damn beautiful. With her bright red lips and long black hair that curls down her back, she looks like wilderness. Like chaos.

Ash should come with a disclaimer. Catlike and beautiful, with random acts of violence. And still, all he wants to do is get close. Experience her light.

Backing up on the rock, she gets into a comical running position.

"Careful," he calls out as he's hit with a jolt of concern.

Those gray-green eyes slice to him.

"It might not be deep e—"

Holding up her middle finger, she runs.

Jumps.

The splash echoes around the rock wall.

Gritting his teeth, he tears a hand through his hair. Waits. Fucking reckless woman.

Seconds later, she sputters to the surface. Hair plastered to her face, she shakes her head like a wet dog. She's smiling. "Fuck. It is fucking cold!"

He almost smiles, but he holds tight to his grin so she can't see it.

For some reason, he's glad. That she likes the water.

Keeping her in his sight, he walks down to the beach. "And I thought *I* liked danger."

She snorts. "Admit it. You were secretly hoping I cracked open my skull."

"No place to bury the body," he says, wading into the water. "How would that look?"

Ash hoots. "I demand a beach run." Her eyes drift over him with heated appreciation. A rush of pleasure hits him. Ash liking his body does more for his ego than he'll ever admit.

Arms arcing, he swims toward her.

"Look at that," she drawls. "No emotion. No scream. Just a robot-like propensity for cold." Ash bobs up and down, goading him as he gets deeper.

The outlines of her nipples are visible through the thin fabric of her bikini top.

Fuck. He's done.

Ash floats backward, arms slicing the water. "This is good for him." She casts a sideways glance at Augustus.

Beside him, Tate is crouched on a rock, gesticulating furiously. Adjusting his glasses, Augustus leans in, gives his grandson his familiar, patient smile.

"I think so too." Nathaniel sighs. "Even if Tate is forcing him to listen to his podcast."

Ash laughs. Water pebbles her face, one bead balancing precariously on her full bottom lip. The urge to lick it away surges through him like a wildfire.

She twists away from him. He follows.

Silently, they swim through the turquoise water until they're in a cove shielded by tall rock walls.

"Wow," Ash says as she takes in the cove. She stands, her upper torso rising above the water. Water sluices over her perky breasts.

Nathaniel tries not to stare. Fails miserably.

"This place is like a sitting duck for a maniac."

A smile tickles his lips. "Always the macabre on your mind."

Those gray-green eyes glimmer. "Don't knock it 'til you've tried it."

"You want to play?" he asks. "Truth/lie?"

Her gaze narrows in suspicion. "Is this your cheat code to getting me to like you?"

"You already like me."

She splashes him. "So cocky."

His feet touch the bottom of the lagoon. Sand and seaweed. "Okay, Bigfoot. If you could be a cryptid, which one would you choose?"

Her eyes light up. He's piqued her interest. For some reason, it makes him happy to see that she's happy.

"Banshee," he asks, "or a fury?"

A burst of laughter escapes her mouth. "I'm sorry, excuse me? You did research. *On cryptids?*" Smiling, she swims toward him.

His ears flame. He did. Last night at the bar before she joined him, he couldn't resist googling the term.

She schools her expression into one of faux seriousness, mouth fixed in a straight line, brow slightly furrowed. "You better take that to the grave, Doctor Whitford."

"I'll be sure to delete my search history," he says dryly.

"Since you're asking…" She searches his face, and he resists the urge to call the game off. Like she's seeing too much of him.

"Neither," she says. "I would choose to be Jenny Greenteeth. A monster swamp hag who lives in a bog. If anyone gets too close, I drown them." Her lips curl. "Then eat them."

He chokes on a laugh. "That can't be a real thing."

"Oh, I regret to inform you, it is very real. And it will terrify you." Expression wondering, she tilts her head. "What about you?"

He shifts, uncomfortable. Again, with her searching eyes, her earnest questions.

He offers a shrug. "I don't know. Maybe a Wendigo."

"No way." She runs her hand along his jaw. The touch of her silk, fire. "I think you'd be Mothman. You act big and scary, but really, you're just misunderstood. You're kind and sweet when you want to be."

When she drops her hand, Nathaniel abandons his fight to stay restrained. He captures her slim wrist. Pulls her toward him. "Is that what you think of me?"

Her teeth sink into her full bottom lip for a second. "I think so," she admits. "I think a lot of things I thought about you were wrong."

"Here's another truth," he says, running his fingers over the thin, delicate skin on the inside of her wrist. The pulse that beats there. "I can't stop thinking about that kiss."

Usually, he wouldn't try so hard. Be so goddamn desperate. But he can't help it. This woman is keeping him afloat on this trip. Keeping him sane. Alive.

She bites her lip, looking suddenly shy and soft. Immediately, he's snared by the contradictions that are Ash Keller. Her girlish flushed cheeks alongside the sharp, dark cat eye. Her quirky love for cryptids balanced by her love for his grandfather.

Now that he's unlocked a little bit of her, he wants more. A hell of a lot more.

Hesitating, she sinks her teeth into her lower lip.

"You do that a lot," Nathaniel says. "Bite your lip when you're nervous."

A cool brow arched. "You notice when I'm nervous?"

The words roll off his tongue before he can stop them. "I notice everything about you."

Her kohl-lined eyes widen. The tantalizing flush on her face ruins him. That's what finally does it. He's officially lost the battle he's been fighting for the last few days. "I liked our kiss."

At his honesty, the wariness in her eyes turns to consideration.

"I liked the kiss too." She ducks her dark head. But rather than swim away from him, like he expects, she drifts toward him.

"So what do we do about it?" His voice is hoarse.

"What if we...kissed sometimes?" Ash suggests. Sunlight falls across her face, highlights the hazy need in her eyes as she seems to battle some internal struggle. "No big deal, right? No big...commitment?"

He nods, suddenly dry-mouthed. "Right."

"A truth just between us," she whispers. "No one else knows. Not even Augustus."

His hopeful heart hammers. "You want to do this?"

They stare at each other, heated, searching. For a long second, the only sound is the lap of water against the rock walls. The splash of the waterfall outside the cave.

And then, her expression turning determined, Ash simply says, "Yes."

That's all it takes.

He yanks her against him. Ready for it, Ash loops her legs around his waist. She's soft and lush against the hardness of his chest. Heat spiraling through his ribs, he lowers his lips to hers. Christ, he loves the way she tastes. Soft and salty and sweet.

She runs her hands through his hair. Whimpers into his mouth. The sexiest, neediest sound he's ever heard.

He palms the curve of her hip. Tangles the tie of her bikini bottom around his fingers. Pressing her tighter against him, he grips her ass, lifting her higher.

She opens for him, legs spreading wide. "Yes," she gasps, the word only for him. "Yes, yes."

Reading her loud and clear, he teases the edge of her bikini bottoms and nudges them aside to slip a finger into her. That tight, perfect pussy.

Ash moans.

Two fingers now. He pushes them forcefully into her slickness. On a gasp, her eyes fall shut. Her lashes flutter. She arches in his arms, riding his hand. The heat of her, the hard clamp of her muscles, turns his dick to steel.

"What if someone sees us?" she gasps.

"I'm beyond caring, Ash," he says roughly, his heart thundering. He's enjoying this too fucking much to care if anyone sees them. To care if he even gets his turn. He wants her to have this. Wants to make her come hard and fast, and he wants to drink in the expression on her gorgeous face.

He adds to the pressure, adjusts the tempo. Swift now.

As she rocks against him in a silent plea for more, he kisses her. Senseless. Endless. He can't be satiated. He's coming undone. Utterly whipped and ruined.

On a growl, she snares his bottom lip with her teeth, tugging savagely.

"Fuck," he grits out, liking her violence. His pulse spikes.

She shakes against him, uneven breaths falling from her lips. Her pupils are big, black and desirous.

He sweeps his mouth against her ear. "So fucking wet," he whispers. "So fucking beautiful."

An aching groan tears from her lips.

Nathaniel's breathing turns strangled. He strokes his fingers over her clit. Faster now. Savoring.

Ash moans at the same moment he does. Panting, she comes. The hard tremble of her body brings a smile to Nathaniel's lips. A rush of satisfaction to his blood. She's beautiful. Fierce face flushed, she continues to moan and rock against him. He slows the pressure on her swollen clit until she goes limp in his arms.

She buries her face in his neck. Saws in breath after breath. He holds her tight. Not wanting her to swim away just yet. When she lifts her face, he smooths away that cloud of dark hair, skims a thumb over the delicate arch of her cheekbone. "Ash."

There's satisfaction in her eyes. She scrapes her hands down the wall of his chest, flashes of black nails and red lips.

"That was…kinda fucking everything," she murmurs. He swears to God she's purring.

"Yeah," he says, unable to tear his eyes from her face. From the red lipstick that still stains her lips. "It really fucking was."

Framing his face in her hands, she kisses him fiercely.

In response, he wraps his fist in all that black hair. A fire erupts within him. Fuck. It's just as good as he expected. She kisses like a monster. Hungry and electric and savage.

Ash dips a finger into the waistband of his board shorts, pulling an unholy moan from deep within him. Her fingers skim the length of his cock. The heavy erection he's sporting begs for relief. Begs for—

"Nathaniel!" Claire calls from the beach, voice panicked.

Ash tears away from him.

"Nathaniel, we need some help here!"

Wide-eyed, Ash jumps out of his arms. "Shit. Augustus."

Heart racing, he tries to get his bearings, calm his erection.

They both splash through the water, swimming fast through the cove.

"Your dick," Ash hisses as they come into sight of his family. His eyes drop to the bulge in his shorts. She smirks. "Your dick, asshole."

Fuck. As they rush onto shore, Nathaniel snags a towel and wraps it around his waist.

He scans the scene waiting for him. Tate sits on a towel, his foot bloodied and cut up. Delaney, Augustus and his mother stand over him.

"What happened?" he barks.

Delaney rolls her eyes. "Tate tried to jump off the waterfall. Instead, he slipped and cut his foot."

"It's called doing a sweet jackknife," Tate says with a scowl at Delaney. "But apparently, we all have our limitations."

"You idiot," Nathaniel rasps, winded from the swim. From the absolute sucker punch of Ash's kiss. Dropping into a crouch, he glares at his little brother. Then he turns his attention to the cut on Tate's foot. It's shallow, but it could get infected if he doesn't handle it.

"Bright side," Ash says to Tate as she sinks into a squat beside Nathaniel. "It won't affect your podcast."

Tate laughs, but when Nathaniel twists his foot, the sound morphs into a groan.

"No," Nathaniel says dryly. "Just your ability to walk for the rest of the trip."

"Here," Ash says, handing him the first-aid kit she must have fished out of his pack.

Gratefulness rises inside him. That she's here. That she's helping.

"Thanks," he says.

Ash looks up at him from beneath thick, fringed lashes. Barefaced, beautiful. Goose bumps dot her bare skin. She's shivering.

Frowning, he removes the towel from around his waist.

"Get warm," he tells her. He drapes the towel around her shoulders, making sure she's covered, and then unzips his kit. "I got this."

He turns to the task at hand. All traces of earlier levity, of him and Ash, gone.

Already, he wants her back.

## Chapter Nineteen

Stupid, dumb reptilian brain. Stupid kissing Nathaniel Whitford. Stupid she's still thinking about it even though it's been approximately five hours since then. And in the meantime, they've had dinner and participated in a sunset water aerobics class so militant that her entire body feels like a rubber band.

She wants to be back in that lagoon. Pressed against Nathaniel's hard stomach, held like she mattered. His frantic fingers inside her, his lush, warm mouth devouring.

*I notice everything about you.*

She's never been looked at that way. Ever. Partly like she's roadkill, but also…with wonder. Wanting.

What does it mean?

Ash walks across the patio into her bedroom.

Nothing. It means absolutely nothing.

It has to. Today, that kiss can't ever matter.

On the nightstand, her phone lights up. She scrambles to answer. Pretends not to be disappointed when the name on the screen isn't Nathaniel's. Or *Tall Asshole*. She should be disappointed in herself. When did she go from *fuck that guy* to *I want to fuck that guy*?

A text from Tessie: **I can't sleep. Again.**

**Calling you.**

"Hi. You okay?"

"I'm so restless," Tessie murmurs. On the other end of the line, the rustle of sheets. "This baby is using my bladder as a trampoline. I swear, she only respects me like 50 percent of the time."

"Are you feeling okay?" Ash sits on the edge of the bed. A

prickle of worry needles its way beneath her skin. "Have you been to the doctor?"

Tessie laughs. "You don't have to worry about me. How was your day?"

"It was…fine."

Even three thousand miles away, her cousin sees right through her. Tessie gasps. "You kissed him."

"What? No." She covers her face with one hand. Then she mumbles, "We kinda, sorta, did more than that."

Remembering Nathaniel's long fingers inside her, the feel of his hard body against hers, sends a rush of heat to her core. Clandestine. Intimate. She wanted it all. Especially him.

It felt good. It felt right. Did he enjoy it as much as she did?

Tessie cheers. "Ash! Does this mean the truce is over?"

"It's a new truce. To maybe sometimes kiss." She's never been good at holding back her emotions. While Tessie's a lockbox, she's always worn her heart on her sleeve. "It's not complicated. Get in and out. Like a drive-through."

Not like she'd categorize it as getting finger-fucked under a waterfall.

It was…more than that. He gave. She took. And he wanted nothing back. Even if she was close to taking the heavy weight of him in her mouth. Because she wanted to.

God, and that orgasm. She *orgasmed*.

Ash lets out a *mmm*.

Tessie's choked laugh breaks her out of her daze. "That good, huh?"

"Shut up."

"I still demand you tell me everything." Over the line, a door shuts. "Solomon is full-throttle snoring. I need some romance in my life."

Ash fights to keep her features, her tone neutral. "I mean, if you want to get all technical, Nathaniel Whitford is a bionic superhuman hiker with above-average kissing skills."

"And he's a doctor."

"And he's a doctor."

"What about his laugh? Is it a red or green flag?"

"Definitely green," Ash murmurs. "Like that red Trans Am that Aunt Bev let us drive down the Pacific Coast Highway."

"Oh my god."

Ash bites her lip. Smiles. Whispers, "He looked up cryptids. For me, I think."

Another gasp. "Ash."

Her cheeks flame. "Stop. It doesn't mean anything. It was just one part of his master plan to corrupt and sway me over to his side."

"Sounds like you like his side."

Ash's heart pounds loudly in her ears. "Okay, I admit I am grudgingly impressed by his jawline, and if he wants to tie me down and whisper his murderous intentions to me while I'm half-naked, then who am I to argue? It's just for the rest of the trip."

"What if this is it?"

Her throat closes up. Her lungs seize. "It's not."

She can hear her cousin's frown over the phone. "You always talk about the universe, Ash. But never yours. Maybe you need to let it in for once."

Ash stands. Paces away her anxiety. "No. There is no universe-ing my love life. Nathaniel and I are a vacation fling. A blip in the stratosphere of it-happened-one-time. If you see me catching feelings for him, please send a carrier pigeon to peck my eyes out." She inhales. "We have a few more days here, then…"

"Maui," Tessie finishes.

"Maui." She swallows hard, suddenly chilled. "I'll be okay."

"Okay like before? When you quit your job, sold your car, started traveling and ate three bologna sandwiches a day?"

Ash squeezes her eyes shut. Embarrassment coats her stomach. She did all that. And then some.

"Lizzo was right. The truth hurts."

"Ash," Tessie says in a soft voice. "I don't want you to push yourself. You take care of everyone else. Don't forget to take care of yourself. If Maui's too much and you need to bail or hide away in your hotel room, do that."

They go silent. But she knows Tessie waits quietly for her to rally. Or snap. Either way, she's there. She loves her cousin so much.

Ash squeezes her eyes shut. All of a sudden, there's no air in the room.

Truth is, it's not even the cheating, the break-up, that haunts her anymore. It's what Jakob said to her the day she packed her bags.

Her deepest, darkest secret. Probably the only one she's ever kept from Tessie. Jakob lingered in the doorway, watching her pack. She was almost out the door when she stopped. Turned. She shouldn't have asked. But she wanted to know. Maybe she wanted closure. Or an apology.

"Why?" she said. "Why did you…" She trailed off. She couldn't finish the sentence.

Jakob let out a great heaving sigh. "Sometimes…you're too much, Ash. Too messy. I just…can't deal."

He said it like he wanted to erase her.

*Don't be too much. Don't be messy. Get your shit together.*

For years, the motto consumed an overwhelming amount of bandwidth in her brain. It took her down psychologically.

She knows she's better off. Jakob never loved her. At least not the real her.

She'll save herself for those that deserve it.

Ash opens her eyes. Lets out a shaky breath. Nods her affirmation. "I'm not bailing on Maui. Or Augustus."

She can get through this. Unless she encounters some sort of force majeure, she's staying by Augustus's side.

"Then you do what you need to get through it," Tessie says. "Alcohol. Weed. Nathaniel's abnormally big—"

A knock at the door makes Ash jump a foot off the bed.

"Someone's at the door."

Tessie squeals. "It's him, isn't it?"

"Goodbye. Good night. Tell Boudica to calm it the fuck down."

Tessie's squeak is indignant. "That is not her name."

Ash hangs up. Gathering herself, she sweeps her hair away from her face. With steady hands, she opens the door.

*Nathaniel.*

And just like that, she can breathe again.

"Hey, Bigfoot." He wears an amused smirk, as if he could hear her and Tessie's conversation.

Oh god, what if he did?

Ash grips the knob. Tight. Forces herself back down to earth. "To what do I owe this displeasure?"

He arches a brow. Leans in the doorway. Between that and his rolled-up cuffs and damp hair, it takes everything in Ash to not let her heart do that *awooga! awooga!* thing in her chest.

She'd give anything for the ability to channel her earlier hatred of Nathaniel Whitford. But she can't do it. It no longer exists.

A sparkle in his eyes, he reaches out. "I want to take a walk."

Ash stares at his hand.

He's infuriating. God, she loves it.

Slowly, she clasps her hand to his. "Then take me for a walk, asshole."

---

When Nathaniel says a *walk*, he means down the beach until they're away from the resort and in front of all the mansions that overlook the ocean.

They settle on a blanket they grabbed from the gift shop. Between them, a bottle of wine and an easy silence.

"I wanted to walk," Nathaniel says, "but really, I wanted to see you."

"I'd never imagine such a heinous thing," she teases, lighting up on the inside.

Nathaniel chuckles. He takes a swig from the wine bottle.

In the moonlight, she studies him. The dangerous angles of his handsome face. He's like an optical illusion. There's so much more to him than meets the eye. He's not a rude, rich trust-fund baby. Not a jerky, opinionated doctor. He's a good man with a genuine heart and a sharp mind. The ridiculously sculpted pectorals are just a bonus.

He passes her the wine. His fingers brush hers in the exchange, sending sparks dancing up her arms.

She takes a sip. "Drinking from the bottle is very heathen behavior." She lifts it in a toast. "I approve."

Nathaniel meets her stare. "Bad habit." When his eyes land on her lips, then trace the remainder of her body, her cheeks flame.

Every memory of earlier, his hands all over her, how good it was, floods her brain. She doesn't know what this is. She doesn't know what to do with her hands. Her lips. She wants them all over Nathaniel. She can't explain her many riotous feelings for this very serious man.

"I have many bad habits," she offers. "I reuse tea bags. I have way too many intrusive thoughts. I bite the heads off gummy bears first, and all doors in my room must be completely shut when I'm sleeping."

"Because of the monsters," he says with utmost seriousness.

"Exactly."

He laughs, and it feels like her favorite sweater wrapped around her hips. Comfortable. Livable. Home.

She rocks herself to the side. Knocks his shoulder. "Don't you have one bad habit? You're so perfect, I have to know."

This time, his chuckle is bitter. "I'm not perfect. Least of all in the eyes of my father."

"Why?" The mood between them has quickly turned somber. "Because you didn't join his practice?"

"I didn't want to burn off warts for a living, and he's been pissed ever since."

Nathaniel's tone is amused, but beneath it lingers bitterness. As if he's covering his hurt. As if he's unburying pain he's pushed down deep.

"I paid the loans for med school, changed my course. I didn't want anything from him that he could use against me. I've seen how he treats my mother, my brother and sister. You've seen it." He slips his hand around hers.

Ash's stomach tightens. She remains silent. Attentive.

"He can't even enjoy this fucking vacation and make peace with my grandfather."

She nods, understanding. So much more than she ever thought possible. He's a son who ran when his father's disappointment became too much to bear. Who moved to the middle of the ocean and cut himself off from everyone completely.

"It's why you stay on that rig, isn't it? To drift. To stay away."

Guilty eyes flick to hers. "I hate seeing what my family's become. They stay and take it." His tone, his face are stone. "I don't even think he knows I hate the name Nate."

The thorns around her heart soften. Ash squeezes his hand.

Nathaniel swallows. Looks away from her. To the ocean.

Ash waits, letting him come to terms with whatever he's wrestling with. When he finally does, his voice is soft. Sad.

"I don't think my father would negotiate a ransom if he received my ear in the mail."

Nathaniel swears. Frustration laces his tone. "And I still can't stop myself from trying to make him proud of me. I have never been able to be what they want. A better brother. The right type of doctor. *I don't even fucking know sometimes.*"

His words settle around Ash. A quiet, dying plea.

She studies him. Arches a brow. "Sure, you could work on the brother part, but your siblings *are* kind of gremlins. And fuck what everyone wants of you. You're doing what *you* wanted to do. And you know what? *I'm* proud of you. Even though I still want to drown you in the Pacific, and who knows? Maybe I still will."

For a long second, Nathaniel sits, his eyes lit with shock.

Then he says, "Do you know you're the first person who's ever said they were proud of me?"

"I'm sorry," she says simply. Her heart aches in her chest. "That would be awful."

"It was," he says thickly.

Both are quiet for a moment. Watching the waves, listening to the crash of them on the shore.

"My wedding." The words feel like an atom bomb.

Ash winces. Looks down at her lap. An ache yawns inside her chest. The thorns constrict. "We don't have to—"

"No. We do." She still can't look at him. He goes on. "You objecting to the wedding made me see that I was living my life for other people. The job, the marriage. Even Camellia."

This time, Ash meets his gaze. Forces herself to face the tidal wave of her wreckage.

"We weren't a good fit," he says roughly. He looks down at his hands. Flexes those long fingers. "I knew it. Went along with it. Mostly for my father. Politics of the business. I suppose some part of me did love her. But…after you interrupted the wedding…I was relieved. Like I could finally be myself. I don't know if that makes sense, but that's how I felt."

Ash does know. All too well. Too painfully.

It would be easy to tell him about Jakob. But why should she? Her past needs to stay dead and buried. It's too intimate, too hers. The truth is ugly and embarrassing, and she wants to shove it back down in the lockbox of her thorny heart before it grows thrashing arms and monstrous fangs.

That's what it is. Monstrous. That unwanted, unloved feeling. The way no one stays when they see the real Ash. They all vanish eventually. Like the sun going down over the horizon. It all ends.

Nathaniel goes on. "When she said she wanted to end it, I didn't fight her. Walking up to that altar was the last time I tried making my father happy."

Ash says hoarsely, "That's a brave thing to do. Live for yourself. Most people don't realize it's what they want until it's too late."

"You did that, Ash," Nathaniel marvels. "You blew up my world. For a long time, it pissed me off. But deep down, I was really pissed at myself. Because I should have been the one to do it." His handsome face creases. "Camellia and I…we didn't notice each other. We didn't talk. Not in any real way. Not like the way you and—"

He snaps his mouth shut. Opens it again to regroup. When nothing comes out, he reaches for the wine.

As Nathaniel takes a long, long drink, the space heats between them. Ash's face flames. She shuts her eyes against the realization of what he almost admitted.

*You and me.*

Fuck. Shit.

There is no *you and me* when it comes to the two of them.

They're existing on a common plane. That's it. Once this vacation is over, they go back to the real world. Reality. He will be in the North Sea, and all he'll be to her is a pirate doctor she once let finger-fuck her beneath a waterfall.

Even if it feels wrong to consider what happened earlier between them a tawdry, illicit fling.

It was better. It was worth it. It was theirs.

Ash picks up the silence. It's best if she controls where they go next.

"It took me a long time to figure out what I wanted to do." She side-eyes him and gives him a sharp smile. "Cons and all."

He rubs his jaw, regret evident on his handsome face. "I never should have said that."

Her cheeks stain with color. "It's okay. Sometimes I feel like a con."

"Don't say that about yourself."

"You may be right. Sometimes." She bumps her shoulder against his. "I don't take on these part-time jobs for fun and games. I need the money, the insurance for insulin supplies. They're expensive."

His eyebrows furrow, making his expression unhappy. "I know."

"And this job? I'm helping your grandfather, but really, he's helping me. With what he's paying me, I'll be stocked for years." Ash wrinkles her nose. "Shit. Is that gauche? To talk about money?"

"No. He should pay you more."

Ash laughs. A sensation beyond electric works its way through her blood.

Nathaniel is quiet. He stares at her until she meets his eyes. "You're worth it."

She can barely breathe. "I am?"

"Yeah. You are."

He leans in, closing the distance between them. Slides a hand into her hair and brings her mouth to his. Kisses her long and passionately. Each of their pounding hearts tailor-made to say words they long to speak.

Ash closes her eyes, savoring his kiss. This endless night. This man.

Nathaniel pulls back. Eyes hungry and heated, he breathes, "Tell me your name, Ash."

She laughs against his lips. Kisses him once more.

"Nope."

Smiling, he tucks her against his side. "Ashley?"

She makes a face. "Rude. And no."

"I poured my heart out tonight. Don't you think I deserve some consolation?"

"No." Considering it, she tilts her head. "At least not in the immediate future."

"Hmm." He runs a big hand down her shoulder. She shivers at the contact. The feel of his body on her. "That would mean I'm included in the future."

"You're Augustus's grandson. As long as that old man's kicking,

I can only assume you'll be buzzing around like a gnat." She gives a casual shrug, keeps a casual tone.

Only the last thing she feels is casual.

Knotted up. That's more accurate. So knotted up inside. Like not seeing Nathaniel again is a kind of death.

"Then tell me something else," Nathaniel says. "Why the boots? There has to be a story."

"There is." She presses closer to him. For an instant, her heart retreats to the hollow of her chest. But she forces it out of hiding to say, "They make me feel powerful." Her eyes flick to Nathaniel's face. He's watching her with a quiet curiosity. Giving her the space she needs.

"My mom bought me a pair after I was diagnosed. We went shopping in Beverly Hills. Tessie and her mom were there. I was allowed to pick one thing I wanted. No matter what the price was." The golden threads of her memory shimmer, easing the tension in her shoulders. "When I saw them, I knew I had to have them. They were badass. They made *me* feel badass. Invincible. Like I could stomp, and everyone could stare, and I didn't care. I could ward anything off when I wore those boots."

Nathaniel idly smooths her hair, gently combing his fingers through it. He's listening. It's obvious in the stiffness of his body. The attentive weight of his stare. She feels all of him.

Ash sighs, burrows closer to him. "Everything about that time was tentative and hard, but those boots weren't. They were my superpower. They were everything about my life I wanted but couldn't find at the time."

She closes her eyes. Exhales the memory.

A soft muttered swear falls from Nathaniel's lips.

"What's wrong?" She blinks back to the moment, takes him in.

"I shouldn't have called you that." He swallows audibly. "Bigfoot." Guilt's etched across his face. His expression turns serious, and her heart stutters as he says, "I didn't know what your boots meant to you. I'm a fucking asshole."

She's momentarily speechless. Touched.

"No, really. It's fine," she says earnestly. It's sweet that he cares, that he feels bad, but there's no need. "I love the nickname. I really do."

After a beat, he touches her shoulder.

Wordlessly, she twists into him, and he takes her in his arms. The gesture so intimate, so kind, that it steals her breath. Ash sighs at the delightful sensation. His hug is like a weighted blanket, or better yet, a hydraulic press.

A breeze kicks up, and despite the balmy temperature, Ash shivers.

Nathaniel cups her jaw. He wipes that dark hair off her face, skims a thumb over the delicate arch of her cheekbone. "Let's go back. Get you warm."

She is warm. Here, in Nathaniel's arms, she's the warmest she's ever been. She doesn't want to go back. She wants to sit on this beach with this man, confessing strange truths, and watch the sun rise.

But instead, she bites her tongue and says, "Okay."

***

"Well, I guess this is good night."

Ash lingers in the doorway of her hotel room. Nathaniel stands on the other side of the threshold like a blood-sucking vampire who hasn't been allowed to enter. She's suddenly flooded with nerves. Why did he have to be a perfect fucking gentleman and insist on walking her back to her room?

"My bad habit," he rasps. "You asked earlier if I had one."

She props a hand on her hip. "I'm not interested anymore."

He blinks, and she laughs. She likes teasing him. Likes watching him come undone.

Then, slowly, he smiles. "It's rocks."

It's her turn to blink. "Rocks?"

"In every new place I'm in, I take a rock."

"That's a right proper nerd, Nathaniel." She tilts her head. "I'm impressed. There's nothing sexier than a rock."

Eyes blazing, he inches closer.

She smirks. "Do you have lots? Of rocks?"

His hands settle on her waist. "Of course. Igneous. Metamorphic. Sedimentary."

"Sedimentary. Sounds sexy."

"Unreasonably so."

"We should probably get to bed," Ash hedges softly.

Neither one of them moves.

Several heartbeats later, Nathaniel leans in. One muscular forearm rests on the wall above her, pinning her against the doorframe.

Ash swallows. Her breaths come out funny. Shallow. Raspy.

Wordlessly, he dips down and kisses her. His tongue teases hers into a stupor, pulling a whimper from her.

He breaks the kiss. Puts one big hand on her hip. Traces one long finger along the line of her waistband to dip below it.

Her hips arch slightly, pressing against him.

"What do you feel when I do this?" His blue eyes sear hers. Hungry and heated.

"Everything," she whispers. "I feel everything."

"Yeah," he murmurs. "I do too."

So heavy, the space between them. In her chest, fluttering warmth. A sensation she hasn't felt in an ice age. Like a candle warming.

She stops trying to fight it. Her hands shoot out and grab his face. She yanks him toward her. Their mouths crash together. Devouring. Frenzied and claiming.

Her brain fizzes. Her lashes flutter. Gasping for air, she pulls back. "I shouldn't want you."

"Because we hate each other."

The thorns around her heart tighten a fraction. "Right."

"Wrong."

"Because of Augustus."

"Right."

"But I want you. Naked." His heated gaze lands on her lips. "You turn me on. So fucking much."

She can't stop the reckless thrill that skitters through her. There's no reason to rush, yet she can't help herself.

She grabs him by the collar, the move so rough she can't be sure she doesn't pop a seam, and drags him into her room. Inside, they stumble over Ash's shoes, her purses and clothes.

Nathaniel's hands are everywhere. His palms caress over her shape, removing her shirt in the process. As it floats to the floor, he cups her breast, a rough moan parting his lips at the sight of her nipple through the sheer material of her bra.

She holds her breath as he strips her down. It's erotic, the primal way he slowly undresses her. Her bra lands on a chair. Then he's on his knees, slipping off her boots, reaching up to untie her sarong.

It falls to the floor in a puddle of silk. Pleasure heats her core.

His big hands travel up her thighs. His warm breath pulses. "I've been wanting a closer look at these." He sounds mystified. It's one of the sexiest sights she's seen, him exploring the roses, the vines, the lilacs on her thighs, before dipping his head to kiss his way up her legs.

One kiss against her lips. Then he stands and takes a step back.

"Fuck." Nathaniel takes her in, looking like he's been sucker punched.

Ash flushes, feeling vulnerable and sexy under his admiring stare.

"Do you know?" he rumbles, blue eyes shining with a gleam of lust, as he moves toward her, "how goddamn beautiful you are?"

"Flattery will get you everywhere," she breathes out as her heart slams against her ribs. "Especially into my bed."

"So fucking gorgeous," he murmurs, taking her in his arms. "My morbid little beauty."

She smiles, liking that.

He slides his hand to her hip and backs her up to the bed. And then she's flat on her back, naked, and Nathaniel's back on his knees. He parts her thighs.

"Twice in one day." She lifts her head, takes in his smirking, gorgeous face. "You're spoiling me."

"Get used to it."

Briefly, he ghosts his lips over the inside of one thigh. Then the other. Her pussy throbs. He licks over her damp slit, and a whimper escapes her.

He drapes her thighs over his shoulders. Tugs her close. Let's out a ragged moan. "Jesus. You're so wet."

"Ugh," she groans, latching on to his hair with one hand. "Please don't use this against me."

He chuckles. "Tell me that again tomorrow."

"Asshole."

"Ash." His voice is hungry. Faintly amused. "Shut up and let me fucking taste you."

Nathaniel twists the tip of his tongue against her clit. Ash gasps. The sound transforms quickly into a moan. That sweet spot detonated.

With his hungry mouth, he takes his time and teases her. Alternates his tempo. Slow, then fast. Honeyed and heated. He eats her deep and rhythmically.

Her face heats, her breasts. Her hips twist and buck, but he holds her to the bed. So close, so close to teetering over the brink, that fine line of excitement, lust and desire.

"Nathaniel," she cries out, twisting his hair in her fingers. The pit of her back arches. "Faster. Just like that."

He flicks his tongue over her clit, that tight bundle of joy. And then every one of her nerve endings liquefies. There's a rush of heat as bliss blossoms over her. Her lower body rockets off the bed as she comes. A beautiful ache of surrender.

Finally, he gives her one last lick. Pulls back.

Ash lies prone, hand to her heart, certain she's taken half of Nathaniel's hair with her.

His grinning face appears above her. "You like to push? Well, so do I." He holds her jaw, keeps his eyes locked with hers. "I like you on edge, Ash. I like knowing I made you come."

Breathing heavily, she blinks up at him. "It's supernatural. Your arrogance."

"And you are so very lovely and wicked."

All she can do is shakily push herself to sitting. It's what he's reduced her to. A whining, trembling woman. But it sure felt fucking good.

But when he reaches for his zipper, her senses return. Her strength. She grasps it first. Her turn to see him naked. It's only fair. This beautiful, jerky specimen of a man.

Smile vicious, hands trembling, she slides his pants and boxers off as one.

"Holy fuck," Ash breathes when she gets a look at his thick, impressive cock. Tessie was right. It is unholy. Good for her. If she's lucky, he'll plow into her like a monster truck.

And then her eyes lift.

Holy shit.

His body is incredible. Pure power. Well-defined contours, the V of his hips, golden skin and his hands. Her favorite part of Nathaniel Whitford. Big, long-fingered, graceful hands. Lifesaving, waterfall-fingering hands.

She really, really wants him on top of her.

But first...

She grasps his cock. Strokes. His eyes turn primal. She likes the weight of him. The pulse.

She repositions herself so she's on her knees in front of him.

She swallows him down. Relishes the groan he emits. The taste of him is heady, making her brain fuzzy.

Heavy-lidded, she peers up at him. Swirls her tongue around the tip of his cock. Pulls back.

At the loss, he curses, squeezes his eyes shut. Clenches that strong jaw. His entire body is tense as a whip. He's losing control, and it feeds her hunger.

Then he takes her chin hard between his fingers, stilling her. Traces her lower lip with one thumb. When he pulls it back, it's stained in red lipstick. His frame shudders. "So it does come off." He sounds pleased.

"Only for you," she purrs.

"I want to fuck you, Ash." A tortured breath falls from his lips. "I need to."

She gives his cock one last leisurely lick, then pulls back. "Yes."

His gaze blazes. "Right now."

"Hold, please." With trembling hands, she stands, grabs her phone and swipes it against her sensor. *Please, please, please, please.*

Nathaniel waits patiently, chest heaving, eyes watching her every move.

Relief blasts through her. The sex gods must be smiling on her tonight, because her blood sugar is perfect.

She turns to him. Her pussy is throbbing again. "All good."

He gives his shaft a stroke, making it spring up harder. "Any way you want, Ash."

"I love ladies' choice," she growls, his words spurring her on.

She launches herself at him. The backs of his legs hit the mattress. He falls onto the bed, taking her with him.

Ash lays a hand on his golden, muscled chest. "We can't get caught."

That flash of a smirk. "I practically own the hotel, remember?"

"Show-off."

He looks at her, pensive. "You okay with this?"

"Yes. I just haven't been—" Ash hesitates, searching for the right words. *Touched, wanted, loved in forever.* Instead, she says, "With anyone for a long time."

"No judgment. I've been on an oil rig sex sabbatical for God knows how long." He sits up on his elbows. "Condom?"

"I'm on birth control."

With a thick swallow, he studies her. Then, without words, he gently lays her down. "Like this?" He hovers over her, strong body braced.

Lust surges through her bloodstream. "Yes."

He grips his cock and guides it between her legs. He nudges at her slick entrance and then pushes inside. Ash gasps. Not because of the hardness of having him inside of her. But because of the way it feels. What it means.

Visibly affected, Nathaniel throws his head back and groans. "Fuck," he pants, thrusting hard.

"Fast as you can," Ash pleads, scratching her nails down his sinewy back. She's already bucking. So eager it's criminal. "Fast, Nathaniel. Don't stop, or I'll kill you."

"Scratch me up, Ash," he grits out, his eyes flaring. "That's right. Fucking wreck me."

Ash whimpers. Her core throbs in urgency.

His mouth captures hers. Lord Jesus, rapture her now. She can't stop kissing him, fucking him, wanting him.

Nathaniel pumps into her. He bears down. Interlacing their fingers, he lifts her arms above her head. Then he sucks one nipple into his mouth.

Ash writhes anxiously. Desperately. And she doesn't even care. Fuck it. The end of the world couldn't stop her.

"I like the noises you make." His rough voice sends a shiver through her. But his words are like silk draped over her skin. "In fact, I fucking love them."

His encouragement, his praise, is pure adrenaline surging through her veins. "Oh," she purrs, lengthening beneath him. Closer to climax. Closer to heaven.

"Fuck," he blasts. He rears back and slams into her again. Harder. Faster. Over and over.

"Yes," Ash moans. "Yes." Her heart's ready to burst out of her chest.

It builds in them. Release. It ignites in the tips of her toes, her core, her soul. Warmth like a sunrise. A golden thread.

It snaps.

And then she's falling. Shattering. Crying out. Trembling her release.

Nathaniel's not far behind. He roars as he erupts, rocking slower and slower against her.

Then, silence. He stays buried within her. "Ash," he breathes, pressing himself in deeper to kiss her neck. To tuck her against him.

She kisses his brow, swiping at a sweaty lock of that honey-gold hair. "I hate you," she whispers, ludicrously exhausted yet obscenely content.

He smiles against her throat. "Little liar."

Ash snuggles into Nathaniel's arms. The action hesitant, strange. The wall around her heart lowered and unguarded. And yet she'll allow it.

For just one night.

## Chapter Twenty

They get to Rainbow Falls early the next morning. Despite their grumbles, Nathaniel's siblings rallied, and everyone is on the bus. Ash sits by herself in a window seat, dark glasses hiding her eyes, arms crossed over her chest.

"Okay, so should I say it like this?" Delaney asks, clearing her throat. "'You stupid idiot. I love you.' Or like this? 'You're a big dummy, but I love you.'" She frowns at the script she has pulled up on her phone. "It's really hard to know if I should improv."

Tate snickers. "Isn't that what you do every day?"

She socks him in the arm. "Jerk."

"It's an easy hike, Dad," Claire says as the caravan comes to a stop in the parking lot. "Rainbow Falls is just over the hill. It's supposed to be one of the five best Big Island waterfalls."

"Think you can steer clear of rockslides, Bigfoot?" Nathaniel asks, keeping his attention fixed on the guidebook even though there's no need. The hike's short. The morning sunny. Prime position to catch a rainbow.

Ash scoffs. "So hostile. Your grandson needs a leash, Augustus." She keeps her voice bored, her face turned straight ahead.

Augustus chuckles.

But the tips of her ears are bright red. Just like her lipstick.

That red fucking lipstick that came off all over his cock last night.

How is it that only four days ago, all he wanted to do was buy her a one-way ticket back to LA? He was obsessed with hating her, now he's just plain obsessed with her. She's so fucking beautiful and mean, it messes with his mind. She's under his skin, and he isn't ashamed to admit he wants her to burrow in deep.

Fuck the hikes. He wants to be fucking Ash in every room of the hotel.

He's not sure he'll survive her in bed again. But damn if he doesn't want to try.

One night with her wasn't enough. He wants everything about last night all over again. Including the conversation. She heard his thoughts; she understood him. It's been so long since he talked to a person who truly listened. It's unreal to him, that this woman gets it. Gets him.

"This is actually a below-average hike, Nate," Don says. He thumbs through his phone, expression bland. "Cliffs. Water. Rainbows. It's all the same."

Irritation spikes inside him. His jaw grinds.

"Funny, that's what the Yelp reviews about your practice say," Ash says coolly, examining her sharp nails. *"Below average."*

Nathaniel smirks at the beet-red expression on his father's face.

After disembarking at the parking lot, they begin the hike up the left shoulder of the falls. Only Don stays in the van to take a client call. Lush greenery surrounds them. Due to the early morning, the crowd's small, making it a leisurely stroll up to the viewing platform.

Behind them, Delaney continues running her lines. "If you want to get out of this alive, trust me."

Nathaniel stops. "Here, I'll run lines with you."

Delaney perks up, pink ponytail bouncing. "You will?"

When she hands him the phone, Nathaniel pockets it.

"Hey!"

Ignoring her, he strides ahead to catch up with Ash.

"Can't stay away?" she murmurs. "Must be a glutton for punishment."

He sighs. "You're somewhat intriguing. I hate myself for admitting that."

Ash laughs and shakes her head. "You're such a tall asshole."

Chuckling, he moves his pack in front of him. Unzips it to deposit Delaney's phone.

"Wait. What's that?" Without breaking stride, Ash grabs the lip of his pack, drags it down to eye level. Spies the cache of granola bars, gel packets and peanut butter crackers he packed.

Shock creases her face. She throws him a puzzled glance. "Nathaniel…what?"

He swallows. Heat creeps up the back of his neck. "They're for you. Just in case." He can't help but want to take care of her. Maybe it's the doctor in him. Maybe it's because he actually cares about this chaotic girl. The thought of her being without sugar terrifies him.

And Ash—she amazes him. After the story she told him last night, he cursed himself a hundred times over for giving her grief about her boots. The entirety of this trip, he's seen it. She's a lesson in strength. Resilience. Knocking down obstacles. But he'd expect nothing else from her. Not after he's witnessed the way she puts everyone first. How deeply she cares. How she's perfect just as she is. That's not his opinion, it's a fact. Anyone who disagrees with him can fuck off into the ocean.

Her cheeks stain with color. "You didn't have to do that."

"Think of it as making me feel better," he says around the lump in his throat.

She considers him, lips pursed. "I'm truly split between adoration and complete violence."

As they continue along the path, silence ripples between them. The only sounds the crunch of their boots on the hard rock path, birdsong. His arm swings side by side with Ash's. Every few seconds, their pinkies touch, sending a shockwave singing down his spine. It's painful how close she is. Her heat. Her scent.

Jesus.

His fucking dick twitches. He clenches his teeth, racks his brain for a topic that will force it back into playing dead.

"Truth," he says, and Ash's eyes bounce to his. "Sunsets or sunrises?"

"Sunsets," she answers. "They're like nature's last scream."

Nathaniel pushes a branch out of their way, letting Ash pass. Over her shoulder, she asks, "Would you rather wear a fedora every day for the rest of your life, or for every beverage you drink for the rest of your life to contain two drops of pee?"

He snorts, catching up with her. "I'm not answering that."

"Why not? The answer is obviously pee, and you know it."

"What's this?" Delaney's curious voice carries. "What are you doing?"

"It's Ash's game," Augustus says.

Ash turns around and walks backward. "It's a question game. One person asks a question. The person who answers it can either tell a truth or a lie."

Nathaniel adds, "It doesn't make sense."

With a grunt, Ash shoves him into a palm frond. "Ignore him. Here. For example, does or does Nathaniel not look like a highly trained assassin in his all-black hiking attire?"

Claire's face pinches like she's trying to hold in a laugh.

Augustus laughs, big and boisterous.

Nathaniel rolls his eyes. Fights a smile.

"Yes, he does, and that is the truth." Delaney howls in laughter. "Okay, okay, my turn. Does anyone else think Dad's just been holding in his farts his entire life?"

"Delaney!" Claire exclaims, eyes wide.

"What? I've never seen him let one loose!"

Nathaniel's mother looks scandalized, but they're laughing. Everyone's laughing. Like some invisible wall has come down. Nathaniel takes each one of them in. Something inside him lightens. Relaxes.

"My turn," Tate says, shoving his phone into his pack.

Even their mother gets in on the action. For the remainder of the short hike, the whole group plays multiple rounds of Ash's game. Finally, they reach the top of the viewpoint.

"Whoa," Ash breathes as they pass a massive banyan tree. Fig vines hang like delicate curtains. She looks up, boots slipping as she turns in a circle to take in the lush tropical rainforest.

Steadying her, Nathaniel places a light hand on the small of her back. Then he guides her up the trail. Now that he's started touching her, he can't stop. Her creamy bare skin, her tattoos, the way her long wild hair falls forward over her shoulders, is a rush of the senses. He's powerless against her. He'd commit arson if she asked.

When they get to the special viewing platform, they all gasp. The scenery is stunning. Water rushes over the falls at great speed and erupts in white water below. Mist and water droplets pepper their skin. Thanks to the rising sun, a dazzling rainbow hovers in the falls like a mirage.

Ash laughs and holds out her hand to the mist. She stretches out on tiptoes, on those squeaky black boots of hers, like she can touch the sky, and Nathaniel almost believes she could.

Augustus grins. "Now that's a wonder."

Nathaniel's gaze sweeps over Ash's face. In bright sunlight, her eyes are more green than gray. Like shards of sea glass he's found on his dives.

She's beautiful. The most beautiful woman he's ever seen.

"It's amazing." Her voice is husky, honeyed. Leaning in, she slings her arm around Augustus's shoulder. "Legend is an ancient Hawaiian goddess named Hina lives in the lava cave below the falls."

Augustus's smile is wide. "Legends are the best things we can leave behind."

"I concur mightily with that statement," Ash says.

His grandfather pulls Ash into a hug. The familiarity between them tightens Nathaniel's throat. He turns away, moving to the railing to let them have their moment.

And then Ash is pulling out of Augustus's arms and heading toward him. "I have something for you."

"Let me guess. A noose."

That gets him a grin. "Here." She slips a hand into her pocket. When she pulls out a rock, his heartbeat turns irregular. Eyes gleaming, she holds it up. A shiny, jagged black rock. Volcanic, he supposes. "For you."

He can't get the words out.

She remembered. Found a way to do this for him. His chest damn near burns from the gesture.

At his silence, she wrinkles her brow. Tilts her head. "You collect them, right? You're in a new place, aren't you?"

His gaze skims her lips before settling on her face, soaking in her beauty. "Yeah." He swallows through his suddenly dry throat. "I am."

That's what he feels like with Ash. Like he's in a new place. He's a new him. Or maybe this is the him he's always been. Maybe it's Ash and her chiseling gaze that have chipped away at him until he's just as shiny as that rock she holds.

She lowers her hand, hesitant. Uncertain. "Do you want it?"

"I do." He rallies his cool, even as happiness rattles inside him. He doesn't want her to think the wrong thing. To fuck this up.

But what is *this*? There's nothing to fuck up, is there?

She drops it into his palm. "There." Her lips curve into a soft smile. "All yours."

All his.

Before she can pull away, he captures her hand. Every inch of him is hot and tight. "Thank you."

Ash is quiet for a long moment before she finally says, "You're welcome."

His heart roars in his ears.

*Better. This trip has been better because of Ash.*

He's been *better*.

A crunching on the ground startles them both.

Nathaniel drops Ash's hand. Delaney appears. She holds up the phone Nathaniel returned to her when they made it to the top, her face damp from the mist. "C'mon, big brother. The selfie light is insane."

"Here." Ash slips her cell phone from her back pocket. She waves at Tater and Claire. "Let me take it."

As Nathaniel's family lines up against the railing, backdropped by the waterfall, Augustus beckons to Ash. "Get in here, my dear."

Shaking her dark head, she steps back. Positions her phone. "This is a family photo."

"You should still get in here," Nathaniel demands, fighting that burn in his chest. To be consumed by the voice in his head that tells him she belongs here.

Ash eyes him, pupils flaring. "Fine," she sniffs. "If it's my doula duty."

She affects the cold expression she's so fond of, her shield, as she settles beside him. She lifts the camera as they all crowd in tighter.

At the last minute, he wraps an arm around Ash's shoulders. Pulls her close. All of his focus narrows when he realizes she isn't stiff like he expects. She's soft, leaning into him. Her breathing jagged. Swear to God, it turns him on. Ash, uninhibited. Because of him.

"Try not to look so miserable," he whispers. It takes everything in him not to bury his face in that cloud of hair.

"Next to you," she hisses back, "absolutely impossible."

"Little liar."

There's a pinch to his ass, the sharp bite of pain making him jump. Beside him, Ash maintains her placid smile.

The camera flashes.

"You play dirty," he tells her, rubbing his right ass cheek.

She bares her teeth. "That's how I like it." Then she gives him a wink. Drops her phone into his hands.

He dips his chin, his heart hammering in his ears as he looks at the photo.

Invisible claws dig their way into his lungs.

They're both smiling.

That's when he knows he's in fucking trouble.

## Chapter Twenty-One

THE DIVE BAR IS LOUD AND STICKY. IT'S AN ON-THE-side-of-the-road hole-in-the-wall box of a bar. Nestled in palm fronds and backdropped by thick, tropical jungle. Augustus wanted to see a local side of the Big Island, so she and Nathaniel offered to take him into town.

Being stuck with Nathaniel isn't so bad. After what happened between them last night, it's easy to convince herself that they got it out of their systems. That there won't be another time, when in fact, she's already thinking about it.

And it scares her.

Desperately.

The sex was too good. Too right. Their bodies fit. They fucked hard, into oblivion. Nathaniel never treated her like she was fragile. Waited for her to check her blood sugar without any annoyed sighs like Jakob used to make.

Her stomach flips over. He cares. And he's showing that to her. Has ever since she met him. She just refused to see it until now. Bringing her that juice on their first day in Hawaii. Today, his pack stuffed with granola bars and glucose gels and her favorite snack. For her. Never limiting her or wondering if she should slow down. He's been beside her every step of the way. As a doctor, he understands her condition. As Nathaniel Whitford, he sees that her diabetes is just a piece of her.

It means a lot.

It means everything.

Ash, Augustus and Nathaniel claim a picnic table beneath the lanai. Stretched out in front of them, the Pacific. The crash of the waves competes with the sound of the live band playing classic rock and '80s throwbacks.

Here, Ash feels at home. While she's enjoying the lavish hotels and opulence, this bar is more her vibe. Relaxed, unfettered, chaotic. A mix of tourists and regulars crowd the space.

Nathaniel sits across from her. He wears the sun, paradise like a second skin. Like it's made for him. Breeze-ruffled hair. Handsome. So damn handsome. Ash catches herself sneaking peeks at him. Then curses her lack of self-control.

*A week and a half. Get through it. Kiss the sexy doctor. Go home. Forget about him.*

Easy.

Messy.

She should feel confused. Should feel guilt. But she doesn't. Life is a short series of commas, and if you're lucky, an exclamation point, and then you die. So yes, she will fuck Nathaniel Whitford. Happily.

Ash groans when she reads over the sticky menu. Laughing, she brings her hands to her face. "This is the worst city to be diabetic in. Mai tais and piña coladas and margaritas. My blood would explode with one drink."

Augustus peers her way, curious. "What if you had one?"

"I could, and correct it now, but it'll inevitably get fucked up later."

"What's later?" A smug smile toys at the edges of Nathaniel's lips.

She glares at him.

Damn this man.

She's saved by the server. They order drinks and homemade crispy gau gee.

"Now you," Ash says to Augustus. Reaching across the table, she covers his hand. "You have a good reason. All the last drinks."

"Until I can't." Nostalgia flickers through his pale-blue eyes.

"I'll never forget that glass of red wine on my wedding day. Or the scotch I had the summer of '79."

Nathaniel smiles like he's heard this story before. "Is that when you were in Scotland?"

"I'm thinking maybe it was an Oban. No." Augustus taps the table like he's sending an SOS signal to his memories. "It was a Bruichladdich. Rosalea and I were on a yacht in the Irish Sea. We drank half a bottle, and when we woke up, we found a couple of common gulls had made a nest of our towels."

Chuckling, Nathaniel pats his grandfather on the back.

Ash's breath hitches at the sight.

Ugh. Why does he have to be just as wonderful as his grandfather?

"Nathaniel," Augustus says, picking up the beer that's just been delivered. "I'd like to talk to you about my last wishes." He nods at Ash. "You too."

Nathaniel grimaces, shifts in his seat. "Grandpops."

"Ten minutes, we talk business, and then we have fun," he says.

Nathaniel stares down into his beer, his jaw flexing. Pain creases his expression.

It's automatic. The need to comfort him.

"It's okay," Ash says softly. Heartbeat accelerating, she covers his hand with hers.

He glances down at it, then up at her. Stunned. And then his entire body unclenches.

If Augustus notices, he says nothing.

"Okay." Nathaniel rubs the side of his jaw as his face fades to a gentler expression. Inhaling a deep breath, he focuses all his attention on Augustus. "I'm here, Grandpops. You tell me what to do, and I'll do it."

He's all stern business now, which makes him even sexier to Ash. Even with the grief in his eyes, she sees why he's a great doctor. Compassionate, caring, even with the cold front. If she wasn't melting before, she is now.

For the next fifteen minutes, Augustus details how Claire and Nathaniel are to be executors of the will. He goes over his plans for cremation and a ceremony that is already bought and paid for. They drink their drinks. Nathaniel inhales his first beer in five seconds flat, like he needs to numb the pain but nods along to every word his grandfather says.

As he talks, Ash fights off a wave of emotion. The vivid, chaotic noises of the bar don't mesh with the somber conversation. And still, the vibes are warm. Like she's wrapped in a calm embrace. So grateful that Nathaniel is here beside her.

They talk and drink all night. Happy memories. Nostalgia is king: Augustus's childhood. Vegas and mobsters. Hotels and starlets.

It's a night she'll remember long after Augustus is gone.

Finally, when the band is blasting its way through a cover of a Deep Purple song, Augustus excuses himself to use the bathroom. Ash tracks his stuttering footsteps, and when she glances over, she finds Nathaniel is doing the same.

Nathaniel checks his dive watch. Lifts those stern brows of his. "It's late."

"Shit," she swears. So absorbed in Augustus's stories, she never noticed the time. "He'll be tired tomorrow."

"I think he needed this, though."

"True."

"I'm glad," Nathaniel says, pivoting his hand so that their palms touch. "That you're here for my grandfather. That you're here for us."

Heat creeps up her neck at his words. "I will be. As long as I'm needed."

"You're needed," he rasps, pulling her hand closer.

His words have her heart racing. She licks her lips. Unsure where to begin.

Around them, people begin to gasp. To point at the sky. Phones come out and sharp exclamations of wonder fill the air.

Ash lifts her eyes heavenward. "Holy shit."

"C'mon," Nathaniel says, shoving up from the picnic table.

Fingers laced, they turn toward the beach. Toward the dark sky stuffed by lightning-white stars. And then they begin to fall.

Shooting stars streak pale across the inky-black expanse above them. Blazing a sparkling path. Ash brings her fingertips to her lips. She's never seen anything so beautiful. Never felt so lucky and happy and free. It's a moment. The universe is saying *right here, right now*. It overwhelms her. How big, how mind-blowing, how beautiful this little life can be.

Like he's felt it too, Nathaniel tugs her into his arms. "Sneak out." His voice is a rumble in the dark. "After my grandfather goes to sleep."

Ash arches a wry brow. "That's very con artist of me. Are you sure you want me to"—she gasps in mock surprise—"con your grandfather?"

"Fucking ha ha. I deserve that." A gleam of heat in his gaze, he says, "I can't stop thinking about you."

She tries hard to roll her eyes. "Because I made you come. Simple man."

"No." He says it with so much seriousness that her heart promptly ceases its beat. "That's not it."

Ash gives him a pensive look. "I don't know if it's a good idea to do it again."

He looks both unhappy and amused.

Ash smothers a smile. She likes that she's the only one who can make him look this way. Boyish and chagrined. It's adorable, if not infuriating.

One big hand finds her hip and draws her into him. "We do have a truce."

Her eyes flick to the bar, on watch for Augustus. "Playing that card, are we?"

"I am."

"No feelings, right?" She tries to keep the words light, but they sink like sludge in her gut.

Nathaniel blinks, something like disagreement washing over his features. "No feelings."

"Just sex," she says, letting her restraints fall away. "Pure, unadulterated sex."

His hand finds her face, cupping her cheek. A dizzying rush shoots through her as the rough pad of his thumb caresses over her lower lip. The way he's touching her is primal. It makes her heat down below. She's only one strong kiss away from paralysis.

"Come to my room tonight. Don't make me fucking beg." He's looking at her like he'll die if he doesn't get an answer. If it's anything but yes.

In her periphery, Augustus appears. He's shuffling along the beach path, a trio of beers in his hands.

"Nathaniel…" She stares into his eyes. "I…"

Again. Again with his thumb stroking slow over her lower lip.

Nathaniel's fierce gaze burns a hole into hers. "Tell me you'll come."

Too many emotions streak through her like those shooting stars. And yet fighting them seems foolish. So she says, breathlessly, "Yes."

One word shouldn't feel so dangerous, but it does.

# Chapter Twenty-Two

I T'S WHAT HE ALWAYS SUSPECTED. SHE IS A CAT.
Beside him, Ash stretches and flexes in the sheets. Wild black hair, long limbs, sunlight on her porcelain skin. Christ. The places he can explore. New details he can uncover. Like the little arrow on the curve of her ass.

"You up?" he asks, leaning over her to kiss her back.

"Mmm." The sheets rustle. "No thanks to you."

Her low, throaty moan has him hard again. He can still feel her on him. When she came to him early this morning after his grandfather had gone to coffee. She jumped into his arms, and they fucked for hours.

And now it's noon. They missed breakfast and the art museum.

He turns to the balcony. The sun is high in the sky. For him, sleeping in is like a foreign antigen. He's always tried to fight it off. Clearly, Ash is a creature of sloth and habit. He leans over again. This time to kiss her bare shoulder. His beautiful creature. His dangerous obsession.

For the last two days, they haven't stopped. Sneaking away to fuck each other after bottomless brunches. Conversations that blow his mind, right before she blows him.

His hands must be magnetized for her, because any hallway, any elevator, he automatically finds her. So absorbed in Ash Keller that it unnerves him to think he's lost his head over a woman like this.

It's unlike anything he's ever experienced before.

She's unlike anyone he's ever known before.

Irascible, infuriating, irritating, and irresistible.

He runs a hand down her spine to the curve of her ass. "You have good bones."

A dark head pops out of the comforter. A smile curves her lips. "Thinking of carving me up?"

He brackets her jaw. "Not anytime soon."

Mischief flares in her gray-green eyes. "You're becoming very aggressive," she murmurs before their lips meet and he kisses her senseless.

Ash moans and tugs him on top of her. Goddamn, he could get used to this. Kissing this woman every day for the rest of his life.

But he can't go there. He needs to reroute his brain.

This is a vacation no-strings no-feelings fuck.

Still, to reduce Ash to that? It makes him feel like a fucking shithead.

A knock on the door.

"Shit." Ash pulls back in a panic and dives back under the covers.

"Room service," he deadpans.

Somehow, they've made it through the last two days without getting caught. He doesn't feel the need to sneak around, but Ash is adamant that no one know. She never stays over. He'd be lying if he said it didn't bother him.

He answers the door, lets in the valet and waits while the food is set up. All the while, Ash stays buried in the mound of pillows.

After tipping the valet, he shakes the bed. "Coast is clear, Bigfoot."

The comforter whips off the bed, and then Ash is blinking into the sun. She's naked, bare-faced and beautiful. The way his body reacts is ridiculous.

"We have food. Hydration." He points at the white-tableclothed table set up with a spread. "I didn't know what you liked, so I ordered..."

Standing, she sweeps a delighted gaze over the table. Coffee. Pastries. Benedicts. "The whole menu." Sashaying past him, she peeks over her shoulder and grins. "You don't have to show off anymore, Doctor Whitford. You already got me into bed."

Frowning, he grasps her hip. "That wasn't the point of this." She eats like a toddler, and if he can give her sustenance once a day, it eases his mind.

"Don't look so serious." She plants a kiss on his lips, then surveys the table, lifting cloches and inspecting the food. "You can tell a lot by a person's breakfast order." Ash lifts the lid on a bowl of oatmeal, makes a face, slams it down with a clang. "What are you, Nathaniel Whitford," she says, holding out an invisible microphone, "choosing to partake in today?"

He plays along. "Wheat toast, eggs over easy, and granola and milk."

"Ah. A simple, practical, extremely boring meal."

He laughs. "It's more to ward off the Whitford family curse of high cholesterol."

When she uncovers a bowl of tropical fruit and Greek yogurt, her eyes light up. Nathaniel takes note.

Ash claims the bowl and pours out two cups of coffee. Once they've both picked their breakfast, they slide back into bed. Ash, naked, curls up against the pillows. They sit and eat. Fall into a simple, easy silence that Nathaniel likes too much.

Nothing has ever felt better than being with this woman.

Beside him, Ash picks through the fruit. Mango. Pineapple. She smiles. Spears a hunk of coconut.

"How is it?" Nathaniel asks.

"Perfection. Did you know coconut's my favorite fruit?" She wrinkles her nose. "Favorite nut?" With a shrug, she kicks her impossibly long legs over Nathaniel's lap. "My mom always made me these snowy white coconut cakes for my birthday. Historic coconut cakes like ten feet tall." She waves her fork in the air above her. "Truly gargantuan. One year, she was taking it from the oven and dropped it. Smashed it all over the ground. She stood there, stunned, and then she started to cry." Color deepens on her cheeks.

"So Tessie and I grabbed forks, popped a squat and ate it off the ground. Then my mom joined us. It was the best fucking birthday."

He smiles at her smile. "Sounds fun."

She nudges him with her foot. "Which reminds me. You still owe me a coconut."

Amusement fills him. "I'll be sure to swing by the grocery store."

Rolling her eyes, Ash flops back against the bed. "Tell me something fascinating about you. Really wow me, Nathaniel."

"See this?" He nods at the scar on his shoulder.

"What's that from?" Her eyes glitter. "Knife attack on the port bow?"

"Patient in the ER stabbed me with his ballpoint pen when he woke up from anesthesia."

"War wound. How tragic." Leaning in, she sweeps her red lips across the puckered scar.

His heart jumps. Not to mention his cock.

Ash's brows draw together. "Did you always want to be a doctor?"

He wraps his hand around her foot. Red toenails. He waits as she tenses and is relieved when she relaxes and doesn't pull away.

"I wanted to be a marine biologist."

"You got close."

"I did. What about you?"

"Junk food taster, age eight. Then trash compactor. I loved smashing things."

He chuckles. These brief, fleeting moments where she drops her guard. He craves them.

"I used to want to be a doctor," she offers.

He tilts his head, surprised, but remains quiet, waiting for the story there.

"If you can believe that." Her laugh is light. "After I found out I had diabetes. Like I could fix myself."

Frowning, he runs his hands over her thigh. Those tattoos

he knows all about. The black rose she got to celebrate her death doula certification. The colorful lotus watercolor to honor her aunt's passing. "There's nothing about you that needs fixing."

She purses her lips, thoughtful, and stabs another piece of fruit. "I don't know. Maybe."

He doesn't like that. Her response, her flat tone make his heart constrict in his chest.

She shifts in the sheets. Sets her bowl down. "All my life, I could never really stay with anything. I had all these jobs. Professional mourner. Wedding objector." Her eyes flick guiltily to his. "I was all over the place. Sometimes, I still feel like that. Grasping at rings, desperate to be the person I thought I was, all while everyone is trying to tell me who they think I should be. I don't know. The sameness of life was always so boring to me. I could never sit still. I liked the dark, the gloom, the weird. But I made bad professional choices." She utters a bitter laugh. "Bad life choices."

"You do that," he says gently. "When you talk about yourself. Put yourself down."

"Observation skills?" She arches a brow. "This early in the morning?" It comes off light, like a tease, even though it's more of a push.

When it comes to Ash, he's learning she has something he can't touch. But he wants to. He wants to open that box.

The wild thrill of Ash Keller is his new favorite thing.

"What would you do?" he asks. "If you could do anything?" He wants to get as much out of her as he can before she clams up.

A sudden shyness crosses her face.

"Honestly..." She laughs, then bites her lip in that endearing yet vulnerable way he's learned is her nervous tic. "This. I love this whole death doula thing. For the first time, I feel like I've found my calling. And like it's enough to..." She trails off, a slight break to her voice.

"What?" he presses.

"To make it a business." Excitement leaps into her words.

"*My* company. Have a whole website and everything. I have ideas. A name." She pulls her knees under her chin, wrapping her arms around her legs. "*A Very Good Death.*"

"I like that."

She laughs. "I feel like a freak even commercializing death, but…"

"Not a freak," he interjects. "You offer a service that's needed. You should do it."

Anyone would be lucky to have Ash by their side at the end of their life.

"Yeah. Maybe." She opens her mouth, closes it. "Like I'd even have the slightest idea where to start. In case you haven't guessed, I'm not that great at organization or business."

He studies her. Suddenly hit by the urge to pull his billionaire card and give her everything. Everything she wants, she gets. No more struggling to pay for overpriced insulin supplies. No more shitty part-time jobs. He wants Ash to have a job she loves. She'd never ask for help or handouts. Little Miss I Can Handle Anything. It's one thing he respects about her, and yet…

"But yeah. That's what I'd do." The wistfulness in her eyes falls away, replaced by a dark and hazy cloud. "Maybe one day I'll be someone with their life together. No mess. No chaos."

"Hey," he says fiercely, pulling her into his arms. Closing the gap between them. "I like your mess. Your chaos."

She shakes her head, her stubborn gaze flicking up to meet his. "You say that now."

"I mean it." He kisses her deeply. The world stops.

Purring, Ash twines her arms around his neck. Rakes her nails through his hair as they kiss and kiss and kiss.

Her smile is feline when she pulls back. She nuzzles once at his neck, bites his lip.

He tucks her unruly black hair behind her ears. He knows he told her no feelings, but he's wondering if that ship hasn't sailed. "Maybe in Maui, we can get an adjoining room."

She inhales sharply, stiffening in his arms. "Right." Twisting away from him, she moves to the edge of the bed.

His stomach gutters. He fucked up. Said the wrong thing.

"How many days until Maui?" Her voice is distracted.

"Two. Why?"

Silence.

Nathaniel's stomach sinks. "Everything okay?" He runs a hand down her back. "Ash?"

Her shoulders rise on a deep breath. She keeps her back toward him. "It's fine."

Not fine. Not the way she's leaving. Not like this.

She stands, finds her black swimsuit cover-up. Pulls it on over her head. Finally turns to face him. "I should go." Her smile is forced, awkward. "Before everyone wonders where we are."

His throat bobs. "All right."

He watches as she goes, his jaw struggling through the words.

*Stay with me.*

He wants to say it so damn badly. But they made a deal. No feelings. The last thing he wants to do is push and scare her away. Even if he is enamored with her. The word *like* is far too simple for Ash Keller.

He's completely gone for this woman.

Questioning it, controlling it, seems impossible.

# Chapter Twenty-Three

"Ash."

Making a sound of annoyance, she rotates like a kebab to absorb maximum Nathaniel Whitford warmth. Hard chest, check. Cleaving arms, check.

Fingertips sweep through her hair, the gentle sensation soothing and wondrous. She sighs again.

Warm lips graze her cheek. "Ash."

Eyes closed, she smiles. She could get used to this. Being held in his arms every morning and night. No cares. Just this very serious man who infuriates her on a daily basis. It's absolutely everything she's ever wanted.

"Ash."

Nathaniel's deep voice calls her back from her thoughts.

Her heart stops. "Shit." She rockets up in bed. Scrapes a nest of hair away from her eyes. "What time is it?"

"Midnight." He's still making those smooth, gentle caresses over her arm.

"Fuck." This is the third time she's been dangerously close to staying over. Which absolutely cannot happen. Staying over is a tripwire to an ambush of feelings.

Nathaniel watches, wearing an amused smirk, as she tosses on her clothes. "What do you think happens if we fall asleep?"

"We turn into pumpkins and then fucking combust," she hisses. "Or worse. Augustus catches us, and I get fired."

An arched brow. "There would be no firing." He's smug, finally cashing in on that billionaire privilege. "Sleeping is a necessity for good health."

She snorts. "Says the man who gets up at four a.m. to jog."

He snags her wrist. Long, tan fingers dance over her pale skin. When he pulls her toward him, his eyes are on fire. "What if you stayed the night?"

"Can't." She kisses him, bites his lip. Nathaniel releases a pleased groan. "Let me go, you tall, handsome asshole."

His eyes turn molten. But he does.

Champagne dinners at five-star restaurants. Jet skiing. Scuba diving in a reserved cove. It's been her world for the last couple of days, yet none of it holds a candle to Nathaniel.

Their time together is bliss. Paradise.

While she packs up her beach tote, the sheets rustle. He sits up, chest bare, frowning as he checks his phone. He's been waiting for an acceptance from the rig in the North Sea. It's had him in a mess for days.

He ducks his head, types out a response. It feels like there's a switchblade in her chest. She wants to grab the phone from his hands, fling it out to sea.

Still, she plays it cool. "You hear back?"

A shrug. "No. Not yet." His eyes are distant, his attention fixed on his phone.

Thank god. The knot in her stomach loosens. She never thought she'd want Nathaniel Whitford safe on shore, but here she is.

Ash chews on her bottom lip, then decides against saying more. She shoulders her bag. Walks toward the door. Pauses. On the minibar is the rock from their trip to Rainbow Falls. Shiny, bright and jagged.

Her heart hammers a warning in her ears. "You kept my rock."

He quits scrolling. Smears a hand over his whiskered jaw. His eyes clear out as he focuses on her. "Of course I did."

She gives a bobblehead nod. Takes in his stern, handsome face. His hair thrashed by her nails. His calm stance, leaning back against the headboard, watching her.

Fuck. There's too much of her in his eyes. Adoration and lust and…and…

Butterflies automatically swoop into her stomach. It's just green flag after green flag with him.

And then her stomach drops.

Too much green.

Too many feelings.

Noncommittal. They have to be noncommittal and cavalier about this.

*It's just sex.* Her mantra the last few days. What she tells herself so she doesn't detach and freak out and self-sabotage. Sleeping over, spending the night, is too intimate. It leads to attachment. And she needs to be very unattached. Even if she is starting to crave him on a level that is no longer strictly carnal.

The first sign of impending doom should be that they're no longer playing the truth/lie game. There's no need. Everything is truth. There's a comfortableness now. Her truths, her musings just spill out.

She is not in the market for a relationship. She and Nathaniel go together about as well as serial killers and normal brain waves.

Mouth suddenly dry, she swallows. "Well, okay. I'll see you."

"You better," he says solemnly, eyes heated.

Her heart somersaults. Perfect response from the perfect man. Good thing she hates it. Good thing it means absolutely nothing.

She slips out of the room, and instantly, she freezes.

Tater's coming down the long hall, headed toward the room she's sharing with Augustus, a carton of cigars in his hands.

Fuck.

Although she supposes it's about time they got caught. The last two nights, she made great lung-sputtering sprints down the hall. Trying to beat the sun and Augustus's alarm in the great race to fuck Nathaniel's brains out. She hasn't snuck around like this since she and Tessie hitchhiked to Burning Man.

"Oh shit," Tater drawls. He holds up his hand and the cigars and gapes at Ash.

Ash narrows her eyes. "Are you sneaking cigars to your cancer-afflicted grandfather?"

Tate darts a look at Nathaniel's door. His shoulders straighten with bravado. "Are you sleeping with my brother?"

They stare at each other a beat. Ash forks her fingers at her eyes, directs them to Tater. "We both have seen nothing," she whispers ominously.

"Roger that." With that agreement, Tater slips into Augustus's room.

Ash stands in the middle of the hall, scarcely able to breathe. There it is. That spark of guilt vortexing deep down in her soul.

*Fuck.*

*Fuck, fuck, fuck.*

Isn't this what she's always done? Make a mess of it? This time, she's determined not to. Because there is no *this*. No her and Nathaniel. Sex on the beach between frenemies with benefits. Nothing more. It's a situationship. Ending when the vacation does. Sure, she'll see him because of Augustus, but that's where it ends.

Or is it? Is that what she wants?

"Ugh, shit." Ash rubs at her eyes. Tries to fight the realization, the fierce want that's rising up inside her like a tsunami.

Block him, delete him from her memory, throw her heart across the Pacific Ocean, do *something* to get Nathaniel Whitford out of her brain cracks.

Now.

She'd be insane to ever play that dirty game of love again.

Even if Nathaniel hasn't shied away from her. She never feels judged when she's with him. He accepts who she is, maybe even likes it.

Trying for something more serious with him wouldn't be fair, anyway.

How can she ask anyone to love her, when all she does is ache to push them away?

She's gnawing her lip, weighing her options, when her CGM alarm goes off. Loud. Sharp. Angry.

She checks her phone. Groans.

Sixty-eight.

Not wanting to bother Augustus and Tate as they puff away, she heads for the elevators.

At the hotel bar, she orders a glass of orange juice. As she waits, she scans the lounge. In a corner booth, Claire sits alone. Her face is free of makeup, and she's wrapped in a shawl. A glass of wine to her left, a closed book to her right.

Ash sips her juice and moves in the direction of Nathaniel's mother. She's still debating about what to say when she stops. Clears her throat. "Claire?"

The older woman startles like she's remembering where she is. Her pale-blue eyes, so much like Nathaniel's, land on Ash. "Ash? What are you doing up?"

"Oh, uh…" God, she can't tell the woman that less than twenty minutes ago, her son was folding her up like a lawn chair. "Juice," she says, lifting the cup like a torch. "Minibar was out." She peers closer. Claire's face is puffy and red. "Are you okay?"

"Are you having fun on this trip?" Fingers on the stem of her glass, Claire spins it in a slow circle. "Because I don't think I'm having fun."

Ash shrugs, goes for nonchalant. "I am surviving as much as the next person, I think."

"I suppose we haven't made it easy on you, have we?"

Ash offers a small smile. "No. But I'm not in this life for easy. And I probably deserve a little hazing after what I did to your son." She looks Claire in the eye. "I apologized to him. I'm very, very sorry."

"I appreciate that." Nathaniel's mother sips her wine.

Taking that as the signal to go, Ash turns. Before she can get far, Claire's shaky voice sounds at her back.

"I don't think I can do this. With my father."

Slowly, Ash pivots. She walks back to the booth. Takes a chance and sits across from Claire. Waits for her to go on.

Finally, Claire sighs. "He wasn't there a lot, my father, but I—I still don't want him to go."

"I don't either. It could be months, or it could be years. All we can do is be there for him." She does her best not to say too much. Most people want an ear, not a lesson. "I know he loves you a lot."

"I wish he would tell me that," Claire says in a sad, faraway voice. She wipes at the corner of her eye. "All the birthdays he missed, the stories he never told me about my mother. All my life, I've felt like I'm made of strings. They're all connected to me but blowing in different directions, and I keep grasping, keep trying to thread them together for—for some connection—and now for some closure before he goes." Claire covers her face with her hands. Groans. "It's weird. I don't expect you to understand it, but—"

"No, I do." Ash laughs, smiles at Claire's words. They almost feel like Ash's own story. "I understand more than you think."

"How do I get through it? There's so much to do. Our family's not good at this." Claire gestures between them. "What you do. Engaging with others. You have something that people like." She fingers the stem of her wineglass and smirks. "Something that pisses off my husband."

Ash arches a brow. "That's really the purpose of this trip, isn't it? Rip Don a new one?"

Claire laughs, a joyous sound of relief.

For a moment, silence settles.

"You know," Ash muses. "Love and death are so similar. The beginning. The end. It's all a mystery. An unknown. Both are always on our minds. We don't control the ride, the ride controls us. And no matter how hard we prepare, no matter how much we think we've got this, we can't escape. Love. Or death." She fiddles with the edge of a napkin, swallows back the emotion bubbling up inside her. "But finding the grace to get back to one another, to understand, to forgive, is another kind of love on its own. It's not death."

"Then help me," Claire says. She sits up, mouth fixed in a determined line. "Tell me what to do. You're here to help; I'm listening."

Ash's jaw drops, and then she takes a breath, attempting to disguise her surprise. "I think you two should sit. Say a lot of big words to each other. Maybe you'll get angry, and it'll be hard, but then it's out. You only get one shot. Chance, life, love are finite.

"And when the time comes..." Her throat tightens. The backs of her eyes sting.

Dear god, no. Not tears. Not now.

"I'll be there," Ash chokes out. "For Augustus and for all of you. If you want." She swallows, but she forces herself to maintain eye contact with Claire. "I'll help. It's what I'm here for. You don't have to go through the fear and sadness of being left alone after his departure. You just feel what you feel and rage how you rage and cry how you cry, and I'll be there."

Claire rests her chin in her palm and considers Ash. "Yes," she says quietly, "I look forward to it."

# Chapter Twenty-Four

FUCKED. THE ONLY WAY TO EXPLAIN THE VIBE SINCE they left for Maui. Their plane was delayed for three hours due to engine failure. At lunch, Tate ate a shrimp cocktail that absolutely decimated him with food poisoning. The Sunrise Above the Clouds tour Augustus had been planning was canceled thanks to the heavy rain. Sure, Ash could chalk all of it up to first world problems, but she also thinks it's Maui problems.

To top it all off, there was a room mix-up, which means she's on the lower level of suites. Away from the Whitfords. Augustus is pissed. He did all he could to move her, but because the resort is fully booked due to a wedding (of course it's a wedding), there's nothing they can do.

Being on her own down here only has Ash feeling more alone. Left behind.

As she walks down the hall to room 1313—even her room number feels like bad luck—she reads Tessie's texts.

**I have a voodoo doll with Jakob's name on it.**

**I'm so proud of you, Ash.**

**Observe, do not absorb. Unless it's Nathaniel's righteous dick.**

Her cousin's warm, supportive words have Ash feeling like she can rally and get through the next five days.

Maybe.

Ash presses her key card against the reader, pushes the door open.

"Fuck," she says, blinking.

Clearly, Augustus saved the best resort for last. The ocean-view guestroom is bright and airy. Gives coastal-chic vibes.

Oversized leather armchairs, a plush J-shaped couch and a hot tub in the living room. The place is as luxurious as it gets.

Tessie would flip her shit if she saw this room.

Ash drags herself over to the balcony. Unlocks the sliding door and steps out. The sky is dark and ominous. Thick, tropical air, the scent of petrichor envelop her. Suddenly, it's hard to breathe. She aches to crawl out of her skin. To teleport back to LA, to Tessie, to anywhere but here.

Despite how hard she's worked to outrun them, move past them, the ghosts from her past have found her. And *boo!* is the whisper in her ear.

She and Jakob planned to honeymoon in Maui. It's where she agonized over every detail. She'd joked to Tessie that it was the one thing she had actually planned in her life after Jakob tossed a hand up and said *I don't care where we go, babe, as long as I don't miss football.*

*I hate him,* she thinks. *And I'm tired, so very fucking tired of thinking about him.*

It's not just the memory of her honeymoon, all those old feelings, wreaking havoc on her emotions. The end of the trip looms. The end of paradise. Of Nathaniel.

The thought is a sharp pain in her chest.

But that's how it works, right? Those are the terms they've agreed on.

In life, everything ends. Especially love. It's foolish trying to keep it.

Foolish trying to hold on to something she'll only lose.

Because that's what happens to her.

She loses.

Blinking tears from her eyes, she peers over the railing. The ocean is so close she could touch it. The fall is so far it's dizzying. With a shaky hand on the railing, she forces herself to remember how to breathe. To remember what it feels like to kiss Nathaniel. Under the stars. In his bed.

She smiles beneath the dark curtain of her hair. Through the sheen of tears.

"Don't jump. I'd miss you."

She lifts her head at the sound of the deep, familiar voice. Inside, her chest is a firefly.

The sight of Nathaniel on the neighboring balcony roots her. Oxygen returns to her lungs.

"What—what are you doing here?" She's so surprised she doesn't even have a barbed comeback.

"Traded rooms with your neighbors," Nathaniel says evenly, hands in his pockets. "Knocked on their door and told them they were staying next to a burgeoning homicidal maniac, and they all but begged me to stay here instead."

She fights to keep a cool exterior. Even though every emotion inside her is a powder keg.

A hand propped on her hip, she tilts her head. "They did, did they?"

Nathaniel rocks back on his heels. "Uh-huh."

"Then get over here, asshole."

With ease, he scales the small drop between their balconies. This tall, thoughtful billionaire, this very serious man who fears nothing. Not even her.

He comes toward her, the look on his face soft, hesitant. "I didn't want you to be alone."

"You did that?" she breathes. "For me?"

He smiles, the corners of his eyes creasing. "Of course I did."

She doesn't say anything. She can't. Instead, she throws herself into his arms and shamelessly burrows into his hard frame. "Thank you," she murmurs. His shirt smells like salt and sea. A hit of calm for every atom in her body.

He smooths a hand down her hair. Then, taking hold of her chin, tilts her face to his. Brow furrowed, he searches her eyes. "You okay, beauty?"

Her stomach somersaults at the endearment. The thorns

around her heart pulse. "From Bigfoot to beauty. How'd I get there?"

Nathaniel's mouth tips in a pleased grin. "Very easily, in fact."

He slips his hands to her waist. As he anchors her to him, he says, "My grandfather isn't here. We're neighbors. I think you know what this means."

"I finally get to throw you off the balcony with no witnesses."

His chuckle is a husky, deep rumble that shakes her frame. "No." Sobering, he regards her, gaze hopeful. Tentative. "Stay the night with me."

"That's dangerously close to feelings."

Frowning, he runs his big hands up her arms. Her body heats at the contact. At the way he keeps her close, connected at all times.

"I don't care. I want some time with you." He says it so quietly that it's nearly drowned out by the sound of the ocean.

A weak laugh pops out of her. "I'm sure you have better things to do than watch me sleep."

He sweeps his thumb over her bottom lip. "On the contrary. I'm pretty sure it's my ideal hobby."

Ash draws a breath. He's softer with her. All his barbs and taunts and evil eyes now come coated in a sheen of affection. He's shown her a different side of him she never expected. So why can't she do that with him? Let him in? Sleep over? Because it's all too close. Too many feelings.

She wants the German shepherd back. Because the golden retriever she sees in his eyes frightens her.

She rests against him flush and lays her head on his chest. That's when she realizes her hands are wrapped in the fabric of his shirt, like all she wants to do is become one with his body.

Shit. Maybe she hasn't been as good at keeping her walls up

as she thought. Keeping Nathaniel out. For once in a long time, it feels like someone sees her. Knows her for who she is.

Because he's more than the fling from a few days ago.

After only a few days, Nathaniel's a comfort. A need. That person who can get her through anything, especially Maui. Already, he's holding her together, igniting dopamine levels so high they edge out her anxiety.

On a heavy sigh, Nathaniel adjusts her in his arms. They stay like that, taking in the tropical scenery. The lush mountains. The thunderous beach.

She can't explain her many rioting feelings for him. So she doesn't try. She just enjoys. For as long as she has him.

---

The bed frame creaks as Ash tiptoes out of bed. She pads, feet bare, across the cool marble floor. With a second look at Nathaniel, who sleeps face down, arms curled around his pillow, she slips into the bathroom and locks the door behind her.

She sits on the edge of the tub and dials.

"Hi," she says into the phone. She cups her hand against the mouthpiece. "It's me again. Third time calling, third time no answer. I promise I'm not stalking you…" She frowns. "Which I realize is something a stalker would say. Would you just…call me back?"

She hangs up and clutches the phone to her body as her guilty heart ricochets in her chest. Squeezing her eyes shut, she pushes to standing. Tiptoes back to Nathaniel. The room smells of sex and salt and sea.

"Ash," he murmurs in his sleep. His muscular back rises and falls with the steady rhythm of his breath. He's the most beautiful man she's ever seen.

In the dark, she smiles. He could eat her name, swallow it

down into that warm, chiseled, tender heart of his and hold it there. Keep her.

She kisses his back. His freckled shoulder blade.

After she gathers her things, she studies his handsome face, boyish in the moonlight. Touches his lips with trembling fingers. Touches her own.

*You, me,* she thinks.

If only it were that easy.

# Chapter Twenty-Five

As Nathaniel expected, Ash is fifteen minutes late. His heartbeat becomes irregular when she appears, slicing through the restaurant. She sits beside him at the round table, amid the clatter of the brunch buffet and his siblings' chatter.

"You look more pale and tired than usual," he remarks, lifting his coffee cup to his lips. She must have snuck out of his room at an ungodly hour. When he woke around three a.m., she was gone.

It's like a vise around his heart. It pisses him off.

She gives him a dirty look while reaching for a croissant. "At least I'm not dressed like a leprechaun."

The sharp tone in her voice makes him want to take her back to his room and bury his cock between her soft, wet thighs. Christ, he craves her banter. Can't get enough of those under-the-breath asides that carve him up.

Can't get enough of *her*.

There's nothing about her that's a passing interest anymore. Or a fling. The awareness is undeniable every time he sees Ash. This is about feelings.

Fucking feelings. He promised he'd steer clear, and look where he is. So obsessed he can't even see straight.

He wishes he could say the same for Ash. Her walls are up. Every time he gets close, she pulls back.

It's Maui. It's obvious. She's been agitated since they got here. The defeated look on her face when he saw her on the balcony yesterday. Unspoken pain in her eyes.

What has this girl survived? That's what he wants to know.

Why does Hawaii make her flinch? And goddamn does that lipstick ever come off?

Whatever the problem, he wants to fix it. But she won't let him.

His father drops his cloth napkin, checks his watch. "Let's wrap this up soon. The boys have things to do."

"The boys," Ash murmurs, popping a piece of croissant into her mouth. "Is that a secret syndicate that fights billionaire crime?"

Delaney, three mimosas deep, looks up from her plate. "That should be a TV show."

Nathaniel's silent as he leans back in his chair. The idea of splitting up from Ash makes his skin itch. They have such little time left together. At that, he frowns. How many days is it again? Four?

At the thought, it's hard to get air.

Needing to touch her, a reassurance he still has time, he slides his hand along her thigh beneath the table. Squeezes.

Ash keeps a straight face. Only the curled edge of her blood-red lips gives anything away.

He slides his hand higher. Over the blooming iris tattoo she got after crowd surfing at Bonnaroo. The tattoo he traced with his lips, his tongue last night, before reaching the apex of her thighs and going in for a taste of her.

Touching her is a necessity. Another way—a better way—to live.

Fantastically beautiful. Like the dangerous allure of the sea. Only it's everywhere he wants to be. Riding those waves, dipping into every deep, dark, secret part of her.

She spreads her thighs, the subtle invite making his pulse quicken.

*Jesus.*

His cock could punch through drywall.

He's pressing a finger against the wet seam of her panties when his father says, "Our tee time's at noon. You think you can swing it, Augustus?" Don smirks. "It's right around your mid-day nap."

Augustus sips his coffee easily. Smiles. "Never too tired to kick your ass in a round of golf, Don."

His grandfather's a good liar. Nathaniel will give him that. The dark circles under his eyes give away the truth. He's fading. Slow, but soon. Although the man could probably muster the strength to take a swing at his father with a golf club. Nathaniel wouldn't blame him. His father is acting like an ass.

"You take breaks if you need to, Dad," Claire says, squeezing Augustus's arm.

In his periphery, Ash's lashes flutter. He sweeps a thumb over the bud of her clit. Her thighs tremble. Through the thin silk of her tank top, her nipples are pinched. He rotates his rhythm.

Ash gasps. Her dark head falls forward. She grips her silverware with white knuckles.

"Enjoying that croissant?" he asks, voice devoid of emotion.

She whips her head in his direction, gives him a deadly glare.

"Ash?" his mother asks, concerned. "Are you okay?" To his surprise, his mother's been cordial to Ash since they got to Maui.

"I'm fine." She huffs out a breath. "All good."

Nathaniel bites back a smile. Withdraws his hand.

Ash flounces back against her seat, breathing heavily. Her eyes are a swirl of green and gray, glassy and glazed. "I hate you," she whispers.

Don shakes out his paper. "Claire, you have my card. Try not to spend it all in one place."

For a brief second, his mother looks irritated. Then she folds up her napkin without another word.

"Designated gender roles." Ash's lips curl. "We love to see it, don't we, Don?"

Nathaniel fights a smile.

His father makes a sound of dismissal and goes back to his paper.

At that, Ash sighs and taps at the screen of her phone.

"What're you doing?" Nathaniel asks, tilting a fraction closer.

"Marking down how often he speaks to me," Ash replies, eyes on the device. "So far, I have been acknowledged once, grunted at four times, and addressed by name negative three."

Nathaniel frowns. She says it lightly, but inside, he's seething.

Delaney drums the table in excitement. "And for the *ladiesss*, spa and shopping day in town!" She lifts her mimosa glass high.

"Wait. What?" Ash's voice is flat. Her panicked eyes rush to his.

This time he doesn't bother to hide his smirk.

"Shopping. Sounds right up your alley, Bigfoot."

"Oh, you fucking Tall Asshole," she growls.

Fuck. It's all he can do not to kiss that sharp mouth in front of everyone.

"Lobby." Don's sharp bark calls the group to order. "Five minutes, Nate."

Ash glowers. "Nathaniel," she says under her breath.

In the lobby, he and Ash hover close, but not too close, to one another. His father calls their separate drivers. Heat rises in the space between them. He's tempted to touch her, but he can't do that right now. Not with his family around. And why does it feel like his heart's getting yanked out by a scythe?

Ash's husky voice sounds. "What's wrong?"

Nathaniel rolls out his shoulders. "I hate wasting a day with my father."

Eyes searching his face, she lifts her hands. "Jaw," she says, tapping his jaw. And it unclenches. "Now shoulders." Another tap.

Nathaniel's body relaxes. The tension eases out of him as easy as that. Because of Ash. She's a goddamn dream.

"Think of it this way," she says. "It's another day with your grandfather."

Nathaniel nods, but he's hyper-focused on only one thing. "You're right. But it's a day away from you."

Eyes wide, she looks startled by his words. Then expertly resets her face into an expression of nonchalance. "We have tonight."

*But it's not enough*, he wants to say. *Four more days with you is not enough.*

"Yeah," he rasps. It feels like there's acid in his windpipe.

Ash grins. "If you do one thing for me today, please kick Don's ass."

"You can count on it."

Behind Ash, his father's gesturing frantically. If there's one thing Don can't miss, it's golf.

Nathaniel blows out a frustrated breath. "I have to go."

Ash grabs the strap of his golf bag before he can walk away. Yanks it backward so sharply he almost lands on his ass. He catches himself. Spins.

She pulls him against her. In her eyes, fire. "Kill you later."

His gaze falls to her lips, then lowers.

Her boots.

"Hold on," he says, and he hits his knees.

For a long minute, Ash is stunned speechless. She blinks down at him.

Eagerly, he slides a hand over her slim calf and looks up at her.

"Watching you nearly die every day is fucking killing me," he growls, tightening her laces. He takes his time. Lets his gaze travel up those long legs. Beneath her short skirt. To the faint dampness of arousal on the inside of her thighs.

Christ. Instantly, his dick's hard as a rock.

He loops her last lace, then looks up. "There."

"My hero," she quips. Her words are clipped. But her face is flushed. Her eyes wild.

He's still trying to figure out how this woman made him go from emotionally unavailable to having feelings and tying her goddamn boots in the middle of a hotel lobby in front of his entire family and a handful of strangers.

One thing's for certain.

He doesn't care.

Not one goddamn bit.

Nathaniel watches his grandfather quietly. The older man is tired. Putting on a good front, a show for his family. But he sits in the cart at all greens. Resting.

With a long breath out, Nathaniel wipes a towel down his sweaty face. Then he tosses it into the back of the cart. He joins his grandfather, settling in the driver's seat. Before he can say a word, Augustus says, "Something on your mind?"

Ash. She's on his mind. Between his backswing and his pitch shot, he's been driving himself crazy thinking of her. He's an asshole for turning her loose with his mother and sister.

"Have you been enjoying the trip, Grandpops?"

"I have." Augustus nods. "I admit, the start was a bit rough, but it's been better than I expected."

*Because of Ash*, Nathaniel thinks.

He reaches into his pocket. Inside, he rolls the rock Ash gave him from Rainbow Falls between his fingers. It's just a rock, yet it feels like so much more.

They watch as Don, at the ninth hole, manhandles his club.

Augustus scoffs. Crosses his arms over his chest and leans back. "Might as well give him a baseball bat."

An easy bark of laughter escapes Nathaniel.

"I want to tell you something," Augustus says, turning to him. "And only you."

Nathaniel tenses, but he keeps his mouth shut. Gives his full attention.

"When I get back to LA, I'm not doing any more chemo."

Nathaniel tugs a hand through his hair, feeling sucker punched. "Grandpops, I don't understand."

Augustus holds his eyes, no bullshit in his gaze. "Yes, you do. You're a doctor."

He does.

He knew early on that chemo and radiation were only

extending the time his grandfather had left. That with this type of cancer, the chances were slim. But it's still not easy to hear. That the hope he had is just that. Hope.

"I'm terminal." Augustus looks out at the fairway. "I don't want to drag this out. So I am pivoting, and I'm making peace with that choice."

He puts an arm around his grandfather's shoulders. "I believe you," he says thickly. He'll never be ready for this. And that hard thought cracks something inside him. Moisture collects at the backs of his eyes. Christ, he doesn't think he's cried since he was a child.

But he doesn't fight it. Instead, he scrubs a hand over his face and says, "I love you, Grandpops."

His grandfather pulls him in for a hug. Nathaniel holds tight to him for a long time.

"Nate dawg!" Tater's goofy voice pulls them from the moment. "Dude, check this out."

In unison, they look over to see him wearing a beer bucket on his head.

Augustus gives a wry laugh. "Please take care of that kid when I'm gone."

Nathaniel rolls his eyes. "Goddamn idiot," he says dryly, though he's secretly thankful for the levity.

"Now don't tell anyone about my plans yet," Augustus orders, coming back to the conversation.

Nathaniel's throat tightens. He curls his fingers around the steering wheel. Squeezes. "What about Ash?"

"I plan to tell her." Augustus's voice is steady, but the tremor in his words betrays his nerves. "I plan to tell everyone at the end of the trip."

Fuck. The last thing he wants to do is keep secrets from Ash. Not now. Not when they're—

They're what?

"I don't want you to worry." His grandfather's somber voice derails his thoughts. "We are prepared. We have Ash." He squeezes

Nathaniel's shoulder. "And after I'm gone, you'll move on. You'll all move on."

Already, he's sick to his stomach. Move on? Is that what he's supposed to do when he gets on that plane? Forget about her? Forget their time together ever happened? Impossible.

Is that what she'll do?

A rush of denial floods his chest as images pop like sunbursts in his head. Ash stretching catlike in a bed that isn't his. Her red lipstick smeared over another man's chest. Those long black nails making their mark down someone else's back.

Fuck. Fuck this.

He's going to have a fucking heart attack. He has to fight the urge to gun the gas on the golf cart and drive like a madman back to town. Track down Ash. Tell her—

"Won't you?"

He blinks his way back to the present. His grandfather's staring at him expectantly.

"What?" he asks.

"You'll move on. The North Sea? It's what you want, right?"

He swallows, making a pained noise. An ache settles behind his ribs. "I don't know anymore."

Last night, he received an email promising they'd have an answer for him soon. It seemed so appealing when he applied. When he had wanted to get away from it all.

Expression thoughtful, Augustus settles back into the seat. "One thing I've learned in this life, Nathaniel, is that if we're lucky, we get one shot. One death. One life. One good love. I only had ten years with Rosalea. But the one thing I'm glad for…" Augustus tilts his head back, absorbs the warmth of the late afternoon sun. "I'm glad I didn't hold back my feelings."

For some reason, Nathaniel thinks of Ash.

For some reason, he doesn't stop himself.

# Chapter Twenty-Six

FOR THE BETTER PART OF THE AFTERNOON, ASH SHOPS until she literally drops. The swanky outdoor mall is drenched in afternoon sunshine. Luxury retailers and high fashion shops seem out of place in the laid-back atmosphere of Hawaii.

"Go," she huffs, plopping onto a bench.

Delaney and Claire blink down at her. She has never been more in fight-or-flight mode than when she's in a mall. All afternoon, she's played her part, not wanting to alienate the Whitfords. Now? She's done. Personal shopper is not in her death doula duties.

"Are you sure?" Delaney asks. Shopping bags hang off her arm. "There's a sale at Gucci."

Ash squints. Sweat beads her brow. "Don't they have Gucci in Los Angeles?"

"You haven't even bought anything," she complains.

Claire gives her daughter an amused look. "I'm going to get a coffee," she says. "Anyone want one?"

Ash shakes her head. "Leave me here to rot."

With that, mother and daughter turn away, in search of clothes and caffeine.

As soon as they leave her, Ash breathes a sigh of relief.

Her feet have hurt less hiking with Nathaniel than they have today. Typically, she'd considered herself well skilled in the art of shopping—how could she not be with Tessie as her cousin?—but clearly, for the Whitford women, shopping is an extreme sport.

Her phone vibrates with a message from Tessie: **How are you? You need me to fly down there and kick Maui's ass?**

As soon as she sees it, the words fold around her like a hug, and that tightness in her chest loosens.

**I'm surviving,** she types back. **But my wallet might not. How are you?**

**Fine!!!**

Ash frowns at the barrage of exclamation points.

**Baby still on your bladder?**

**No, I think I'm just dehydrated.**

A swell of music, and Ash looks up from her phone. A woman with a ukulele is in the center of the square.

Smiling, she stands and drifts through the crowd. She tips the musician and then heads back to her bench. Only, she doesn't get far. As she passes a pink brick storefront, she stops. And even though gasps are more Tessie's MO, it's exactly what she does.

In the window of the boutique, on a mannequin that no normal woman could even hope to emulate, is a long white silk dress. Spaghetti straps, a sweetheart neckline. The exact opposite of vampy. Feminine, flowy and delicate. When was the last time she wore something so girlish?

"That's hella cute."

Ash startles at the voice in her ear.

"I don't know," she says, twisting around and telling her heart to settle. Delaney's like the ghost of shopping past who keeps popping up when Ash least expects it.

"It's pretty." A new shopping bag hangs off Delaney's wrist. Lifting her hot pink sunglasses, she says, "Virginal beach vibes. I like it."

*But would Nathaniel like it?*

The thought pops into her head so fast she cringes.

Jesus.

What is wrong with her? Dressing for a man like some Stepford woman? What kind of hell has she wrought? Still, it brings a smile to her face. Imagining his reaction. Because isn't that how he's made her feel this last week? Vulnerable. Delicate. Sexy.

When she arrived, she wasn't sure she'd survive this vacation.

Now all that's on her mind, day in and day out, is seeing Nathaniel. Bantering at brunch. A good-natured race over the boulders on a sunset hike. Sneaking to each other's rooms at night.

She doesn't feel so alone on this trip. Not anymore.

She needs him. Especially in Maui. The on-edge feeling she's had since they landed in Hawaii disappears when she's in his arms.

A week ago, she was so sure this was a fling. A truce with the enemy. But it's quickly become far more intimate. Special. Like it's hers.

The thought's sharp, cutting. A sensation she wants to hold on to.

Which means they have to end when the trip does. Continuing this relationship isn't a possibility. Ash isn't in the market for love or anything remotely related to the romance realm.

"Let me get it."

"What?" Ash jumps, spins around. Claire has appeared, an espresso in her hand. "No. I can't let you do that."

"Please." Claire smiles. "We both know nothing would piss Don off more."

Ash laughs, then shakes her head. "I really appreciate it. I do. But I'm a fully grown woman. I can buy my own dress."

"Then do it," Delaney goads.

Ash narrows her eyes.

"Delaney," Claire chides. Sips her drink. "We've talked about this. There's no peer pressure in shopping."

But Ash takes the bait and, on a whim, buys the ridiculous dress. It's more money than she should spend, but what is savings if she can't treat herself and then spiral guiltily afterward? As she leaves the store, the fancy boutique bag feels like a bomb in her hand. Only a good type of bomb. One loaded with rainbows and confetti and happiness. It's been a long time since she's felt this way. Like she's belonged. Like she has it together.

"How about manicures before dinner?" Claire asks, her wispy

voice smoking between them. "My treat." Her eyes land on Ash, and she gives a little nod as if to say *you too*.

Oh.

Stunned, Ash follows Claire and Delaney into a tiny nail salon. The room is half-empty. Tropical fish swim in wall-to-wall tanks. TVs play episodes of *The Real Housewives*. Crystals dangle from the ceiling.

They're quickly ushered into chairs. Glasses of champagne magically appear in their hands.

Is this what it feels like to be let into the Whitford circle of excellence? Manicures and mimosas? Either way, she'll take it.

Ash sits in the middle of Delaney and Claire. Her mind swims, searching for something to say. An appropriate topic.

Her mind lights on Nathaniel. Of course it'd be Nathaniel. Everything she likes about him. Everything she's trying not to like too. His hard exterior full of broody frowns and stern brows. But inside, he's like a Cadbury egg. All gooey and soft. How it's an honor to crack that shell and scoop out his goodness. His thoughts. How he's a stickler about time, a hard-ass to his siblings, but it's only because he cares so much. He doesn't know how to show it any other way. How every night, he fucks her senseless and leaves her begging for more.

But yeah, no. That's not the way to Claire's heart.

Thankfully, it's Delaney who pipes up.

"By the way." The pink-haired woman claps her hands. "I got the part in *Adieu, My Friend*. I just heard from my agent. I fly to France next month." A squeal bubbles out of her. "My entire résumé is going to be slasher flicks."

"I approve of this," Ash says, lifting her champagne in a toast.

"I'm so proud of you," Claire says, leaning forward to smile at her daughter. "That you're making your own way, DeeDee. That nothing has stopped you."

Delaney flushes. "Thanks, Mom."

When the conversation quiets, Ash asks, "Why didn't you

ever take over Augustus's company?" She bites her lip, hoping she hasn't atom-bombed what little headway she's made with Claire.

Delaney puts her phone down and shifts to face her mother, interest lighting her expression.

Claire takes on a faraway look. Like she's shuffling through memories. Reliving the past.

"I don't know. I suppose I had babies. And then…your father didn't want me to work."

"Ugh," Delaney groans, rolling her eyes at Ash.

"Oh, trust me, I wanted Fox Hotels. I have a degree in business. But life happened." She exhales as she sticks her feet in the foot bath. Her blue eyes return to Ash, Delaney. "Girls, sometimes it's a shit lesson to learn this late in life."

The curse word feels out of place coming from Claire's mouth, but both Ash and Delaney stare, riveted.

"But…I wish I'd had the courage to live a life true to myself rather than focusing on what others wanted of me."

Instantly, the air in her lungs ceases, every inch of her chest stinging.

Her job, this trip, Nathaniel, those are true things. After all those years she spent searching for purpose, for herself, she's finally found it. She's put herself first.

"It's never too late to unstick," Ash tells her. "To change."

Claire's chin dips as she smiles. "Maybe so."

The women settle into silence as their nail techs take their seats in front of them. Ash accepts the ring of nail colors, even though she's going with her tried and true.

"This color," Claire says, tapping a nail against a swatch of black. She looks at Ash, looks at the salon tech. "Like hers."

Ash's jaw drops.

Laughing, Delaney claps her hands. "Fuck yeah, Mom."

Ash's heart is a balloon on a string. Lightening, lifting. For once, she feels like Maui might just be okay. Like she can get through it. Survive.

# Chapter Twenty-Seven

SHE'LL NEVER SURVIVE THIS.
    Not tonight. Not this dinner.
    Not this fucking restaurant.

A Hui Hou, a sleek, subterranean space located a block from their hotel, has quite the haunting history. In fact, it used to be a morgue. Bodies were carved up here. Right where upscale servers trot around with bread-and-butter carts. Not like the Whitfords know that—they're more focused on the Michelin star and the white tablecloths—but Ash does.

It was one of the stops on Ash's honeymoon itinerary. A morbid stop among Jakob's parasailing and scuba diving demands. As she takes in the sign, all those old feelings bubble up until her vision swims.

The synchronicities of her life and this life are stacking up in ways she really isn't vibing with.

"Ash?"

She shakes herself out of her daze. Delaney and Claire wait for her at the entrance to the restaurant.

She forces a smile. Slivers of anxiety slice up her gut like shrapnel. "You go ahead. Bathroom break."

Seconds later, she's locking herself in a bathroom stall and sending an SOS text to Tessie.

"Fuck. Fuck, fuck, fuck."

She's suffocating. She's sweating in her beautiful silk dress. Fuck. This is why she doesn't wear silk. Because she's the wrong kind of woman.

Despite her meltdown, she pulls it the fuck together and gets back out there. *Raise hell, Ashabelle,* her father always says.

The restaurant is tiny, with brick walls and dim lighting. She scans the room. Finds the Whitfords seated around a long rectangular table by the window. The men brood silently while Delaney and Claire are animated and chatty. It seems a little spa and shopping day worked wonders. Her gaze finds Nathaniel, whose mouth is a flat line as he listens to Don. As if her attention is a physical caress, he senses her. His head swivels. His entire face changes. His eyes widen and a crooked grin tugs at his lips.

Then he's standing, crossing the room, moving toward her.

A hook snags Ash's heart. He looks achingly handsome in pressed khakis and a black T-shirt stretched tight over his muscular chest. His golden hair is ruffled from his day on the golf course. If she could craft herself a blueprint of the perfect man, it'd be Nathaniel.

Eyes locked on her, he comes to a stop. "Ash."

"Hi," she breathes, suddenly shy. "I'm late. I just—"

"It's not that." He runs a hand over his mouth. His blue eyes are wide, startled, dazed as he gives her a thorough once-over. When he zeroes in on her face, warmth pulses through her. "Your dress—"

"Was an impulse purchase." Her laugh is awkward. "I know it's not me. It screams virginal beach prom queen, but I saw it on a mannequin in a window and thought it was pretty."

"I think you're pretty," he says, and all her objections fall away. He slides a finger along one strap and stops at her neck. Thumb caressing her throat, he dips closer, his voice low. "No matter what you wear. Stomping boots. Vampire garb. White dresses that fuck up my heartbeat. I love it all."

"Even more than your rock collection?" She keeps her tone cool, controlled to hide her emotion. What his words mean to her.

He closes his eyes, and when he opens them again, there's something heated and raw there. "Even more than that. Although igneous is a pretty close second."

A warm sunset blooms inside her. But a heartbeat later, she remembers where she is, and the sensation fades.

Nathaniel studies her face. Frowns. Asks, "Are you okay?"

"Peachy," she lies.

"Thank God you're here," he mutters. "Don's espousing the virtues of flat earth theory."

"He is not."

He grins. "Guess you have to come sit by me and find out."

The hand that goes to the small of her back as he guides her to the table has little fires building inside her heart. Those damn thorns twitch.

He pulls out the chair between his and Augustus's, waiting. Ash lowers herself, smooths her dress. Don eyes her like she's a fourteenth century rat with a bad case of the plague.

"I ordered a piña colada for you," Nathaniel says, as he settles in his own seat.

Her gaze goes to the creamy white drink in front of her place setting.

"I had them make it with sugar-free syrup and go light on the juice. I hope that's okay."

She opens her mouth. Closes it. There's a fucking rockslide happening behind her ribcage.

He drags a hand through his hair, his face suddenly tentative. "It might not be as good," he says abruptly, all business. "But—"

"No." She grabs the icy glass and locks her lips around the straw. Sucks a mighty sip of rum and lime juice. Hopes he can see how much his thoughtfulness means to her. "It's delicious."

"Delaney, Ash, and I had the loveliest day," Claire tells the table.

Ash perks up, says, "Can we all please take a moment to acknowledge Claire's nails. Because they are fabulous."

Claire stretches out a hand. Everyone *oohs* and *aahs*. Except for Don.

Dinner's delicious and insufferably long. But the

drinks—bottles of wine, too many to count—cut the sting. The conversation ranges from the injustices of the housing market to today's golf game. Claire and Augustus get to talking business, whispering softly about Fox Hotels.

Through it all, Ash's entire body is tense. Not because of where she is. But because of Nathaniel, sitting beside her. One long arm stretched out across the back of her chair. Her body heats at the slow sweep of his thumb across her shoulder. The boneheaded man isn't even trying to play hands off. It's infuriating. She loves it.

They're always moving for each other. Reaching. Touching.

It's too much.

It's not enough.

And it never fucking will be.

"Tell your father what you told us at the spa," Claire says to her daughter when the waiter's finished taking their dessert orders.

"Oh, uh…" Delaney twists her napkin, sits up straight, looks at her father. "I got the role in that French slasher film."

Tate pounds her on the back with so much force her body jolts. "Congrats, dude."

Don looks at her over his phone. Cocks a brow. "Do you know French?"

Delaney lowers her chin, swallows. "No, but I'm planning—"

"This is what I mean. You jump before you think things through." A sigh. "Just like this little job of yours." Don sets his phone down. "Don't you think you should go back to school and get a degree?" he asks, while Claire stares at him dagger-eyed.

"I don't know," Delaney mumbles. "I guess."

Ash saws her lower lip between her teeth, ready to taste blood. The crestfallen look on DeeDee's face cuts like a knife. She knows what it's like. To always be trying. To never feel like enough.

"It's not a little job. It's a lead role," Nathaniel says, speaking up.

Delaney blinks, clearly surprised at her older brother's support. "It's her career."

Excitement radiates from Delaney. "It could be a breakout

role." Her hands form a makeshift camera. She pans the restaurant. "Just like Jennifer Aniston in Lepra—"

"Delaney, please," Don snaps, holding up his hand.

Augustus smiles fondly at his granddaughter. "Chin up, my dear."

"I don't understand my children and these"—air quotes from Don—"careers."

Ash narrows her eyes at him. This is textbook schoolhouse bullying.

Nathaniel smothers a sigh. "Pretty sure we're all employed, Dad."

"You had it all, Nate," Don blusters.

The way Nathaniel cringes at *Nate* makes Ash cringe too. "The career. The girl. And you threw it all away."

"Dad." Nathaniel's needling his brow now.

"It's not too late to get back there. Be a real doctor again. Find a nice girl." Don cranes his neck and scans the restaurant.

Ash's stomach sinks. He's no doubt picking out the perfect woman for his son. She can picture it perfectly. Blond. A fine pedigree. Heels. Pearl earrings. A 401(k) and organic cotton sheets and absolutely no anxiety coursing through her system.

Eyes still on a slim, blond waitress, Don crosses his arms. "Maybe download an app or a—"

"I don't need an app, Dad," Nathaniel grits out.

"We're Whitfords." Don glances at Ash. Focuses on his son again. "You can't slum it your entire life."

Directed at her or not, it fucking stings.

Ash's face burns. The piña colada, the rum, the coconut milk settle like five hundred pounds of sludge in her stomach.

Beneath the table, Nathaniel takes her hand. Only, it slips like a limp noodle from his grasp. She can feel his burning gaze on her face, but she refuses to look at him. What is she doing here? What is she doing with him?

The realization sinks into her skin like acid. She isn't meant for this. She doesn't belong here. With the Whitfords. She's too different. Especially for Nathaniel. Suddenly, everything feels wrong. Her dress. Her skin. Nathaniel's hand grasping hers again.

Claire forces a smile, desperately searching for a topic. "So, uh, Nathaniel, are you all set for Peru?"

Silence.

Nathaniel glares at his father.

Ash takes a sip of water, then sets down the glass. "Did you know this used to be a morgue?" she says, trying to help out Claire. Trying to take that awful look off Nathaniel's face. Trying to salvage what's left of this dinner party from hell. For Augustus. That's why she's here. For him.

Claire's face creases in distress at the news, and then she fakes a smile. "Really? That is fascinating. Don't you think, Don?"

Ignoring his wife and Ash, Don leans forward. "Let me tell you something, Nate. You go out and hide yourself away on a—"

Ash slams a hand down. Every person at the table jumps.

"Nathaniel," Ash snaps.

She can't take it anymore. The botching of his name.

Don rears back. "Excuse me?"

"Your son's name is Nathaniel." She enunciates each syllable. Glares. "He hates being called Nate."

The table's silent. Barely breathing.

Every eye is on Ash, but she stares at Don calmly.

He reddens, embarrassment staining his expression. He looks directly at her. Hell must have frozen over, because it's the first time Don's acknowledged her existence.

Then he chuckles scathingly. "Augustus, why is she here? I know she's one of those weird woo-woo types, but I could do without." His nostrils flare as he draws forward again. "You've already ruined things for my son, but there's no need for you to ruin this vacation too."

There's an audible gasp from Claire.

Even seated, Nathaniel's stance turns bodyguard-like. His eyes narrow dangerously. "I know you didn't say that to her."

Tater winces. He slumps low and lazy in his chair, his gaze bouncing from Nathaniel's furious face to his father's. "That's a good way to get smacked, dawg."

"Stop acting like a tyrant, Don, and shut up," Claire snaps.

Don blinks at the fury in his wife's voice.

"Leave the poor girl alone," she says. "One nice night. It's all I asked for."

Ash squeezes her eyes shut to block out the noise. She can feel her villain era returning to her like a rogue wave.

"Apologize," comes a hard voice.

Ash opens her eyes, certain the demand is directed at her, but it's not.

Nathaniel's staring daggers at his father. "Apologize to her now."

"It's fine." Her heart hammers with adrenaline. Her chest is tight with rage. "I'm fine."

In fact, she's only getting started.

She's not doing it again. Letting someone knock her down for being her. She's fed up with every single word that comes out of Don's stupid ass mouth.

"I'll take weird, quirky and hilarious over rude, pretentious and self-absorbed any day." With each word Ash lets out, it's like a pressure releasing from her chest. Her heart. "If my presence is hard for you, then you're a bona fide piece of shit. Live with that or choose to be a better person."

Gasps from Claire and Tate. Delaney has her napkin pressed to her face, hiding the permanent scream that is her mouth.

Ash keeps going. She can't stop.

"All your offspring want is a speck of your attention. That's like a pebble in the sea. And you're so focused on tits and asses and your own Machiavellian dreams and schemes that you don't see it.

This isn't the Thunderdome, Don. It doesn't matter who fucking wins. It's a family. *Your* family."

Expression caught between outrage and embarrassment, Don opens his mouth. Probably to bluster.

Ash won't let him. Lurching in her chair, she points at Nathaniel. "This is *his* life. His." Her finger swivels to Delaney and Tate. "Their lives. They only get one. They shouldn't live to please you. If you don't get that, that's your loss. But you're missing out. Because Tate has an amazing podcast about potatoes. Delaney is killing it—well, getting killed. And Nathaniel…well…Nathaniel is someone to be proud of." Her voice cracks. "So, so proud of. Do you know he put his own life at risk to save his entire crew? He could have died, but he did that. And then he stayed, knowing it could happen again."

Don's eyes slowly flick from her face to Nathaniel's.

Her panting breath shakes from her frame. Leading to a knockout blow.

"And you don't know that because you're too pissed off about them not living up to your hustle-culture standards. Which is just so weird. You can be proud of your children for living their lives and being successful without all the weird judgmental bullshit."

Delaney and Tater glance at each other, wide-eyed.

Don doesn't respond. His jaw is so unhinged it's on the table.

Nathaniel stares at her in stunned silence, his expression indecipherable.

Her gaze settles on Augustus. "Please do not fire me. Even though I really need this job, I adore you and will be heartbroken." Looking around the table, she says, "Claire, you are too sweet for this insufferable man. Tater, always stay stupid. You are the himbo of my platonic dreams. And Delaney, you get murdered all you want. I heartily support the bloodlust."

Augustus wears a bright smile, glass of wine held loose in his hand. "I couldn't have said it better myself, my dear."

Ash inhales. Everything inside her feels wobbly. "And now...I will show myself out."

When she rockets up, Nathaniel wears a strange, stricken look on his face. He grasps desperately for her hand. "Ash—"

"I'm okay," she tells him. "I need a minute."

She takes two steps from the table, rips around, finds Nathaniel's sister. "Get your tarot."

Delaney springs out of her seat, nearly falling in the process. "You mean it?" The joy blazing across her face carves out Ash's soul.

"Fuck yes." Ash grabs a bottle of red wine. "We're taking this." She looks around the shell-shocked table. "And we're going to go see the fucking future."

Nathaniel stares up at her with an expression of worry and amusement.

She drags her fingertips across his warm palm, touched by his concern, and then she walks out of the restaurant.

What the hell did she just do?

Whatever it was, it felt really goddamn good.

# Chapter Twenty-Eight

"Holy shit," Delaney crows as they walk down to the beach. "Did you see Don's face? He was fighting for his life at that table."

Ash's mouth pulls up into a smirk. "Humbling a stranger in public has been on my bucket list for years."

"You didn't even take a slow spiral down. You took a leap off a cliff. I love it!"

Delaney passes her the bottle of wine. Ash takes a swig, passes it back.

She doesn't even feel embarrassed. All she feels is purged.

DeeDee whoops, whips around and walks backward, focus still set on Ash. "Conflict resolution queen!" she shouts, pumping the wine bottle in the air.

The night is balmy, the sun almost set. They wander past the resorts and the expensive houses until they come to a spot on the beach that Delaney deems worthy. Their hotel in the distance, minutes away.

With tired huffs, they sit on the sand. Ash nestles the bottle of wine so it stands up, and they take turns drinking from it. A big grin on her face, Delaney pulls the tarot deck out of her large woven beach bag. She unveils a silk scarf and places it on the sand, small ripples beneath it.

"How long have you been doing this?" Ash asks. She's never been one for organized religion, but the spiritual, the woo-woo, the weird, has always helped her ground herself. She loves the mythology of it. That blend of magic and supernatural.

"Since I started acting," Delaney says, adjusting to cross her legs. Her turquoise earrings glint in the fading sun. "I taught myself tarot between shoots while I was waiting on set." The cards slip smoothly between her fingers as she shuffles. "At first, I did it because I was bored. Scared the shit out of Zendaya once."

Ash laughs.

"I'm not a psychic, and I don't have the gift of clairvoyance or anything. It's meditative for me. It forces me to think about things I maybe wouldn't. We decide our future, yes, but the cards can help us to make that decision." A shrug of her slender shoulder. "It helps me work out the kinks."

"The kinks. I like that."

They share a smile.

Delaney's face loses some of its brightness. "Maybe I'm not good at it, but..."

"But," Ash clarifies, unwilling to let her do this. "But you like it, right? Bare minimum, no one says shit about it. Best is they support you. It's not hard to support a hobby that someone you care about loves."

"Yeah," she says softly, smoothing a square of sand beside her. "That's true." Then she inhales and straightens up. "Let's keep it easy. Three-card spread."

Ash lifts a brow. "Sounds sexy."

Concentration creasing her face, Delaney lays three cards on the sand. "Do you have a life crisis?"

Ash chuckles. "Doesn't everyone?"

"Past, present, future, then."

Ash admires the cards. With their ethereal images and moody jewel tones, they're stunning. She thinks about the time she and her mom had a reading done at a cheap strip mall. It was a terrible experience and not at all real, but it still made her giddy about the what-else-is-out-there.

"Ooh, this deck is sassy," Delaney breathes, a myriad of emotions playing out on her face. She hovers her hand over the cards. The second she does, a gust of wind sweeps up, threatening to upsend them. With a squeal, she tosses her body over the scarf and the spread to shield it.

Ash's eyes meet Delaney's. Electric awareness crackles between them. "If the ocean pulls back," she whispers, "we run."

Mouth ajar, Delaney nods. Then she straightens, inspects the cards. Her glazed nail moves, taps a heart impaled with three swords. "This is the three of swords. Your past."

"An impaled heart. It's perfect." Her throat is burning.

"It means loss." The energy between them kicks up. As does the wind. "You have said goodbye to more things than you have cared to in your past. Things you still grieve for. Things that taught you what life costs, and that's made you…pull away."

Her words have ice sinking in Ash's gut. Brief flashes of the past. Microbursts of loss. Her health. Aunt Sophie. Jakob. Tessie.

Delaney moves on to the second card. Taps it like she did the first. Her eyes have taken on a strange glassy quality. "Your present. The Tower."

Ash winces at the image of figures falling from a flaming stone tower. She drinks from the bottle of wine.

"New things are coming into your life. Things that scare you." Delaney's gaze flickers to Ash's. "You simultaneously like it and want to run from it. You're not sure how to work your feelings into the story you've told yourself. You're fighting them because you're scared. There are cracks in your life, and something about the here and now is filling them."

Heart hammering hard, Ash digs her fingers in the sand. All this woo-woo, this introspection, this life, it resonates.

Delaney nestles her elbows on her crossed thighs. "I think it means my brother."

Ash's laugh is sharp as a blade. "No way."

With a flat yeah-right look, Delaney says, "I don't need a tarot deck to tell me that. Tonight, you two were all over each other. Even if you physically weren't."

Her cheeks flame with embarrassment. So much for remaining inconspicuous.

"He and Camellia..." Delaney's voice kicks up an octave. Full of anger. "Their couple's spark was not sparking like it should be. They were like Barbie and Ken robots. Pretty packaging, but she wasn't the one." Her expression shifts to smug satisfaction. "Let's just say I wasn't super upset when I saw you in that church."

It means a lot to Ash. That maybe she did something right, even if it doesn't feel like it.

"It's different with you." Delaney searches Ash's face. "*He's* different with you."

Ash holds her breath. She doesn't want to ask, fights it, but eventually, the question pops out. Curiosity has always been her downfall. "How is he different?"

"I've never seen him so soft for someone else before."

She's soft for him too.

The knee-jerk thought sinks into her stomach like ice.

Oh god. Is it possible? She likes him? In a more than temporary way?

A brilliant smile fills Delaney's face. "See? I'm right."

Ash looks down, heart racing. "Right is relative."

"You're honest with everyone but yourself, you know that?" Delaney sounds amused.

Ash narrows her eyes. "I don't like you very much."

Delaney sticks her tongue out. "Last card," she says. "The future."

It's the Devil.

Ash groans, anxiety coiling in her stomach like a snake. "So do I shit my pants now or later?"

Delaney smiles, one brow arched high. "It's reversed, so it's not as doom and gloom as you think." She leans down low, cocks her head. Listens as if the cards are telling her all their secrets.

Ash holds her breath. Holds her hope. Her heart.

Delaney opens her mouth, pulls in a breath. But before she

can speak, a gust of wind picks up the card. They scramble to catch it, but it's too late. They watch in horror as it's danced across the beach and into the water.

"Holy balls," Delaney says, her jaw dropped.

Ash doesn't know how she feels about that. Losing a card to the sea.

Eyes wide, she looks at Delaney. "Does that still count?"

"It does." Delaney's tightly drawn brows ease. She closes her eyes, whispers, "What you escaped in the past is not what you will find in the future. What held you back will release you."

Emotion clogs Ash's throat. Tears sting her eyes. For a reason she can't understand, the reading's landed like an arrow. Maybe because she believes. Maybe because she wants to believe.

Because Delaney—the tarot—is right. She does hold herself back. She pushes other people, but never herself. Her legs have roots in her sadness, her heartbreak. She thought she had grown from that, but what if she hasn't?

Delaney regards her, expression intent. "What do you think?"

"I think... I drank too much wine."

With that, Ash flops onto her back on the sand. Rum and coconut juice and red wine slosh around in her belly. Above, the stars blink. Delaney settles beside her. Slips her hand into Ash's.

Ash closes her eyes. Somewhere, there's the ping of a phone.

Emotions stir in her. Heavy, full of longing. An aching chorus of courage.

*Maybe you aren't a mess. Maybe you could do this with Nathaniel. Maybe you want to.*

*Maybe he does too.*

## Chapter Twenty-Nine

SHOULDERS COILED, NATHANIEL PACES THE HOTEL lobby and types out a message on his phone. **Where are you?**

**Sand. Where are you?**

"Ash," he growls. The cryptic messages he keeps getting back from her aren't helping.

It's been two hours since she grabbed Delaney and the bottle of wine and stormed out of the restaurant like a Visigoth marauder. In that time, he and his family took an extremely awkward ride back to the hotel. From there, they disbanded. But they didn't go their separate ways like he expected. He and Tate went to the bar. His mother and grandfather took a walk on the beach. Only his father was left blustering in the lobby. No one paid him any mind.

And they likely won't for the rest of the trip.

**Please tell me you're okay.**

**You're okay.**

"Christ."

His fucking father. He'll never forgive him for what he said to Ash. He wouldn't blame her if she hopped the next plane out of here. Even if the thought makes him sick to his stomach.

Her leaving—it wouldn't feel right. They're in it together now. Whether she knows it or not. She's made this trip better for everyone. Especially him.

**Commit a murder or clean up the evidence?**

He chuckles at her text, drags a hand through his hair. Thinks back to Tate's theory about a woman texting the one she wants when she's drunk.

He hopes.

Christ. He's never wanted anything more.

The lobby door slides open, and in strides his sister. The wine bottle cradled in her arm like a flower bouquet.

"She's on the beach," DeeDee says when she reaches him. "Straight shot south."

He gives her a look. Tips her chin. "You okay?"

"I'm fine. But you now owe me a tarot deck and your firstborn daughter." She slugs his shoulder. "Go get her, big brother."

He leaves the hotel and walks the twenty yards to the beach.

His heart beats hard until he sees her. It slows to a steady rhythm as he takes her in where she's sprawled out on the sand like a sexy, lazy starfish. In her white dress, in the silver moonlight, she glows.

"The wine has absconded," Ash drawls. Her eyes are closed.

He sinks down beside her. Smooths her black hair from her face. "The wine has been drunk."

Her long lashes flutter open, focus on him. He takes her hand, helps her sit up.

"Hi," she murmurs happily.

"Hi." He angles in and kisses those red lips. Like it's natural. Like there's no other earthly choice but to be drawn to her. He searches her dreamy gray-green eyes. "Did anyone ever tell you you're hot when you're angry?"

"Just my creepy uncle."

He can't stop the growl that escapes him.

"Kidding." She quickly turns shamefaced. "I'm sorry," she breathes, her eyes big and beseeching. "I shouldn't have said what I did to your father."

A quiet smile tugs at his mouth. "If it makes you feel any better, I almost hit him in the parking lot."

"Open hand or fist?"

"Fist."

"Yeah," she purrs, leaning in to sniff his neck. "That does make me feel good."

He kisses her again, running a hand through her untamed black hair.

A soft murmur against his lips. "Still, I'm sorry."

"It's okay." The last thing he wants is for her to feel guilty.

"No, it isn't." She worries her lower lip between her teeth. "I'm getting blacklisted right now, aren't I? Your family is going to tar and feather me poolside tomorrow."

He chuckles softly.

"I did not observe, I absorbed, and now I'm in it." She tilts her head back to look at him. Cups his cheek with a savage tenderness that makes his heart swell. "No one should talk to you like that, Nathaniel. It's not right, and it's not cool."

Nathaniel's heart thumps a strange beat. His mouth turns dry, but he manages. "You're right. It's not."

It's all he can say. When the truth is, there's so much more. On the tip of his tongue. Burning like a forest fire through his heart.

The minute she lurched out of her chair, he knew he loved her.

That fierce defense of him, teeth bared, lit something inside. No one has ever stood up for him before. The tremble in her voice as she ripped his father a new one. The soft sheen in her eyes as she looked at him. He's never seen anything more beautiful, never felt emotion for anyone like this.

Eleven days together, and already, she feels like the home he's never had.

Which is why losing Ash before he even has her isn't an option.

It's fast. Fuck, he can't argue with that. But he has to figure something out. Has to tell her.

But not here. Not tonight. Not when she won't remember in the morning.

He laughs, snags her purse off the sand. "You know what was cool? You calling my dad a bona fide piece of shit."

She groans again, slumps into his chest. "Oh god, let the sea take me at this point."

"I can't lose you to the sea."

"And why's that?"

He gives her an affectionate grin. "You do better terrifying the people on land."

Nathaniel scans the ground, making sure he has her phone and purse. Then places his hand on her back, one arm already threading under her knees. Scoops her into his arms and stands.

"I knew you wanted to carry me like a caveman," she murmurs. "Another check off my bucket list."

She closes one eye, peers at him with the other, her head resting against his chest. "Am I drunk?"

"A little. But it's okay. I think everyone's getting drunk tonight."

She sighs contentedly. "Are you drunk?"

"No. I should be." He's silent, then says, "I listened to my brother's podcast." It's what he and Tate did at the bar while they nursed shots of Jack.

Her pleased smile is bright. "You did?"

His chest aches when she looks at him that way. "I did."

"And?"

"You were right," he says softly, remembering the happy expression on his brother's face. "It mattered."

He carries her back to the hotel, cutting across the grass to enter through valet and take the elevator up to their floor.

He doesn't bother asking. She's going to his room.

When he reaches the door, he slips his key from his back pocket and enters. Carefully, he sets her on her feet, only leaving her side to snag a bottle of water and to text his grandfather that he's found her.

Ash strips down to her panties and bra. Wobbling only slightly, she crawls into his bed. With a great tired sigh, she flops against the pillows and burrows in deep. "Ugh," she says. "This buzz would be better without eight thousand calories of dairy sloshing around in my guts."

A smile battles at his lips. She's adorable. Soft against the pillows. A needy glow on her face. Her smoky halo of wild black hair.

He removes her sandals. Digs her phone out of her purse and swipes it against her sensor monitor. Satisfied with her blood sugar reading, he places the device on the nightstand. Sits on the edge of the bed, beside her.

"Am I okay?" Ash lifts her head from the pillow. Scrunches her nose. "Is it a mess?"

"It's perfect."

"I don't want to be a mess."

He frowns when he realizes she's not joking anymore. "Who says you are?"

"I say I am. And Maui says I am."

He knew it. The way she acted prior to getting here. Tonight, the coiled shoulders, the nerves.

"It's Maui," he says. "Being here…something's wrong."

She sniffles. "How do you know?"

"Because you're not you. Haven't been since before we arrived."

Ash swallows. "You act like you know me." She turns her face away.

"Ash." He takes her chin, gently forces her to look at him. "I do know you. Whether you want to admit it or not."

"But does it matter?" She sounds distraught now. Her full red lips pull into a tiny slice of sadness. "I'm not the girl who wears pearl earrings, Nathaniel. I'll never be her. I'll never fit…" She moves her hand between them.

He grabs it and holds it to his chest. Presses it against the pang there.

What she's saying is ridiculous, but it's her truth. It kills him that she feels even the least bit left out. Like she doesn't fit in. Like she's too weird, when she's proven her weird is exactly what his family needs.

"I don't want you to fit," he says roughly. "You're Ash. You're—"

*Mine.* But he doesn't finish the sentence.

She thrashes her head, her long hair falling around her bare shoulders. "I'm not that person for you. I'm too different. I wear boots. I'm a stomping, chaotic mess. I can't hold a job. I can't do anything right."

He frowns. His heart sinks. "You're not a mess. Who told you that?"

Jerking out of his grip, she buries her face in the pillow. Her voice comes out muffled. "No one."

He runs a hand down her back, soaks in the warmth of her. "You have it right. You are right. Do you not think that?"

"No." The admission is a whisper so soft he can barely make out the word. Melancholy lingers beneath her tough surface. "Not all the time. Usually, I do. But sometimes, especially here, tonight, I don't."

God, all he wants to do is shake her. Tell her she's perfect the way she is. Kiss her, hold her tight, never let her fucking go.

"But you're right. I don't like Maui." From her shuttered expression, the ice in her voice, it's clear she's done talking about it.

Emotion jackhammers at his chest as he covers her with a blanket. Talking with Ash sometimes feels like trying the password to a vault. Unless you get it right, it'll stay locked up tight. But that doesn't mean he'll stop trying.

She slips a hand out from under the blanket and searches for his. "Will you stay with me?"

He links his fingers with hers. Squeezes. "You know I will," he says thickly.

"No couch," she grunts, tugging on his arm. "Bed. With me."

He slides into bed beside her, tucking a slash of inky hair behind her ear. His room's a mess. There's sand in his sheets. But all he cares about is the riot of a girl in his bed. All bare skin, feral hair, red lips. Curled up like she belongs there.

"This doesn't count, you know."

"What?" Her voice is soft, tired. She'll be asleep soon.

He lays a hand on her hip. "Staying over."

She grins at him, eyes closed. "Why? Because I'm too sloshed full of alcohol?"

"Something like that."

"Will you wake me?" she whispers, nuzzling close to him. "If I don't hear my alarm?"

"I'll wake you up." He has no intention of sleeping tonight. He'll stay up, make sure her blood sugar's okay, so she doesn't have to worry.

He squeezes her to him. His mind still locked on her words.

*I'm not that person for you.*

They're like a punch to the stomach. He hasn't made her feel secure. Given her any indication that this is more than a vacation fling.

He'll do whatever it takes to make her believe the truth. That she's the one he wants.

He has no doubt of that. And he wants to be the man she needs. The man she wants. To take care of her, to protect her always—especially from assholes like his father.

His grandfather's words ring out in his head.

*I'm glad I didn't hold back my feelings.*

He won't. He won't shut down like he did with Camellia. Or give up like his parents did.

Instead of worrying about how they'll make it work, he's ready to figure it out.

First, he has to tell her.

Nathaniel closes his eyes, presses his mouth against her brow. "You are that person for me," he says softly. "And you don't have to wear pearl earrings."

Only he doesn't know if she hears him.

She's already asleep.

## Chapter Thirty

Ash wakes in a soft bed, blankets tucked up to her chin. She snow-angels her arms in the cool sheets, blinks her eyes open to blazing sunlight. "Ugh, fuck," she groans, dropping a hand to her face. It feels like the morning after a night out with Tessie when they were young. Bleary eyes, dry mouth, throbbing head. The holy trinity of their best drunken nights.

That's when the night comes back to her. Tearing Don a new one at dinner. Delaney and the tarot reading that rocked her world. Nathaniel plucking her from the sand like she was a drunken damsel.

Nathaniel.

She sits up and scans her surroundings.

It's not her room, but it's the spitting image of it. On the nightstand is a bottle of water, a mini bottle of orange juice with the cap missing, two ibuprofen and her phone. A flash of memory hits her. Nathaniel waking her, cradling her in the middle of the night, making her take a few sips of juice.

Phone in hand, she checks her blood sugar. Her texts.

**Tessie: Can you talk?**

"Shit." Ash rubs her eyes. It's her day to call her cousin and catch up on the trip.

Footsteps snag her attention. She looks up.

Nathaniel appears at the doorway to the balcony.

His lovely mouth quirks.

Ash smiles as her heartbeat thunders. He is a beautiful man, and she is never getting over him.

"How are you feeling?" he asks.

"I hate my liver, the sun and myself." She wrinkles her nose. "Listen, about last night—"

He holds up a hand. "You don't owe me an apology for last night."

Setting her phone down, she studies him. "I don't?"

"No. You don't owe anyone an apology." He half grins. "Don's probably rightfully banished from the family for a day or two."

He pours her a cup of coffee, comes to the bed and sits beside her. "But you know what I would take?"

Ash grins. Her attention dips to the waist of his boxers. "Rough, wild sex?"

"Later." He stills her hand when she reaches out to cop a feel. Searches her eyes, his look blistering and concerned. "How about an explanation about Maui?"

Fuck.

She forgot about that part.

Heat climbs into her cheeks. She glances at the window, then down to the sheet covering her. "I want to let you in…"

She does. She truly means that. But can she get through it without falling apart? Or feeling weak? Those are the parts she hates.

He taps her chin, bringing her back to him. "While you're considering it, let's go."

Her breath hitches. "Where?" Her eyes go wide. "Wait. What time is it?" She shifts, gaze landing on the nightstand clock. "Shit. We missed the tour."

"We haven't missed anything. Plans have changed. Our plans, at least."

She narrows her eyes in suspicion. "Where are we going?"

He smiles. "Pack a bag. I'll show you."

<hr />

The helicopter takes them from Maui to Kauai. A picturesque four-hour thrill ride where they're gifted perfect views of the lush scenery of Hawaii. She and Nathaniel talk about everything—except

Maui. When they land, they take a taxi from the airport to the tip of Kauai's northern shore.

When they arrive, backpacks in hand, she gapes at where he's brought her.

"Nathaniel," she says softly, shocked. In the distance, Kilauea Lighthouse stands tall, overlooking the Pacific Ocean.

"You said you wanted to see a lighthouse." His grin's lopsided, like he hasn't figured out how to use it. "I reserved it for you."

She stares at the lighthouse and its bright red roof. Her breathing goes shallow. "You can do that?"

"For you, I did," he says seriously. He watches her face closely. "Do you like it?"

Her heart thumps so hard it hurts.

Nathaniel did this. For her. Whisked her away on an impromptu trip. A sweet excursion that's tailored to what she wants to do. It's such a kind, thoughtful gift that she wants to cry.

To scream.

Because she can feel it. The slow dissolve of the walls of her heart. It's all breaking down. Like bones in acid.

Suddenly, she can't contain it anymore. Her joy.

She flings herself at him, wrapping her arms around his neck. "Thank you," she says, clasping her hands to his face. She stares into his eyes. Kisses his lips. "I love it."

His throat bobs, his face heavy with emotion in the hazy sunlight. "I thought we'd stay for the sunset, then head back. It'll be late, but…"

She nods. She wants every second of this day. A world, a memory she gets to share with only Nathaniel. "I don't care."

Hand in hand, they walk the trail that leads up to the lighthouse. Seabirds—kestrels, petrels and boobies—swoop over the waves.

A thousand bonfires ignite in her heart. "Look at it." She points up at the structure, fascinated by how big it is, how small she feels. There's an electric energy to the place. A meant-to-be type of feeling. "It's like a great looming giant."

She turns her head, and her breath hitches. Nathaniel is watching her, gaze intense. Heat slicks up her thighs.

She wiggles her brows. Squints up at the tower, the beacon and the viewing platform, and a chill creeps over her spine. "Do you think the ghosts want to meet us?"

A kind of amused laugh escapes him. "I don't know how I feel about being offered up to the spirits."

"I'll be the first sacrifice." She tugs at his hand. "C'mon."

Feeling giddy and reckless, she opens the door of the lighthouse. Inside, it's part gift shop, part museum. They look around, reading plaques and various other displays, and then Ash drifts to the circular staircase.

"Up?"

Nathaniel nods. Hand on her back, he follows as she takes the stairs carefully. They climb. Up and up.

"Be careful." His voice is hard. She knows now that he's being cautious. Worrying. When they get to the small circular walkway that lines the beacon tower, he holds tight to her waistband.

They step out onto the observation platform. Salty sea air hits them in the face.

Ash takes a deep breath, inhaling. "Oh my god," she breathes, grasping the railing.

Their surroundings are stunning. Panoramic ocean views. The sunset dipping beyond the horizon. She can picture it. Kilauea's guiding light giving early sailors safe passage from the dangerous bluffs and guiding them home.

Nathaniel wraps his left arm around her middle and pulls her back against him. She snuggles against the hardness of his body. Tips her head back to look up at him. "Now's your chance," she teases. "Three days left to murder me."

The mention of the end of the trip kills the light in his eyes.

A muscle works in his jaw. Then he husks, "How about I kiss you instead?"

He turns her toward him, crushing her against his chest. He kisses her. Hard. Almost angrily. Her heart knocks at her sternum as she sweeps her tongue over his. Runs her nails through his wind-ruffled hair. She digs them in, earning a sharp curse of pleasure from Nathaniel.

He's evil. The way he makes her want him.

Without breaking contact, he coasts his hands over her ass, squeezing, yanking her against him tight. Every ounce of willpower inside her shatters.

Ash whimpers against his lips.

Nathaniel pulls back. They're both breathing hard.

"Tell me what you want in life," he whispers, kissing her hair, her temple, her throat.

"I want cats. I want a place in the forest or on a boat near the water. I want to travel to witchy woods and tremulous oceans and take lazy naps in a cabin in one of those big blankets with the loops that are so ridiculous I can already see your eye roll. But I...I want all that. I want to be healthy and have good sex and maybe live in a lighthouse."

Heat kindles in his eyes. "Your weirdo dreams are my absolute favorite. And you are my absolute favorite weirdo."

"Really?" His words do something swoony to her insides. Like he could know everything about her life and never run from it.

"Really." He cups her face. "I'm insane for you, Ash."

He's nodding, nodding, nodding, his lips moving around her name, and then he's moving into her.

"Ash," he breathes. Fingers shaking, he cradles her face. "Tell me a truth. Tell me your name."

"No," she laughs, too happy to ward him off, to scoff, to joke. "Not yet."

Satisfaction flickers in those pale-blue eyes.

A ping on her phone. Quickly, Ash silences the text. It feels wrong to interrupt this moment. Whatever it is.

Nathaniel, immaculately backlit by the sunset, leans in. "What if I told you…I want to live in a lighthouse with you?"

"I'd say…" Emotions swell and bubble in her throat. "Maybe I'll let you."

It's that *maybe* that does her in.

Her heart's in this. Whether she likes it or not.

Whether she can admit it or not is a different story.

Is it stupid, silly to want? He's conventional, a doctor with a game plan. She's unconventional, a death doula with no direction. Complete opposites. Sure, they can commit, whisper sweet nothings. But they can't escape real life. Or their differences. Reality's creeping up on them.

Three days, and they're all over.

"My turn," she whispers. "Tell me a lie."

Right now, the truth terrifies her the most.

"I don't like you," he says hoarsely, and her chest wrenches. "I don't think I ever will."

She takes him in through lust-addled eyes. Her heart feels heavy. Like a one-hundred-pound weight sinking in quicksand.

No one else on earth has ever seen her so completely. It's terrifying.

She shivers as the wind kicks up. The sky's turned dark and ominous.

"Cold hands." Nathaniel gathers her hands in his and brings them to his chest protectively.

She steps into him, slipping her thigh between his. "Colder heart."

"But I have warm lips. Very, very warm lips." He drops a strong hand to her skirt, roughly pushes it aside. "Ash." His voice is intense, velvet. His eyes drugged and dark.

She lets out a whimper. "I need you." God, she hates begging, but she's a flame.

Approval fills his eyes. "Fuck."

With urgency, he unzips his pants. His long, muscular body hovers over her as he backs her against a portion of brick wall. Roughly, he grabs her leg and drags it up to his waist.

When he shoves her panties aside, Ash closes her eyes.

And then he slips into her. She cries out silently, head falling back. He's so hard, fits her so right. She rides him, grinds against him in mindless desire.

His eyes blaze with hunger. Hand tangled in her hair, he brings her mouth to his and whispers, "Come with me."

At his words, something sharpens inside her.

Her heartbeat pulses in her gut. Desire rises like a wave inside her. "Yes, yes," she breathes. She falls forward, that strong chest holding her up as they rock wildly—together.

The thorns around her heart release. Then constrict.

Not loose. Not quite yet.

# Chapter Thirty-One

IT'S NEARLY TEN BEFORE THEY RETURN TO THE HOTEL, and they have to be up early for a tropical island excursion his grandfather has pulled strings for them to participate in. As they exit the van after dinner and Nathaniel tips the driver, he tucks Ash tight against him.

Letting go of her proves a feat impossible.

After today, he's never seen clearer in his life.

She's the woman he's going to marry.

And not someday.

Soon.

Nothing else matters. *Them*. Fuck the North Sea. Fuck his hike in Peru.

He hasn't loved anyone in five long years.

But he remembers what it feels like.

It feels like Ash.

The knowledge burns through him.

She makes him want to stop running. To make a home. But unless it's with her, it's not worth it.

"Come to my room," he tells her. He can't explain this inexplicable pull to keep her close. To hold on.

"And do what?" Her eyes twinkle.

"Whatever you want."

A mischievous smile tugs at her lips. "Then we're escaping to the roof and howling at the moon."

He feels breathless as she laughs and tugs him forward. This is one of those fleeting moments where she drops her guard. He craves them.

How has he lived without her his entire fucking life?

Different. She is different. Unlike anyone he's ever known. She offends his family. Makes little kids cry. Once upon a time, he'd say they'd never work. They're different in so many ways, yet they get each other. Belong together. A car can't be wired without two opposing wires. And that's what she is to him.

Feral, mean, *his*.

He's trying not to think about it. What happens when this trip ends. But suddenly, it's the only thing on his mind. While Ash dozed in his arms in the helicopter, he worked through scenarios. Ways to make it work.

How he *will* make it work.

Whatever he does next, all he knows is he can't let her get away.

It was inevitable. Falling in love with Ash. He'd have a million babies with this woman. He'd also be content living in a lighthouse at sea with fifty cats. Whatever Ash wants. She owns him completely.

"There you are," his mother says, coming toward them when they enter the lobby. Her eyes land on his arm around Ash's waist.

He doesn't let go of her. He's stopped caring about who sees them. Let them say something.

"Have a nice time?" Claire asks.

Nathaniel angles his head to Ash. "We did."

In return, Ash pokes him in the arm. "He's a show-off with that helicopter."

Nathaniel asks his mother, "What are you still doing up?"

She nods her head toward the bar. That's when he picks up the sound of Delaney's great giggle of a laugh. "Late night chess match between Tater and your grandfather. You two should come."

Nathaniel murmurs to Ash, "What do you think?"

"I think I'm betting on Augustus."

His mother gives him a quick smile, then focuses on Ash. "Someone's been calling the hotel trying to get a hold of you. He's very…growly."

Nathaniel frowns.

"Who?" Ash asks, her brows pinched in confusion.

"He said his name's Solomon."

Ash pales, goes rigid in his hold. "Fuck." She slips out of his grasp. Then she's moving so fast, speed walking for the elevators, that Nathaniel has to jog to keep up.

"What's wrong?" he asks immediately.

She's shutting down. Tense expression. Tight voice.

"I never called her. Tessie." Her lips are pressed flat. Storm clouds enter her eyes. "It was my turn. And I forgot. I put her off."

In silence, they take the elevator up to the thirteenth floor. The minute they pass through the doorway of her hotel room, her phone's at her ear. "Shit. Shit, shit, shit." Her curses are soft and panicked. She hangs up. Tries again. "I forgot to call her."

"Ash," he says, alarm rising in him too. "What can I do?"

Wide, worried eyes on his, she shakes her head. Then she startles, like maybe the other end of the phone finally picked up. "Solomon? What happened?" A pause as she listens. Then, "*What? Oh no.*" Ash presses a hand to her chest, worries her lower lip between her teeth. "Is she okay?"

Nathaniel sets his backpack on the counter. He moves to stand behind her, running his hands over her shoulders. Ash, eyes closed, leans back against his chest like she's absorbing a blow.

"Fuck." She sniffles. "Okay. Call me if anything changes." A growl of warning in her voice. "*Anything*, Solomon."

The moment she hangs up, she turns around and buries her face in Nathaniel's chest. His entire body jolts, stiffens when wetness coats his neck, his shirt. Fuck. She's crying. Her tears do something violent to his heart. Why does he feel like he's drowning?

"Hey, what is it? What's wrong?"

"Tessie went into labor." Her voice breaks. "They stopped it, but it's too early."

"Fuck." His stomach sinks. "I'm sorry."

"She told me she wasn't feeling well yesterday, that she was tired and dehydrated. I didn't think anything of it…" She trails off, her eyes lined with silver.

"It's not your fault." He pulls her closer, crushing her to his chest. Their hearts hammer together. He rubs her back in slow circles. Keeps his voice calm and steady. "They'll give her terbutaline to stop the contractions. Then bed rest. She'll be okay."

Wiping her eyes, Ash pulls back. Drops onto the couch. His heart clenches when she turns away from him. "Please, go see your family. Let me ugly cry in peace."

"Right now, I don't give a fuck about a single human in existence but you."

He won't let her do this. Push him away.

Her smile's wobbly. "Then can you bring your shoulder closer so I can cry on it?"

"Absolutely." He sits beside her, pulls her onto his lap. "Let me guess. Tears of rage because your one and only keeps scaring you to death."

Her smile is thin. "Something like that." She curls up against his chest. "I don't like this," she whispers.

"What?" he murmurs, stroking her wild hair.

"Life. It's not nice. It hurts too much." Her words are anguished. "She's all I have. My York Peppermint Patty. I'm not scared of death. But I am scared of losing Tessie. She can't die. She's mine. She matters."

"She'll be okay." He has to say it. Because the woman he loves is crying, and he feels so goddamn helpless. All he can do is hold her tight and let her rage.

Ash blinks up at him with big green eyes. Tears sparkle in the dark flutter of her lashes. "Sometimes I think death is easier than love. With death, all you have to do is survive it. And in the end, it doesn't hurt. Love…you have to chase it. Tend to it. Work for it. Give it back. And sometimes it's so, so hard. To love someone."

"It is," he says, desperate to ease her pain. "It's hard to love. It's hard to hurt. It's hard to see *you* hurt," he amends. "But I'm here, okay? I'm right here, and I'm not going anywhere."

A wobbly laugh shakes out of her. "Lie?"

"No, Ash. That's the truth." He looks into her eyes. Wills her to see how earnest he is. "It is always the truth when I'm with you. I hope you believe that."

Ash considers him. She wipes a hand over her swollen face and nods. "I do."

Nathaniel hugs her, cradles her in his arms, rocks her side to side. When her breathing's evened out, he loosens his hold but keeps her on his lap.

For a few long seconds, silence.

Ash leans into him. Puts a hand above his heart. "The reason I hate Maui," she says in a small, resigned voice, "is because I was supposed to have my honeymoon here."

His eyebrows shoot into space as his stomach drops to the floor. He couldn't be more surprised if he tried.

She inhales a deep breath. "Jakob. He was my fiancé. I was twenty-nine. We both liked to travel. Shitty music. I thought he was the one for me." A shrug. "At the time, I was trying to do something right in my life, and having a serious boyfriend with a good job...it felt steady."

She licks her lips. "A month before the wedding, I came home early from work, and he was home." Her eyes flick to his. "In bed with someone else."

"Jesus," he swears. His heart crumples in on itself.

"Yeah. Nothing beats walking in on your fiancé balls deep in another woman." She gives a long, tired sigh. "We called everything off. I was so fucking pissed. So embarrassed. Heartbroken. You name a gamut, I ran it."

It pains him to think about Ash seeing that. It pisses him off to think a man dared to do that to her. He wants to find the guy and put his head through a wall.

Ash's expression softens. "That's why I interrupted your

wedding. It was like a bomb went off inside me. Back then, all I wanted to do was destroy. It's so stupid. For letting a man make me feel so fucking insane, and for such a long time." She lets out a bitter laugh. "One thing about me? I'm gonna make everything about my trauma."

"You could have told me," he says softly.

A shake of her dark head. "No. It's gross. I didn't want your pity or the sad looks. It's bad enough he's haunted me this long."

Ash inhales an angry breath. But the tears are back. Seeing them fucking kills him.

"It's not even that he cheated. Not anymore. I couldn't care less. I dodged a fucking bullet. I should have known he was bad news when he spelled his name with a fucking *K*." She makes a sour face. "We weren't right for each other. He never asked about my diabetes. He didn't know if thirty-five was death spiral or A-okay. Thinking back on it, he didn't know anything about me." She bites her lip. "Not the way you do."

Finally. Someone said it aloud.

"Then what is it?" he asks. "What haunts you?"

"It's what he said to me. That last day at the apartment, when I was packing up my things. I asked him why. Why he did it. Like maybe it would give me closure. Like there was some fucking answer that would take away the sting. And he told me—" Her voice breaks like she's reliving the memory. "Oh fuck." She grinds her fingertips into her eyes.

Nathaniel curls his hand into a fist, reins in his anger.

Ash ducks her face. Big tears slip out of her eyes to slide down her cheeks. "He told me I was too much. Too messy. That everything about me was too messy. My hair. My life."

"He fucking did not," Nathaniel growls. Cheating on a partner then gaslighting them to think they're the one with the problems is a whole different level of disrespect.

Ash's lower lip trembles. "He did."

"That man deserves to be fucking flayed and tortured for saying that."

"See?" Her laugh is wobbly. "Medieval violence is the answer."

He draws her tighter against him. Tilts her chin. "He's an idiot. You know that, right?"

"Sometimes," she admits. "Sometimes I think he was right."

Shame, sadness, stains her voice, slumps her shoulders. Dims her light.

"I've always felt like I didn't belong," Ash says. "Not because I'm not good enough, but because of my weird interests, or my diabetes. Take your pick. What Jakob said cemented it in my head. And I hate it. I hate that I let a man like that, a man who couldn't even stay faithful, who didn't even see the real me, make me feel like that." She gives him a sad little smile. "I know who I am…but sometimes I think people don't want me because of who I am. That they don't see me."

Nathaniel inhales a deep breath. "I see you, Ash. I see someone who comforts others, but not herself. Someone who wants the best for everyone else, but not herself." He pushes a damp lock of hair behind her ear. Stares into her wide eyes. "Do you know how you make me feel? How you make others feel? Someone has you in their corner, they're fucking lucky. You are fierce and you are loyal and you are extremely, extremely mean. And I'm glad to be on the receiving end of all your *assholes*."

That pulls a laugh from her.

"Nothing about you is messy," he says. "I love your wild hair and your mean mouth. They are impossibly perfect. *You* are perfect."

Her answering smile is wobbly but true.

He cradles her face in his hands. "And fuck that guy," he says roughly. "He doesn't deserve you."

She meets his gaze, her eyes softening. "I know."

With a deep breath out, he pulls her closer. "It's late." They have a long day tomorrow.

"Nathaniel…" Ash peers up at him through wet lashes. "Will you stay with me?"

The rare, shy vulnerability on her face spears something deep within him.

"Stay. Please." She catches his shirt, twists it in her hands. "I want you to. And it's not because I'm sad and lonely and don't want to be alone." She cups his face in her warm hands. "It's because I want you, Nathaniel." Her wet eyes search his face. "I want you more than I can stand it."

"I'll stay," he says hoarsely.

*I'll stay as long as you'll have me.*

"Thank you," she breathes.

He dips his head and kisses her, fingers knotting in her hair.

This time, the sex is slow, needy, purposeful. Unbreakable. A link snapping taut in the middle of them. When they're finished, they lay on the couch in the dark, tangled up together, Ash's breathing steady and her face content.

*I love you*, Nathaniel thinks.

He stays awake until the sun rises.

# Chapter Thirty-Two

"How are you feeling?" Ash asks.

Tessie sits in bed, hands on her bump, propped up by no less than ten throw pillows. No doubt Solomon's doing.

"I'm on bed rest. And Solomon is activating the absolutely most insane protector mode." Tessie sounds unhappy.

Ash snorts. She wouldn't be surprised if he was pacing outside the bedroom right now.

"He's just worried. We all are." She doesn't think her heart rate has come down since last night.

"I'll be fine." Tessie rubs her stomach, brow wrinkled, as she settles back into the pillows. "We'll both be fine."

Ash tosses a handful of granola bars and energy chews into her backpacking bag, then makes a sudden decision. "That's it. I'm coming to Alaska."

Tessie gasps and pushes herself up higher in the bed with one arm. "You will not." Before she can argue, Tessie continues, "I will have Solomon escort you from the airport."

"Good luck," Ash shoots back. She snatches up her suitcase. "You forget I took jujitsu in third grade. My arm bars are nothing to scoff at."

"Put the bag down." As Ash paces, Tessie tracks her movement with watery brown eyes. "Stop and listen to me. If you don't, I will go into labor so I can travel and kick your ass."

An icy pang of guilt threads through her. She feels like shit for not being there. For putting off that phone call, those texts. All because she was distracted by a man. She closes her eyes. It could have been worse. So much worse.

Slowly, she sets the bag down. She doesn't trust that fate won't let Tessie follow through on her plan. "I need to be there. I need to be there for you and little Delilah—"

A giant scoff. "Absolutely not."

"You can never die." She swipes at her eyes, the stupid moisture that's decided to make an appearance. "I only have one of you, and if I'm there, the universe might throw me a bone and right whatever fucked-up nonsense they're planning."

"I know you want to be here for me, but you can't be." Tessie smiles sadly. "There will always be a just-in-case. There will always be tragedies. And there will always be you and me. You are my six-inch stiletto. I will always need you. But you can't put your life on hold to take care of me. It's your life, Ash. You have to live it."

"I don't know how," she admits.

The tarot reading, the trip, her past, Nathaniel. It's chasing her down, popping up when she least expects it. Like evidence at a crime scene. She's been trying to hide it before it convicts her.

"Your heart is so soft, Ash, and you hide it away from those who want it." Tessie's voice wobbles. "I'm not the only one who deserves your heart."

"But…" She licks her lips. Trails off.

"You need to stay," her cousin urges gently. "For Augustus. For Nathaniel. To see where it goes."

"There is no seeing where it goes. It just…goes. When we leave, whatever is between us will be over."

Tessie arches a brow. "So there *is* a whatever."

Ash groans. "No. It's just sex."

She guffaws. "Last time I had just-sex, I married the guy." Tessie's face turns serious as she regards Ash. "Stay, okay?"

Ash thinks back to last night. Her hands twisted in Nathaniel's shirt, her heart hammering against her rib cage as the word dripped off her lips, thick as honey. *Stay.*

"Okay," she says, even as she knows her heart has already made its decision. Now it's her brain that has to fall in line. "I will."

Ash, shouldering her pack, makes her way out onto the deck of the ocean catamaran. Being stuck on a boat with eighty random people is a nightmare, but here she is. A private excursion and a private guide for the Whitfords and four other families from the hotel. A private beach where they can explore and day drink.

The quarters are tight and chaotic. With so many people on board, it's hard to pick out her party. But finally, she spies Augustus, Tate and Delaney curled up in a corner of the boat, practicing lines from Delaney's script. "Grandpops," Delaney squeals. "You're a natural."

"With a gravitas that suits Brando," he says, chest puffed out with pride.

As she comes to the front of the boat, she stops.

Nathaniel. He stands at the bow, gazing out over the ocean.

The sight of him knocks the wind out of her.

In the glow of the golden morning light, that strong, stern jaw is accentuated. It's made even sexier by the stubble he's let grow the last few days.

Handsome. He's so handsome. So calming. He is like the best soft sweater on a rainy day.

Ash's lips turn up and her stomach flips.

That heart in her chest.

It's slipping away.

Last night, she let him see the most private, sad parts of her. And it didn't feel so bad. It felt…beautiful, actually.

He made her feel safe. Understood. Heard.

Nathaniel Whitford likes the weird. Her weird. The good and the bad about her. The thought causes her heart to lurch so violently she places a hand to her chest.

After Jakob, she believed she'd never have anyone else. Find anyone who truly saw her. She never thought she'd want to try again.

And maybe she doesn't. Maybe she just wants it with Nathaniel. Maybe he is that little invisible string, that universal gotcha, that man she never saw coming.

"Voyeurism isn't your strong suit, Bigfoot."

She scowls. He's caught her in the act of lurking.

But then he turns. A lopsided grin splits his lips. Her heart turns to a firefly in her chest. All warm and glowing and hopeful.

Behind him, the sky is indigo and without clouds. It stretches the horizon. Endless. It's how Ash feels. How she feels about Nathaniel.

She could go on and on and on.

"Secretly ogling you is my new kink," she says. "You just have to deal with it."

"Fair enough. How's Tessie?" he asks, his eyes full of genuine concern.

Ash strides toward him. "She is being bossed around by a very brawny mountain man, so I think she's in the mid-to-late stages of being frustratingly horny."

He chuckles. Traces the strap of her bikini with those long fingers. Heating her. "Glad to hear it."

She tips her face up. Grasps the front of his shirt. Holding tight. "I almost flew to Alaska," she admits.

His throat works, over and over. Then he says, "I would have fueled up the jet."

Her entire body sparks with warmth. Nathaniel's willingness to move mountains to make sure she could get back to her best friend has Ash melting. If she thought her heart had cracked before, now it's wide open.

Nathaniel pulls her against him. Their hearts hammer in sync. "I'm glad you didn't go." He chuckles, then lets out a relieved sigh. "You're the best thing on this trip. I would have missed you."

"I would have missed you too." She wants to be angry with herself for this lapse, for this softness, but it's impossible. It's getting easier. To drop her guard. To say what she means.

Eyes turning molten, he angles her toward his mouth. Kisses her. Ash rakes her fingers through his disheveled hair and drinks him in.

He tastes like coffee and sunlight and the sea. He runs his tongue over hers, and his enormous paw of a hand skims the curve of her hip. Ash moans. God, just the man's hand is an entire love language.

When they untangle, he wraps his arms around her. For a long moment, they're quiet, watching the horizon.

"You know," she says. "When I was younger, I was sure I'd have to worry a lot more about the Bermuda triangle and Atlantis."

"The '90s let down a whole generation," he says.

She leans forward over the railing, squinting at the ocean beneath them. Her heart bottoms out when Nathaniel grasps the waistband of her shorts. Steadying her. Protecting her.

"You still owe me a coconut, you know."

He snorts. "I'll make it my life's purpose." Lifting his free hand, he points. In the distance is an island. "There," he says, kissing her brow.

When the catamaran docks, they all disembark and drop their packs and belongings on the sand. The manmade island is full of lush tropical vegetation and white sand. A cheesy wooden sign that reads THE BEACH IS CALLING has been hammered into the ground. Beach chairs, umbrellas, and coolers of water and beer line the sand in rows.

Brad, their guide, steps up and hands out maps and beers to each one of them. In each beer's mouth is an umbrella. "All right, everyone," Brad says, enthusiastically clapping his hands. His head piece fills with feedback.

Ash winces.

"We have some fun excursions planned for today," he continues. "Take a look at your beer bottle. Anyone with a purple umbrella is going bird-watching with Amanda. Yellow, you'll be with me, and I'll be showcasing the botany of the island."

Ash clutches Nathaniel's arm. Her umbrella is purple; Nathaniel's yellow. Panic lances through her stomach. "Wait, what the fuck?"

It's worse than she thought. They're being split up. Into groups. Into activities. Into group activities.

Nathaniel's gloomy expression matches hers.

Into his ear, she whispers, "Can that tsunami take me now?"

He catches her gaze for a moment, that lush mouth of his fighting a smile, and a warm rush of familiarity passes between them.

"Or better yet," Ash replies, "let it take Brad."

That garners a dirty look from the woman to her right. She holds a finger to her lips, and Ash rolls her eyes.

Brad lifts his hands in the air. "And when we return, we'll have an island lunch. Coconut shrimp. Rice and beans. Ice cold beer."

Cheers go up in the group.

"Fuck this," Nathaniel growls when Brad launches into island *dos* and *don'ts*. He grabs a towel from the sand. Snags her hand. "I'm not spending this day without you. C'mon. You want a coconut. Let's go look."

A thrill of adrenaline zips through her. He's right. They only have two days left. And spending the majority of this one without Nathaniel is absolutely not happening.

"Wait. My pack," she hisses. Sneaking forward, keeping low in the crowd, Ash grabs her pack from the jumble of bags piled on the sand.

Then, together, they melt into the tropical jungle. The sun's heat fades away beneath the canopy of trees. Nathaniel, map in his hands, leads them up wet, winding paths. Thirty minutes into their great escape, they hear it. The rush of water.

Hand in hand, they cross a small stream. When they push through dangling vines and palm fronds, numerous lagoons and a waterfall greet them.

With a laugh, Ash claps her hands. "Magellan would be proud."

Nathaniel tears off his shirt, pulling a small hum of approval from Ash.

"And I am now horny."

"Do I need to fight Magellan?" Nathaniel asks, grinning. "For history's sake."

Smiling, she surveys the beauty of the lagoon. Even with ample shade, it's hot, making the water that much more tempting.

"You want to swim?" he asks.

Ash nods, slips off her cut-offs. "Mm-hmm." She sticks her shorts and her insulin pen beneath her pack to keep them out of the sun.

"Here." Nathaniel crouches and unzips his bag. He brings out a packet of clear adhesive patches and stands. "Let's try this for your sensor. It should keep the water out so it doesn't get loose."

She bites her lip, stares up at him wordlessly as her heart swells. Every little thing he does stuns her. If she could absorb his handsome face, his kind heart into her bones, she would.

Nathaniel frowns in doctor-like concentration as he adjusts the patch on her arm. Gently, he smooths his fingers over the material to help it adhere.

"There," he murmurs. "That should do it."

She clears her throat. Checks out her sensor. "Looks good, Doctor Whitford."

When she goes to move away, he snags her arm.

"Ash."

Heart thundering, she looks up into his face.

All day, he's looked as on edge as she's felt. Utterly and completely undone.

"I'm going to die if I don't touch you," he rasps.

The raw edge to his voice has her breath whooshing out of her.

"So dramatic," she teases, laying a hand on his muscled chest. Beneath her palm, the echo of his heart.

Eyes blazing, he draws her into him. He palms her sacrum, that smooth expanse of skin above the lush curve of her ass.

Then his mouth meets hers, and the world stops.

His lips melt against hers, like a sugar dissolving, a sugar she can't get enough of, a sugar that's good for her, never bad.

*Nathaniel.*

Ash twines her arms around his neck, twists herself ever closer. Like trees that grow, that fuse together.

Breaking their kiss, they move. Wordlessly, Nathaniel spreads a towel on the beach of the lagoon. Lays Ash down. He drags his calloused fingers over her breasts, her hips, between her thighs. Good. She's never felt so damn good.

"Fuck," she whispers.

He kisses the base of her throat. "I love this bikini," he husks almost reverently. "Yellow's my new favorite color."

She rakes her nails through his hair, down his back. Enjoys the growl of approval he makes. Slowly, her top is peeled off her. Her nipples pucker in the clammy air.

Nathaniel takes her breast in his mouth. Warm. Heated. Hungry. She moans. Next, he removes her bikini bottoms. Licks up her thigh, the arousal that's built there.

As he comes back to her, he hovers over her. The hard weight of his body a grounding calm. His kiss delicate against her cheek, his whisper in her ear. "I love your hair."

His trembling fingers run over her scalp, firing every nerve ending. Unraveling her.

He draws back, drinking her in. "I love—" A hard breath rattles out of him. "I love everything about you, Ash."

She's smiling so big and dumb, but she can't help herself. The scent, the closeness of him, travels down her body and into her heart. She pushes his board shorts past his hips. She's desperate to have him inside her. Desperate for him to fill her.

"You're perfect," Nathaniel whispers against her skin. "You're perfect for me."

His eyes meet hers. And then he sinks inside her body.

Ash gasps. So good. So fucking right. Their bodies like ley lines. Connected. Moving toward one another in a course bound for the heart.

"I could stay like this forever," he rasps. "With you." He grazes her throat, brushes a hand over her veins, her pulse, her skin. "My morbid little beauty."

She swallows back the emotion crashing inside her. "Me too," she whispers. "Me too, me too."

Silence falls. Nathaniel moves inside her, his breath warm and pulsing. He grips her neck, brings her mouth to where he wants her. She lets him. Own her. She's never wanted anything more.

"Ash." At the plea, she palms his face, rakes a hand through his hair.

His voice like velvet. His hands like silk. Nathaniel surges deeper. Thrusts.

The sex isn't frantic or wild or rushed. It's slow. Claiming. Meant to be.

Just like them.

Ash cries out to the sky. Her lashes flutter as the hearts between them pound in sync.

There's that bloom in her chest again.

That bright bloom she can no longer ignore.

## Chapter Thirty-Three

THEY SNEAK OUT OF THE JUNGLE LIKE WILDCATS. ASH is on the prowl as she treks through the brush, sweaty and flushed and damp.

They swam for hours at the lagoon, and as late afternoon fell, they made love again. Reluctantly, they redressed and set off for the boat.

Nathaniel shoves a fallen tree branch out of their way. He lets Ash pass first, taking in the tropical backdrop of the island. A bright orange butterfly flitters in the air. Vines and flowers and lush vegetation make it a paradise. And still, Nathaniel has the best view in the world.

Ash.

From his position behind her, he has a prime view of her perky ass. She's in her bathing suit, smiling, her long black hair dripping down her shoulders. In the dappled sunlight, she's shivering.

"Truth," Ash says, glancing over her shoulder at him.

"Give it to me."

"Last meal. What would it be?"

He hurries to catch up. Grabs her hand. "You and a cloth napkin."

Her kohl-lined eyes flash. A feline grin tips her lips. "Absolute carnage."

He's in a goddamn great mood. Waterfall sex, the beach, Ash. Nothing can beat this day with her. Except the next one after it.

"You?" he asks curiously, stroking a thumb over her knuckle.

"Mushroom and Swiss burger, rare. Fries. The sweetest, most mouth-puckering root beer."

"No hesitation. Savage." He chuckles. "Why are we talking about food?"

"Because I'm hungry." With a laugh, she skips over a rock. Her backpack bounces on her shoulders. "I shot up in anticipation of lunch. Brad was hyping it up so much I can already taste it."

They wander down a path, this one bordering a rock wall. A few feet ahead of them is a cave. Spiderwebs and leaves cover the entrance.

Smirking, Ash shoves him. "Go in that cave. See what's in there."

"You first."

Grinning, he grasps her wrist and pulls her toward him. She squeals, twists in his hold, then loops her arms around his neck and pulls him in for a vicious kiss. The light reflects the green in her eyes, the bright red of her lips.

It's like illuminating every feeling he's ever had.

Her.

She is mean and feral, and fuck it if he doesn't love it.

Fuck if he doesn't love her.

He almost said it earlier, on the bank of the waterfall. Buried inside her, all that dark hair wrapped around his fist. But it wasn't the time.

Moments later, they're on the beach. The heat of the sun sears.

"Ugh," Ash grumbles, lowering her sunglasses and scowling. "Welcome back to the sauna."

Nathaniel appraises her as she pulls her pack off. She's covered in chill bumps. She needs a change of clothes and sunscreen.

"Nathaniel," Ash says. "Why are there porn magazines in my pack?" She's peering into her bag with a frown.

"What?" He takes it from her. Looks inside. Sighs. "Fucking Tate. You must have grabbed the wrong pack."

Her head snaps up. She scans their surroundings. "Wait. Where the fuck is everyone?"

At the tremor in her voice, Nathaniel goes rigid. He follows her wide-eyed gaze, turning his attention back to the beach. His heart stops.

"Shit," they say at the same time. The beach is empty. All that's left are the grooves in the sand from the chairs and umbrellas.

Ash takes a step toward the ocean. "Where's the boat?"

He drags a hand through his hair, gaze on the horizon.

"Oh my god. They left us." Her wide eyes race to his face, her expression more panicked than he's ever seen. "They fucking left us, Nathaniel."

His stomach drops, but he forces himself to cling to logic. "They'll be back. They'll notice we're missing."

Hawklike, he scans the beach. Shields his eyes from the sun with a hand, mentally preparing in case they're stuck overnight. They have three bottles of water. Two towels. And one Ash.

"We were the only tour of the day. This island is private." Ash is on her knees, digging through the backpack. Her voice is strained. "What if they don't notice? What if—"

"Don't do that," he orders. He lifts his phone high, then swears. No service.

"You don't understand." Her voice trembles. "My sugar, my granola bars, were in *my* pack."

Fuck.

His head whips up even as his stomach plummets. "You have your insulin, right?"

She stands, nods. "I do, but…"

Swallowing, she trails off. He knows the *but*. But without sugar, it doesn't matter.

"Tell me." Her eyes are pleading. "Where am I on the fucked scale?"

"You're not fucked." He goes to her. Takes her in his arms. "In fact, you're a long way from it."

"Really?"

His chest aches. He can feel the waves of fear and hope radiating off her. "Here's why we don't worry."

"Why?"

"I have a granola bar in my pack."

"You do?" Relief shines in her wet green eyes.

"I do. I had three. But Tate ate one on the way here. And so did Delaney." Fuck, he's an idiot. And so are his siblings. "So I have one. What was your last reading?"

"I was high when we went on the hike," she says, digging her phone out of her back pocket. "But I didn't give myself any insulin until a few minutes ago because I thought we were going to eat." She swipes her phone against her sensor. They both stare at the reading. Eighty-two. It's already lower than he'd like.

Even as his mind runs wild, Nathaniel forces himself to stay calm. For himself. For Ash. If he learned one thing working in the ER, it's that life is never as simple as one thinks. Shit happens.

It's a two-hour boat ride from Maui to the island. He calculates it. How long she has, how much sugar she has. Every second counts. Once his family notices they're missing, they still have to get back here. And how long will it take before they notice? The boat was full, their bags were with them. Maybe at dinner tonight, but...

Fuck.

Nathaniel tears a hand through his hair.

If her blood sugar gets too low, she'll go into hypoglycemic shock. Without treatment, without sugar, she could pass out. Or worse. Coma. Seizure. Death.

This is all his fucking fault. He took her on that goddamn hike.

Ash tears out of his arms and paces across the sand. "Oh god. This is a horror movie. We snuck off to fuck, and now we die." Her lower lip trembles. "All I wanted was a fucking coconut on this trip."

"There's sugar in coconuts." He strides over to a palm tree, gives the stalk a fierce shake. Above, the coconuts sway. "See? If we run out of granola bars, I'll climb that tree and fight it for a coconut." That gets him a laugh. Tears sparkle on her lashes. Her full lips try to pull into a smile.

"C'mere." He dips down and grabs the towel. Wraps it around her trembling form. "I've got you, okay?" he says, coiling his arms around her.

She nods against his chest, her slender frame relaxing.

Nathaniel sweeps his mouth over her dark head, murmurs, "I won't let anything happen to you." He's on autopilot. Emergency mode. All his focus on Ash. Getting her what she needs. Getting her safe.

Until he gets her back on that boat, he won't relax.

Ash pulls back, her face determined. "What do we do?"

"We make a shelter," he says. "We get out of the sun."

Her brow furrows as she looks around. "Should we walk?"

"No." The last thing she should do is use up what little energy she has. "We stay where we got left."

She inhales a hard breath. Then she turns and wanders toward the water.

"What are you doing?" he asks around the boulder lodged in his throat.

She lifts a hand. "I get one good scream a year, and I'm going to use it to full max."

He watches as she walks down to the surf, opens her mouth and lets out a full-throttle scream.

His heart hammers as he stares at her.

He can't let her see.

How fucking scared he is.

# Chapter Thirty-Four

"Well, it's official," Ash says as she slips Tater's T-shirt over her head. She holds her arms out, the huge black T-shirt hanging off her body. "I'm going to die wearing a *Big Johnson* T-shirt."

Nathaniel's face clouds. "Jesus. You're not going to die." He hasn't sounded this disgruntled with her since they first met.

"Just let me have my misery."

He opens his arms. "Come be miserable over here."

With a smile, she crosses the sand, then lies beside him on a towel stretched out under the starry sky. They used the last few hours to collect supplies and make a shelter. Well, really, Nathaniel did. He made her sit in the shade while he set up an abandoned beach umbrella he'd stumbled upon. They don't need shelter, but it makes her feel better.

The Hawaiian night is balmy and as beautiful as she's ever seen it. A light breeze makes the palm trees sway. The noises coming from the jungle—snuffling animals and crunching sticks—are unnerving, but being curled up in Nathaniel's arms eases her fears of being devoured in the dark.

She smiles up at the stars. "This is kind of nice," she murmurs. "You know, minus the whole stranded at sea thing."

"Except we're not actually at sea." Nathaniel drags a towel over her bare legs. Holds her tight, as if he can't bear to lose her.

"You love this, don't you?" she asks. "The adrenaline. The wilderness survival skills."

He gives a short, low laugh. "I'd love it more if you weren't involved."

"The skills will come in handy in the North Sea. Dodging vortexes. Fending off pirates."

He kisses her brow. "Yeah. Maybe."

She swallows hard. She still hates the thought of him leaving.

There's a hand on her brow. "How do you feel?" His voice is low, concerned. Experiencing the doctor side of Nathaniel Whitford up close and personal is extremely sexy. He's calm, so she's calm. It makes her feel a little better, at least.

She checks her phone. Her blood sugar's sixty-eight. The battery on her phone is at 20 percent. So is the granola bar. She had a few bites of it earlier to boost her blood sugar after the hike and her injection.

There's one bite left. But what happens when it's gone?

She shows Nathaniel her reading. They both stare at her phone like it's a bomb. That tick of a green line down, down, down. After a beat, she palms his hard chest. Nods at the granola bar. "You should have a bite."

"Ash," he says, brows stern and so serious. "I'm not eating your fucking food." He lifts himself from the sand to look down at her. "Promise me if you feel sick, you tell me." That muscle in his jaw flexes. "Don't be tough. Not about this."

She nods. "I promise."

Slowly, she chews the last bite of granola bar.

He's given her the food, the blanket, the water. No one's ever cared this much for her. She's trying to hold on to that. The knowledge that he won't let anything happen to her. Even as she pushes away the alternatives haunting her. Being stuck here potentially for days. Her mind screams it's impossible. Right? Someone will notice. Someone will come. But what if they don't?

Her blood is already on fire. It's what happens when her sugar is low. Sweating and lightheadedness. She muted the shrieking alarm on her phone. She couldn't take it anymore. Because she knows. It's all no good.

Still, despite everything, she's glad she's here. With Nathaniel.

Using his change of clothes as makeshift pillows, Nathaniel lies down again. He reaches for her, his big, possessive hand landing on her waist.

She snuggles in closer, into the curve of his arm. "This is the best kind of terminal burrowing."

His laugh is choked. "Let's not get morbid."

"Tell me a truth. Zombie apocalypse skill."

"Being able to drive a manual transmission. You?"

"Mine would be the very powerful skill of annoyance."

Silence falls. The crash of waves thud onto the beach.

Snuggled into Nathaniel's broad chest, Ash rises and falls with the sync of his breaths. She closes her eyes.

"What if no one comes?"

"They'll come." He answers fast, certain.

*What if no one comes* in time.

More silence. He strokes her hair. Slow, calming strokes. She can't be sure if they're for her or him.

"Nathaniel?" She chances the question. "What do you think happens when we die?"

His body goes stiff, and he makes a kind of pained noise. "Ash."

"No, I'm serious. I want to know." Clearly, dark times call for baring all.

He's quiet for a long second, then concedes with a sigh. "I think…I think your life is like a spark running down a fuse. And when it fizzles out, we're just…done. Blackness."

"Wow," she says drolly. "Boring and not at all hopeful."

He snorts. "What's the Ash Keller explanation, then?"

"I, and this is my personal hot take, like to envision ghosts or reincarnation. I don't think it's the end." She shrugs, allows a little peace to seep into her. "It's what gives me hope. It's what lets me do my job without turning into a blubbering mess. That there is something else out there waiting for us. That big secret at the end of our life that we finally get to find out about."

"I hope your theory is right," he tells her, voice thickening. "I really do, Ash."

"What do you want in life?" Her eyes flick to his. "You asked me at the lighthouse. But you never told me what you want."

Nathaniel shifts, pulling her in closer. His voice is low and rough. Fierce in its intensity.

"What I want is to get off this goddamn island," he swears quietly. With a hand on her chin, he holds her gaze. In the dark, his eyes burn. "I want you to be warm and safe and most importantly…be mine. Be mine, Ash."

His words knock the wind out of her. His voice is convincing and firm, as if he knows what they are when even she doesn't.

There's a weight in her chest, and it's increasing its pressure.

She wants to stop it, wants to tamp down the blooming feeling inside her. Wants to continue telling herself it's easier to be tough, to put others first, to close herself off because of what happened to her.

But she can't. Not anymore.

No more pushing. No more heart of thorns. No more fear.

Here, in Nathaniel's arms, it's okay. Okay to be herself. Okay to let herself move on with her life, to cobble together some semblance of happiness and embrace it during the time she has left on this planet.

Lifting up on her arm, she traces gentle fingers over his handsome face. Those cheekbones. Those lush lips. Nathaniel's beautiful, thumping heart. He whimpers as she leans in, barely sweeping her lips against his.

"I am," she whispers. "I am yours." Cups his cheek. "And you're mine too."

The thorns around her heart release.

It blooms.

Nathaniel stares into her eyes. Makes a rough sound in the

back of his throat. Palms her face with both hands and crushes his mouth to hers.

They're both breathing heavily when she pulls back. She looks at him in wonder. Feeling so light she could float away. Like there's never been any kiss, any man, any love to exist except Nathaniel. And then she takes a hard breath and says, "Ashabelle." Her voice wobbles. Her eyes sting. "My real name is Ashabelle."

"Ashabelle," he echoes, his tone full of amazement. No humor or mockery.

"My parents couldn't decide on a name. For two weeks after I was born, they called me the baby. Just the baby. My mother liked Ash, but not Ashley or Ashton. My father liked Isabelle. So, they combined what they liked and got Ashabelle."

"Ashabelle," Nathaniel says again. In the darkness, a glimmer of a smile. "It's so Disney princess. So, so, so…" His wondering gaze scours her face. "You."

She laughs. "Excuse me?"

"It's you. Crispy outside, chewy center." He palms her cheek, tucking a lock of wild, salty-sea-waved hair behind her ear. "Tough. Mean. Beautiful. I love it." He kisses her brow. "Every single part of you is perfect."

Her lips part. But she can't find the words. Instead, the walls around her heart crumble. Prisons collapse in her rib cage. She couldn't stop it if she tried.

Without another word, they settle on the sand. Nathaniel pulls her onto his chest and holds her. She doesn't have to ask. She already knows he's staying up.

She's exhausted, but she lies there, thinking. Contemplating the big, wide universe above them. Tessie's words echo in her head. *See where it goes.*

God. What a fucking fabulous notion.

Suddenly, she feels lightheaded. There's a tight, stressful feeling in her chest. Low blood sugar or heart attack, she can't tell.

She closes her eyes. The stars wink out.

It's not a heart attack.
*Fuck.*
It's love. It's Nathaniel.

---

Morning comes. Too soon. Too bright.

Groaning, Ash tucks her chin into her chest and covers her eyes. She feels like shit.

Dammit. By the smell of the salty sea air, they're still on the island.

Beside her, Nathaniel wakes with a lurch and a whispered *shit*.

A big, tentative palm lands on her back. Like he's gauging her breathing. "Ash?"

"I'm alive." Slowly, she rolls over. Sand digs into the knobs of her elbows as she sits up and scans the beach. "Anyone?"

A rattle of a breath shakes out of him. "Not yet."

With trembling hands, she grabs her phone. Tosses it back on the sand.

"My phone's dead," she tells him. But she doesn't need a phone to know she's fucked. She can feel it. The edge of her blood sharpening. Clammy skin. Blurry vision. Numb lips.

Still, she forces a smile. "I'm okay."

"That's the first lie I think you've told."

She huffs a laugh. "Yeah, well, let's just say a twinkie sounds fabulous right now."

"We'll get you a twinkie," Nathaniel says, slipping his sandals on. "All the twinkies you want."

His words blur as her head, her whole body sway a little.

"Ash?"

She blinks herself back at the sensation of his hand on her shoulder.

"It hurts, Nathaniel." Fire. It's the only way she can describe how her blood feels.

Pain flashes in his eyes. "I know it does."

He scoops up his phone. "I'm going to walk east again. Try to get a signal." Expression grim, he takes her chin, angles her head so she's forced to meet his gaze. "I *will* get a signal."

Ash licks her dry lips. "Okay. What can I do?"

He dips down so they're eye to eye. Kisses her brow. "Stay here. Stay in the shade. Save your energy."

Ash nods.

After one last long look at her, Nathaniel jogs off. He's panicking but trying to keep it under wraps. For her.

As she watches his broad-shouldered form determinedly jog across the sand and disappear, she doesn't move. She scans the beach. The gravity of the situation dawns.

If she has to go another day here, she's fucked.

More than fucked. She's dead.

On shaky legs, she stands and stretches, leaving the cool shade of the umbrella. She doesn't know what her blood sugar is, but it feels like that time she fell to a precarious all-time low of forty-five. Her mom fussed over her, and she got to drink an entire Dr Pepper and hoover a Moon Pie, and it was fabulous.

Sunlight warm on her face, sweat beading her brow, she crosses the sand. She's boiling. Her clothes stick to parts of her body she'd forgotten about. On a sigh, she leans back against the thick trunk of a palm tree.

Can she freeze time and become one with the tree? She looks up. The bright blue sky above is shielded by thick fronds, heavy with coconuts. It all feels slightly surreal, impossible. Like any second, she'll wake from a fever dream. Is this what it's like? Is this how it ends?

She's going to die. Trapped on an island with Nathaniel Whitford. All because she snuck off to have the best sex of her life.

And she won't even get a coconut before she dies. A weird laugh pops out of her mouth. The unhinged kind. Clearly, she's losing it.

"Fuck," she says, pushing off the tree. Another wave of dizziness nearly knocks her over. Squinting, she scans the ocean for a boat, a ship, anything.

Who is she kidding? No one's coming. At least not in time.

Shit. Just when she was getting the hang of this love thing.

If it is the end, if it is her time, she has to tell him. That he's the tall, serious asshole she loves.

Ash's heart flutters. She smiles at that. Then sways.

She has to get back to her shelter. Nathaniel will flip his shit if he returns and finds her walking around, wasting the precious energy she has.

With another step forward, she shields her eyes against the bright glare of the sun. As she does, the wind kicks up and the leaves on the trees around her rustle.

There's a *thump*, then a *crack*.

Instantly, pain radiates through her—skull, eyes, face. "Fucking ow," she growls.

The world goes hazy. Her body feels weird. Discombobulated, she looks up, blinking, rubbing her head.

*The stars.*

*Oh, wait. No.*

*Shit.*

Her vision blurs.

*The ground.*

# Chapter Thirty-Five

NATHANIEL RUNS LIKE HIS LIFE DEPENDS ON IT—only it's not his life.

It's Ash's.

Phone held high, he hikes to the east side of the island. But he still has no service. "Fuck." He stomps into the wild brush of the jungle. "Fuck."

Where the hell is his family? When he gets back to Maui, he'll murder every single one of them. He's never been so fucking terrified. His blood is on fire; he can barely breathe.

Panic's set in. He's trying to hide it for Ash's sake, but they both know it's a nightmare scenario. She needs sugar. She needs sugar very fucking badly. Cold permeates him at the thought of what happens if she doesn't get it.

Her life is at stake.

He squeezes his eyes shut. Fights for calm. Emotion is a luxury he can't afford.

This is why he works out on that rig. *Stay away. Stay unattached. Stay emotionless.*

But he can't. Not with Ash.

That woman activates every fight-or-flight reflex ingrained in him. He wants to take care of her. He's protective of her. He cares for her. The thought of leaving her, the thought of her getting sick on his watch when he's fucking helpless to help, carves up every inch of him.

*I am yours. And you're mine too.*

Her words last night threw him off balance, right before they aligned within him so completely.

He doesn't want to go back. Not to work. Not to his rig. Not on his backpacking trip. He wants more than the memory of this vacation with Ash. He wants a life with her.

There will be time to think about the future later. First, he has to get them off this island. Remain calm for Ash's sake.

Nathaniel clenches his jaw. *Stop it. Pull it the fuck together. She needs you.*

Crossing a stream, he waves his phone in the air. One last desperate attempt for service. He freezes when four bars appear.

A heartbeat later, his phone lights up. A barrage of texts.

**Dawg, you better not be off banging.**

**Where are you? Dinner's at seven.**

**You're late. You're never late.**

**Nathaniel, I'm afraid to admit that I'm beginning to get worried.**

He homes in on one text in particular. His mother: **We're coming.** The time stamp reads four a.m.

He checks the time on his watch. It's six.

*Any minute.*

*Any minute, they'll be here.*

Adrenaline coursing through him, he dips his head and blows out a breath. In the stream in front of him, a Coca-Cola bottle bobs. He crouches down and picks it up.

It's half-full.

Breath held, he twists the cap. A weak hiss. The soda is nearly flat. It's possible it's only been here since their tour yesterday. Regardless, it's sugar. It's disgusting, but it's sugar, and it'll work.

He's never been so fucking thankful for litterbugs.

Bottle in hand, he runs full speed back to where he left Ash. As he crests the final hill before the beach, she comes into view.

She's on the sand.

*Lying* on the fucking sand.

Not moving.

His world tips sideways. His head goes quiet.

It's supernatural how fast he moves. He charges across the

beach. His heart thunders wildly. When he reaches her, he drops to his knees.

Her body's slumped face down. Grabbing her by the torso, he rolls her over. Brushes black hair from her pale face. Her eyes are closed. He places two fingers to her throat. Rapid pulse. Clammy skin.

With force, he shakes her. "Ash," he rasps, desperate for a response. "Ashabelle, wake up."

Fear blooms in his chest, but before it can take root, a soft groan leaves her lips.

Her eyes flutter, then open. She lifts a hand to her temple. "Something bit me."

"Yeah," he says. His attention shifts from her to the small brown orb beside her. He tips his head back, surveys the tree, gauges the height of the fall. "A fucking coconut."

He picks her up and carries her over to their shelter. He gets her comfortable, then crouches in front of her. "Look at me," he orders, checking her eyes. Her pupils are fine. "Do you have a headache?"

"No." She wrinkles her nose. "My brain feels like mashed potatoes."

"Yeah, well, it's still in your skull." He exhales, relieved. If she's concussed, it's minor.

"You sound glad about that."

He lets out a strained laugh. "I am glad, Ash. I am very fucking glad about that."

For a long second, he can barely breathe. This is his job. He's a doctor, but this is almost more than he can take.

He strokes her hair. "Stay still, okay? Stay awake."

Ash squints at him. "You are the tallest tree trunk I've ever seen. Did anyone ever tell you that? No, I suppose you're too worried about being carved up into paper products."

"Okay," he says slowly, torn between laughing and crying. "We're going to sit here."

He props himself up against the rock and settles Ash between his legs, her back to his chest. Her skin is clammy, and it's not from the sun. She has all the symptoms of someone in hypoglycemic shock. The crack on her head isn't helping.

Leaning back against his shoulder, she looks up at him. "Should we make a swim for it?"

"With a head injury?" The thought fills him with amusement and pant-shitting fear. "No. Help's on the way." He pulls out the soda bottle. Tears off the cap and brings it to her lips. "I found this. I want you to drink it."

Her eyes narrow in suspicion. "Where'd you get that?"

"From the 7-Eleven on the hill," he says. "Really doing a piss-poor job of bringing in business, if you ask me."

She pouts. "I don't want any."

"Now," he orders, staving off the frustration threatening to take over. Irritability and confusion are both symptoms of low blood sugar. "Right now, Ash." He all but manhandles the bottle to her lips.

She gives in, takes a small sip.

"Good girl," he whispers. "Good fucking girl."

Ash stops and sighs, as if the effort's exhausted her.

He's holding her, heart beating fast, ready to pour it down her throat, when she whispers, "Nathaniel."

"What?"

"Tell me, even dying, am I still an absolute fox?"

He laughs, low and rough. "You're not dying. I refuse to let you."

"Mmm. You didn't…answer my question."

"Ashabelle Keller, you are without a doubt the most stubborn, morbid, mean woman I've ever met." He strokes her cheek, sweeps a lock of tangled dark hair back. He keeps talking, his blood roaring in his ears. "But you're also a beautiful, brilliant pain in the ass. *My* pain in the ass. You make this bullshit world better."

"I do?" Her voice is soft, slurred.

"You do, beauty."

"Why?"

"Because with you, it's not bullshit. Because you are all I have ever wanted. You make six hours feel like ten minutes. And when you're gone, I miss you. It's absolutely ridiculous." He smooths a lock of sweaty hair from her brow. "I think you're the greatest thing to ever exist."

"Really?"

"Yes. Bigger than Bigfoot." Nathaniel extends the bottle. "Now be quiet and take a drink."

Silence.

"Ash?"

He ducks his chin, takes her in. Her pale cheek rests in the palm of his hand. Her eyes are closed.

Panic twists in his throat like a blade. He sits up straighter, his heart racing. Brings the Coke bottle to her unmoving lips. "Ashabelle, don't go to sleep. *Ash.*"

No response. She's slumped against his chest, eyes closed.

His heart plummets.

*No. Please, God, no. He can't lose her. Not now.*

"Just one more sip, Ash," he murmurs, adjusting her in his grasp. "Do you hear me, beauty? One more sip."

She sags in his arms. Nathaniel swears. She can't drink if she's unconscious.

Heart pounding in his ears, he lays her on the sand, rubs her sternum with his knuckles in a desperate attempt to wake her. Panic, fear, a primal raging beast inside him.

A horn startles him.

Nathaniel whips his head to the ocean.

Oh, thank fuck.

A ship.

Strike that.

A fucking pleasure yacht. The words MARGE THE BARGE stenciled on the side in bright, brash, glittery letters.

And it's already docking.

Nathaniel scoops Ash up. With her clutched tight to his chest, he rushes to the boat. His lungs burn. His heart thunders. He doesn't stop.

He won't.

Off the ship come his mother and Augustus. They're wearing matching looks of shock. He charges past them, hustling down the dock and up into the boat.

"I got her," he tells the medic when the man tries to take Ash from him. Over his dead body is she leaving his side.

He lays her on the bar of the sun deck. Her eyes are closed. She's still and unresponsive. There's no time to waste.

"She needs glucagon," he barks at a second medic, who is waiting with a first-aid kit. "Sugar. Tell me you fucking have it."

At his side, his mother's face is pale. "Oh no, Ash." She looks near tears.

The second the medic opens the kit, Nathaniel snatches the pre-filled syringe from it. He doesn't trust anyone else to touch her. Quickly, he pops off the cap and jams the needle into Ash's upper thigh.

He stands at her side, unmoving, barely breathing, as the glucose is injected into Ash's system. Soon, much-needed sugar will flood her veins.

"Open your eyes, Ash. You have to get up. Please. Come back to me." The only plea he hears. In his head. His heart. His lungs. The backs of his eyes burn.

Augustus leans forward, face ashen and etched with concern. "Is she—"

"She'll wake up in about fifteen minutes," he tells his grandfather. With shaking hands, Nathaniel strokes Ash's dark hair. Watches the slow rise and fall of her chest.

His brave, brave girl.

He takes her hand in his and feels the beat of her pulse, that bright bloom of life that's made his world come alive. Only when her fingers flex and tense in his grip does Nathaniel remember the steps to breathe again.

---

Nathaniel paces. The sandwich, the bottle of water he's been given lie forgotten on the bar top. He's too keyed up, too fucking worried, too pissed off to stop moving. To do anything but think about Ash. As soon as the medic took her down to the infirmary to wait for her to wake up, his mother explained what happened.

"I'm so sorry." Claire worries her lower lip between her teeth. "We didn't know that the guides hadn't taken a headcount." Fucking Brad. "And when we disembarked, we thought you and Ash had already gone ahead to…" A little laugh pops out of her mouth. "You've been sneaking off this whole trip. We thought it only logical."

He blinks at her. "You knew?"

"Oh, honey." She places a hand on his arm. "Everyone did."

Jesus. He tears a hand through his hair. "It's not your fault, Mom." That's the least of his worries.

Claire explains that it was midnight before Tate noticed he had Ash's backpack. That's when the Whitfords realized Nathaniel and Ash were truly nowhere to be found.

"By the time we got ahold of someone, the charter company was stalling, trying to figure it out."

He clenches his fists, seething. "Fucking ridiculous."

The amount of time it took for their absence to be noticed, for the charter company to help, is unforgivable.

Ash could have died.

He's already planning retaliation. "We should sue them. Buy their company. They're fucking done."

"I think your grandfather is already on it." Claire gives him a sympathetic smile. "We didn't wait around for help. It was clear the charter company was trying to evade responsibility, so your father went down to the pier and bought a yacht."

"*What?*" Nathaniel lurches to a stop. "Dad?"

Claire nods. "You know that man. Any way he can get something, he'll do it."

Nathaniel peers over at his father. Don sits with Augustus at the bar. Their voices muffled, glasses of whiskey in their hands, despite the early morning hour.

Don looks over, catching his gaze.

Gratefulness seeps into him. Nathaniel gives his father a nod, and in return, Don lifts his glass.

"Doctor Whitford?" The medic's coming up from the lower deck. "You can see her."

He doesn't remember moving. Doesn't remember taking the stairs two at a time or opening the door to her room. All he knows is that suddenly he's inside and she's there.

She's okay.

Ash is in bed, a blanket pulled up to her waist. A glass of juice sits on the nightstand. At the closing of the door, she stirs. Opens her eyes. Smiles.

"Hi," she says.

His legs almost give out. His shoulders uncoil. His fists unclench.

"Buried or cremated?" he asks.

Those wide gray-green eyes blink. "What?"

"Buried or cremated?" He shrugs, fighting the urge to unravel. "You look like you've thought about it."

"Neither. Lampshade," she says with a smile. "Courtesy of Ed Gein."

He chuckles. That's his girl.

Itching to be close to her, to touch her, he crosses the room and sits beside her. With her tousled black hair, big black T-shirt and pale skin, she looks like the death's door heroine of an Edgar Allen Poe novel. To Nathaniel, she's never looked more beautiful.

With a relieved exhale, he cups her jaw, evaluates her face. Her pupils. "How's the head?"

He gets that droll, snarky smile he loves. "Concussed by a coconut," she rasps. "I'll never live it down. It'll forever be on my medical record."

He gives a low laugh of disbelief. "You're lucky it's not a skull fracture." Slipping her hand into his, he asks, "How's your blood?"

"Oh, it's practically vibrating." A graceful arch of her brow. "If you've been waiting for me to be weak and defenseless, now's your time for murder."

"And not have it be a fair fight? I wouldn't dream of it."

She laughs. The sound is the most incredible thing he's ever heard.

He looks down at her hand curled in his. His mean, beautiful girl. Pushes through the tightness in his throat. "I'm glad you're okay."

"I am too." She smiles at him, but there's a fragileness behind it. A hesitation. "Thank you," she says softly. "For making me feel okay out there. Not so afraid. For taking care of me."

He squeezes her hand. "I always will."

Ash squints at him. "Are you okay?"

Nathaniel opens his mouth. Looks into Ash's eyes.

He doesn't know how to tell her. That he's not okay if she's not okay. That he'd give his own life to keep her safe. That she's endgame. In his head, heart, blood, soul. She owns him.

Finally, he gets the words out. "I am. I am more than fine now." His lips twitch. "*Ashabelle.*"

"Oh god," she grumbles, covering her face. "Can we just pretend I never told you that? I will claim you took advantage of me in my weakened condition."

Grinning, he leans in and kisses her through her fingers. Her warm cheek, her delicate jaw. "No. Never going to forget."

A kind of whimper escapes her. Then he's engulfing her in a hug. He crushes her tight against his body, breathing in her hair, her scent of sun and juice. For a long second, he just holds her. Overcome. She's okay. She's alive.

"We're about twenty minutes from Maui," he says hoarsely, his lips brushing her temple. "We'll get you back and get you some rest."

Settling against the pillows, Ash thins her lips. "It's our last night. I'm not resting."

"Ash," he growls, ready to hog-tie her to a bed. Or better, his body. "You almost died. Which means—"

"Which means I'm not missing the luau." Her eyes flash with determination. "Augustus and I worked hard to plan this night." Before he can protest further, she holds up a hand. "I'll be okay. All I need is a cheeseburger and a very long, very hot shower."

"Done." In his head, he's already arranging room service. A soft bed. A fully stocked minibar. Lots of rest.

Toying with his fingers, she looks at him from beneath heavy lashes. "Lost at sea. That's our story now. We can take it to our grave or tell the *National Enquirer*."

*We can tell it to our kids.* The thought leaps into Nathaniel's mind, but he bites his tongue.

In an ultra-soft voice, Ash says, "We go home tomorrow."

He swallows hard, interlacing his fingers through hers. "Yeah. We do."

She bites her lip, lowers her gaze. "I wish we had another day."

"Me too."

Their eyes meet. A sharp emotion passes between them. Their night on the beach, but also this entire vacation. They've endured the good and the bad of the trip together. Shown up for each other. That matters.

He's not ready for this to end. Not when he's had the best days of his life. Not when he has an emotional connection with this girl that rivals their sex, bests it. Not when being with her feels like home. Not when he…

Not when he loves her.

He whisks his thumb over her knuckles. Takes a hard breath. "Ash. Listen…"

The door opens. Augustus pokes his head in. "I hope I'm not interrupting."

"No," Ash says, smiling bright. "Not at all."

Nathaniel leans in to press a kiss to her forehead. Shoves up to standing and turns to his grandfather. "She's all yours."

He's almost to the door when his grandfather lets out a smug, knowing chuckle.

Augustus turns to Nathaniel, his eyes soft and bright. "That's where you're wrong, my boy. That's where you're wrong."

## Chapter Thirty-Six

It's a night of lasts. Last sunset. Last mai tai. Last kiss.

When they get back to the hotel, Nathaniel all but bullies her into climbing into bed and resting. His will, not to mention that stern, furrowed brow of his, is too strong for Ash to fight, especially in her weakened state. After a hot shower and a weepy telephone call with Tessie where she tells her best friend about her close call on the island, it's time for the luau.

Wrapped in a fluffy white towel, Ash stares at herself in the mirror. Instead of the myriad of worries and anxiety carousing through her brain, all she can think is:

*Nathaniel.*

A hum that warms her blood.

No one has cared about her like that in a long time. Sure, she was improbably close to lapsing into a coma and dying, and he is a doctor, but his Hippocratic oath didn't cause the tremor in his voice. The fear in his eyes.

He cares about her.

For ten days, she's been trying to ward it off. Now, she doesn't want anything else.

Suddenly, she craves the sight of him.

Oh god. It's madness.

Ash slips on her sandals, pulls on a simple black dress. Gold jewelry. Black cat eye. Red lipstick. She checks her blood sugar (fine, thank fuck). Then grabs her purse, her room key, then walks out the door.

The sight of Nathaniel brings a smile to her face.

He's leaning back against the wall in the hallway, arms crossed, waiting for her.

So handsome it makes her heart stall.

He pushes off the wall and exhales, attention locked to her face.

"You're staring," she says.

His eyes sharpen. "You're beautiful."

She blushes. Her heart takes off at a sprint.

"You okay?" he asks. He tucks a lock of hair behind her ear, using the move to check the temperature of her skin.

"I'm more than okay." She narrows her eyes at him. "But if you ask me that again, you won't be."

"Threats before dinner," he says dryly. But there's heat in his gaze. "I see you're just fine."

He offers her his arm, and, heart squeezing, she takes it. Together, they walk to the elevator.

It's silent as they ride down. A kind of intense manic energy radiates between them. Like when they first met. Except instead of ripping his face off, all Ash wants to do is tear off his clothes. Say everything that's been bubbling inside her for so long now.

But she waits too long. The elevator doors slide open.

Nathaniel, hand on the small of her back, guides her through the lobby out to the beach.

The farewell luau dinner is a stunner. Tiki torches line the entrance. An elegant long table sits in the center of the space, decorated with tropical flowers and pitchers of rum punch and iced tea. Hula dancers and a small band warm up for the evening. In one corner is a bar, where a bartender shakes up cocktails. In the other is a plush black couch and a firepit, where the Whitfords hold court.

Delaney hops up, eyes wide. "Oh my God! We were so scared." She throws her arms around Ash, shaking. "We thought you were swept out to sea."

"Not quite," Ash says as Delaney slips a floral lei over her head.

"Gotta get you on the podcast," Tater says. "I'm thinking next season...coconuts."

"I don't fucking think so," Nathaniel snaps, that jaw of his grinding his molars into fine dust.

She tilts her face up to him, placing a hand on his chest. Instantly, he relaxes. Covers her hand with his.

She blushes, noticing Augustus watching them with a smile.

"You're just in time for sunset," Claire says, saving her.

They have champagne on the beach while Nathaniel grudgingly recounts their time on the island. Even when he's talking to family, he doesn't let go of her. As Tate howls over Ash wearing his Big Johnson T-shirt, a hula dancer joins them. She's beautiful, with thick black hair, big brown eyes and a basket of orchids in her hands.

She gathers the women. "Don't forget a flower for your hair, ladies." Her soft lilt of a voice floats in the evening air. "If you wear it on the left, it means you're taken or unavailable; wear it on the right and you are looking for love."

Delaney and Claire gasp as they peer into the basket. Delaney selects a white orchid, Claire a yellow. Ash is next.

Hesitantly, she reaches into the basket and chooses a dark purple blossom. She can feel Nathaniel's heated gaze on her as she brings the flower to her ear.

Her right ear.

She assumes nothing. Keeps her expression shuttered and unexpectant. Even as her heart feels like a lead weight in her chest.

"Wait." Nathaniel's voice, low and rough, rings out.

Stunned speechless, she freezes.

He strides toward her, and blue eyes darkening, looks down at her. "You have it in the wrong spot."

He plucks the flower from her right ear. His big hands deftly affix it behind her left.

*Taken.*

Flushing, she tips her head back to look at him, arches a brow. "Heavy on the *there are people around*," she warns.

"I don't care." He runs a finger across her cheekbone. "Not anymore. Not when it comes to you."

She moistens her lips, opens her mouth, but nothing comes out.

His words make her heart stutter. So does the intention in his eyes. Because there's more. So much more they both need to say.

Only dinner's ready. At the sound of the drums, they take their seats and are immediately presented with a feast. Chicken long rice, poke, salmon, roast pig. The food is delicious. The conversation a mix of nostalgia and camaraderie. It's not the awkward family dinner it was when they arrived. Even Don's phone is nonexistent.

After their meal, the luau begins. The music is an up-tempo beat, competing with the slow crash of the waves on the shore. Ash wills herself to concentrate on the show, but her mind is elsewhere.

It's hard to remember why she's on this trip. She's here for Augustus, to be a source of support. And yet she found her own. In Nathaniel.

And it fucking figures. It figures that only Nathaniel Whitford would affect her like this. Irritatingly irresistible.

As the last plate is cleared and dessert plates and utensils are swiftly set in front of them, Augustus rises. "All right, you know the drill," he begins.

Nathaniel laces his fingers through hers. "Last dinner means…"

"A Grandpops speech," Delaney pipes in.

Augustus laughs, his eyes twinkling. "It certainly wouldn't be the end of the trip without one. You love these, don't you, Don?"

Don chuckles, his response more good-natured than she's seen from him.

Augustus sobers. "I'm happy tonight. Do you know why I'm happy? Because I have you here with me. My family. Which brings me to something I'm afraid I have to tell you."

Nathaniel eyes her, anxious.

"I've decided to stop treatment."

Claire covers her mouth. Even Don blinks silently, stunned. He reaches over and takes his wife's hand.

Ash sits frozen. Sucker punched. She wants to weep, to scream. But it's Augustus's choice. It's her job. All she can do is support him. Even if she's not ready, he is.

She gives him a wobbly but encouraging smile.

"I have less than six months until I die of brain cancer. Before I move into the unrefined stage of forgetting your names and spilling food on myself, I want to be sure you're okay. Because I am. I've had a good life. The goal of this trip was to make sure you had everything you needed before I go." He smiles around the group, his tender eyes stopping on Ash, then Nathaniel. "I hope a connection has been made between all of you that lasts longer than I do."

Silver in his eyes, Nathaniel pulls her hand into his lap. She squeezes back.

Tate slings his arm around Delaney, who rests her head on his shoulder.

Augustus holds up a hand. "But tonight is not about me. It's about Claire." He finds his daughter, smiles warmly. "Honey, I have done many things wrong in life. I was absent, I was cruel, I was unavailable."

"Dad." Claire shakes her head. Tears stream down her face.

"I knew after a month that I loved your mother, but it took thirty years to realize I hurt you." His voice cracks. "I'm so sorry, Claire Bear. I've missed many of your birthdays. And I will miss more. But not tonight."

Fighting back tears, Ash twists in her seat and gives a nod to the server.

In come birthday cakes. All the birthday cakes. Small and squat, towering and behemoth. Vanilla, chocolate, funfetti, every flavor imaginable. Bavarian cream, fondant, royal icing. Some are decorated with marzipan roses, some have real flowers, some look like a child's birthday cake, some resemble an elegant wedding cake.

Claire gasps as they're set on the table. Ash sees it in her eyes. Awe. Joy. It's obvious. It's all she's ever wanted. It's just cake, and yet, it means so much more. What Augustus missed out on. What he's making up for.

A hand on her shoulder. Warmth and comfort. Ash turns to Nathaniel.

"You two made her world tonight," he says, his voice breaking.

"I'm glad," she agrees, nodding.

The night goes on. Cakes are cut and devoured. More tears are shed. Even Don is teary-eyed. Every face is etched with pain, but also comfort. Words like *I fucked up, but I'm sorry; I'm fixing it* go a long way.

As hugs are passed around and the group lingers, hesitant to break the spell of the night, Ash is hit by a sudden pang of emotion.

She sees. What could be. What she wants.

Throat tightening, she turns abruptly, to get away from the sight, to chase away the pressure in her chest. She walks briskly down the beach. The urge to burst into tears is suddenly overwhelming.

At the lip of the surf, she takes in the great, vast ocean. Feels the sand between her toes. The touch of warm night air.

She has all this back in LA. But what she doesn't have? Nathaniel.

They're going their separate ways in less than twenty-four hours. The thought is like a knife to the throat.

She's sick of pretending. She wants to make what they have real. Make them real.

But could they? Where do they go from here? From this fantastical fantasy of a vacation? The real world? The real them?

They *have* been them.

He's seen her. She's seen him.

And he's everything.

He saved her life out on that island. She trusted him to get her out of there safely. And that trust came easy. It's a triumph, knowing she can trust someone again.

She closes her eyes, brings her hand to the flower in her hair. Two weeks with Nathaniel has mattered more than two years with Jakob.

With him, she doesn't have to be invincible. Even if he makes her feel like she is. He makes her feel safe. Secure. Happy. So damn happy.

She hasn't had that in a long time.

At her back, Nathaniel's warm, velvet voice. "Midnight swim?"

Her heart does a backflip. "On the contrary. Just contemplating flinging myself into the sea."

"Don't think it would take you."

She spins. "Oh, no?"

With a firm shake of his head, he steps closer. Takes her hand. "No. Because you belong here. With me."

She gives a wobbly smile. "Tonight was a really nice night."

He draws her into his arms. Hums thoughtfully. "It was."

On a sigh, she rests her head against his shoulder. "You knew about Augustus."

He strokes her back, his big hand warm, comforting. "I did. I'm sorry I didn't tell you."

"No. It's okay. I understand." Guilt squeezes her chest. Augustus is allowed to have his secrets. And it's admirable. Nathaniel holding them for him. He's a better person than she is.

She straightens. Shudders out a shaky sigh. "It's hard to believe that, one day, he won't be here."

"It is." His throat works. A soft sheen to his pale-blue eyes. "But you'll be there for him. And so will I. All of us will." He sounds certain. Happy. About his family. Her chest expands at the notion.

Ash lays a hand on his muscled chest. "I like your family. Augustus the best, for sure." She smiles. "But you're a close second."

He holds her tightly, his eyes blazing.

She's caught in his orbit, mesmerized by his gorgeous face.

The night wind whips her hair. But neither of them makes a move. The world pauses.

Ash moistens her lips. *Just tell him. Tell him you...like him. Care for him. Are falling faster than the Hindenburg.*

Only she doesn't get that far.

One hand cupping her face, Nathaniel lowers his head. Kisses her.

Slow. Steady. Tremulous.

Ash's knees go weak, and she grips the front of his shirt to hold herself up.

Pulling back, he touches the flower in her hair. "When I saw this," he rasps, "I knew that I'd waited too long."

Her breath hitches. "Too long for what?"

"To tell you what you mean to me."

Emotion clogs her throat. "Nathaniel—"

"Tomorrow, that plane," he whispers. "It's not how I lose you."

Her head spins. Her heart pounds against her sternum. "It's not?"

"No." A shudder of a breath shakes out of him. "I don't want this to end, Ash."

"You don't?"

God. Clearly, her brain's been taken over by a robot who can only ask breathless, inane questions.

He chuckles, presses his forehead to hers. "No. I don't."

For a moment, silence.

Fresh tears sting her eyes. Her heart feels too heavy for her body. Her mind works out the kinks, and suddenly, it seems so seamless. Maybe the coconut to the cranium cracked something loose. Sure, she almost died. But it's more than that. It's an ache. A bone-deep knowledge that death is always there. That risk is something to be leaped at. Because the end result in life is that time runs out. She has to live while she can. Love while she can.

Love. Nathaniel.

She does.

She loves him with all 206 bones in her body.

"Ash?" he asks, when the silence has gone on too long. His eyes are worried, begging. As if her answer has the power to undo him.

She gasps it out, opening that place inside herself that's been closed off for so long. "I don't want it to end either."

"Thank fuck." He grasps her arms, skims his hands down them. The grooves of his fingers indent in her flesh, muscle, like he's terrified she's already gone.

"But how?" Heart racing, she searches his eyes. "How do we do this?"

His face is intense, as if he's been planning this. Resolve races through his voice. "I still have two weeks of leave."

"What about Peru? The backpacking trip?"

"It doesn't matter anymore." He cups her face. "The thought of not being with you makes me want to die."

"So morbid," she teases.

He chuckles but sobers quickly. "I'll come back to LA," he husks. "We'll figure us out there."

She thrills. *Us.* All her stupid emotions shaken and stirred. Real world. They go back to the real world and try this.

All she can do is nod. A hard stab of want, of hope, spears her through the stomach.

"Yes," she says. She's unhinged. In the best possible way. "Yes, yes, yes."

A brilliant grin fills his face. "Monosyllabic sentences are very off brand for you, Bigfoot."

She laughs. "Shut up."

And then, expression heated, he's stepping into her, pulling her against him, cradling her jaw as if they're the only two people in existence. And for a long second, she wishes it could be like that.

Her and him, together. Fantastical.

End times.

His lips are hot and wet on hers. His hands beneath her ribs sliding up, over her heart like a secret to be captured. And it is.

Because that lovely ache in her stomach is gone, as if she's finally put a claim on what she wants.

"This is fucking insane," she murmurs against his mouth. "What we're doing."

Nathaniel cups the back of her head and stares into her eyes. "I don't care," he says roughly. A grin tips his lips. "I want you, Ashabelle. I'm not running away from any of it. From any of you."

Her name. Her full name rolling off Nathaniel's lovely lips is too beautiful for words.

Ash grins back, slinging her arms around his neck and yanking him back in for a mind-blowing kiss.

She's allowed to have happiness, and it looks like Nathaniel.

In every universe, it will look like him.

# III.

# BLOOM

## Chapter Thirty-Seven

THE ENTIRE WHITFORD FAMILY, PLUS ASH, TOUCHES down in LA the next day.

Ten days ago, she'd have rather been put in the luggage hold than be seated near Nathaniel Whitford. And now look at her life. Snuggled up next to him on the Whitford private jet.

At the private terminal, Claire gives her a special marmalade from the Big Island and a tight hug. "I've enjoyed getting to know you." Her smile is bright, warm. "I'm grateful you're there for my father. And my family."

As Nathaniel shakes hands with his father and kisses his mother, Ash gives Augustus a bone-crushing hug. "Thank you," she says against his ear. "For everything."

"My dear, I should be thanking you."

"You're not mad at me for banging your grandson?" She winces.

Augustus laughs. "On the contrary."

Heart aching with appreciation, she squeezes his hands. "See you soon. Tea and whiskey?"

Augustus lifts a brow. "And chess."

More hugs. Delaney and Tate, and then it's just Ash and Nathaniel.

"Ready to go?" he asks softly.

Caught off guard, she blinks. It's then that she realizes where they are. Not Hawaii. Not paradise. The real world. They're doing this. They're trying. Whatever *this* is.

She looks at his handsome face, that adorable half smile, and breathes, "Yes."

Hand in hand, they exit the hangar and make their way to

the long-term parking. Nathaniel digs keys out of his pocket, and soon, they're standing in front of a vintage Bronco.

Ash arches a brow. "Figured you for more of a Benz guy."

"Nah, I'm not a show-off." He takes the bag of gifts for Tessie and Bear from Ash and loads it carefully into the back seat. Into the cargo space goes their luggage. As he slams the hatch, he casually asks, "Your place first?"

Her brain fizzes out, then clears. Her place. God. She hopes it's clean.

Panic, anxiety, make a mess of her nerves. Suddenly, all of this is daunting. What if Ash Keller post-vacation is not what he anticipated?

She and Nathaniel, they haven't talked about commitments, expectations. They're just doing it. They used their time on the plane to snuggle. Not talk about next steps. Jump first and think later. Which is all very Ash Keller of her. But now…plans seem of the essence.

Two weeks together in LA. She has a place; he has a place. It makes perfect sense. Until they stay together. One never truly knows whether they're compatible with another person until they discover if they have an overreliance on throw pillows or sleep with the TV on.

Like he's read her thoughts, he tugs at her crop top. Bringing her back. To him. "Beautiful brain compute."

"Listen, if you don't like this, you can leave, okay?" she says, her voice a sharp challenge. "You can bail at any time or any place and—" At the grin that splits his face, she falters. Her brain fumbles. "What? Why are you looking at me like that? Why are you smiling?"

"I'm smiling because you're adorable when you're nervous."

She scowls. Damn his charm. He's too perfect and he knows it.

"What if I scare you away?" she breathes, voicing her fear. She searches his face, his pale-blue eyes, for any hesitancy, any *what the fuck am I doing here?* regret.

But there's none.

"You won't." He cups her face, running that big thumb over her lower lip in a tender way that leaves her breathless. "I carried you on a beach, saved you from a mountain, stabbed you in the thigh with a needle. You think I'm leaving now?"

Oh god. Her heart.

"Very true," she says, flicking a cool brow. "You had your chance to kill me multiple times, and you failed. It's a shame."

He scoffs. "I could kill you any time I wanted. Maybe this is all a ruse to get you to let your guard down so I can smother you in your sleep."

"There's one thing you don't know about me."

"What's that?"

"I sleep with knives."

"I look forward to it." He sobers, stepping forward to take her in his arms. "I want to know you, Ash. Here and there. Wherever you are, I want to know you."

It sounds too good to be true. Just like him. Just like the last two weeks.

Shit. That's what she's doing. Waiting for it to end, to break, to snap. Isn't she? Treating him like temporary when every single one of his words, every action proves otherwise.

Her eyes flutter closed briefly. "Okay," she says, her throat tight.

A hint of a smile curves his lovely lips. "One thing you should know about me…I drive like a very tall asshole."

---

Nathaniel Whitford's in her apartment.

It still feels surreal to say that.

Quietly, methodically, he inspects her tiny one-bedroom in Culver City. The moody black gallery wall of art prints. The Victorian highboy she and Tessie thrifted years ago. On top, it's decorated with flower prints and teacups found at antique stores.

Nathaniel studies it all in that steady, stern way of his. Like he cares. Like it matters to him. It should freak her out. Letting him poke around her apartment feels like she's opened up all her gory inside parts and put them on display. But it doesn't scare her. Not with him.

In fact, the situation feels far less strange than she expected. It feels like the last two weeks. Like home. A sense of belonging.

She wants Nathaniel to see her in real life. All the seasons. Her apartment. Every mood. To prove to herself he's not just a mirage or temporary.

Ash follows his gaze as he looks over a shelf of framed photographs. When he stops and studies one in particular, she says, "That's me and Tessie." A dark-haired girl and a blond, mid-laugh on Venice Beach.

She shows him the bedroom with its brick walls and electric-purple velvet headboard.

He eyes the half-made bed, the blankets and sheets rumpled like she left mid–air raid, and says, "I expected nothing less."

She bites her lip. Tamps down the nerves fluttering through her. "I'm a horror story. I leave caps off the toothpaste too."

He crosses his arms. "Good thing I'm an expert at putting them back on."

She tugs him back into the living room. "Now for my favorite part."

Nathaniel lifts a brow. "Head in the freezer?"

"Better." Ash stomps to the windows and opens the doors to her small vine-covered patio. "Ta-da!"

The sun slices through the apartment. Far off in the distance, beyond the smoggy LA skyline, is the Hollywood sign. It's barely discernible, but it never fails to make her smile. Her home.

And now Nathaniel's in her home.

He joins her. Wraps an arm around her waist.

A calm silence passes between them.

Tilting her head back, Ash looks up at him, at his handsome

face cast in sunlight and shadow. Every hard angle a perfect chisel in stone.

"What do you think?"

"It's you."

She arches a suspicious brow. "So do I disassociate now or…"

"Take the compliment, Bigfoot."

"It's weird. You being here," she says, quickly adding, "but I like it."

"I like you," he husks. His eyes have that lustful, hungry look to them. She knows that look. It means she'll be naked in a matter of minutes.

She slices her nails through his hair. "Does this mean the truce has ended?"

His eyes are heavy-lidded now. "The truce ended about ten days and a hundred kisses ago."

Ash purrs as Nathaniel's mouth meets hers with a hard urgency. He slips his strong fingers up the hem of her crop top and palms her breast. She bites that lush lower lip of his, tugging him toward her. Arched bodies, frantic hands.

The exquisite ache in the center of her chest blooms. Making room. A space for Nathaniel.

"Christ, Ash." He shudders. One hand is on her hip, teasing at the waistband of her skirt.

From inside the apartment, her phone chimes. The sound of an incoming FaceTime call.

"Tessie," she gasps, tearing away from Nathaniel. But he's still kissing her, his lips moving instinctively for her throat.

*Oh fuck, Tessie.*

"I have to get it." She twists in his grip, lunging for the door. Her heart drops to her boots. "If something's wrong…"

Nathaniel nods in understanding. Eyes still dazed, he adjusts himself and his rumpled shirt. He follows her inside as she scurries to the device and positions himself in direct view of the camera.

"What are you doing?" Ash waves an arm at him, frowning.

She texted Tessie before she boarded the flight, but she hasn't given her the details of the conversation she and Nathaniel had last night. "Get out of here."

Nathaniel smirks. "Hiding me already?"

"Shut up," she hisses. She holds a finger to her mouth. He rolls his eyes.

Exhaling a hard breath, she pivots her position, then swipes Accept.

"Hi," Tessie chirps. She's in bed, as beautiful as ever, a book balanced on her belly. "You made it home."

"We did." Her heart pounds against her chest. "I mean *I* did."

To her right, Nathaniel rolls his eyes and mouths *smooth*.

Ash glares murder at him.

"Are you okay?" Tessie asks, her brow pulled low in confusion.

"I am." Ash forces a smile. "Are you?"

"No. I am on strict nonmoving orders."

"From who? The doctor?"

"No. Solomon. He won't let me out of bed." She smiles. The look is full of love and amusement and annoyance. "So entertain me. Tell me everything about Nathaniel. Did you get one last vacation lay in?"

Ash flushes. Nathaniel leans against the wall, smug. Arms crossed, eyebrow raised. *Well?*

She shakes her head. "It actually, uh, didn't end like I thought it would. I kinda, maybe, sorta smuggled something back with me."

Tessie wrinkles her nose. "Can you do that? I thought that was illegal?"

"No." Ash lets out a breath. "Nathaniel. I smuggled Nathaniel back."

An ear-splitting shriek pierces her ear drum. Tessie's phone tilts, then lands with a muffled thud on the comforter.

Solomon's rushed boot steps echo through the phone, his panicked baritone of a boom. "Tess?"

The phone's righted. Tessie's laughing, waving Solomon off.

"It's okay. I'm okay." Returning to the camera, she jabs a manicured nail at Ash. "I demand proof of life."

Solomon appears on the screen. Scowls. "You know what? I'd like to see him too."

"But I get to interrogate him," Tessie argues.

Ash tosses her head back and groans. "No one's interrogating anyone."

Tessie levels Ash with a look. "Show me."

Eyes flicking to Nathaniel, Ash nods her affirmation. Then she turns back to her cousin. "You're a pregnant pain in my ass."

Tessie sticks her tongue out.

Nathaniel steps up beside her. "Hi."

Ash's face flushes as he curls a big hand around her neck. The touch of him is calming. It's the perfect reminder to her mind, her heart, that she's made the right decision. Because she's obscenely, disgustingly happy. All her emotions are screaming at her to admit it. That she's down bad for this man.

"Oh my God." Delight shines in Tessie's wide brown eyes. She waves. "Hi."

"He lives, he breathes, he annoys. He is Nathaniel Whitford." Smirking, Ash shrugs. "He's obsessed with me, so I kept him."

Nathaniel laughs and kisses her shoulder. "She isn't wrong."

Despite her cavalier words, she can't keep the stupid smile off her face. Now that everyone knows about them, it feels too good to be true.

Tessie's eyes narrow. "What are your intentions with my cousin?"

A grunt of agreement from Solomon.

"Tessie. Stop," Ash commands, covering her face. To Nathaniel she says, "She's an angel among us, but she doesn't know much about minding her own business."

Nathaniel chuckles.

"Ash," Tessie breathes. "The universe did its thing."

Her face heats. "Yeah," she says, looking up at Nathaniel. "It did."

Life. It just happens.

They spend the next week together, doing Ash's choice of activities around Los Angeles. She takes Nathaniel to her favorite five-dollar theater, where they watch a double feature. *Frankenstein* and *Frankenstein's Bride*.

They buy popsicles on Venice Beach and pay too much for mushrooms at the farmers' market. Nathaniel helps her fix a broken table leg that she's been putting off since the last blackout. They meet Augustus for patty melts at his favorite greasy diner, Lancers. Drive him to his weekly doctor appointment, where they learn about his next steps. They meet her parents too. Her mother pulls out baby photos. Her father his trains. Nathaniel's a good sport. They talk travel and coconut cakes, and at the end of the night, her mother is mouthing *we love him* from the porch, and Ash has to lasso the giddiness blooming beneath her skin and control it.

They do the tedious, boring things like picking up her insulin at the pharmacy or grocery shopping. Then there are the lovely glimmers of happy. Eating dinner in Ash's tiny kitchen, watching the sunset from her patio with ice-cold glasses of wine, making love at midnight and in the early hours of the morning when a lilac dawn is just breaking.

It's not paradise. Not anymore.

It's normal life stuff, and, somewhat shockingly, it's just as nice. Better even. Because it's real.

On day four, Ash gives Nathaniel an unofficial tour of Hollywood Forever Cemetery. She tells him about the old Hollywood actresses, points out the almost unnoticeable grave of aspiring actress Virginia Rappe and tells him the chilling tale of her death.

Afterward, they go to the Hollywood Roosevelt Hotel for drinks.

"This is my absolute favorite spot in LA." She tugs him into the lobby. "Overpriced drinks and celebrity sightings."

He leans into her, curling an arm around her shoulders. "How many ghosts?" His warm breath sends shivers down her spine.

She laughs, delighted. "Not ghosts, *the* ghost," she recounts spookily. "Marilyn Monroe lived here for two years. They say she still haunts room 1200."

They claim a seat at the Rosy Café at the Tropicana Bar and order bar bites and cocktails. Surrounded by lush greenery, they have a prime view of the art deco pool and its eclectic crowd. A poolside DJ spins the latest hits at ear-blasting decibels.

Nathaniel looks perfectly placed, perfectly sexy in his casual slacks and linen shirt with the cuffs rolled up. His devastatingly beautiful face carves up her heart a little more each day.

"Feels like I'm back in Hawaii," Nathaniel murmurs, scanning the space.

"I miss it," she says. "I didn't think I would, but I do."

He reaches across the table and links his long fingers with hers. His eyes darken as he looks at her. "We'll go back."

She swallows back the lump forming in her throat. "We will?"

"Or we can try someplace new. Whatever you want."

His promise eases the uncertainty that plagues her when she thinks about what happens after this. Nothing to misunderstand about that statement. They're together.

"What if, after this, we go back to your place and pack a bag? Go to my place."

"See how Doctor Nathaniel Whitford lives?" Ash teases. "I picture your entire place wallpapered with scrubs. Maybe a jar of hearts on the mantel."

He smiles, but he's visibly distracted with checking his phone. He's been that way since the cemetery. Checking it like he's waiting for a text or a call.

A pit opens in her stomach. A reminder that this is all still temporary. In a week, he could be on his way to the North Sea. Aside from these next few days, they haven't discussed how this will work. If it will.

If *I love you* is in their vocabulary.

She's practiced. Saying it in front of the mirror in the middle of the night while Nathaniel sleeps. It should be easy. *Let's do this. Let's do this forever. Let's tell the universe that we are in love.* But the words stick.

Brows bunched, Ash asks, "Everything okay?"

He nods, running a hand over his flexing jaw. Inhaling a hard breath, he leans in, as if he's about to tell her something, but he's interrupted by another voice.

"Ash?"

She stiffens. The sound cuts through her like a knife. Rocking her with memories she'd rather set on fire.

Nathaniel sees her expression and tightens his hold on her.

Jakob. He's walking toward her, coming from the pool bar. Her stomach dips, knots, flames.

*No fucking way.*

The bright smile on his face confuses her, pisses her off. Reminds her that he's a forever gaslighter. Reminds her of the text he sent her two weeks after she ended things. The message that said "can we be cool?"

The fucking audacity.

Quickly, she stands. The last thing she wants is for Jakob to get the wrong idea and sit down. Nathaniel follows suit. He pulls up alongside her. Tall, towering. She's vaguely aware he's moved closer to her, his warm palm splayed over the small of her back. His shoulder-to-shoulder solidarity a welcome comfort.

She looks up at him. He's already watching her.

Suddenly, the adrenaline, the anger tearing through her like a cyclone, just…

Quiets.

Every lawless emotion inside her has turned off. All she feels is nothing. Nathaniel's presence cancels out Jakob. Every little awful thing he ever did to her, all the ways he made her feel bad…gone.

It's all just gone.

He's just Jakob, and she's just Ash. They no longer exist in the same universe.

"Ash! How the hell are you?" Jakob comes to a stop in front of her. The dimple in his cheek deepens as he smiles, then rocks back on his heels. "I saw the hair, and I knew that was you."

"Jakob," she says, making herself smile. "Hi."

"Holy shit. I don't believe this. It's so good to see you." His gaze skims her body for a second too long, then bounces back to her face.

Beside her, Nathaniel stiffens.

"You look phenomenal," Jakob says. He drags a hand down his smooth jaw. "Jesus. I mean, really, really great. I swear, you've never looked better than you do right now."

*Because of Nathaniel.*

Keeping her well fucked and well loved.

"Thanks, I just got back from Hawaii." She looks up. "This is Nathaniel. He's my—"

"Boyfriend," he cuts in, causing something warm and gooey to flutter in her stomach. Nathaniel's upper lip curls. "And you must be Jakob."

His cold, stern tone, the steel posture of his body say it all. He knows about Jakob and is unimpressed.

Jakob looks taken aback, but he recovers quickly. He nods. "Nice to meet you, man."

When Nathaniel doesn't return the sentiment, her ex turns his attention back to her. She tries not to feel smug when he zeroes in on their linked fingers, the way Nathaniel has her hand cupped in his and held at his ribs.

Ash dares herself to ask. "How's Keleigh?"

Her ex drags an almost-sheepish hand through his hair. "I, uh, wouldn't know. We ended things last year."

"Oh." She grits her teeth against the smug smile that wants to take over her face. "Sorry to hear it."

Jakob extends a hand. Touches her elbow.

In her periphery, she can see Nathaniel's face tightening. He looks murderous.

"So what's new in your world?" Jakob asks. "You still doing your little side businesses?"

*Little.*

*Asshole.*

"Or whatever." He gives Nathaniel a look like the two of them are in on some inside joke that only the manliest men would understand. "I swear, this girl always had a hand in something. Am I right?"

She opens her mouth to light him up with her flamethrower tongue. Only Nathaniel gets there before she can.

"You sure have a lot to say for someone who's currently unemployed." Nathaniel says it evenly, but his flinty gaze holds that stern, cold edge she's come to understand means business.

Eyes wide and her heart rate picking up, she looks at the man beside her. This is the first she's hearing of it. Apparently, he's done his research.

Jakob, pink-cheeked, holds up his hands. "Hey, man. I didn't mean anything by it."

"Good." In one smooth move, Nathaniel opens his wallet and tosses two hundred-dollar bills on the table. His eyes are the blackest she's ever seen them. "Ash has her own business. She's top tier at her profession."

The smile on Jakob's face flatlines. "Oh, well. Glad to hear it."

Tension cements the air. Ash resists the urge to chew a nail. She looks from one man to the other, her eyes bouncing like a pinball. She shouldn't like it as much as she does. Two grown men swinging their dicks. But the way Nathaniel is sticking up for her? It's distracting and, if she's honest, incredibly romantic.

Solidarity, support. It's a comfort she's never known with a man.

Her heart swells.

"And you?" Ash asks, smiling bright. "You still shitting out your alt-lit novels? Trying to get published?" She can't resist the dig.

Jakob makes a guttural noise of disagreement. "It wasn't bullshit, but, uh, think what you want."

"Oh, I will." She lets out a shallow laugh. Grabs her purse. "Have a nice life, Jakob."

Chin up, she tugs on Nathaniel's hand. They march out of the pool area.

Minutes pass before they speak again. Her mind is spinning. Nathaniel pulls her to a stop in the narrow alleyway that links the pool to the lobby.

In the shadows, he's all hard angles, tense muscles, a pulsing jaw. "Little fucking prick," he mutters. Anger's entrenched in his eyes. "You've never looked better than you do right now." Agitated, he shoves up his sleeves, glares over his shoulder. "Let me go back and disembowel that guy."

His protectiveness has her swooning.

"No." She slides her palm up his chest. "Not disembowel. The pool's perfect for a public drowning."

Nathaniel bursts out laughing.

Flattening her palm on his chest, Ash narrows her eyes. Tilts her head. "Tell me how you know he's unemployed."

"Here's a truth." Nathaniel takes her chin between his long fingers. A triumphant gleam enters his eyes. "I'm low-key petty. If you thought for one second that I wouldn't keep track of the asshole who hurt you, you're wrong."

A warmth sweeps through her body as his gaze lands on her lips. He always knows the right thing to say. To do.

She loves this man. God, does she love him.

Smiling, Ash loops her arms around his neck. "Did I ever tell you vengeance turns me on?"

"Then I better get you home," he says. And then he's inhaling her. Devouring her with a mind-melting, panty-dropping kiss that sends her into a whole new orbit.

"Yes," she murmurs against his lips. "Home."

# Chapter Thirty-Eight

THE WAY SHE LOOKS IN HIS BED SHOULD BE CRIMINAL. Nathaniel sits at his desk, laptop open, but he's not looking at it. He can't take his eyes off Ash. Buried in the rumpled sheets. One slender, creamy leg kicked out from beneath the covers, her long wild black hair a tumbled mess.

She's so beautiful it actually fucking pains him.

It still blows his mind. How totally unexpected she was.

The power she has over him, it's deafening. All he can hear, all he knows: this girl has made his life better. Every day he's alive will be better because of her.

Ash is the kind of woman who makes a man feel like he's fucked up for taking so long to discover her. She comes with warnings and arrows, and he loves every single one of them.

This vacation will be worth it. If he gets to keep her.

A soft moan. Ash jerks in her sleep. And then sits up with a jolt.

Amusement courses through him. She sleeps as chaotically as she lives.

"Shit." Groggy, she focuses on the window, then Nathaniel. "What time is it?"

He moves to sit beside her. "We're in no rush."

"Says the man who's already dressed for the day," she drawls, running a hand through her sleep-mussed hair.

"My mom called. She wants to have lunch." He runs his palm over her tattooed thigh. "If you're up for it after the hike."

She groans and grabs her phone off the nightstand, checking her blood. "Still determined to kill me, I see."

"You can survive it."

Satisfied with her reading, she flops back down on the bed. "You are a lovely liar, but I'll take it."

Arching in the sheets, she takes in his bedroom. On a windowsill near his bed is the collection of rocks and gems he's brought back from his adventures. Ash's included. It's the only one that actually matters.

After the scene at the Roosevelt, they barely got through the front door of his penthouse before they were fucking. He couldn't get her here fast enough. Seeing that prick Jakob fed his fear, his anger. Had him wanting to put a claim on Ash, even though, if he said it out loud, she'd rip his balls off.

That toxic prick took her trust and her sweet heart and wrecked them completely. For that, Nathaniel refuses to let it go. He'll keep tabs on that asshole for as long as he lives in LA.

"This feels like a hotel," Ash says, flicking on a light above the bed. "I didn't expect your apartment to look like this."

He knows what it looks like.

Rich.

He and Ash couldn't have more opposite living situations if they tried. He's in downtown LA in a penthouse with a doorman. Her tiny apartment could fit inside his bathroom. His place is barren, sterile, while hers is moody and expressive. It's that juxtaposition he loves. Has craved since the day he met her.

Being with Ash feels like freedom. Like his suit, his last name, his money, hell, even his career, don't matter. If he gave it all up, she wouldn't bat an eye.

Her lips quirk. "It's not as soulless as I thought it would be. It's sturdy and meticulous. Like you."

"Hmm. Minimalist robot. Got it." He moves to stand.

She purrs, tugging him back into bed with her. "You leave, I kill you."

Hovering closer, he kisses her lips. "You act so tough until it's time to cuddle in bed."

"Shut up."

He cups her pale cheek. "I'll be right back."

When he returns, he sets a tray on the bed.

"Fascinating." She taps the acrylic. "You have a tray. I don't even have a tray. I'm a trayless vagabond." She scours the items set before her. Chamomile tea. Peanut butter crackers. Coconut chews. All her favorites.

Ash sinks her teeth into her bottom lip for a moment. Then she looks at him. "Nathaniel…when—when did you get all this?"

He sticks his hands in his pockets. "I sent out for it last night."

"Sent out? So fancy." But she's smiling.

"I want to make you look like this all the time."

Her lips part. She blinks. "How's that?"

"Happy."

Her eyes soften. "Keep this up, and I'm never leaving."

"That's the plan."

A ping from his laptop.

Ash sits straighter. "Did you hear back? About the job?"

Her voice is steady, but she can't hide the concern in her tone. He leaves soon.

Fuck. He has to tell her.

He doesn't know how she'll take it. He doesn't know about anything except for her.

"No," he says, moving to grab his laptop. He clicks into his email. "It's not about that."

He settles into bed beside her.

Ash curls up against him, feral and beautiful. She kisses his shoulder. "What is it?"

He turns the computer screen her way. His heart rate accelerates. Fuck, he hopes she likes it. "It's your website."

She blinks. Sits up. Her fingertips go to her lips. "Nathaniel…"

"I called in a favor," he explains. "I thought this would help you get started on your death doula dreams. If you don't use it, no big deal."

Worry creases her face. "It is a big deal. It's too much."

"It's not too much." He presses his lips to her temple. "I can do things like this for you, Ash. So let me."

He's got her back. He believes in her. What she did for his grandfather, his family—he's nothing short of thankful.

He runs a hand down her silky arm. "You were born to do this. I have all the faith in the world in you. I think you'd change a lot of people's lives. You've already changed mine."

He stares, worried he overstepped. Worried she hates it.

Expression incredulous, she inspects the computer screen. She pulls the laptop onto her lap, clicking through the site. The moody colors, the gothic font.

She smiles, and his breath hitches at the sight.

With a sigh, she throws her arms around him. "No one's ever done anything like this for me before," she whispers, burying her face in his neck.

Emotion clogs his throat. When she's hard, she's hard. When Ash lets go, she's an absolute softie.

"You deserve it." One hand cupping her cheek, he gazes at her gorgeous face. "Just do what you love, and I'll make sure you're happy."

Her eyes fill with a softness he's rarely seen. "I love it. Thank you, Nathaniel."

Grinning, he adjusts her in his arms. "Should we get ready?" He's already picturing a shower. Ash. Soap suds. His slippery hands on those gorgeous, tattooed thighs.

Her lips twitch mischievously. "Not yet. Now I want to give you something."

He cocks a brow. "What's that?"

Rather than reply, she swings herself onto his lap, straddling him.

"I didn't do it for this," he says with a chuckle. Even as his dick screams at him to shut the fuck up and enjoy.

"I know you didn't, but you deserve it."

"Well, I won't turn it down."

Eyes glittering, she reaches for the hem of her T-shirt and pulls it off.

Christ.

Perfect breasts. Beaded nipples. His dick springs to attention.

No free will with this girl. He only wants to fill his veins and blood with her. Obsessed.

"Ash…"

Tits swaying, she reaches back to squeeze his rock-hard dick.

"Fuck me," he groans.

A feline smile on her face, she lowers her blood-red mouth to his and whispers, "That's the plan."

---

Needless to say, they don't make the hike.

It's two by the time they meet Nathaniel's mother at Musso and Frank's in West Hollywood.

Claire looks different, casual, in a sundress and heels. Her blond hair's been darkened slightly and that tight knot of tension in her shoulders has eased.

She stands when they arrive, hugs Ash first, and then kisses Nathaniel. They each order a signature martini, appetizers.

"How have you been?" Claire asks, fanning a napkin over her lap.

"We've been keeping busy." He looks at Ash. The morning still burns fresh in his mind. Her hair. The feel of it dragging over his back, around his cock, fisted in his hand as he used the momentum to bring her bright red lips to his.

Ash smiles at him over the rim of her martini glass like she can read his thoughts.

"You've been hiding Ash away," his mother chides.

He chuckles. It's just as he expected. Everyone loves her as much as he does.

"How about you?" Ash asks. "Recovering from the trip?"

"I needed a week of sleep after that vacation. But I've never had so much fun." His mother's expression sobers. "I have some news, Nathaniel."

"Oh?"

"Your father and I are separating."

His jaw drops.

Ash sits beside him, frozen, her wide-eyed gaze darting between Nathaniel and Claire. "I'm...sorry?"

His mother bursts into a laugh. "Oh, Ash, no. It's fine. In fact, it's long overdue. It's not sad or bad, it just is. The trip to Hawaii was just the icing on the cake. It showed me a lot of things. Things I've been missing or putting off in the interest of our family."

"Such as?"

She smiles at him, the expression surprisingly warm for the topic of conversation. "You're grown. All my children are grown. I want to do something for myself before...well, before our time's up."

Ash leans in. "Do tell."

His mother beams at him. "I'm going to help your grandfather with his hotels. We don't have a lot of time, but we'll make the best of it. It's our family business, and I want to keep it like that." She inhales hard, swallows. "If your father shapes up, great. If he doesn't, that's fine as well. I have my life."

There's a brief shared glance, a smile between his mother and Ash.

His mother lifts her martini glass. "To change."

"To change." Ash winks.

"I'm proud of you, Mom," he tells her.

She tuts and pauses as the waiter refills their waters. "Let's talk about how proud I am of you." Reaching across the table, she pats his hand. "I ran into Doctor Moser the other day. He says you got that transfer you wanted to the North Sea."

Nathaniel goes rigid in his chair. Ice floods his veins.

Ash turns to him, her eyes full of shock and hurt.

*Fuck. This isn't how he wanted to tell her.*

His mother sighs. "I know it's dangerous, but I know you really wanted it."

"Yeah." His voice is gravel. "I did."

His mother looks hopefully between them. "I suppose you two have a lot to figure out."

"I suppose we do," Ash replies coolly, narrowing her eyes at him.

His heart cracks when she slips her hand from his.

Everything was perfect.

And he's the asshole who ruined it.

---

Ash sets her bag on the counter. She hasn't uttered a single word since his mother dropped the bomb. Even now, she's completely expressionless.

He shuts the front door to his penthouse.

"We need to talk," he says on a sigh. Her cold shoulder is unbearable, and he's so fucking pissed at himself. He should have known better than to keep it from her.

He won't let her do this. Shut down. Ice him out.

"Do we?" she replies, turning to him and dropping her shoulders. "It seems clear what this is. Where it's going. We knew it was a possibility, right? That it wouldn't work? I just wish you would have told me."

She laughs, the sound sad, dejected, and it tears a hole in his chest.

"Stop," he orders, refusing to let her do this. "The last thing I would ever do is hurt you. Lie to you."

"But you did. Why?"

"I was planning to tell you." Regret eats at him from the inside. "I didn't want you to find out like that."

"But I did find out." She shakes her head. "I'm not mad you're going—I'm upset you didn't tell me."

"I know. I'm sorry." He exhales a hard breath, pushes away the frustration threatening to overtake him. "I didn't tell you because I didn't take the job."

She rubs her face. "What? I don't understand."

"I turned down the transfer."

"Nathaniel, you can't do that. You can't shirk your responsibilities for me."

He arches a brow. "Shirk?"

"Yes, shirk."

Hands pulled to her heart, she paces. "This is your career. And even though I don't want you to die out there on the fucking high seas, I don't want to fuck up anything else in your life." Her voice is shaky. Full of fear. "I fucked too much up already, okay?"

"You didn't fuck up anything."

Guilt clouds her face. "I did."

A sick feeling crawls through him. She still blames herself.

Tears fill her eyes. Fuck.

Ash crying scares the hell out of him. She's tough, she's mean, but right now, she's hurting.

How does he tell her he's been busy working out the details, the plans, and then chickening out, panicking that what he wants isn't what she wants? He's been berating himself for assuming that Ash can be tamed. That Ash would want him.

But fuck that. Because he wants her.

Suddenly, he finds himself crossing the room to take her in his arms. "Don't you apologize for that. Never again. Do you understand me?" His voice thickens. "This is where we are now. You're mine. I wouldn't change that for anything or anyone."

She scans his face, sadness in her eyes. "You gave up your job, Nathaniel."

He grasps her chin, forcing her to look at him. "I used that job to run. I don't want to run anymore." His heart pangs. A muscle flexes in his jaw. "You have made me brave enough to live the life I want. And it's with you. *You* are what I want, Ash."

She shakes her head, arching a brow. "I'm messy and I'm mean."

"I love your mean. I know I will always get the right order at a restaurant because of you."

She laughs, but it's a sad sound.

"And I love your mess."

Her eyes blaze. "We're too different."

"That's bullshit," he says simply.

She is absolutely perfect for him. Why can't she see that? See that she is all he wants.

He takes her face in his hands, says roughly, "Ashabelle, I have thought of nothing and of no one since I first set foot on this vacation and laid eyes on you."

The sadness slides from her face.

His throat is tight with emotion. But he pushes through it. "I love you. I am utterly and unfathomably in love with you, Ashabelle Keller."

At his words, she closes her eyes. Takes a shallow breath, the action rocking her body.

He means it. She's his. She will always be a sharp object. And he will never stop loving her.

Her mouth works. Those bold red lips part. But nothing comes out.

"You don't have to say it back." He stares at her, thumbs whisking over her sharp cheekbones. A heavy ache pierces his gut. And yet, if she's not ready, he won't push. "I'll love you enough for the both of us."

Ash lays a hand on his chest. She peers up at him. A kind of vulnerable earnestness on her face. "Unfathomably, you say?"

He clears his throat. "Very much so."

And then she smiles. "I love you too, Nathaniel."

The wind's knocked out of him. He stands there, stunned. Processing the fact that this fierce force of a woman loves him back.

Ash smirks. Cups his jaw. "Speechless? I didn't think you had it in you."

Steadied by her voice, he stares. Then crushes her in his arms, unable and unwilling to let her go. "Christ, Ashabelle," he says hoarsely. "You more than anyone." He pulls back. Cradles her jaw. Kisses her lips. "You more than anything."

"I like it when you call me that," she whispers. A shy smile crosses her gorgeous face. "Ashabelle. It makes me feel like I'm yours."

"You are," he promises. "You are mine."

"Yes," she breathes. Tears sparkle on her lashes. "I'm sorry I didn't let you explain."

He shakes his head. Rests his brow against hers. "No. I'm sorry I kept it from you." He pulls back to look at her. "I applied for jobs at Cedars-Sinai. I have to finish out the next two months on my rig, but then I'll be back here." He's making this real. He's in this for the long run.

"Really?"

"Really. I want to be the only man in your world, Ash. The only man you want to kill. Kiss. Fuck." His eyes turn molten. "Love. If that's what you want."

When she smiles, her eyes are filled with tears. "Yes, yes. I want you, Nathaniel." She laughs, the joy on her face making his chest tighten. "I love you. Until this world ends and our sun is nothing but a shriveled, dead star, I will love you."

He laughs. Damn if that sentiment isn't the sweetest thing he's ever heard. "God, that is sexy." He leans in, whispering, "I love you," and kisses Ash again. Then he's dipping his hand between her thighs, and she's smiling at him as her eyes fall closed, and soon, they're both gone.

## Chapter Thirty-Nine

NATHANIEL WHITFORD LOVES HER.

The reminder, the cult chant, runs through her head over the dream of the last few days. This stern, serious, kind man loves her. And she loves him back.

Yes, he has to leave in less than twenty-four hours for an oil rig in the Pacific. But he'll be back.

And they'll be together. For the first time in a long time, she feels like she can live happily. Live bravely.

Nathaniel makes her feel like she already is. She's still that defiant girl who's maybe made too many mistakes, but she keeps getting back up and trying again anyway. Like all the trials and doubt she's faced to get here were worth it. Meant to be.

He moved mountains to be with her. She'd never ask him to, and yet he did. He supports her hobbies, her business. He believes in her. He's the epitome of constant reassurance wrapped up in the perfect package of a man.

Which really fucks with her state of mind.

Her old anxiety, the concerns about what they were, are soon edged out by a new one.

Like all good things, it could end too soon. What if he goes back to the rig and realizes he's made a mistake? What if her absence makes his heart wander? What if all they are is puppy love in paradise?

Ash has to remind herself, a continuous loop of positive feedback in her head—in a voice that sounds a lot like Tessie's—that it's not ending. It's only just beginning.

"I think my father wants to kidnap you and keep you in the basement with his trains," Ash says one night after another long dinner at her parents' house, where her father and Nathaniel set up a new train track. They drank red wine and listened to Nat King Cole until Ash had to drag him away.

Nathaniel's reflection appears in the mirror. Toothbrush in hand, he comes up behind her to nuzzle the curve of her neck. "I would be honored to sleep in the train basement."

She tips her head back against his chest. "Brown-noser."

He kisses her brow. "Are you going to be okay when I leave?"

Twisting in his arms, she tips her chin. Takes him in. Inhales a steadying breath.

"Yes," she says. "I have Augustus. And my business." Dread and excitement churn in her stomach. "I'm going to talk to a lawyer and see what else I need to do before I launch."

It's nowhere close to being in her wheelhouse. Planning. Organization. All for *A Very Good Death*. But she wants it so much. And she'll get it. The future. *Their* future.

"I'm proud of you." He tucks a strand of hair behind her ear. "We have service on the rig. I'll call as much as I can."

Gripping the front of his T-shirt, she says, "I want you to be safe out there, okay? I'm the only one who kills you. Understand?"

Nathaniel barks a laugh. "Duly noted."

Ash brushes, rinses her toothbrush off, spits in the sink. Nathaniel slips his hand into the blue-and-white kimono she bought in Japan and cups her breast. She purrs in his arms. The playful touches, the heated glances in the mirror. Even the act of brushing their teeth is foreplay.

In the mirror, Nathaniel crosses his muscular arms and leans back against the wall to watch her.

His expression is curious. Attentive. Always. She'll turn to tell him something, only to find he's deep in thought, considering her. That big, beautiful brain of his is working overtime. Her Very Tall Asshole who plans.

"Do you want kids?"

She freezes at the abrupt question. Wide-eyed, she meets

his gaze in the mirror. Then turns to face him. "I, uh…I would. I want to travel first."

He nods, grins. "Me too."

"Girl or boy?"

"Either. Healthy. Happy. Not Chucky."

Humming, he crosses his arms. "What did your wedding plans look like?"

She narrows her eyes. "Why?"

"So I can do it right."

She almost faints dead away.

He chuckles softly. "Don't look suspicious. I just love you."

"You know what?" She smiles. Her heart hurts too much to possibly be good for her. "I'm just going to let you love me that much."

"Good," he says, taking her hand and tugging her into him. "Because I do."

With a sigh, she lays her head on his chest and wraps her arms around his trim waist. "Sometimes I feel like I'm jinxing it."

No matter how good things are going, she'll always overthink it.

"You're not," he murmurs, stroking a hand down her back. "But I understand."

Of course he does.

There's a long second of silence as they hold each other.

"When I come home," Nathaniel says, "I'll have about three months off before I start back at Cedars."

Her heart thrills at the prospect. "What should we do?"

"Travel. Let's go to Tibet."

"I've always wanted to go there." She wiggles her brows, smiling. "Death vultures."

"Ash." His expression sobers. "I need you to tell me. When it gets bad for my grandfather. When to come home."

"I will." She holds his handsome face, her heart aching for him. "Of course I will."

He dips his head to kiss her palm. "Thank you," he says, blinking back the silver in his eyes. "For being there for him. And for me."

He picks her up in his arms, buries his face in her hair and lets out a shuddering breath. His gratefulness seeps through his tight hug and into her. "I love you," he whispers, and the only sound after that is Ash's thundering heart.

---

Augustus lives in the heart of Beverly Hills. An enchanting little stucco cottage covered in vines with prime views of the Hollywood hills. Earlier today, she gave a cemetery tour and then put the finishing touches on her website. While she worked, Nathaniel went with Augustus to the hospital to discuss in-home hospice plans.

Now they plan to have one last lunch before Nathaniel leaves for the *Sophia Marie*.

Ash shuts her car door and jogs up the hill. This is the best part about being here. Walking straight into Augustus's house. No knock, no doorbell, just home.

Inside, it's an homage to all of the man's travels. Photos of the places he's been and the people he's met line the walls. Thailand. Vegas. South Africa.

Augustus comes around the corner. "Ash!"

"Hi," she says, dropping her backpack with the goodies she brought on the foyer table.

She enfolds Augustus in a hug. He smells like lemons and thyme, fragrant herbs from his garden out back. "I brought whiskey," she says, pulling away.

His eyes twinkle. "I made tea."

Nathaniel appears then, stepping through the back door.

"How was it?" she asks, giving him a soft smile.

"It's done." He sets a tray of charcuterie on the table. "We arranged hospice. When the time comes, they're ready."

She reads so much in his face. Concern, worry, but also resignation and that stoic calm she's come to love.

"How long?"

"Six months."

A knot of sadness rises in her throat. It's a harsh reminder that Augustus isn't infallible.

As if he reads everything on her face, Nathaniel slides a broad palm down her arm, squeezes. Ash blinks back tears.

Fuck. She's too damn attached. To everyone.

Augustus tuts. "None of that."

They eat in the garden. A simple meal of meats and cheeses and veggies. Whiskey and wine. Afterward, they go inside and spin records. The Beach Boys. The Bee Gees. Ash sits on the huge green sofa and plays chess with Augustus.

"I'm determined to beat him," she tells Nathaniel.

He looks on with an amused expression, silent.

She can't help but grin. "Just once."

Augustus guffaws. "Just wait until the old brain is rotting. Then it'll be easy to take advantage of me."

She rolls her eyes. "You cannot play that card."

Nathaniel settles beside her. A wide smile breaks across his face. Then he's squinting, just like Augustus does when he's pondering a deep thought. Smirking, he taps her rook. "You have to tighten it up, Bigfoot. You're embarrassing yourself."

She elbows him. "Hush. Let me lose in peace."

Chuckling, he clutches her thigh with one enormous paw. Squeezes.

Without a doubt, she loses. After, Nathaniel and Augustus go at it. Grandson and grandfather battling it out for the win. Whiskey is poured. Some of the lightness ebbs. They make plans. They talk about how Ash will stay here near the end. About plans for his funeral. Who to invite. When to read the will.

Nathaniel's brows get more and more furrowed until he stands and paces. Every so often, he stops and rubs her shoulder like she's his touchstone. His way to cope. She soaks in the contact. She understands. He's hers as well.

A mischievous smile on his face, Augustus rises from his chair. "Now I have something for the both of you," he says, shuffling over to a photo on the wall. "But I need you to keep it on the down low, as the kids say."

Nathaniel sits beside Ash, rests his elbows on his knees. "What is it?"

Without a word, Augustus tugs at the frame of the photo to reveal a safe.

Ash nudges Nathaniel's shoulder. "Did you, uh, know about that?"

"Not a clue," he mutters.

Augustus's hand trembles as he twists the dial on the safe. It's expected. The doctor told them his fine motor skills would be on the decline. When Ash meets his eye, Nathaniel makes a move to rise. Asks in a light tone, "You need help, Grandpops?"

The safe pops, and Augustus crows. "Ah-ha. Still got it."

Nathaniel sits. Augustus returns, his eyes dancing with mischief. The object in his hand flashes gold for an instant before he deposits it in Ash's palms.

She gasps, gapes at it. "Oh, holy shit, Augustus. Are you serious?"

To the bright sunlight of the window, she holds up a gold money clip with a mother of pearl inlay. Though polished bright, its age is evident. Weathered by time. She flips it over. Engraved on the front side are the initials CG.

"Grandpops…" Nathaniel's eyes are wider than Ash has ever seen them. "Is this what I think it is?"

"It is." A fond smile twists Augustus's lips. "It was a gift from Carlo Giacomo. After I gave him a room at the Ambassador. It's now yours."

Ash hands the clip to Nathaniel, whispers, "We're not going to get our legs broken just by looking at this, are we?"

Nathaniel laughs, a bright, brilliant sound. Blue eyes lit with wonder, he runs a hand over his square jaw and evaluates the piece of history in his hands. "Grandpops, I need this story."

Right then, Ash's phone blares in her purse.

"Shit." She hops up and heads for her backpack. As she brings out the device, her breath stalls in her windpipe. "Fuck."

Nathaniel's head snaps up. Stern brows furrowed, he asks, "Everything okay?"

*No. It's not.*

Because of course. Of fucking course the universe has its own plans.

Instead, she forces a smile. And a lie. "New client. I have to take this." She waves a hand. "Go ahead with the story. I'll catch it later."

With that, she heads for the backyard. Heart pounding, she winds her way through the roses and gardenias until she comes to a stone bench next to a small koi pond.

She steadies herself. Hits talk. "Hey, there."

"Ash?" comes the hesitant voice.

She closes her eyes. "Camellia, hi."

An image of Camellia forms in her mind. Beautiful. Sleek blond hair. Pearl earrings. Designer clothing as she walks the halls of her McMansion.

"I'm sorry it's been so long," Camellia says with false sincerity. "Time completely got away from me. How can I help you?"

She's tempted to hang up.

In Hawaii, she wanted to know. Why. She wanted to know for herself. She felt like she owed Nathaniel. Now, though, she's blissfully happy. By asking, would she be doing the right thing or the wrong thing? Is she meddling again, or is this some sort of fucked-up self-sabotage?

"Listen, I had a question." Dread and anxiety join forces, stake a claim in her gut. But she goes on. "That photo you gave me."

Camellia's breath hitches on the other end of the line, but Ash ignores it, powers through.

"It was Nathaniel's sister."

There's a long, telling silence.

Ash swallows the burn in her throat. "But you knew that, didn't you? You knew it was Delaney."

"Ash—"

She closes her eyes. "You told me he was cheating on you. You hired me to break up your own wedding. You did that to your fiancé. To Nathaniel." Her words come out in short, shaky bursts of anger. "Why? Why would you do that to him?"

"Because I didn't want to marry him," she snaps.

Ash freezes. Holds her breath.

A long silence, then— "I didn't love him."

"Fuck," Ash breathes, pressing a hand to her heart. It hurts. She hurts for Nathaniel.

"Look, you don't know what it was like," Camellia protests. In the background, the sound of a baby crying. "Our parents wanted it. We had a big write-up in the LA times. Everyone had flown in." Desperation laces her voice. "I put four years into that relationship. How would it look if I ended it?"

Heart pounding, Ash shakes her head in disbelief. "I think it would look like you were considerate enough to sit down with your fiancé and tell him you wanted to end it. Treat him like, you know, a real human being? Be a mature, reasonable adult."

"I couldn't. I couldn't do it. It was better this way. I didn't want to hurt him."

"So you let me do it instead?" Ash asks with an incredulous laugh.

Fury boils her blood. Camellia and Jakob, they're the fucking same. Gaslighters to the end.

"You let me destroy your wedding, let the world think he was a cheater, let Nathaniel think god knows what for all these years. That's incredibly fucked up."

Camellia's tone is chilly. "I did what I had to do. I don't expect you to understand it."

Bristly protection rattles her spine. "Nathaniel's a good man."

"Look, why do you care? It was just a job, right?"

"Right. Just a job." Ash lets out a drained breath. "You never deserved him anyway," she tells Camellia. Without waiting for a response, she hangs up.

## Chapter Forty

AFTER AUGUSTUS'S, THEY STOP AT NATHANIEL'S TO grab his bags. Then they're off to the airport.

Between his imminent departure and the phone call with Camellia, Ash is struggling to keep it together. She feels carved open. Raw. A great, gigantic, messy secret burrowing a hole in her gut.

But that's the real world. Full of mess and exes and heartbreak.

Ash stands in the middle of his living room while Nathaniel retrieves his bags from the bedroom. A hollow ache builds in her gut.

"I was thinking—" Nathaniel returns and sets his bags down. Leans back against the counter. He crosses his tan arms, the sunlight from the window slipping across his hooded blue eyes.

The sight of him makes her go soft.

"What if," he says, wearing a tentative frown, "we got a place together?"

She shakes her head. Clears her daze. "What?"

"Maybe I should have saved this conversation for when I return, but I don't want to wait." He sweeps a hand over her shoulder, kisses her throat. "My place is paid off. I can pay the fee to break your lease. Or we can keep it if you need a place to work."

Her brain scrambles. Her throat closes up.

"There's a house on the beach in Venice. Close enough to the ocean I bet we can hear it from the bedroom." He grins, his face lighting up. "It's ten minutes from a cemetery. But you can look too," he tells her. "I trust you. All I care about when I get back is starting our life together."

Her phone buzzes a warning on the table. She ignores it.

Palm cupping the back of her neck, he kisses her brow. "I like knowing you're in my bed," he teases. "Pining for me."

She doesn't smile. She can't. All she wants to do is break down and bawl.

It sounds perfect. A life with Nathaniel. Beach walks, cemetery walks. Waking with him in the morning, going to sleep with him at night.

But it can't be perfect. Not with this living, breathing thing called guilt. How can she do this? Move forward with him? Be in the now. She has to settle their pasts first. Her mess. It's always her mess that comes back to bite her in the ass. If she doesn't tell him now, he'll only find out later, and she'll lose him.

She can't fuck with the integrity of her love for him. She owes him the truth.

"Ash?" He's peering at her, confused.

Panic fizzes. Explodes.

"I can't do this," she blurts.

"It's too fast," he says slowly, patiently, even as a flash of fear crosses his face. "I get it."

"No." Her throat, the backs of her eyes burn. "It's—it's everything. But I'm not."

His eyebrows slant low. "You're not what? What are you talking about?"

"You can't take care of me, Nathaniel. You don't have to. It's not your job." She's rambling. She can't stop.

"Ash. Ashabelle, what is it?" He cups her face with those big, warm hands, sweeping his thumbs softly over her cheeks to banish the tears. "You're scaring me."

"I can't do this anymore. I have to tell you the truth. I have to tell you who hired me."

His shoulders tense. And with a sigh, he drops his hands. "I don't need to know that. Not anymore."

She backs away from him. "You do, you do. Because I can't do this if you don't know. You're owed the truth, Nathaniel. If I keep it from you, I'm no better than Jakob." She inhales a breath. "It was Camellia."

He goes still.

So painfully still.

Ash gulps air. Her heart feels like it will combust any second. "She hired me. She gave me that photo. She knew it was Delaney. But I didn't. And I—I did what I did. Because I'm an asshole."

He stares at the ground, the strong line of his jaw pulsing. "You're not an asshole."

"Yes, I am. She hired me because she was too scared to do it herself. To tell you that she didn't want to marry you." She has to get it all out. Every last bit.

His head snaps up. The pain on his face is so visceral he looks like he's been stabbed in the throat. "She said that?"

She licks her dry lips. She's sweating. Ungodly amounts. God, what's wrong with her?

"Yes. She said that."

Utter silence.

Ash wipes her eyes. "I'm so sorry."

"Sit."

Her heart lurches at his stern tone. "What?"

"Sit down."

She stands on shaky legs, wanting to go to him, but she's just frozen. Unbalanced.

He looks at her over his shoulder, opens the fridge. "Ashabelle, would you fucking sit down? Please."

Finally, she does. She covers her face, hiding from him as best as she can. "You're upset."

"I'm upset, yeah. But not at you. Your blood sugar's low." When she looks up, he's setting a glass of juice in front of her. "Drink that."

She brings the glass to her lips. Sips. Heat returns to her face.

Sweeping concerned eyes over her, he slides the chair back to sit beside her. Rests broad palms on the table. Those long fingers tan and perfectly shaped. "Listen to me. I'm in love with you. The past doesn't matter. I don't know whether you need to fucking hear it, but I forgive you for what you did." He grasps her hand. "No more punishing yourself."

She shakes free of his hold. "You say you forgive me, but what if you—"

He looks frustrated, amused. "I know my heart. Don't tell me how I feel about you. Don't shut down because you made one mistake."

She takes another sip of juice, runs her thumb along the lip of the glass.

"It was a big mistake."

"It wasn't a—" He breaks off, blinking, his features contorting into pain. "Saying you breaking up my wedding was a mistake completely negates what we have. Don't you fucking get that?"

She shakes her head, over and over. "I don't know," she mumbles.

He swallows. "You cannot be serious."

Her voice is gone. Completely mute.

"Get that shit, get Jakob out of your head." He's angry now. Fury etched all over his handsome face. "I'm not upset about Camellia; I'm upset because you doubt us. I'm in this, Ash. I'm in love with you. And I don't know why your morbid little brain won't let you see it."

She gives a humorless laugh. "Maybe it's because I'm not right for you. Maybe you need someone else. Someone different."

He stares at her, roughs a hand through his hair. "Don't do that," he says hoarsely. "Push me away."

"I mean, can you see me as a doctor's wife? Going to galas? Charity functions? Your father's country club?" Ash breathes heavily. The walls are closing in. The doubt, the despair of losing Nathaniel in the future. It sideswipes every bit of rationality, joy, love.

"Ash—"

"You need someone who wears pearl earrings. Who fits your family. Because I don't."

"Fuck," he whispers. "You're doing it again. You're taking away what you want because you're scared," he says, voice stricken. "Because you think I want something other than you. When you've never been more wrong in your life."

Tears blur her vision. As she blinks them back, she takes in the stoic, masculine living room. Pieces of herself scattered around Nathaniel's apartment. Her boots on the rug. A tea bag and a cold cup of tea on the coffee table. Scattered throw pillows from the night they fucked frantically until they both fell apart, gasping for air in each other's arms.

Her anxiety has claws. The thorns in her chest ready to regrow, ready to rehome her heart, somewhere far away and dark.

Ash scrunches her eyes tight. Gulps air. Her head and heart throb.

Is she going to fuck all this up? Let her anxiety tell her that they never should have agreed to continue this? That she and Nathaniel should have left what they had in Hawaii?

It would be easy to be scared of this. To allow herself to push love away.

But she won't.

She is better than her past. Better than her bullshit brain telling her lies.

"Ash? Beauty?"

She opens her eyes. Back to earth.

Back to *them*.

When she says nothing, Nathaniel threads his fingers through hers. Lifts the back of her hand to his lips. "You are more than your mess. You're the love of my fucking life." His blue eyes, full of hurt, are locked on hers, intent. "I wish you'd see that. I wish you would trust me."

"I do trust you," she promises. "More than anyone."

Relief flashes on his face.

Eyes misty, stomach a ball of pure anxiety, Ash stands and climbs onto his lap. Fiercely, she wraps her arms around his neck, kisses the top of his hair. Inhales his scent. His love. The tight hold of his arms wrapped around her waist. The nerve of this perfect, stern man, sitting her down and talking it out.

"And you're right. I'm so fucking sorry. I'm scared. I'm stupid."

His voice is thick and scratchy. "You are."

"I love you. I don't mean to push you away." She looks into his eyes. "I won't. At least, I will try," she amends. "So damn hard."

He squeezes her tight. "I can live with that."

She burrows her face against his neck. Whispers, "Did I ruin things?"

"No." A light chuckle shakes them both. "Never."

"Are you sure?"

"More than." He pulls back to look her in the eye, his expression serious. "The sun will rise, and I will still love you tomorrow. Understand?"

She sighs and clings to him. "Yes."

He kisses her shoulder. "We will be fine, Ashabelle." He glances at his bags set by the front door. An unhappy noise escapes his lips. "I have to go."

A deep ache spreads within her chest. "I know." Ash blinks rapidly, tears lining her eyes. She squeezes him once more. "Please be careful. Come back to me."

When she drives him to the airport sometime later, she waits until the helicopter takes flight, carrying Nathaniel off to the *Sophia Marie*.

She can still feel him.

Because he's in the air. He's everywhere.

## Chapter Forty-One

HE CAN'T DO THIS ANYMORE. BE AWAY FROM ASH. It's been two weeks since he left LA, and every day, he feels like he's slipping farther into insanity. It's painful being away from her. It doesn't help that the connection on the ocean is shit. He keeps missing her calls. The way they left things taints every conversation. Like they tossed a stick of dynamite into their relationship right before he left.

Nathaniel radios for a helicopter to take him back to the ship and heads to the upper deck of the *Sophia Marie*. He's been called out to the rig at some ungodly hour. A crew mate thought he was having a heart attack when, really, it was a classic case of overeating. And now he's up. Awake.

Hands clenched around the rail, he looks out over the Pacific. The ocean is choppy. Far off, the bright lights of LA twinkle. Pure torture. He's this close and can't touch her.

He should be thinking about his grandfather and his limited time on this earth. Instead, there's only Ash. Every solitary thought inside his head is Ash, telling him to go home to her.

The way they left things eats at him.

Couples argue. He understands that. But Ash struggles with trust. Her guilt over him and Camellia. Thinking about him not being there, about how they left, it's like razor wire lining his gut. Ash and that beautiful brain of hers is no doubt overthinking. Worrying. He loves that about her. That she feels. That she cares so damn much.

It's his job to be there to support her. And he isn't.

Two more months at sea feels like an eternity. He's already talked to his supervisor about finding a replacement. If he can, he'll be on his way home sooner than anticipated.

A wave rocks the boat. Instead of steadying himself, Nathaniel digs his hand into his pocket, turning a velvet box over in his palm. Meant to be a gift for Ash the night he left, but it wasn't the time. Now it's burning a hole in his pocket. A reminder of what waits for him at home.

God, he's pathetic. But he doesn't give a shit anymore.

He's ready for a normal life. On land. With his morbid little beauty. Her gallows humor, that massive black cloud of hair, and her fierce, kissable mouth. That black cottage on the beach. Bringing breakfast to the girl in his bed. *Cryptozoology Monthly*, peanut butter crackers, whatever it is that will make her happy. He'll overpay for helicopter rides to any and all haunted locations. And most of all, he can't wait to hear her call him her Very Tall Asshole until the end of their days.

He misses her.

Right now, he has to suck it up and do his job. The crew needs him. He has to get his head on straight.

Their love stretches that distance. Can she feel it too?

That Ash-shaped space in his heart won't change because they're apart. If anything, the time away has only cemented how much he loves her.

Another wave hits, and the *Sophia Marie* sways, violently tilting sideways. Nathaniel grips the railing to stay afoot. Rather than righting itself immediately like it should, the rig is pitched, and now the ocean is closer than it was before.

As he searches the black sky for the helicopter, he realizes it wasn't a wave that hit it.

A siren sounds through the rush of the wind. Crewman scramble onto the deck.

Alert, Nathaniel whips around. There's a glow on the rig that wasn't there earlier. And it's spreading. Fire.

"Fuck." Nathaniel grabs his radio and sends an SOS to the ship. And then he's moving, heading into the chaos, even as Ash whispers in his ear.

*Be careful. Come back to me.*

## Chapter Forty-Two

Barely two weeks without Nathaniel, and she's already looney tunes.

After another restless night of sleep, Ash wakes at nine. Changes her clothes and makes a pot of tea. She eats a six-day-old slice of cake for breakfast, because YOLO dumb ways to die, and takes a scalding shower. Then she heads to Augustus's cottage.

After a lunch of tuna salad sandwiches and chips, Ash cleans the dishes in the sink and rinses them in hot water. She sets the fine china back inside the curio cabinet and dries off her hands.

She needs these moments full of tediousness and monotony. When she's not with Augustus, she's preparing *A Very Good Death* for launch. She met with a lawyer about setting up an LLC and a contract to protect herself and her clients.

Anything to take her mind off Nathaniel. Off why every conversation they have is stilted and awkward. Why it's been so damn hard to get ahold of him out on the rig. He said he'd have service, a connection, but for the last two days, there's been radio silence. What if…

Ash swallows back the trepidation rising inside her, grips the countertop tight. Stares out the window at Augustus's lush backyard.

What if he doesn't want to talk to her?

Ash growls at herself, wipes down the counters and stove. God, she's like one of those frontier women perched at the window, waiting for her hero to return from war.

Her anxiety is a riot. She can't stop overthinking all the ways she ruined what they had. What if he's realizing she's a mess he doesn't want to clean up? What if he's reconsidering his options? What if he'd rather have the North Sea than her? What if he doesn't trust her anymore because he believes she doesn't love him?

The thought has her gasping for air.

Where is her hard shell when she needs it? Her anger? Her spite? All she has in her head anymore is Nathaniel. Brain space, brain waves, he occupies every last bit. She wants him here beside her. Wants to rest her head on his shoulder and inhale his salty sea scent. That hit of calm for her senses. Her heart.

She dissects the argument in her head. What he said. What she said. She wants to apologize. Craves it so badly it's a soul-deep ache.

She hurt him. It was evident in the look on his face when she said they shouldn't be together. Blue eyes glassy, shoulders defeated. That sharp jaw moving over and over. Her stomach roils at the memory. At the knowledge that she was the cause of his pain. It breaks her little black heart that they spent their last minutes together arguing when they could have spent them making love or planning their future or threatening bodily harm upon one another.

Most of all, she wishes she could take it all back.

"Ash?" Augustus hovers in the doorway, gripping the frame tightly. Holding himself up. "Chess?"

"I'll set it up." She doesn't want him to struggle with righting the pieces like he did yesterday. "I need the practice."

Augustus scoffs. "I know charity when I see it, my dear, but like I told Betty White in 1972, I'll shut up and play along."

Ash laughs and flicks a towel at him. "Go rest. There's a recliner with your very fancy name on it."

Ash sinks into the big green couch. As she sets up the chessboard, Augustus wanders off and prattles around in the kitchen. She sighs and shakes her head. The man won't sit still. Which is a good thing. He's strong. He's not ready to kick it yet.

With dexterous hands, she moves the brown and white pieces.

Focusing on the board and the board alone. Because dammit, Nathaniel's all around her.

The jacket he left here when they had lunch two weeks ago. A notepad full of instructions for his grandfather sits on the coffee table. A new photo framed on Augustus's wall. The selfie taken of all of them at Rainbow Falls. Right before she pinched Nathaniel's ass. As he pressed her in close, like he already knew she belonged there. He's smiling so big and beautiful it makes her chest hurt.

Their time spent together is like the melody of her favorite song. So clear it kills.

"Your pick of poison," Augustus says, hobbling into the living room. He sets a tray with a pot of tea and small glasses of whiskey on the coffee table.

Ash smiles. "You have a tray too." It's identical to Nathaniel's. Goddamn these men.

He raises his bushy eyebrows as he settles in front of her. "Something on your mind?"

Ash hesitates. She doesn't want to cross client/employee boundaries with Augustus, although she supposes she's already in too deep. Cheeks fusing with heat, she says, "Nathaniel and I— we had an argument the night he left. We fixed it, but…" Her voice breaks a little, her heart cracking as well. "I'm worried that I messed up. That he won't feel the same way about me when he gets home."

Augustus casts her a wry look. "My dear, in every phone call, you are a topic. *How's Ash? Is Ash planning to maim someone today?* He speaks about you so often, I'm afraid he is, what they called back in my day, twitterpated."

She laughs wetly. Feels just a fraction lighter.

"He's always been stubborn. A thinker. A wanderer deep down. Most of his adult life, he's pushed people away because he doesn't know how to let them in. But with you, he doesn't fight it. You challenge him. My grandson's come alive these last few weeks, Ash." His blue eyes, so like Nathaniel's, twinkle. "Because of you."

His words only intensify the guilt, the love in her heart.

"Same." She tucks her hands between her knees. "He made me feel the same way."

With a hum, Augustus nods. "Have you tried telling him that?"

She shakes her head. "I tried calling. He didn't pick up. I just miss him, is all."

Augustus leans back in his recliner, considering. "I see."

"I'm sorry." She sits up straight, willing herself to get a grip. "You're the one who needs me, and here I am, putting all my bullshit on you."

A fond smile curves his lips. "You're not just a person I hired. You're family, Ash. You've given all of us a light to follow. And you'll give them one after I'm gone."

She brings a hand to her mouth, like she can steady her trembling lips. "I'll miss you."

"It will be great to be missed," he says. His smile is wide and his eyes are bright. "It will be an honor."

Ash leans forward. Eyes this incredible man. A man she's built such a wonderful familiarity with, and says, "You know, I might not be great at this whole love thing, Augustus, but…I love you. Very much."

"And I love you too, Ash."

For one long moment, they watch one another, silent. Hope, love, sorrow rising in her chest like the most brilliant sunrise. One she'll remember forever.

"Now," Augustus says, flexing his gnarled fingers. "Allow me to kick your ass."

Her phone rings the minute she reaches for her pawn.

She blinks down at her device. It's Claire.

She answers.

"Ash?" Claire's voice trembles, borders on hysterical. "Are you with my father?"

"I am." Suddenly alert, Ash grips the phone tighter to her ear. "What's wrong?"

Claire lets out an unearthly sob. "It's Nathaniel. Something happened on the rig."

It's instantaneous. The disintegration of her heart. Just dust. Disappearing into the ether.

She closes her eyes. "What kind of something?"

"I don't have many details yet. All I know is there was an accident."

"Fuck." She opens her eyes, seeks out Augustus. Her vision blurs. Her hand shakes around the phone. It's like the death of herself with just one phone call. "Fuck."

*Not him. Not Nathaniel.*

---

Chaos. Mess. For once, it's not Ash's.

The Whitford family fills Augustus's cottage, making it headquarters for Operation Nathaniel Whitford Rescue. They won't give up until he's found and brought home.

They came together impossibly fast. Delaney jetting back from France in record time. Tate leaving his studio in downtown LA halfway through his podcast recording. Don and Claire, each on their phones, pace the living room floor. It'd be comedic if the situation wasn't so terrifying.

Ash's heart's stopped a thousand times since they got news that Nathaniel was missing. The audacity of her Very Tall Asshole to make her worry about him.

"He can swim like a shark, dawg," Tate tells Delaney. Despite his cavalier tone, his face is drawn. "Look on the bright side. At least he's not in the North Sea."

Ash, hovering over the table where a map of the California coast lies, glares at him. "Not helpful."

"Idiot," Delaney snaps, looking up from her tarot spread. She's on hands and knees on Augustus's Moroccan rug. Her lower lip wobbles. "That isn't funny."

Claire hangs up the phone. She's pale. "I just heard from the coast guard." Tears roll down her cheeks. "The *Sophia Marie* collapsed after it was hit by a cargo ship. Most of the rig crumbled. A fire broke out."

Ash covers her mouth, smothering a scream. She knows, she *knows* Nathaniel went back. He wouldn't leave anyone behind. Especially not if there was an accident.

Ash tries out her voice. "Are there any survivors?"

"Two people were rescued from the water," Claire whispers. Don reaches out to steady her. "Four others are presumed dead."

Every person in the room gasps in unison.

"They're taking survivors to Cedars-Sinai."

Delaney gulps. "We need to go there."

Tate runs for the keys.

"I'm the one who's supposed to go first, damn it," Augustus says, his voice in fissures. "Not my grandson."

"Sit down," Ash commands. Gently, she helps him into a recliner.

He obeys, but he curses and grinds a fist against his temple, a sure sign that a migraine's begun.

Awful. It's all awful. She's frozen, helpless. She doesn't know whether to scream or to fall apart or to put herself to work.

Don speaks, crossing the room. "We have a search and rescue going out." Though his expression is stoic, there's the faintest tremor in his voice. "I hired an additional team to help with the search."

For once she's thankful for Don's bluster, his billions. If it finds Nathaniel, if it finds any survivors, she'll never gently bully the man again.

"If he's in the water, it's warm enough, right?" She doesn't even recognize her voice. High pitched. Shaky. "To survive?"

She looks at Don, and Don looks at her. "I'm not sure," he says bluntly.

Blood draining from her face, Ash sinks onto the couch and buries her face in her hands. Her shoulders shake. Those fucking thorns around her heart are gone, forever, but right now, she'd do anything to get them back.

To live means death. But she's not ready to face this life without Nathaniel.

"Ash."

Sniffling, she looks up. Don stands above her, holding out a glass of whiskey. She wipes her face with trembling fingers.

Ash gives him a wobbly smile. Accepts the glass. "Thanks." With that, she swallows it in one long gulp. Savors the sting. Anything to take away the panic. To keep her from thinking the worst. She's doing her best not to imagine Nathaniel unconscious, horribly injured. Lost in the ocean. Burned alive.

Eyes closed, she sends out an SOS to the heavens. To whatever or whoever is up there to hear her plea.

Let the water be warm. Let him not be lost. Let him be so, so very lucky. Let her be bashed with a coconut a thousand times over. Let her pillow always be hot and her socks always slip off her feet. Anything. She'll give up anything and everything if he's just okay. Please let him be okay.

He absolutely cannot be at the bottom of Davy Jones's locker right now. She won't allow it. The only one who kills Nathaniel is her.

Death has always lingered in the margins of her life. Her aunt, Tessie, her diabetes, made her more comfortable with death than she should be. It's a part of life she's supposed to come to terms with in her career as a death doula. But now...

It's too close. Nathaniel could be gone.

*This is the real world, Ash.* She takes a deep breath. Life is full of pain and panic and heartbreak and death. And yet, if it's with Nathaniel, she'd take it on always, forever.

It's all so clear. How much she loves him.

She used to believe it cost too much to love. But it doesn't. It costs too much not to take risks. For so many years, she was anti-love. So against it that she objected to weddings for a living.

Love almost broke her. But Nathaniel makes taking the risk easy. Worth it.

There's no end to what she feels for him. She knows that now. Memories, so many memories, threaten to take her down.

Nathaniel carrying her off that rock ledge, long talks on the beach. His lips against hers beneath the waterfall. The way he saved her when she didn't know how to save herself, checking her blood sugar at midnight and never making her feel like a burden. The luau that last night in Hawaii, heated eyes dark as he leaned in to adjust the orchid in her hair. The glow of his face in the sunlight when he tucked her into his body on that beach and told her he wouldn't lose her.

Ash closes her eyes.

God, she loves him.

She has never loved anyone more on the earth than her Very Tall Asshole.

He has to still exist. On this earth. On this planet. In her universe. Because there is no world in which she wants to exist without the Very Tall Asshole that is Nathaniel Whitford.

Ash rests a hand over her hammering heart. Its beat fills her fingertips.

She would feel him, right? She would feel if he was gone. Far from her.

*Truth?* she asks her heart. But all she gets is silence.

## Chapter Forty-Three

ASH WAKES TO THE SCREAM OF HER CGM ALARM. Blearily, she reaches for her phone, sandwiched between her right hip and the couch cushion. After checking the reading, she silences it.

It takes all her effort to drag herself to the kitchen for a glass of juice. At five a.m., and after yesterday, her blood's the last thing she cares about. Even if Nathaniel's stern voice sounds in her head, telling her to take care of herself.

She stands at the sink. Numbly, she drinks her juice. Augustus's house is a cavernous type of quiet. The silence is matched only by the rush of blood in her ears. The glow outside, the rising sun, feels like a taunt. A new beginning, a new morning, but does it matter?

All the Whitfords—with the exception of Augustus—are at the hospital waiting for word on Nathaniel. It kills her to not be there, but Delaney's promised to send updates. Ash's duty is to Augustus. Nathaniel would understand. He'd want her here.

Her heart balloons when her phone rings. *The hospital?*

Then slowly deflates.

It's Tessie.

Ash picks the FaceTime call up quickly, not wanting to wake Augustus.

"How are you doing?" her cousin asks. She sits in bed, Solomon beside her. Sympathy lines both of their faces.

"Hanging on by a thread," Ash says morosely, propping her phone up on the counter.

"Still no word?"

"No."

"I'm so sorry, Ash."

She shakes her head. Tears well in her eyes. "How are you?" she asks, needing a distraction from her agony. "Still on bed rest?"

"Two more days." By the force of his growl, it's clear Solomon is not happy about that.

Bear, cradled in Tessie's arms, lets out a tiny wail. Her lip quivers. "Same here, kid."

"It sucks." Tessie's voice cracks.

"Fucking sucks. I keep thinking, *what if?* Lasts. I know I deal in those…but right now, all I want is love. I just want Nathaniel."

Tears spill from Ash, cascade down her cheeks. She can't stop them. She's a rose bush that's been overplucked and de-thorned. She might still go on, but she'll never be herself.

"I told him my name, you know," she whispers between shaky, gasping breaths.

Tears fill Tessie's eyes. "You did?"

"I did. And he didn't laugh."

"Oh, wow." Now Tessie's voice is wobbly. "He's a keeper."

Ash wipes her cheeks with the pads of her fingers. Even now, the thought of never hearing her full name from Nathaniel's mouth again has her wanting to fall apart.

"I know." Fanning her face, she says, "I don't know how to do this, Tessie. This love thing anymore. Maybe I never did."

"You do," Tessie disagrees gently. "You so do, Ash."

She shakes her head, feeling broken.

The bed shifts as Solomon tucks Tessie's body against his. He gives Ash a kind smile, but then his adoring gaze returns to his wife.

"Grief and love coexist," he says, resting his massive hand on Tessie's belly. His rugged face creases with pain. "You can't have one without the other. You have to take the good with the bad. And when you do, you'll find the bad doesn't matter as much as the good."

Ash's chest constricts at his words, making it hard to breathe. Solomon's right.

Life doesn't give us what we expect. And in all those moments, we find joy, terror, and ourselves. She found Nathaniel.

He gave her something she hasn't had in a long time. Trust in a man. Trust in herself.

He's seen her. Maybe more than anyone.

No matter what happens, she will always have that to hold on to.

"Okay, I'm done being a crybaby." Ash sniffs and exhales a shaky breath. "Tell me some good news. Because I need it."

Solomon looks at Tessie, and Tessie looks at him.

"We finally picked a name." Tessie touches her bump. Her brown eyes shine with tears. "Willow."

"Oh, Tessie. I fucking love it." She looks at her best friend's belly. That little life. That little baby she will love with her entire soul. "Willow."

Tessie's smiling and Solomon's smiling and Ash's heart is a great balloon in her chest. Nothing is right. But for one long second, it all feels like it will be okay.

---

Ash wakes to the sound of the front door opening.

Heart thudding, she rockets up on the couch, smearing her palms across her bleary eyes. She shakes her head to rid herself of the fog of sleep. Reality, her surroundings come back into focus. Footsteps. Down the hall.

Wait.

Shouldn't all the Whitfords be at the hospital?

The footsteps get closer, and then a broad-shouldered form stands in the parlor.

Ash looks up. And up.

An unholy strangled sob leaves her throat.

Nathaniel.

"Ash," he says softly.

For one long second, she's sure he's a mirage. A hallucination caused by lack of sleep. Even though her heart, her brain, the two best annoying parts of her, scream otherwise.

He's here. In front of her. Whole. Alive.

Ash cries out. And then she launches herself up and covers the distance between them.

He catches her in his arms. Instantly, a sense of calm, of rightness, washes over her.

He glues her body to his like he'll never let go. "Ash," he breathes into her neck like a mantra. "Ashabelle." He's shaking. They both are.

She burrows into him, presses her face to his chest, absorbing his heartbeat. "Oh my god," she gasps. "You're alive."

Nathaniel collapses to his knees, wrapping his arms around her waist and pressing his face against her stomach.

"You're hurt," she says, alarmed. Her hands, unsure of where to go, hover urgently over him. "You need to go to the hos—"

"No." A miserable sound wrenches out of him. He shakes his head over and over again. "Let me hold you. I just need to hold you."

The scent, the sight of him hit straight to her heart like a flood. *He's here. He's here.*

"I've got you," Ash whispers. "I've got you." Trembling, she runs her nails through his damp hair. She doesn't have any bones left in her legs.

"God, you feel so fucking good," he rasps, hands tracing over the curve of her back. "You're all I thought of, Ashabelle. Getting home to you. I had to make it home."

*Home.*

Ash feels the tears rise. And then she's crying, nodding, wrapping her hands tight around those broad shoulders to stay standing. "You're here," she sobs. "You're here." She doesn't believe it. This beautiful second chance. A do-over of the highest order.

Gripping her hips tightly, Nathaniel pushes to standing. "Don't cry," he says, cradling her face in his hands. He whisks his thumbs over her cheeks, wiping away her tears. "Don't cry, my morbid little beauty."

"I thought you were dead, you asshole," she hisses, voice shaking with emotion. "I'll cry if I want to."

"I told you. That honor is yours alone."

She sob-laughs and pulls back, taking him in. His face is haggard and his hair disheveled. His scrubs dirty and water-logged.

"What happened? How are you here?"

His face sobers. "When the rig was hit, I was thrown overboard. I stayed adrift on a piece of wreckage for a few hours until I was picked up by a fishing boat near Catalina."

She lets out a watery sob. "So you're telling me it was a pirate rescue?"

With an exhaled laugh, he grips her waist with one hand. "When I got back to land, I came straight here." He bows his head. "All I kept thinking about was you. How I couldn't leave this world without seeing you one last time."

Tears roll down her cheeks. Ash shakes her head. Her fists make a home in the hem of Nathaniel's scrubs, yanking him closer. "I was so worried. The way we left things…" She gulps air, swallows her tears. "I'm so sorry, Nathaniel. For freaking out. For pushing you away."

He kisses her hard, passionately. "Never apologize for that. There's nothing to forgive."

A thousand explosions happen in her heart. His trust in her, his love nearly make her knees give out.

"I don't doubt us." She exhales raggedly, pulling back to look him in the eye. "I choose you, Nathaniel. In every universe, in every afterlife, I will always choose you. I love you."

"Fuck," he rasps. His eyes shutter like her very words have carved him up. "I love you. I am so fucking in love with you, Ashabelle."

With tremulous hands, they trace each other's features—lips, cheeks, jaw—in wonder, as if they've been split apart by time, long lost. Like they're memorizing each other in case. So close, so needy, a crowbar couldn't pry them apart.

Whimpering, Ash tightens her hold on him, refusing to let him go. She can't get any softer. She can't love him enough.

In the span of two weeks, they got to know each other's strengths and scars, fears and weaknesses. With each piece of herself she showed him, Nathaniel never once shied away.

Love isn't about fixing yourself so that someone loves you. It's about finding the right person to love you as you are.

She will never have to be less with Nathaniel. She is fine the way she is.

Ash. Just Ash.

Fiercely, she kisses him. When she pulls back, she grips him by the throat. "Never do that to me again. I thought I lost you."

"Never," he rasps against her lips. "You will never lose me." He laces his hands beneath her lower back. Tugs her closer. "I'm in this no matter what it takes. The long run."

"For better or hearse?" she teases.

"For better or hearse." The corner of his mouth curves. "We're going to do this, do us, and we're going to do this good, okay?"

She's nodding, nodding *yes*, nodding her happy.

"You just have to know one thing. The rest we can work on as we go."

She clings to him. "What is it?"

"I will give it all to you, Ash, but you have to fucking let me."

A smile blooms across her lips. "I will," she says simply, staring into his handsome face.

One lifetime won't be long enough to love Nathaniel with all she is capable of.

Somewhere in the house, the crack of a door.

Air bursts out of her in a silent scream as reality hits her. "Oh my god, Nathaniel. Augustus. Your parents. Everyone thinks you're dead. We have to—"

He snags her hand before she can bolt for the door. "Hold

on. I want to give you something first." With that, he reaches into his pocket and pulls out a black velvet box. Damp from water, a little worse for wear, but there's no mistaking it contains jewelry.

Ash gapes at him. Opens her mouth. But nothing comes out. When she closes it again, tears mist her eyes. "What—Nathaniel..."

"I wanted to give this to you the night I left," he says hoarsely, hands shaking. "I may or may not have carried this with me for the last two weeks."

She doesn't know whether to laugh or cry or scream bloody murder. She wants this, but...

It's too early. Too soon.

And yet, she'd still say yes.

In every universe, yes.

He stares at her, amused. Reverent. "I'm going to open the box, Bigfoot."

"Okay," she whispers, clasping her hands at her chest. Ready or not, here it comes.

Brows furrowed, his attention exquisite and stern, he does.

"Oh my god."

She inspects the box, what's inside, for a long time. Eyes too hot, throat too tight. And yet love fills her.

Pearl earrings. But not just any pearl earrings.

Her teary gaze lifts. Nathaniel watches her anxiously.

She gives a watery laugh. "They're black," she says, awed.

Gorgeous pearlescent black pearls. Pearls that scream *Ash*. That will always remind her of who she actually is.

He leans down, finding her mouth, and whispers against her lips. "Just like your pretty little soul."

She kisses him then. Kisses him like there's no tomorrow, like the universe is smirking down at her in that *I told you so* way. And she'll accept it. No more fighting it. She drags Nathaniel closer, her tongue smoking over his. In response, he digs his fingers into her hips, shifting her until they're flush, until all she can feel are his tall bones and brooding muscles.

When they pull apart, she doesn't release him. She can't let him go. "I'll wear the fuck out of them."

"Good." He considers her, his expression growing serious. His voice is choked, damp. "They'll have to tide you over until I buy a ring."

She nods. "Yes."

This time, there's no ache, no fear in her chest. It's a light, brilliant and blooming. It's not a sigh, it's an exhale. Letting go, letting it out.

Time doesn't wait.

And neither will they.

# Epilogue

*One year later*

"All these leg muscles I've built up on these damn hikes of yours," Ash huffs as she climbs the steep, rocky terrain of the mountain. Stones crunch beneath her clomping boots. "Going to use them to snap your neck one day."

Smirking, Nathaniel glances over his shoulder. His sun-bronzed skin is rosy from exertion. He looks like a sexy GQ model in hiking gear. "Best way to die. Your legs around my face."

Ash rolls her lips against a smile. Adjusts the straps of her backpack, hefting the weight inside.

Nathaniel stops and turns. Eyes simmering with emotion, he reaches for her, pulls her into his arms for a brain-melting kiss.

"I'm sweaty," she says, though her protest is weak. It only takes a heartbeat for her to go pliant and melty against his ridiculously hard body. Apparently, she'll never stop swooning for her Very Tall Asshole.

"I love your sweat." Amusement dances in his pale-blue eyes. "It's very kissable. I never know where my lips are going to slip."

"Mmm. We have a deadline," she murmurs, as his mouth sweeps over her overheated skin.

"We'll make it." Her husband's broad palms smooth over her hips, move to cup her face. "We always do."

He's right.

They do.

It's week three of their two-month-long around-the-world honeymoon. And so far, she's run through two airports to make connecting flights. She nearly got run over by a Vespa in Italy and chased down by a highland cow in Scotland. And still, she'll take it. Every last death-defying memory. She'll relish them all, because she's making them with Nathaniel.

They were married seven months ago. Nathaniel never went back to the *Sophia Marie*. They were married at a boutique Fox Hotel, a small ceremony on the rooftop overlooking LA with their immediate family and friends. Augustus's garden was the perfect location for their reception. Fairy lights, a string band, and a coconut wedding cake with bride and groom Bigfoot toppers.

They didn't want to wait. They wanted to wed while Augustus was with them.

Two months later, he passed. It feels strange to say his passing was beautiful, but it's the truth. They were all with him at the end. Claire and Nathaniel holding his hands. The memory of Augustus going quick, quiet, in his sleep, is now a part of her.

Ash sighs in Nathaniel's arms.

Tucking a lock of hair behind her ear, he smiles down at her. "Ready?"

She inhales. "Yeah."

He releases her, takes her hand. Together, they scale the last mile up the mountain. For one more adventure.

That's what the last year has been. Never knowing what will happen, but taking it day by day.

They bought that little house on the beach. The best mix of the both of them. Minimalist morbid, she calls it. A traditional cottage painted black with white shutters. Every night, time disappears. Nathaniel smothers her in stern, serious kisses. They breathe in the salty sea air. Take midnight swims. They cook coconut pancakes on Saturday mornings, hike to the Hollywood sign. Sundays are for lunch with her parents or Nathaniel's.

Her death doula business has grown. She takes on two families at a time. Despite the heartbreak, she adores her work. Assisting people in unearthing the love that wants to be expressed is her favorite part. There's no blueprint for what she does, so she's always recentering and refocusing on how to do it better.

Death has taught her that having the chance to say goodbye, to find joy in the sad, truly can change a life.

Per usual, Nathaniel slays at everything he does. As head of Cedars-Sinai ER, free time is a rarity. Their days fly by, changing shape, squeezing through their fingers. But they always make time for each other. Their life together feels perfectly crafted. Like the wait to get to this place, to find what she needed, was worth it.

This man who never fails to have her scoffing or sighing. Who calls her by her full name when he's serious. Who has never asked her to change herself or put her life on hold. Who holds her dreams and helps her chase them. Every day, he makes her love herself better than she ever has.

When they reach the summit, they still.

"Fuck," Ash breathes.

Nathaniel wraps an arm around her shoulder, his handsome face stern, his hair windswept. Ash relishes the sight. Commits it to memory.

They're quiet as they stand near the cliff edge. Look out at the lighthouse below. The Pacific and its lazy, rolling waves. Her breath hitches. The Hawaii sunset is a brilliant and bold mix of oranges, pinks and reds. A fitting tribute to one of the best men around.

"I wish he were here to see this," Nathaniel says, emotion choking his words.

She sends him a wobbly smile. Squeezes his hand. "He is."

As she surveys the horizon, a rush of emotion sweeps over her. Like Augustus is here with them. Seeing what they're seeing and feeling what they're feeling.

It's a sensation that's stuck with her since he died.

Ash lowers her backpack to the ground. She kneels and retrieves the urn inside. Gently, she settles it on the ground. Nathaniel squats beside her.

"You go first," she says, uncapping the urn.

A shadow passes over Nathaniel's face, clears.

Reaching in, he grabs a handful of dust. Ash follows suit. On a sigh, Nathaniel stands and walks to the cliff ledge. Ash waits at a respectful distance while he speaks to his grandfather in hushed tones.

And then he lifts his hand and gives a fierce throw. Dust and sunset become one.

Ash rises, moving to stand beside him.

"I want a good toss," she says. "Help me?"

He grasps her wrist. "Do it," he says fiercely, despite the mild concern on his face. "I have you."

Out in front, by her side or watching her back, he always does.

Smiling, Ash inches closer to the cliff edge. The sparkling ocean calls to her, the blue sky bigger than life.

Her vision blurs and her eyes sting, but with a steady heart, she leans out.

She hangs there, suspended partly off the ledge, into space, into the universe. Nathaniel's hand, viselike, wrapped around her wrist. Never letting her go.

The wind carries and dips. Ash closes her eyes and inhales. Lets life wash through her. Lets the pieces of herself click together.

"I beat Nathaniel at chess," she says to the nothingness. Her laugh is wet. "Barely. And just between you and me, I think he let me win. But god, Augustus, I adore that Very Tall Asshole." She lifts her eyes to the sky. "I've never loved one like him. So thank you. For everything."

Heart thundering, she opens her hand and lets go entirely.

Of Augustus.

If it's possible for the ocean to get louder, the sunset more brilliant, the wind a fiercer rush, it does.

She's crying, and she doesn't want it to stop. Tears stream down her face until her soul feels wrecked while at the same time at peace.

And then rocks crunch, and a warm, steady presence is behind her, pulling her into his arms. Back to him. On a gasp, Ash buries her face in Nathaniel's muscled chest. They hold each other. Hearts, breaths, sighs in sync.

"Ashabelle." He strokes her hair, calling her back to him.

She lifts her face. Her entire body, down to her bones, warms. "I'm okay. How are you?"

He tightens his hold. "I'm good." His pained eyes move to the cliff edge. "He'll miss a lot. But he gave so much too."

Ash smiles.

He gave more than anyone expected.

The stunner of a surprise in Augustus's will was the gift of his love of travel. Five years' worth of reservations at his Hawaii hotels have already been booked, ensuring all the Whitfords can spend time together every year.

One more way he's pulling the strings from the beyond.

"What time does everyone get in tonight?" she asks, slipping her leg between his.

A rough grunt falls from Nathaniel's lips. "Six." He cups the curve of her ass, primally pulling her closer. "My mother's made reservations for a ten-course tasting menu."

Ash groans. "You monsters."

Kidding. Those monsters are now her in-laws. And she loves them, despite their annual turkey trot.

Claire's thrived since she began working for Fox Hotel Group. Heading into her second year as co-owner, she plans to double the number of resorts worldwide. Tate's on his third season of his *Tater Talks* podcast. This time the subject is the spice trade with a special emphasis on pirates. Delaney's made a name for herself in the horror movie circuit. There's never been a better final girl.

And Don—he's still his belligerent billionaire self. Albeit tamed a little. He and Claire have made it work, and these days, he's only an asshole 2 percent of the time. But they all reserve the right to ban him from activities as they see fit.

Ash lowers her gaze to her wedding ring—a brilliant dark

blue sapphire, almost as dark as the pearls she wears—then looks up at Nathaniel. "Tell me the escape plan now."

He sweeps a kiss over her lips. "We bail mid-dinner. Shimmy out the bathroom window with a very big bottle of wine."

Ash strokes a finger over his cheekbone, marveling at how lucky she is. Monsters, myths, legends. She has never held someone so heavy in her heart the way she holds Nathaniel. "And do what?"

"Go live in a lighthouse."

"Hmm. That's the dream."

His smile is smug. "Dreams have a way of becoming reality, Bigfoot."

She gasps, twists in his arms. Narrows her eyes. "Did you buy a lighthouse?" She's always shocked at the lengths he goes to make her happy.

"You never know," he murmurs, stubbornly dodging her question, "what you'll get in this big old universe."

Pure happiness has her giddy. "I do," she says. "I got you."

The edges of his lips curve, a beautiful smile that steals the breath from her lungs.

And then he captures her mouth, kissing her deeply. Decadently.

Slowly, so slowly, Ash inhales him. Like there's never been any kiss, any man, any love to exist except Nathaniel. She scrapes her nails over his back, rakes them through his hair. The heated rumble in his chest, his hardness down below are a promise of what's to come when they make it back to their hotel room. *If they manage to wait that long.*

Ash growls, that delicious hunger blooming in her stomach. Nathaniel Whitford's the absolute worst. In the best possible way.

Breathing heavily, Nathaniel pulls away. Need lives in his eyes. Those pale-blue irises that never fail to have her in a chokehold.

Ash lays a hand on his muscled chest, feeling the heart that thunders there. Thunders for her.

"Tell me a truth," she says.

His eyes flare as they meet hers. "I love you. Absolutely. Desperately."

"You're a horny madman," she breathes, nipping at his lips. Desire pricks and pulses in every warm part of her. "And I love you too. With every beat of my pulpy heart."

Nathaniel angles in until their brows touch. His voice is low and rough. "Tell me a truth, my morbid little beauty."

"Truth is overrated," she says. Curling her arms around his neck, she yanks him toward her. "We only end with the cold embrace of death."

Nathaniel laughs, tugging her closer. Into him. Meant to be. "I am wildly in support of that."

Ash drinks him in, this memory, this speck of joy in time. The rush of the wind. The burn of the sunset as it settles its beauty for the night. Nathaniel's heart, pounding against hers. His big hand on her cheek, his salty sea scent staining her skin.

The ebb and flow of life. Death. Love.

That's the joy and the beauty of it.

The unknown in a world of certainties.

It's all kinds of fucking perfect.

And it's all theirs.

Thank you for reading!

If you enjoyed the book, please consider leaving a review on Goodreads and the site you bought it from. Every review means the world to indie authors.

Don't miss out on Ava Hunter's upcoming books! Sign up at www.authoravahunter.com to be the first to get the latest book news and bonus content.

# Acknowledgments

What can I say? Except I loved, loved, loved writing this book. And I love, love, love those who have been along for this writerly ride of mine.

First, thank you to Leni Kauffman for slaying the cover. She brought my morbid mean girl and her very tall, handsome asshole to life. Beth, at VB Edits, thank you for reading all my rambling words and making them sharp and pretty.

To all my amazing beta readers: Anna, Mary, Yolanda, Rachel and Tabitha, thank you for reading this book and making it the best it can be! Thank you for loving Ash so damn much. Thank you to Claudia for your beautiful edits and letting me pop into your DMs with random questions. You are a gem.

To all the bloggers and bookstagrammers who've taken a chance on my words—thank you! I'm so grateful for your support.

Thank you to my family, but especially my husband. Thank you for letting me poke your brain (and pancreas) about type 1 diabetes. You're so much more than your condition and to allow Ash to take that on in her story—it's an honor.

Last, but never least, thank you to my readers. I always say it, but it's true. I can't do this without you.

# About the Author

Ava Hunter is a strong believer in black coffee, red wine, and the there's-only-one-bed trope. She writes contemporary romance with healthy amounts of angst where the damsels are never quite damsels, but the men they love (good, bad and rugged) are always there for them. Married to her high school sweetheart, Ava loves crafting strong, stubborn women that only make their men fall harder, adores all things pink, and can never ever get enough of protector romance.

CONNECT WITH AVA:

WEBSITE: www.authoravahunter.com
NEWSLETTER: www.authoravahunter.com
FACEBOOK: facebook.com/authoravahunter
INSTAGRAM: instagram.com/authoravahunter
TIKTOK: tiktok.com/@authoravahunter

Milton Keynes UK
Ingram Content Group UK Ltd.
UKHW042014190924
448461UK00008B/95